ANCIENT GUARDIANS

The Legacy of the Key

S. L. MORGAN

Pasidian Press 2012

ISBN-10: 0615736742
ISBN-13: 978-0615736747
(Pasidian Press)

The Ancient Guardians novel
Series is Dedicated to

My sister, Amanda.

Chapter One

The fall semester of Temple University's medical program in Philadelphia had finally come to an end. Reece handed in her last final and walked out toward the area where her friend Jack was meeting her to drive her to the airport. She had been dreading this day, not because of the finals, but because she was flying back to San Diego. Halfway through the semester, Reece had been notified that she would have to return home to settle the last of her father's estate.

Two years ago, the summer after she graduated from college, her father died of a massive heart attack. He left her alone, with no one she could call family.

She had planned to stay in San Diego to pursue her medical degree, but it took nearly everything she had to stay and cope with her father's death. In the end, she could no longer bear to live in the city that reminded her so much of him and their years together.

After his passing, she fled to Philadelphia in search of a new life. She had settled in quickly, making a couple of friends who helped take her mind off what she had left behind. Her grades were excellent, and she could not have been more proud of how well she was doing on her own. She felt strong.

Now, she had to return and face the reality of it all again; the painful memories and feelings of weakness that she had so successfully suppressed.

She was determined not to let this trip tear down the strength she had found. She refused to let the past haunt her anymore. The trip would not be a long one; she would quickly handle the paperwork regarding the sale of her father's home, and then return to her life in Philadelphia.

"Hey, Reece," a familiar voice called out, pulling her out of her distant thoughts. "You're out early; I was just going to wait out at the benches for you."

Jack was getting ready to start his internship. He was an even-tempered guy and enjoyable to be around. They had developed a quick and entirely platonic rapport from the moment they met, and he always made her feel comfortable.

She smiled. "Thanks for taking me to the airport, Jack. I hated to call you so late, but Lori's cancellation was kind of last-minute." Lori and Reece had shared an apartment since Reece's arrival in Philadelphia.

5

Jack placed his arm around her shoulders as they started walking. "So, when is Lori going to admit she's in love with me and get rid of that geek, Mitch?"

Reece chuckled. "When you get over yourself and you've shown you can stay in a relationship longer than one night."

He stared back at her. "Figures. Why do women always wait for Prince Charming to come along? I could be Prince Charming, if that's what it takes." He laughed at himself.

"Jack, I'm sure you could. I think many of your girlfriends thought you were!"

"Well, whatever dork Lori wants to date is her problem, not mine. I've never been the type to attract the brunettes anyway. It's always the blondes that seem to be attracted to men like me."

Reece stared at him incredulously. "You're unbelievable."

He laughed. "Actually, come to think of it, there is *one* blonde-haired, blue-eyed girl that hasn't fallen for my charming sensibilities." He looked at her and smirked.

Reece shook her head. "And that's not going to change either! I don't get it."

"Get what?"

"The fact that you have to stereotype every female you come across. How shallow can one person be? You're actually judging your relationships with women by the color of their hair? It's stupid, and it's half the reason you can't stay in a relationship longer than one day."

Jack laughed. "Aww, Reece, that's what I love about you, always trying to keep me in line. And you know what? You're probably right."

"I'm always right."

Jack dropped her off at the airport about two hours before her flight. *Airports, ugh.* If there was any place that she dreaded, it was an airport full of rush and chaos. On this trip, she had enough to contend with without additional stress.

She gritted her teeth through the security inspection, then shouldered her backpack and made the rounds of the shops, hoping to keep her mind occupied. She studied what seemed to be every souvenir in the terminal, then headed over to her departure gate and found a seat. She had at least half an hour before boarding.

As she sat back, she noticed two young businessmen walking toward the gate. They were dressed immaculately, in perfectly tailored suits that gave off an air of absolute supremacy. It wasn't their magnetic and powerful presence that had her studying both of them, but there was something strangely familiar about them. Even so, she couldn't place their faces from any class she'd been in. *Well, it's obvious they wouldn't be in college, Reece; they're dressed like they own the airline company. Who are these guys?* It was bothering her that she couldn't identify where she had seen them before.

One was dark-haired. *Tall, dark, and very handsome*, she thought, with an internal chuckle. He was probably in his late twenties, but he had an intimidating presence. He walked as though he commanded the entire gate, perhaps the entire airport. She frowned, trying to figure out whether it was the way he held himself or the odd sense that she knew him that caught her attention.

The blond man beside him was about the same height and equally stunning, but less intimidating. The good-humored expression on his face set him apart from the other man. He looked as though he was recalling the punch line to a good joke. The men walked through the waiting area and stood near the large windows, away from the crowd.

7

Without warning, the dark-haired man looked away from his friend and stared directly at Reece. Their eyes locked, and she became startled, but she tried to continue gazing casually around the room. Her eyes didn't see what was in front of them, though; she was wondering why these men seemed familiar.

She could not resist another glance back toward the window. The blond man was already staring directly at her. *Busted.* Perhaps she hadn't been as discreet as she'd thought. He smiled vibrantly at her to confirm it.

Oh, well...

She gave him back a smile and looked past him at the sky outside. Thankfully, boarding was now announced. Reece stood and turned away.

Knowing this would be a long flight, Reece had opted to fly first class. She was one of the first to board, and she found a comfortable aisle seat.

Two uniformed pilots sat in the front row. Perhaps they were going to take over the flight after Chicago, where more passengers would board. As soon as the airplane moved away from the gate, Reece rested her head against the leather headrest, closed her eyes, and allowed herself to drift off. It seemed now that the long week was finally catching up with her.

She woke enough to refuse when an attendant approached her to ask about refreshments. As she laid her head back, the two pilots in the front row stood and walked toward the cockpit. *That's a bit out of the ordinary,* Reece thought sleepily.

She heard a step and looked backward down the aisle. Through the curtain that separated first class from coach stepped the two young men she had seen earlier. They didn't stop, but walked toward the cockpit. Now she was a little concerned. Both men looked extremely somber. She noticed their blue eyes. Very blue eyes. They were almost—they *were* glowing, like sapphires reflecting the light.

Reece looked around at her fellow passengers, but no one seemed to notice anything strange. In fact, no one seemed to notice anything at all; they all stared straight ahead like mannequins, and the flight attendants were nowhere to be seen.

Now the two men were in the cockpit. *Must be crowded with six in there*, Reece thought nervously. Her heart beat faster.

The aircraft then went through an odd array of motions. It banked hard in one direction, and then immediately dropped. Reece's stomach reacted instantly, and she gripped the armrests so tightly, there should have been finger dents in them. The plane was climbing now. She looked for some comfort from the other passengers, but found none. Everyone in the cabin was expressionless and stoic, staring blankly ahead. Reece began to wonder if it could all be some strange dream.

Just then, the plane lunged sharply forward; it felt as though they were in a nose dive, speeding back down toward the Earth. Suddenly, a flash of light lit up the cabin, blinding Reece. While she was still dazed, another blinding flash lit the cabin.

After the two bright flashes, the airplane started to level out. The lights in the cabin flickered. It seemed the bright lights were the cause of the electrical malfunctions in the aircraft. Or was it the other way around? At any rate, they were not heading downward anymore.

Reece began to calm down. The plane flew smoothly without any more abrupt movements. Quiet conversations sounded around her, and she felt as though she were waking from a trance. The cabin was dark, and the people around her were talking to each other with concern.

A voice came over the intercom. "Good evening, passengers. This is your pilot speaking. It seems that our aircraft is experiencing various forms of technical difficulty. There is no need for any undue concern, but to err on the side of caution, we have requested, and have been granted, clearance to return to Philadelphia. We are en route there now. I ask that all passengers remain seated until we return the aircraft safely to the ground."

Reece remained quiet; she did not know what to believe. Shortly after the pilot made his announcement, the airplane began its descent. Once safely on the ground again and the airplane slowly returned to an open gate, the pilot came over the intercom again, thanking the passengers for their cooperation and expressing his apologies for the inconvenience. Reece sat in shock and wondered if it had been a dream. *Dream or reality, I want off this plane*, she thought, and she grabbed her backpack.

As she followed the group back into the airport, she noticed the two young men again, walking ahead of her. The blond man was acting as if he had just gotten off a plane in Las Vegas after a winning streak, but the dark one seemed uninterested in his friend's enthusiasm. They stopped, both of them staring down at some object in the dark one's hand. Reece looked at them speculatively. They raised their heads simultaneously, looking directly at her. She could not pull her questioning eyes away from them, wondering if they were the cause of the airplane's malfunctioning. They returned her gaze, seemingly as interested in her as she was in them. Everything in her wanted to stop and question them, but for fear of making a fool of herself, she turned her attention back to the crowd in front of her and continued to walk past them. Before turning the corner, she turned back one last time. They were both staring intently at her. The dark blond smiled at her warmly. There seemed to be more behind his smile than just politeness.

After Reece managed to secure another flight out for the next morning, she called Jack for a ride home from the airport. She hated to bother him again, and she thought she should probably just take a cab ride home, but she'd rather not be in the presence of strangers after what she had just experienced. Jack had wasted no time returning to pick her up, and she was grateful for it. The distress of the strange flight started to diminish as soon as she was away from the airport.

Jack dropped Reece off at her apartment. "Marti's later?" he asked.

It was their usual coffee shop. "Sure." She smiled at him. "Lori will bring Mitch; think you can stand it?"

He clasped his hands dramatically. "Ah, my broken heart!" Then he reverted to his normal voice. "Pick you up at six, okay?"

Reece dumped her backpack at the door, plopped down onto the sofa, and turned on the television. She dropped her purse to the floor next to her and grabbed the remote. Flipping through the channels, she found a sea life documentary to watch. Graceful dolphins, swimming, swimming...suddenly, she felt as if it were three in the morning; she could hardly keep her eyes open. She let her body relax and closed her eyes.

She woke abruptly from a dreamless sleep, thinking she'd heard the door. She sat up, looking toward the door, expecting Lori to enter. There was no sign of Lori, and no sign the door had been opened. The deadbolt remained in the locked position.

Old building noises. She sank back into the sofa, pulling over her the blanket they kept draped over the back. She leaned over to grab the remote control from the coffee table.

Something moved. In the kitchen? It was just a glimpse, out of the corner of her eye. She sat back, taking slow breaths. *Probably nothing.* She stared into the kitchen—open to the living room, with a counter in-between.

Phone. She picked up her purse and fumbled around for her cell phone. As she retrieved the phone, she looked up and was stupefied by the figure standing in front of her. She tried to blink it away, but it remained; solid, unmoving.

"Dad?" she whispered.

She stared in amazement at the image of her father, standing in her living room. He didn't move or respond to her. He stood there, expressionless, as if he were studying her.

Reece felt as if a heavy weight had landed on her, instantly paralyzing her. She could not do anything except stare at him. He was wearing the clothes he had worn the last time she saw him; dark brown slacks and a crisp blue shirt.

Suddenly, he smiled his heartwarming smile.

Reece's eyes filled with tears, and the image blurred. She'd forgotten how much she missed him. She felt a flood of repressed emotions far greater than those she'd feared her trip to San Diego would evoke. His face, his presence, and his smile brought back vivid memories of him and their life together; memories she had tried to set aside so she could function without him. These were the memories that made her wonder how she could go through the rest of her life alone.

Frightened by the realization that her deceased father was standing in front of her, she squeezed her eyes shut, hoping this image would go away. Strangely, the weight lifted slowly, and she regained control of her large muscles.

When she dared to open her eyes, he was gone. She felt both frustration and relief. Was her perpetual anxiety over her impending trip causing hallucinations now? She needed to get hold of herself.

Slam! Reece leaped off the sofa and turned back toward the door.

"Geez, girl! What are you doing here?" It was Lori, jumping back into the doorway and dropping her keys.

With her hand over her heart, Lori stared at Reece in shock. Reece was the mirror image of Lori, with her hand covering her chest. She took a deep, calming breath. "Sorry, Lori, my flight was pushed out until tomorrow. The plane had issues or something."

Lori let out a sigh of relief and bent over to pick up her keys. "Well, that's..." she started.

"Never a good thing, I know," Reece finished her sentence.

An hour later, they were all in Jack's car. He drove the car as if he were in a high-speed chase.

"Slow it down, Jack," Reece said. "I knew I should have taken my own car," she muttered to Lori, who sat next to her in the back seat.

Lori smiled and leaned forward to put a hand on Mitch's shoulder. "You're driving next time, honey."

"Hey," said Mitch, "I'm actually enjoying myself. It's not every day I get to jump into a classic '67 Camaro SS. I'm curious, how fast can these cars really go?"

A large smile stretched across Jack's face. "I can fix your curiosity, if you'd like."

Lori exhaled ostentatiously. "Why don't you do that after you drop us off, Jack? Then you both can go kill yourselves together. What is it with men and cars?"

Reece shrugged her shoulders. More talk about cars would just encourage Jack to do something stupid. "Hey, what do you guys think about going to dinner instead of coffee? I'm not really in the mood to sit in a coffee shop right now. School's out, and we've spent enough time there studying for finals."

Lori smiled. "Good call, Reece. I'm hungry anyway. Let's go to that new Italian restaurant. It's supposed to be nice."

Jack laughed and responded. "Whatever you women want, I'm just the driver." He looked toward Mitch. "You cool with that, Mitch? Oh wait, never mind, you're always cool with anything."

He tried to make eye contact with Reece in the rearview mirror. Reece ignored him pointedly, looking out the window.

They were stopped at a red light, a block south of the restaurant. Pedestrians hurried past on the sidewalks. Two of them—*what?*—two of them were the young men who'd been on the airplane. Reece's heart raced.

"Reece? What are you staring at?" Lori had grabbed her arm.

"What? Um, well, there was…it's just..." She turned back to look out the window, and the two men were gone.

"Just what, Reece?" Lori said, trying to look past Reece out the window.

"Oh, nothing. My mind was somewhere else. I'm sorry, what were you saying?"

Lori laughed. "Girl, you need a cocktail or something! You're starting to act delirious." She laughed, but her eyes showed concern.

"I just need to eat something; it's been a long day."

The restaurant's parking lot was full. "Well, of course this place is packed! Hopefully, the garage we passed has a spot available." Jack huffed. "You girls need to learn how to cook dinner or something. By the time it takes me to park, you both could have cooked and served us men a nice, healthy meal." He spun the car back down an alley to find more parking.

"We 'girls'?" said Lori. "You 'men'? Learn to cook yourself, Jack! Until then, just park the car and quit complaining, or you can wait with it until we finish." They pulled into an extra parking area and found a spot. Before he was out of his car, Jack noticed another car nearby. "Are you serious!" he said, walking up to it. "Check out this car, guys. It's like some prototype or something."

Mitch walked over to the car while Reece and Lori stared at them both, annoyed by the delay.

Lori called out to them, "It's nice, Jack. What is it, a Porsche or something?"

Jack laughed as he walked the length of the sporty black car. "It's not a Porsche. I've never read, or heard, about anything like this! I wonder whose it is; this car has to be worth well over a hundred thousand bucks!"

As he walked closer, the car emitted a warning sound. Reece crossed her arms. "Jack, can we GO? You are most likely about to meet the owner; I'm sure it has some kind of pager. I'm ready to eat."

Jack's head snapped up, and he walked away from the car, turning back over and over, as if he wanted to check it out one more time.

Once inside the restaurant, they were seated in a secluded, candle-lit nook behind a red brick archway. While waiting for their orders, they engaged in conversation about their challenging finals earlier that day. As usual, Jack entertained the group with his natural humor. It was definitely the environment Reece needed to take her mind off the strange events from earlier.

In the midst of her laughter, Reece glanced up to see if the waitress was returning with their meals, only to be frozen in shock. Across the way, the two men from the plane were sitting at a table that faced theirs. The blond man was staring directly at her, and when she tried to act as though she hadn't noticed them, he raised his wine glass in her direction and smiled.

She looked back to Lori and Mitch sitting across from her, trying to shake herself into reality. *Are they following me? Who are these guys?*

Lori looked at her quizzically. "Reece, are you okay? You look like you've seen a ghost."

Reece shook her head and tightened her fist angrily. This could not be happening.

"What do you need?" Jack said. "I'll get the waitress. Why are you so tense?"

Reece heard all of their voices like echoes in the background as she pulled herself together. She closed her eyes and unclenched her fists. "Water," she said softly. "I just wanted to see if refills were coming."

She had to pull it together, and she would do it now. Reece would not allow these men to intimidate her in any way. Whether or not these two interesting men had anything to do with the strange occurrences on the plane or were following her now, she would prove to them she wasn't afraid of them. Inwardly she was concerned, but she would not let *them* see that.

Jack was the one to break the silence. "All of this over a glass of water? Stay here; I'll go get the waitress." Reece clutched his hand. "Sheesh, Reece, can you release the death grip? I won't make a scene, but Lori's right; you look like you've had a paranormal experience or something."

Shortly thereafter, the waitress appeared with refills, followed by other staff with their plates. Jack sat back, and once the staff left, Reece laughed. "Sorry, guys, it has been a very long day. I think I just need to eat. This food smells delicious, doesn't it?"

Her friends looked worried. She knew they'd never seen her act this way. And quite frankly, she was beginning to worry herself.

Reece ignored their discomfort. She started in on her plate, took a bite, and smiled brilliantly. "Guys, stop staring at me, we don't need any more drama." She laughed as she took another bite. "Now, what were we talking about before I almost melted down over a glass of water?"

Jack didn't hesitate to break up the awkward moment. While he continued to relax everyone at the table with his humor, Reece reached for her glass of wine. She felt the eyes of the men stealing glances at her, and now it was time to show them they didn't intimidate her.

She looked over at their table. Both men were engaged in conversation, but they must have noticed Reece watching them. The dark haired man looked over at her, bringing the blond one's eyes to follow his gaze. After Reece had the blond man's attention, she arched her brow, raised her wine glass to him, and smiled with confidence. The darker one's lips turned up slightly while he brought his attention back to his friend, the one who Reece was gazing directly at. The blond chuckled softly and returned her smile with amusement. Then, without another glance back to Reece, he returned to his plate before him.

Handsome or not, Reece was annoyed that these two mysterious men were playing games with her. It was best if she just ignored them from here on out. She knew if she didn't, it would not take much for her to walk over to their table and start demanding answers. With that in mind, she engaged herself in the lively conversation her friends were now having and ignored any desire to return her attention back to the men.

The rest of dinner was uneventful, and Jack entertained everyone so well that they seemed to forget about Reece's odd behavior.

Back at the apartment, Reece wished Lori a good night and fell into bed. The alarm clock would ring soon enough.

Chapter 2

After all of her worries and false starts, Reece found the trip to San Diego went a lot better than she'd expected.

She had convinced herself that the bizarre occurrence on the flight and encountering the vision of her father were strictly due to stress and worry.

She forced herself to view this as a business trip. After three days, the business was promptly handled and she returned to Philadelphia. A few tears while going through the storage locker, and a few difficult decisions. She finally got rid of Dad's favorite old chair. But on the whole, it was almost an anticlimax.

She walked out of the airport to find Lori's car, which was first in the line of cars to pick her up. Reece wasted no time in getting into the front seat, ready to get home.

"Whew. Sorry to arrive during rush hour."

Lori smiled sympathetically. "It's okay. How did it all go?"

"A lot better than I thought. I really think it was the closure that I needed."

Lori pulled the car into the traffic leaving the airport. She looked back over at her friend. "Reece, you really are one of the strongest people I have ever met. I'm happy it went well for you."

The women spent the entire evening at their apartment. Reece was happy to pick back up where she left off, having girl talk with her friend. It was after midnight when they finally headed for bed.

Reece found she was so tired that she considered sleeping on the couch. She reluctantly got up from it, clicked off the end table lamp, and walked into her room. She quickly changed into a T-shirt and her flannel pajama bottoms and crawled into bed. She let her mind drift off to memories of Dad.

Reece lay in bed, completely relaxed. She stared out of her window, watching light snowflakes being pushed around like feathers in the wind. Her eyes fell closed, and she was almost asleep when she heard a shuffling noise in her room. Trying not to panic, she lay still and scanned the room.

It was Dad, standing in the corner of the room. He walked over to her bed, a bright smile on his face. But there was something extremely odd about his eyes. They seemed vacant, as if no one was home. Reece had to force herself to keep looking; the little-girl part of her wanted to close her eyes and pull the covers over her head.

But as he drew closer, she began to experience an odd sensation of comfort. She pulled herself up in bed, sitting and facing him.

His smile widened, and he spoke. "Reece, do not be afraid. I am not going to hurt you."

"I know. I'm not afraid. Dad, why are you here? Am I dreaming?"

He smiled and sat on the edge of the bed beside her. "No, you are not dreaming. It's me, I am here." He smiled and reached to touch her, but pulled back his hand quickly, as if he had burned it on something.

"I've missed you so much," she spoke softly to him. "I have thought, over and over in my head, about what I would say to you if I only had that second chance. How I would tell you goodbye the right way, how I would thank you for all that you did for me. So many things." She sat there trying to gather her thoughts, but the weird sense of calm was almost controlling them.

He stood up and walked toward her window. Her confused eyes followed his every move. As he stared out of the window, he said quietly, "Reece, my beautiful daughter, there is no need for such talk. I am here now, and that is all that matters for us. I have been given what you could call a second chance; I choose to spend it with you. I have been watching over you since my death, but I was not able to manifest myself for you to see me. I have been with you this entire time."

He continued to stare out the window. Reece could not understand why he would not look at her anymore, and her fear began to build again.

When he finally turned around to face her, smiling, the strange calm returned to her. "Reece, I must leave, and you must rest. I will return again soon. Until then, my sweet young girl, appreciate what we both have been given."

His voice seemed odd. It was her father's voice, but there was something strange about his tone. He stared deeply into her wide eyes. "Close your eyes, precious daughter, and sleep."

Overwhelming exhaustion overcame her. She lay back and fell into a deep, dreamless sleep.

The next morning, Reece woke in a state of panic. Had it really been her dad's ghost? Was she losing her mind? She checked out her bedroom window to see if the previous night's snow had accumulated much. Just a sprinkling. Good. If there was any day she needed a morning run, this was it.

She went to her closet, put on her usual running attire, and then a warmer track suit over it. She pulled on her running shoes, scribbled a note for Lori, and was out in the crisp air fifteen minutes after waking.

She was thankful no one stopped her on the way out; she was in no state for conversation. She needed to be alone and let the therapy of running take her mind off everything.

She did some minor stretching, and then set off toward her favorite park. As her muscles loosened up, she picked up her pace. At her favorite running path, she increased speed even more. In the exhilaration of the run, she felt the tension from the night before leave her body. Her heart was beating fast, but it was the strong beat of exercise, not the flutter of fear. Her stomach unknotted itself; her leg muscles, given a job to do, forgot to tremble.

It had been nearly thirty minutes when she came to her usual resting place, an open area with park benches. In warmer weather, the benches would be occupied, but today they were empty. She slowly jogged toward them, bringing her heart rate down in the process. She stopped and leaned over, hands on her knees, and caught her breath. She luxuriated in the comparative calm of her mind. Hallucinations weren't always a bad thing. Maybe her subconscious was telling her she could let go of Dad—or telling her that she could think of him without pain.

She straightened up and headed for a bench. Two other runners—or possibly walkers—were coming toward her. They were men, dressed for running, but a surprising number of casual strollers dressed that way. The sight of two men together made Reece a bit apprehensive. As they came closer, she noticed that they were regular, fairly homely men; not the two from the airplane and the restaurant.

Relieved, she smiled at them.

When their paths crossed, Reece was suddenly grabbed by the upper arm. Before she could react, her other arm was gripped, too, and she was being moved rapidly along the ground. She did not have time to react, as it was the last thing she expected to happen. All she knew now was that she had to find a way out of the man's grasp.

She struggled to free herself from the man's tight grips. She was successful in freeing one of her arms and reached out to his face. The man violently caught her loose arm and brought her back into his secure clutches. Reece screamed and found his hand tightly over her mouth. It was all too much; the man was faster than any sudden move she could manage. She fought as hard as she could, tried to scream, kick, scratch, but was unsuccessful. The harder she fought, the weaker she became. She had nothing left, and the man knew it.

One of the men spoke into her ear. "We were paid a pretty high price to capture you. You must be one important person."

"Let's get her out of here," said the other. "This was too easy."

Just as Reece felt she might pass out from terror, she heard a deep voice call out, "Let the woman go."

She had never heard the voice before, but when she saw its owner, somehow she wasn't surprised. Coming off the path toward her was the dark-haired stranger from the airport. The mysterious man was sharply dressed in a dark suit and overcoat. His eyes were fierce and intently focused on the man holding her.

As he approached their location with an air of authority and command, Reece felt a twinge of hope that this mysterious man might in fact save her. His features darkened. "Release her…now!" His voice seemed to boom, even though he had not shouted.

He continued to approach them, confidently and slowly, with a calculating look in his eye.

"This isn't any of your business!" one of the attackers shouted out to him. "You would be wise to get out of here, now!"

The man ignored him and again ordered the captors to let Reece go.

"Get rid of him!" one said to the other.

One of the men holding her released his hold, pulled out his knife, and lunged aggressively toward the man from the airport. Without any effort, the dark-haired man disarmed his attacker and left him on the ground, writhing in pain. He moved so quickly that Reece had no idea how or what he had done to defend himself from the attack. She used this opportunity to wrench away from the man who held her, but he twisted her arm painfully.

The mysterious man turned his darkened gaze to the man restraining Reece. "You will join your friend," he said lowly, "if you don't release her this instant."

The man grabbed his knife and held it to Reece's throat. "You don't know who you're messing with. Back off, or I *will* kill her."

The familiar man's eyes narrowed, his expression now lethal. Then he did—something. He went through a series of movements that Reece couldn't follow. Suddenly, two men lay on the ground, and Reece was in the arms of the man who had saved her. She looked up into his vibrant blue eyes. She didn't know what to say to him.

"Are you all right?" he asked, unsmiling.

She nodded. He helped her regain her balance and suddenly looked back at the trees behind her. His face darkened. "I must get you out of here."

"What?" said Reece. "What's going on?"

"You're being followed."

"What?" *Brilliant, Reece.*

His face was extremely grave, and his eyes kept returning to the trees at the edge of the clearing. "Come," he said.

Reece told herself she had no option but to trust him. It wasn't true, but it was true that she did trust him, with some instinctive, animal trust.

"Okay," she answered softly.

Her legs were still searching for strength. He drew her arm into his and led her at a rapid pace away from the trees.

"Why do you keep staring back into the trees?"

"Someone is waiting for you there, and I just complicated his plans. You need to get safely out of the park this instant."

Reece felt her heart racing again. "You mean this was planned?"

He kept walking them toward the opposite side of the park at a quick pace. "Explanations will have to wait. For now, I need you to trust me and allow me to protect you."

Reece felt tears welling up in her eyes. She softly spoke, only to herself, "Why me...why now...what's going on?"

He looked down at her. "You've been through quite a lot recently. I'm sorry for that."

"What do you mean? How would you know what I have been through?"

He continued walking them at a brisk pace. "It's my job to know these things."

She froze in place, forcing the young man to stop with her. She looked up at him questioningly. "What are you talking about? Know what things?"

He looked down into her eyes sympathetically. "Miss Bryant, I know you have a lot of questions, and for those I'll give you answers. Right now is not the time."

Reece's eyes filled with tears. She swallowed and asked, "How do you know my name?"

He turned down to her; his eyes seemed to be searching for something in hers. He exhaled softly. "As I said, it's my job."

He resumed their walk and headed off the path and uphill, toward and through a grove of mixed trees.

"Could you at least tell me who you are, then?"

Looking straight ahead and forcing them into a faster walking pace, he answered, "My name? I must have forgotten my manners; forgive me." He looked down at her, but seemed distracted. "My name is Levi."

The trees were becoming denser. It was obvious they were nowhere near the park. She had no idea where they were and began to have second thoughts. She stopped dead, forcing him to stop with her. "How do you know my name?"

He sighed impatiently. "Tell me, Miss Bryant, do you believe in ghosts?"

Reece stared at him in alarm, her mouth open. She swallowed hard, and her answer, when it came, was a very soft and questioning, "No."

"Good, because they do not exist; at least, not the way you might imagine them to. Last night in your room—that was not your father."

"No." Not Dad. She had known that, though, hadn't she?

"Reece, you'll get the answers you seek. I would love nothing more than to give you those answers right now." Levi looked back along their path. "Right now, you must make a choice. You can choose to seek your answers from the one who is pursuing us, or you can trust that I'll give them to you when we're safely out of his reach." He stared somberly at her and waited.

Reece returned his gaze speculatively. Did she trust him? She wasn't terrified of him, as she had been of the men who'd grabbed her. But she also didn't feel the unnatural calm that the apparition of her father had seemed to turn on at will. She was scared, and she knew she had reason to be. If Levi were capable of forcing him to trust her, he hadn't shown it. Nor was he trying to intimidate her, though he surely could have done so.

She looked up at him and nodded.

They resumed their quick pace through the woods. The thick clouds had begun to drop light snowflakes. Reece felt a chill coming over her. Reflexively, she brought her free hand over the exposed hand that she had resting on his arm. She absently leaned closer into him, trying to stay warm. Noticing immediately, he covered her hands with one of his.

She looked up at him. "Are we almost there?" she asked as they reached a clearing.

"Yes, just a few more feet in this direction. My cousin, Harrison, is waiting."

Once in the clearing, Levi led Reece out toward a street where she recognized the same black car Jack had raved about at the restaurant. As they crossed the street and approached the car, the dark, tinted window where the driver sat rolled down. Reece was unsurprised that the driver was the other man she'd seen at the airport, the blond man who'd raised his glass to her in the restaurant. With one arm slouched over the steering wheel, he smiled. "You took long enough, Levi!"

Levi hustled Reece into the front seat and got in the back seat, behind his cousin. Instantly, the car was in gear and they were moving. The car went from a dead stop to what seemed to be the speed of light; yet, it felt like they weren't moving at all. The trees they were passing, a complete blur in her vision, were the only thing that gave relevance to the fact that they were moving. None of it made sense. *Is this even a car?* She looked at the driver, wondering how he was managing to keep the car on the road. He didn't slow the car once, not even to take a sharp turn.

The driver looked over at Reece, his eyes piercing in their light silver-blue color. "I'm Harrison, by the way. Relax, Miss Bryant—I drive rather well." He looked out at the snow; it had gone from a light flakes to heavy clumps hitting the car. "Sorry we had to interrupt your lovely morning in the park."

Reece nodded. Harrison was as superbly dressed as Levi. She questioned who these men really were. "Do you work for the government or something?"

Harrison glanced over at her and subtly grinned. "I suppose you could say that, yes."

She looked back at Levi; he was intently focused on a transparent object in his hand. "Where are we going?"

Levi didn't answer. Instead, Harrison responded. "We're taking you to a safer place, Reece. I'm sure my cousin hasn't explained much. Unfortunately, explanations take time. I can give you the lighter version of the facts; however, I need you to promise you will not do anything crazy, like jump out of our car."

Reece looked at him quizzically. Her anxiety soared, but she hoped her expression didn't show it. "I won't be jumping out of any cars; I understand basic physics, thanks."

He chuckled. "We'll see about that!" They were leaving the city and going into the more rural areas. "Tell me something, Reece; have you ever considered the existence of other worlds, apart from your own?"

Reece swallowed hard. "You mean, like Mars? Not really, why?"

"The man in your room—you thought he was a ghost, correct? Or possibly a bad dream?"

"I'll admit, I've considered both options."

He chuckled and glanced at her with a mischievous grin on his face. "Reece, he was neither. He was not of your world."

Reece stared at him in shock.

"Maybe a little too much information?" He smiled sympathetically. "You should relax. Where you are going

31

will be much more welcoming than where you were about to be taken."

He looked into the rear view mirror. "Levi, we're almost to the vortex. Make sure Javian has sent for Areion and Saracen. We should get Reece to Pasidian quickly."

Did he just speak in a different language? Reece rubbed her forehead disbelievingly. The car grew silent, except for the low purr of the engine. The road they were traveling on was long, winding, and very narrow. Considering the high speed they were driving, combined with the sharp turns, Reece expected to have her body weight thrown all over the inside of the car; yet, gravity had no effect on her.

Even so, she started to feel sick to her stomach. She didn't really trust the two men, but she'd burned her bridges. She decided to stop asking questions. The answers she was receiving were more than she could cope with right now.

The road curved around a hill, and as she watched, the car left the road effortlessly, heading straight for the hillside. It appeared as if they would crash directly into it. Reece took a quick breath and was blinded by a bright flash of light.

Chapter 3

he paved road they traveled on now was shiny black and lined with trees unlike any Reece had ever seen. Their trunks were white, with vivid red leaves beaming on their incandescent white branches. She looked deep into the dense forest of these peculiar trees and noticed that they appeared to be glowing in the darkness. The bright, lime green grass that carpeted the grounds of the forest took on a glowing quality as well. It was strange; it was as though the radiant grass and leaves illuminated on their own, in total darkness.

It appeared as if everything was glowing in color. A drop of water on the windshield sparkled like crystal. The sky had a sapphire quality to it. She felt as if her vision had changed entirely. *What is this place?* All she saw was the illumination of the nature all about her, and none of it seemed real. Wherever they were now, the skies were vivid, bright, and sunny; a far cry from the snowy streets of Philadelphia.

She looked at Harrison, then back at Levi, to see if their appearances had also changed. Nothing was unusual about the two men. She held her hand up and examined her skin. *Normal.* It was very odd; it was only the nature around them that had shown this interesting radiance.

When she turned her attention back to the road, she saw a large, shimmering gate ahead. It was fashioned with beautiful patterns, circling throughout. She could see that there was no longer a road on the other side of it, and they would most likely have to stop. She wondered how they would manage to bring the car through, or if they would? As soon as she questioned the thought, Harrison turned the car into a dark area, which seemed to be a cave or something of that nature. As he parked the car, she noticed that the area they were parked in was filled with sleek, black motorcycles and other cars like the one she was in.

When the car shut off at Harrison's vocalized command, Reece reached over to his arm to stop him from stepping out of the vehicle. *Time for answers.*

He looked back at her with concern. "Reece, we're almost to our destination. I know a million questions are probably swirling around in your head, but you need to try to be patient."

"Fine." She took a deep breath. "But before we go any farther, I really need to know who you both are. You should understand my apprehension about going any farther with you two. We should have crashed into that mountain a moment ago, and now I'm seeing trees and grass that seem to sparkle and glow. I'm sure you both know that I was well aware of what happened that day on the airplane, too. I know you both had something to do with it. I want answers before I concede to go anywhere else with you."

Harrison sighed. "Levi and I are from another dimension known as Pemdas. For many years, our people have protected those on Earth, and many other dimensions as well."

Her eyes narrowed. "Pemdas? I'm in another dimension?"

Harrison nodded. "It is why we did not crash into the hillside when we brought you out of Earth. We went through a vortex, which leads into the outer boundaries of our dimension."

Her heart raced. "My friends. What about my friends? They'll be expecting me. What will they think happened to me?"

Harrison stepped out of the car and walked around to open her door for her. "Your absence will go undetected. There's been a—a stand-in—created to take your place. It's perfectly programmed; no one will question it."

Reece had lost the power to keep her confident expression under control, and she stared at the man in disbelief.

He watched her speculatively. "As we have both mentioned earlier, we are prepared to tell you everything; but please, not here. Allow us to bring you to a more relaxed environment." And with that, he turned and walked to the back of the car, leaving Reece standing there, speechless.

She started to become angry. He still hadn't answered her about the bizarre events on the airplane. "But—"

Before she could speak up, she was interrupted by Levi, who had gotten out of the car and had been staring down at the object in his hand. He dropped the object into a side pocket and walked over to her. His expression was commanding and extremely serious. "Miss Bryant, we have every intention of answering all your questions. Unfortunately, it's more than a five-minute conversation, and we have another short journey ahead. I ask that you will have a little more patience and that you allow us to get you to a more comfortable place. My father is waiting for us, and he will explain everything. There will be a lot for you to try to comprehend. Anything we tell you now will only lead to more questions. Please give us the opportunity to make you more comfortable…for your sake."

Reece looked up into the handsome man's somber face. Concern was apparent from the way he stared down thoughtfully into her eyes. She gazed at him, and after a moment she conceded with a nod.

"Very well, then. Allow me to escort you to the gates, and we will be on our way shortly." He turned to his cousin. "The horses will be here momentarily."

He offered his arm to Reece. As she slowly placed her arm in his, he looked down to her and asked, "I hope you don't mind traveling by horse from here?"

She stared at him in astonishment. "Would it matter if I did?"

He laughed softly and escorted her toward the gate. "No."

She remained quiet as Levi led her through the gates. She was now able to see what was beyond the end of the black, glossy road. She assumed the reason they were waiting for horses was that beyond the gate, there was only a dirt trail that cut through bright green grass, with trees scattered here and there. Some of the trees looked ordinary; some were white-barked with red leaves. The place breathed peace, like a new morning. It had to have been the fascinating glow of the foliage and trees throughout the forest, or maybe it was how much lighter the air felt here; whatever the reason, Reece didn't feel as tense as she had been.

"Why do we have to ride horses? Just because the road ended?" It seemed odd that this would be their method of transportation after just having been in a technically-advanced vehicle.

Levi chuckled softly and turned to look at her. "That is part of the reason, yes. Our land is surrounded by a protective barrier that can only be crossed on our horses."

She looked at him quizzically while contemplating his response. Before she could ask any more questions, a loud noise echoed in the distance. Out of nowhere, two of the most beautiful horses she had ever seen came thundering toward them. She watched with amazement as she observed a cloud of gold dust sparkling in their wake.

Reece, who had never cared much for horses, was in awe of the magnificent animals upon their approach. The two black horses halted a few feet from where they stood.

"I believe you will be more comfortable upon Harrison's horse," said Levi. In one swift motion, he mounted the taller of the two horses. It was obviously as impatient as its master, lifting each leg up in turn and biting down on his mouthpiece, as if trying to break it in half. "Ready to go?" said Levi. "Areion tends to be impatient."

Reece looked over toward Harrison, mounted on the other horse. She walked over to him, trying to stay out of range of its hoofs. "I've never ridden before."

Harrison smiled at her comment as he reached out to help her onto the horse. Once she was seated behind him, he answered, "I'll guide him. All I ask is that you hold on and not jump off his back. Saracen is patient and calm, unlike Areion. I fear you would never wish to ride a horse again if your first experience on a horse was riding him."

As she sat into the swell of the tall horse's back, she tucked her legs up under the edges of the tall, black saddle that Harrison sat in. She was reasonably comfortable, if one could be comfortable while completely helpless.

Harrison pointed down the dirt trail. "We will ride through the line of trees until we reach a great divide. The divide is the location where we cross over into the inner lands of Pemdas, where we live."

She peered around him. The trail seemed to go on forever.

Levi, who was patiently waiting on his impatient horse, moved a few steps nearer and nodded at Harrison while he spoke to Reece. "You may want to hold on to Harrison. Pemdai horses are faster than Earth horses."

She nodded. Levi's horse backed away and reared up. Reece instantly wrapped her arms tightly around Harrison's waist.

Harrison laughed. "Not that tight, friend; Saracen will not be showing off for you today. Just keep a good grip is all you need to do." He turned back to her. "This may seem frightening at first, but try to keep your eyes open. You will not want to miss this journey."

And with that, Harrison leaned forward and his horse lunged ahead. Reece grabbed Harrison tightly again. Levi's horse led the way down the trail, the horses thundering and echoing their way through the trees. Reece could feel Saracen's muscles move powerfully under her.

The ride was more comfortable than she expected. She began to loosen her grip. Harrison grabbed her hands before she separated them, startling her. "You're not going to want to do that just yet!" he shouted over the thunderous gallop of the horses.

Reece clasped her hands tightly again around his waist. She leaned a little sideways to look ahead and felt her heart nearly stop. In front of them, the land ended in a gray mist. Saracen gained even more speed, then she could feel him gathering himself. With a surge of muscle, he leaped into nothingness.

She looked down and saw nothing underneath them but thick, gray mist. She looked back and saw a trail of fiery red leaves slowly falling into the nothingness below.

The horses landed gracefully. Their front hooves beckoned the ground as they drew closer to the other edge of the great divide of emptiness. As they reached it, anxious front legs grabbed the ground as if they were pulling it beneath them, and grateful back legs followed. The horses then resumed their thundering gallop, faster than before.

The sound of hooves seemed muted now. Reece looked down; they were riding on firm, black sand, although they were moving too fast for her to be sure. She decided to bring her attention to the change of scenery before her eyes. The forest of trees with the vibrant red leaves had been replaced by bright green meadows.

Reece gasped at the beauty of the open areas surrounding them. There were flowers with colors so unique and vibrant that they reflected the light of the sun, just as gemstones would. *The sun…do they have a sun here?* She looked up at the brilliant blue sky in search of it.

She saw that the sun was a round object, similar to Earth's, except it had a unique brightness and light about it, and strangely, it did not hurt her eyes to stare at it. Brilliance, fire, and ice would accurately describe the round image that illuminated the skies of this interesting world.

Snowcapped mountains lined the horizon. The terrain they were traveling through was becoming less flat, and the flowers in the meadows were being replaced with tall trees and thicker vegetation. The trees became plentiful as they headed into a dark forest. She watched in amazement as this forest became denser and the plant life began to mysteriously glow; just as the foliage in the forest of red-leaved trees had. So it appeared to be that whenever this unique environment saw a hint of darkness, it glowed.

The weather cooled as the last of the sun's light was blocked by the forest they were riding through. Everything was glowing now. Greens, blues, and yellows illuminated the grounds all around them. She saw pink and white twinkling lights fluttering above the ground…*fireflies?* She looked out around Harrison to see what was in front of them and where they were going. As they crossed a stone bridge, she gazed in awe at the site of a sparkling, silver-colored river beneath them.

They steadily made their way over the smooth surface of the arched bridge. Once safely across it, they began a gradual ascent up a hill. She held tighter to Harrison as the horse lunged up the hill abruptly. Once at the top of the hill, they were quickly out of the darkened forest and entering a valley, surrounded by rolling hills.

She glanced around to check for signs of buildings, but there was nothing. Where were they taking her? They couldn't have ridden for more than thirty minutes or so, yet she was ready to get off the horse. She sighed with relief when the horses came around a hill and a small village came into view.

The village sat in the valley they were riding through and was surrounded by more wooded hills. Up the hills and above the village were a clearing and what appeared to be another city. *Finally!* she thought as they quickly approached the small town.

The horses slowed as they entered the bustling streets. Reece looked around, wondering where they would stop.

The houses were made of stone and covered with dark green ivy. Some people stood on the street, waving and cheering as the horses walked past.

What she saw reminded her of the places she loved reading about in historical novels, from the cottage-like buildings to the long gowns she noticed the ladies wearing. Some women wore aprons with their hair tied up in tight buns, while others wore long dresses with capped sleeves and ribbons tied around their waists. There was too much to take in. Horse-drawn wagons filled with produce, different people wearing clothes from another time period scurrying around, carrying fresh baked breads, and crates filled with various types of food. *Is this real?* Did they time travel somehow? People didn't dress like this anymore.

These thoughts were soon interrupted when Harrison shifted in his saddle and turned his head to the side. "You doing okay back there?"

"Um, yeah, I guess…is this where you're taking me?" Reece answered.

She felt Harrison laugh before answering, "No, our destination is up the hill from this village." He pointed toward a magnificent structure that was sitting impressively on top of a bright green hill, overlooking the village they were in. "That is where our journey ends. It will not be much longer now."

Once they were through the small village, the horses picked up their pace, heading up a steep road and bringing the magnificent structure into better view. Reece studied it while the horses followed the cobblestone road, which was winding around and upward. *Is that a castle?*

As they slowly rode up and around the hill, she saw different views of the enormous, gray, stone structure. Countless windows took advantage of the view from the hill. It was a palace, not a castle—castles don't have *that* many windows. Countless steps led down from the front doors to the perfectly manicured lawns. Gardens of flowering bushes and topiaries surrounded the Palace on all sides.

Once at the top, the horses rode over a stone bridge. Reece glanced down at the crystal clear water, seeing easily to the bottom. The river wound its way through the Palace's landscaped yard, disappearing into the thick forest of trees to their left. She looked around and found that the enormous palace appeared to be the size of a whole town. *Maybe it's a city, and not just a palace? Who knows what to think anymore?* Reece thought, as she was at a loss for words. Whatever this place was, it was situated perfectly, with a forest of trees with pastures rolling into hills behind it and an excellent view of the valleys below.

Harrison rode to the side of the Palace. Levi had already dismounted and was talking with the man who had come for their horses. Harrison threw the reins over the horse's head. "Here you go, Javian. I think he deserves a snack. Areion was showing off for our new visitor, I think." He turned back and lent his arm to help Reece down off the horse before dismounting himself. Her legs were a little weak, but not as bad as she thought they'd be after riding a horse for the first time in her life.

Levi stood at the bottom of the steps that led up to the front entrance. He grinned at Reece, searching her expressions, and then he laughed softly. "Thank you for all of your patience with us. We have finally reached the place for explanations. Let me be the first to properly welcome you to Pasidian Palace," he said as he formally offered his arm to her.

Chapter 4

Reece reached out and took Levi's arm. As he led her up the marble steps, she could not help but look up at him and marvel at how old-fashioned he, and each experience she'd has thus far in this land, was. It was as if she had stepped back in time; riding on horseback, small villages, and being escorted by a perfect gentleman were not things she ever encountered.

As they approached the entrance to the Palace, two servants opened the two massive, ornately carved doors, which led into a large hall. Reece gasped at the grandeur of it. The hall was well lit by enormous windows, which displayed the gardens in front and back. Pairs of white marble columns flanked each side of the windows. The walls were a matching alabaster and extended up into a barrel-curved, shimmering, emerald-colored ceiling. Reece stared up at the ceiling with amazement.

She looked over at Levi, who looked amused, as if he had been watching her reaction.

Harrison laughed light-heartedly, startling Reece. She'd forgotten he was behind them. "Are you still doing okay up there, Reece?"

"Um, yeah, I guess." She had no other words.

They turned left, and Levi opened a large door into a long hallway, which was lined with numerous doors and passageways that had staircases leading off into unknown places. Candles, now their only source of illumination, lit up the walls from their sconces. These candles were intriguing to gaze upon. A soft white glow replaced the natural effect of a candle flame. After closer inspection, she confirmed there was no dancing flame, only the iridescent glow. *What is it with the glowing colors everywhere in this land?* she thought to herself.

Queen Anne-style chairs, with brass cabriole legs, and tables ornately carved out of rich wood were arranged throughout the elegant hallway. Each doorway they walked past was closed, leaving Reece to ponder where they led and what they held. As they approached an open door, she absently squeezed Levi's arm and slowed their pace. She glanced into the room. It was elaborately furnished throughout and had arched windows of impressive proportions, which displayed the entire front lawns of the palace. She had never seen such a magnificent place.

"Wow," she whispered. "So, this is your king's palace?"

By now, she could not help but ask such a question. She was feeling utterly underdressed and ridiculous.

Levi politely answered, "Yes. My father, Navarre, is the Emperor, and he rules the entirety of Pemdas. This palace is our home; it is located centrally within the land and has many villages around it. My father, whom we are taking you to meet, is a very knowledgeable man; he is highly respected by all who depend on him, especially all of the Pemdai. Never before, in all the dimensions we've visited, have I seen anyone generate such respect from their people." He smiled down at her bewildered expression.

Reece began to understand why Levi held himself so imperially. The man was definitely a significant individual. It should probably intimidate her to know she was on the arm of such a man; however, it did not affect Reece's opinion of him. She was more concerned with what he had just proclaimed, and that was that they have visited other worlds besides Earth. *Not possible,* she thought.

"All of the dimensions...you've visited?" she questioned with doubt.

Harrison laughed. "Indeed, all of the dimensions! However, I must clarify. We have not only visited them, but we have served to protect them, too."

Reece nodded her head. She was convinced these two were, in their own way, making fun of her. She decided to remain quiet until they reached the man who would give her the answers and explanations she required.

They passed a few more closed doors, and then Levi stopped before leading Reece out of the hallways and into an atrium.

He turned to face her. "Reece, before going any farther, I wanted to give you an opportunity to freshen up a little." He motioned toward a closed door. "Take your time, I know this has been a long day for you. Harrison and I will be just across the way," he pointed to a closed door across the hall, "in that small sitting room when you are finished."

Reece faintly smiled with appreciation and politely thanked him.

Upon entering, the room promptly lit up without having to turn on a switch. She glanced around the magnificent bathroom. *Thank goodness, indoor plumbing!*

The idea of traveling into this land on horseback had her believing this world might be lacking other forms of modern technology as well. So, she was surprised to see that their restroom functioned like the advanced ones on Earth. Everything was motion-activated, the lights, the lavatory, and the sink. She could have easily stood in awe at the elaborate marble sink, the impressive mirror, and golden fixtures, but now was not the time to marvel at a bathroom. *It's a palace bathroom, Reece. Just because you don't see one every day—or have ever seen one before—doesn't mean you should be surprised.*

She tried to ignore the distraction, wanting to make her visit quick. But having been alone for the first time since agreeing to leave with these men, she became dreadfully overwhelmed. She was weak in the knees and almost trembling.

She splashed cool water on her face to help remove her from this state she was in. Fortunately, as quickly as this feeling had come upon her, it left. She was back in reality, and now the answers she wanted were the only things consuming her thoughts.

She grabbed a soft cloth, patted her face, and shook her head at the image of herself in the mirror. The usually bright-blue eyes that were staring back at her were tired and worn. Her face was pale, replacing the healthy glow it normally had. The ponytail she tied for her morning run was in disarray. She could not help but laugh at her appearance, it was pathetic. *Very classy, Reece!* She figured she would just pull the tie out of her hair and allow it to fall loosely down her back. *Ha! THAT was a bad idea.* It was a tangled mess from being whipped around during her horseback ride. Her lips twisted up on one side, defeated in every way. She studied her sorry appearance in the mirror, trying to conjure up a way to make herself look presentable. *Well, what are you gonna do?* She arched her brow, and then quickly brought her hair up into a knot on the top of her head. She chuckled. *Sadly, that actually looks better,* she inwardly concluded.

She quickly turned to leave and headed out to the sitting area where the men waited.

Both men were conversing when Reece entered the room. *They consider this to be a small sitting room?* she thought when she entered the room, only to find another large room, adorned with even more fashionable furniture arranged around a large stone-like fireplace. She did not have long to study the room before both men stood in unison and proceeded to make their way over to her.

Again, Levi offered his arm, and she accepted. They followed Harrison out of the room and back into the hall, which brought them to a grand staircase. As they climbed the staircase, Reece was in awe of its beauty. This majestic feature, with its imposing proportions, was surrounded by pale walls and columns. The white marble of the staircase was complemented by an iridescent, ruby-colored banister. With everything that Reece had viewed so far, she found its colors and rich design flowed together so well, it gave the impression of perfect harmony.

Once they reached the top, they walked a short distance before turning toward two large doors, which opened immediately upon their arrival.

They walked through the stylish entry and followed steps down into its lower level. At the front of the room, white square pilasters framed a bank of tall, multi-pane windows. Dark green sofas and chairs were arranged for conversation in front of the windows, giving anyone who sat in them a perfect view of the gardens that surrounded the back of the Palace. Beyond the neatly groomed and manicured gardens, rolling hills and pastures disappeared into a thick forest of tall trees.

A tall man stood up from one of the sofas and turned to meet his guests. He had black hair, with hints of gray. His blue eyes were as penetrating in their gaze as Levi's were. As he approached, his smile widened and his eyes sparkled; even so, Reece found him to be an intimidating authority figure. It was the way he held himself, she thought; a picture of complete and absolute confidence.

Without a doubt, she knew this was the Emperor of Pemdas. He wore clothes as extravagant as the Palace they were in. It was the attire anyone would expect a man of such importance to wear. *Well, maybe in 1800s England, anyway,* she thought. He was smartly dressed in a rich velvet cutaway coat that perfectly outlined his lustrous black silk waistcoat. His neck was concealed by a black silk cravat, which had been tied in an intricate knot and embellished with a ruby stone in the center. She had to resist the urge to curtsey at the sight of him.

The noble man approached and extended his arm out to her. Levi gently took her hand and loosened the tight grip she hadn't realized she had on his arm. He placed her hand in his father's outstretched hand. "Father, this is Reece Bryant. Miss Bryant, allow me to introduce my father, the Emperor of Pemdas, Lord Navarre Oxley." Levi looked down at her, smiling. "Reece has many questions, and unfortunately, various circumstances thus far have delayed explanations."

Navarre smiled at Reece, gently brought her hand up, and kissed the air over it. "Miss Bryant, it is a great honor to have you here safe with us in Pemdas."

He led her towards the luxurious sofas, never dropping her hand as he guided her to a seat. Harrison and Levi both found empty chairs to sit on.

"Allow me to offer you some tea, as I understand this has been a very trying morning for you." At that moment, a servant girl carried a tray in. Her flaxen hair was twisted up in a bun, and she wore a long white gown, confined at the waist by a braided silver band. She smiled and gently set the tray on a glass table in front of the windows. She poured hot tea into steel mugs and carried them around, providing one to each of them.

As Reece brought the mug to her lips, she inhaled its fragrance, a mixture of spices—cinnamon? Ginger? Bergamot? Peppermint? She wasn't sure, but it was almost intoxicating. Before she took a sip of the tea, Navarre politely asked, "Would you care for something to eat? I can arrange for food to be brought in if you are hungry; it will be a few more hours until we have dinner.

Even though she hadn't eaten a bite all day, she had no appetite. Food was the last thing on her mind at this moment. Reece set the mug on a side table. "Dinner? Will I be staying here that long?"

Navarre nodded, stood up, and walked over to gaze out the windows. "Miss Bryant, I'm afraid you will not be returning to Earth anytime soon. Please allow me to explain, and try not to be too alarmed. This is for your safety, and for the safety of your friends, and all those on Earth."

He turned from the windows to face the room. His expression was serene, yet grave.

She was at the end of her tolerance of all of this. Now she couldn't go home? She looked straight at Navarre and spoke very sternly. "Please explain to me what is going on, immediately," she demanded. "I feel that I've been extremely patient so far, and before I try to find a way out of this place on my own, I want answers."

She looked directly at Levi and Harrison. Levi was leaning back in his chair, looking concerned. Harrison leaned forward, elbows on his knees, and spoke earnestly, "Reece, under today's circumstances, we couldn't break any of this to you gently. It wasn't our intention to shock, upset, or frighten you in this manner. We could have—

perhaps we should have—tried a bit harder to explain things, but our first priority was getting you here safely." He smiled at her. "I, for one, did not want to take any risks that might have resulted in your jumping out of the car, or off the back of the horse for that matter. Please allow Navarre to explain what is happening and why we feel you should not return home so hastily. Have no fear, Reece; you will be able to go home once we're sure it's safe."

Reece sat rigidly, staring at Harrison.

"Yes, Harrison," said Navarre. "You both should have taken a few additional moments with Miss Bryant to prepare her as best you could. But what is done, is done. Miss Bryant, I ask that you forgive us. I plan to explain as much now as you are able to tolerate. I understand that this will be a lot for you to attempt to comprehend, and that is perfectly reasonable. At the very least, I should like to explain to you why you should feel safe among us." He smiled, then sat in an empty chair by Harrison.

"Let me start by saying you were in grave danger this morning before these two young men intervened. There was no time for them to elucidate the situation. By the time Levi reported to us how swiftly the situation had become dangerous, we had little time to react to ensure your safety."

"We were rapidly losing our control over the situation, and we had to decide quickly how best to protect you," said Levi.

Navarre watched Reece carefully before going further. "I can, however, completely understand why they felt the need to wait for more detailed explanations. I believe you'll appreciate their motives as well, when the whole sequence is laid before you."

Reece sat back, eyeing him with some skepticism. She thought he probably meant well, but well for him might not be well for her.

A tiny smile drew up the corner of Navarre's mouth, and he went on. "First of all, it's natural for you to be completely overwhelmed with the realization that there are worlds and dimensions outside your own. Some of your people have chosen to keep secrets from others of their own kind. It is something I have never understood about Earth."

He relaxed back into his chair. "You seem to be the type of person who appreciates being fully informed, be it good or bad news; is that so?" He waited for her reply.

Reece sat up, giving him her complete attention. "Yes, and the sooner, the better."

Navarre nodded. "For all of its existence, Earth has had countless visitors from different worlds and dimensions. You see, the planet Earth is a conduit, a gateway."

"Like an airport? A hub?"

"Yes!" said Harrison.

"Only, sort of," Levi interjected.

Navarre leaned forward. "Our kind, the Pemdai, have sworn to protect your kind, and your world, for as long as we have existed. Our whole way of life depends upon it. To understand this, you must be aware of why Earth is so important, not only to us, but to all other realms outside of it."

Reece swallowed hard.

"I know it isn't easy to believe, Miss Bryant, for someone in your position, with your lack of background in this area, I do hope the experiences you have faced by coming into Pemdas have helped you accept that you are truly in another dimension. If you can accept this, everything else I tell you will be easier to believe."

She had accepted it. Somewhere between the park in Philadelphia and this palace, she had come to believe the impossible.

"Earth serves as a center point to all other worlds and dimensions. Most dimensions exist only because of the unique way Earth spins on its axis. If this is altered, it could either imprison the inhabitants inside their own dimension or make the dimension itself nonexistent. If Earth were manipulated in a particular way, our dimension would suffer the latter. It would destroy our world entirely." He narrowed his eyes, as if trying not to imagine what he spoke of.

Reece looked at him, confused. "So this world…I mean dimension…only exists because of Earth?"

He nodded. "Not only because of Earth, but because of the position of Earth as it spins on its axis. Unfortunately, there are ways to manipulate, or shift, that position. If the

Earth's position is changed, then it will destroy all of the vortices, or portals, of other dimensions. This would imprison the people in their own world. Because of Earth, vortices are opened and inter-dimensional travel is possible."

"But you said your dimension would be destroyed?" Reece asked, still doubtful of what he was informing her about.

"Yes, that is correct. You see, while there are many other dimensions out there, Pemdas is the only dimension that is *on* Earth. That is why it would destroy us, instead of imprison us to our land. You will find, and may have already noticed, that even though there are differences between Pemdas and Earth, there are many similar qualities as well."

Reece's lips twisted as she tried to understand what he was telling her. "This doesn't make sense to me. So, I'm still on Earth…but in a completely different world…I mean, dimension? How is this possible?"

Navarre looked toward Levi and Harrison, who both sat listening as intently as if they'd never heard the explanation before. "Miss Bryant, I can explain all of the properties of dimensions and how they exist, but that is not what I want you troubled about right now. Allow me to address your initial concern. The reason you are with us is because many years ago, Earth faced the danger of being altered. The individuals who sought to manipulate Earth are our greatest enemy. They are the Ciatron; they come from a dimension known as Ciatris. These beings are extremely intelligent. They have many mind-altering powers, and they can shift into any form they wish. Your father, in your room that night, was not your father; it was a shape-shifting Ciatron, there to gather information about you. Of course, as soon as Harrison and Levi became aware of his presence, they intercepted him and removed him from Earth."

Reece's mind was beginning to hurt. "Something from another world was in my room?" She remembered the day of her aborted plane trip. "It wasn't the first time, though. My father—or whatever that thing was—came to see me before, right?"

Navarre confirmed. "Yes, Miss Bryant, we know. That threat was removed as well. These two young men here have been pretty busy watching out for you in the last week or so."

"But, what do they want? Why do they want anything to do with me? I can't give them anything; they have no reason to be concerned with me!"

Navarre exhaled softly. "Oh, but they do. They believe they know who you are."

"Oh? Who am I, then?"

"You are the descendant of a very important man, and within your mind you have a vital piece of information that the Ciatron need. They will stop at nothing to obtain this information. You are the one that all worlds and dimensions refer to as 'the Key'."

"What? My ancestor? This doesn't make sense! I'm a Key? Key to what?" Reece's heart was pounding again. She wasn't sure she wanted to hear any more.

Navarre nodded. "I know this is a lot of information to take in. You must understand, the knowledge I have about your ancestor, and your current importance, was not learned in one night. I can't explain it all in one night either. But I can tell you what you need to know to be able to trust us, and the decisions we've made on your behalf. I understand your fears and concerns, and I will not have you ignorant while you remain in Pemdas. I need you to be comfortable living amongst us and to understand why you are safer inside our borders."

Reece closed her eyes and inhaled deeply, trying to bring her thoughts under control. This was too much. She was still having difficulty believing she was no longer on Earth. She did not feel threatened by the Emperor, nor by Harrison or Levi, but what she was learning more than her mind could bear. She felt a tear run down her cheek and quickly wiped it away.

Levi stood up. "Father, I believe it would be best if I escorted Miss Bryant on a short walk. Fresh air may help her gather her thoughts."

Navarre nodded in agreement as all three men looked toward Reece sympathetically. "Perhaps that would be best. We can continue this discussion later. My dear, please do not worry. You will understand soon enough. When that time comes, I believe that you will come to appreciate the security you have been given." He smiled sympathetically.

Harrison approached her. "This has been a lot for one person from Earth to take in. Not only are there other dimensions and worlds out there, but you are forced to live in one of them. It's a lot for anyone to absorb. Although, if it helps, once you are able to accept most of this information, I would be surprised if you weren't begging to take up residence in Pemdas." He smirked and winked playfully at her.

Reece nodded in return. Maybe Levi was right, maybe she did need to get outdoors. Although given the way she was feeling now, she would rather be alone.

Levi smiled at her as he offered his arm.

She was immediately entrapped by the way his sapphire blue eyes glistened as they stared down at her. She had not yet been in a position where their eyes had locked in such a way. In fact, she hadn't really had an opportunity to see just how handsome the man truly was.

When his full lips parted, they displayed his perfect teeth and offered her a brilliant smile. The tiny cleft in his chin highlighted his strong jawline. His dark hair was long enough to display a natural wave, and it lay perfectly in place. His hair alone would tempt any woman to run her fingers through it and draw his lips down onto hers… *Ugh, why does this guy have to be so good-looking? How am I supposed to think straight?* Reece thought as she tried to force herself to quit gawking at the man. This was not like her, and she wasn't about to act like some foolish love-struck girl. *Stay focused,* she demanded herself.

Levi looked down at her with concern. "My apologies, Miss Bryant. I feel that all we have done in the past few hours is force decisions on you. If you do not care to join me on a walk, I will completely understand."

Reece looked up into his eyes and sighed. "Actually, I would really appreciate the walk. Thanks." And she took his arm.

Chapter 5

As Levi led Reece out of the room, two men wearing cream and gold livery opened the doors for them. Harrison and Navarre were still in conversation when the doors closed behind Reece and Levi.

Levi led them back down the staircase, remaining silent at her side. Reece was grateful; she was in no frame of mind for conversation. When they reached the bottom of the stairs, Levi led them to the back of the room, which displayed only substantial French-style windows and exhibited an expansive view of the outdoor gardens. Two men stood at attention and immediately reached to pull the doors open for them. Reece watched Levi as he politely nodded, thanking the men for their service.

She turned her attention to the steps that led down to the courtyard. At the bottom, a stone path wandered past an enormous, three-tiered marble fountain. The outdoor garden was decorated with statues, flowering bushes, and uniquely trimmed greenery, which appeared to lead to a maze.

Levi led her past the courtyard to a black iron gate. He unlatched it and led her out and away from the grounds of the Palace. They walked downhill until they came to a swiftly flowing river and turned to walk along it. It was the same river Reece noticed on their ride in.

Reece broke the silence. "This place is so beautiful, but I can hardly believe any of it is real. I feel like I'm dreaming." There was no waking explanation for the unique beauty of this place, for how every color dazzled and glistened.

"Miss Bryant, I can appreciate your lack of belief in everything you've experienced today. I suppose, when you find you don't wake up, you'll have to acknowledge the reality of Pemdas." He led her toward a narrow stone bridge. A waterfall thundered down from the hillside to their left. The pool of water below it was crystal blue, and the spray from the splashing water sparkled like diamonds as it reflected the sun's light.

Where did that waterfall come from? "I feel like I'm lost in paradise," said Reece. "As much as I want to believe this day has been a dream, I don't think my mind is capable of making up this place." She turned to Levi. "I'm having a hard time accepting that I'm here—and then to be told I am some kind of a special person—it's just too weird. How can any of this be possible?"

Levi looked back at her with concern. "We're all aware of the distress we've caused you. We couldn't help it, but that doesn't make it easier for you. Let's sit, and I'll try my best to explain more."

Once over the bridge, Levi led Reece over to a mound of grass. He motioned for her to sit, and he followed as well. They sat overlooking a large pool of clear water, surrounded by ferns, and a forest of trees all around them.

Levi stared at the pool. "To understand why you're here, you must first be aware of who you are." He turned to her. "This will most likely be difficult for you to accept."

He was right about that, anyway. *I know who I am,* thought Reece. "Why?" she asked.

"Because who you are relates to things you've never known, or even believed are possible. It will help that you do keep an open mind." He seemed to marshal his thoughts for a moment. "My father spoke earlier of the importance of the manner in which Earth currently spins on its axis. And about how Earth went through a time of vulnerability to being altered. The Ciatron took advantage of that, and they set up a domain on Earth. They were in the beginning stages of a full invasion of the planet. Have you ever heard of Atlantis?"

Reece frowned. "Sure…that place was real? It's the city that's underwater, isn't it?"

Unexpectedly, Levi grinned. "That would be one way to put it. It was completely destroyed, but before that it was a land created and ruled by the Ciatron. The people of Earth believed the Ciatron were a higher being, sent to bring them knowledge and power. During this time, my ancestors tried to convince those of Earth about the dangers amongst them. They also battled relentlessly against the Ciatron and found themselves losing."

"And that's why–?"

"Yes. Fortunately, there was an extremely intelligent man on Earth who saw the Ciatron for what they were— foreign invaders. He worked closely with the Pemdai people, and with his knowledge, and our help, a peculiar stone was created. This stone had tremendous power. It was used only once—to destroy the city, and the Ciatron there as well. Then it was hidden."

"Probably a good thing," Reece said. "It doesn't sound like anything you'd want to fool with."

"More than you know. The stone not only destroyed Atlantis, it held the power to stabilize Earth on its axis. When hidden, it does its job quietly. But anyone who should find, possess, and control the stone would have power over Earth. All dimensions and worlds are safe as long as the stone remains undiscovered."

"This man…who was he?" Reece asked, unsure about why she wanted to know. Aristotle? Euclid?

Levi arched his brow sharply. "His name was Paul Xylander. He was your ancestor, Reece. He is the reason you are an extremely vital person."

Reece exhaled, "Are you serious? He must have thousands—millions—of descendants! I can't be the only one, there is no possible way."

"Miss Bryant, you can try to calculate the odds and complicate things more, if you desire. However, none of it matters; you are his last surviving heir."

Reece cocked her head to the side, trying to follow him. "Okay, fine. So if this is true, and I am, then I'm significant because I'm related to the man?"

Levi nodded. "For the most part, yes. You see, after the powers of the stone were known to every world and dimension, your ancestor hid it away, never to be found or discovered again. But he genetically imprinted a map to its location within his mind. He also fashioned it to pass down through all of his direct descendants."

You've got to be kidding me, she thought. "I have a map in my mind?" Reece's voice rose. "That's what these people want?"

Levi chuckled. "In a manner of speaking, yes. As my father said earlier, you are known throughout all the dimensions as 'The Key'; the special one who holds the knowledge within their mind to the location of the stone. The map is not so easily accessed, though. When your ancestor created this unique way of passing down information, he also protected any mind that carries it. Your ancestor considered this and designed a defensive barrier around the information you carry; this way, no one, not even one who possesses the talent to read and alter minds, can access the information within yours."

Reece swallowed hard. "Well, should I know where this stone is, then? I mean, it's in my mind, right?"

"Yes, it is in your mind, but no, you don't have free access to it. Frankly, we're not sure you'll ever be able to see the information locked inside your mind."

"Oh." She thought a minute. "Well, how do you know these Ciatron people haven't already taken the information from me? Maybe it's not even there anymore."

Levi exhaled softly. "Miss Bryant, the Ciatron are not the only individuals who can see into people's minds." He stared intently at her.

It took her a moment to understand what he was saying. "You're telepathic. You've been reading my mind all this time?" She edged away a little.

Levi laughed, but he looked concerned, too. "It's not as you imagine, Reece. Yes, we have that capability, but we have control over it. We would never intrude into anyone's thoughts unless their safety demands it."

Reece lowered her head. "And just when I was starting to appreciate your stories."

"You have nothing to fear, your mind is protected. Your thoughts are constantly rewriting themselves; they are scrambled to those with the ability to read them. Trying to read your mind is disorienting, to say the least."

Reece turned back to him. "So—you've tried?"

Levi stared at her intently. "As I said, only for protection. We had to see if the Ciatron had found a way into your mind and discovered you were the one they were searching for. The one disguised as your father—we saw the effect he had on you. We had to make sure your mind hadn't let down its defenses."

"The thought of having my mind read—ugh. Well, at least good old Granddad thought ahead and protected me from that." She gave a small, bitter laugh. "So the Ciatron guy didn't get his information from me, then?"

"No, and that's what was happening in the park. They planned to take you into their world and retrieve the information through other methods."

"Other methods? Um, what other methods?"

Levi's countenance grew dark. "Methods that don't include consideration for your well-being, Reece. They would find a way to scrape the information out of your mind. The Ciatron don't care if they leave a brain intact when they're done either. This is why our ancestors swore to yours, and all other worlds, that we would protect the Key. Since you are the last of your ancestor's bloodline, the map is within only you now. You are the Key. We couldn't take chances with your welfare. It is why we brought you into our world. No other being, including the Ciatron, can pass through the defensive barriers of Pemdas; you are perfectly protected here. I hope you can see why we felt it necessary to bring you here."

"Defensive barriers? Was that the bright light that flashed in the car earlier, when we should have crashed into the mountainside?"

Levi grinned. "No. That was the vortex we drove through from Earth into the dimension of Pemdas. We use our cars to pass through vortices; our horses are the only way to pass over the protective barriers of Pemdas."

She remembered the horses jumping into the air. "The gray mist was the protective barrier?"

Levi nodded. "Yes. And with that knowledge, I hope you will feel that you are safe here. Nothing can cross over those barriers without our horses."

"Uh, yeah, I guess. So, why do the Ciatron want to destroy all the dimensions anyway?"

"It is not destruction they seek, but control...destruction is merely a by-product of this control."

Reece stared at Levi quizzically. "Control? Control of what?"

"Control over all of the dimensions out there. The need for total power has always consumed the Ciatron. If the stone was in their possession, they would have the power they need to destroy any dimension that refused to serve under them. Right now, with the stone hidden away, the Ciatron cannot achieve their greatest desire."

"Unless, of course, they find it...with the map that's in my head? Well, isn't that just fantastic for me?" Reece returned sarcastically.

Levi nodded. "Unfortunately, yes."

Reece drew her knees up and wrapped her arms around them. "It's all kind of stupid, if you ask me."

Levi looked at Reece in confusion. "I am not sure I follow you?"

Reece laughed. "Finally! Now you know how I've been feeling for the last couple of hours."

"Reece—" Levi looked at her with remorse.

She arched her brow, challenging him with a proud grin. *Got him!* Levi's eyes suddenly changed. They glistened with humor while his lips curved up slightly, leaving Reece momentarily stunned by the beauty of his perfect face. Her breath caught, and soon after she felt the blood rushing to her cheeks, instantly betraying her. She had no other option but to look away and regain control of her emotions. *Perfect, Reece! Now you really look like an idiot.* She demanded herself to pull it together. Strikingly handsome or not, she could not allow herself to be captivated by the man.

When Reece brought her attention back to him, she noticed he had returned his gaze out to the water in front of them. *Nice job, Reece, way to make an unnecessarily awkward moment for both of you.*

It was up to her to break the silence. "You may not agree with me, but if you think about it, it was kind of stupid for Paul Xylander to create the map. I mean, why would he do something like that? Why would he leave something so powerful, vulnerable? It doesn't make sense to me that he would hide it away and then leave the possibility of it being found again. From what you've told me about him, the guy seemed smart, but I'd have to argue with his intelligence about creating the map," Reece stated confidently.

Levi looked at her and answered her directly, "He was not sure if the stone's powers would ever be needed again. He and my ancestors feared that there might possibly be a day when the Ciatron would return and find some other way to do damage or control the Earth. The map to the stone was fashioned to protect Earth should another Ciatron invasion arise."

"And if that day should happen to come—you guys would have to kill me and scrape my mind, or whatever, to get the information?" She stared at him suspiciously.

Levi's expression went quickly from appalled to saddened by her remark. "Reece, please understand, the Pemdai would never attempt such a thing! Not for any reason whatsoever. "There are other ways of retrieving the information without causing you harm. However, your mind must let its defenses down in order for that to happen."

"Well, how do I do that? Maybe if I can get you the information, you can take control and I can go home."

Levi chuckled. "Miss Bryant, I understand this is difficult for you; however, it is more complicated than that. But with what I have told you, I do hope you have developed a better understanding of who you are and why you are here."

Reece's mouth twisted. Oddly enough, it made sense to her. Part of her was starting to accept what he said, although she still didn't understand all of it. A thought came to her. "Why are the Ciatron only now trying to get to me? I mean, I've been alive for over 24 years now, and I've never been noticed by them before. Why did they suddenly take an interest in me?"

"I must admit, that's partially our fault. We were watching you a little too closely. The Ciatron were watching us, and..."

Reece looked at him quizzically. "Exactly how close were you following me?"

"Never closely enough to intrude upon your privacy; although, in the last week or so we may have seemed to do so. We were forced into the open when the Ciatron tried to carry an entire aircraft into their dimension."

"That's why you both were on the airplane, and everything was so...weird?"

"Yes. We were keeping a closer watch on you then. We had just been informed that the Ciatron were planning your abduction. If we'd not been alerted to that, we would have simply made sure you got safely on the aircraft, and other Guardians would have been waiting to watch over you in San Diego. With the threat of the Ciatron, we could not allow you out of our sight for that amount of time, and definitely not aboard a vessel that is so easily transported into other dimensions."

Reece stared at him in concentration. "What really happened on the plane? Why didn't anyone else notice it but me?"

"We have tools—devices to alter what seems real to other minds. Due to the defensive barrier within your mind, none of our devices work on you. That's why you were aware of everything, while those around you were not. If they had been, we would have had the entire aircraft in disarray."

"And the bright flashes of lights?"

Levi nodded. "The bright lights were a result of us removing the two Ciatron men—the ones dressed as pilots— and sending them back to their dimension."

"And then today…how did you know about the park? How did you find me there?"

Levi's lips turned up slightly. "We always know where you are, Reece. But to be aware of the danger you were to possibly face? That information was revealed to us by the presence of the Ciatron in your room the night before. They had many plans to gain access to you while you were alone, one of which you discovered this morning. They followed you to the park and tried to throw us off by hiring two human men to capture you instead of doing it themselves. They used other Ciatron invaders to distract us. Initially, their plan worked, and that was why I was almost too late getting to you. They knew we were focused on one particular threat and that we were not considering any human danger. It was when we realized they were being too obvious with their distractions that something was not right."

"Yeah, that was pretty terrifying." She shuddered at the memory.

"We should have never let it go that far; however, I'm grateful that you're here now, safe."

Levi studied her, and this time Reece didn't let it affect her thought process. Instead, she studied him as well. Something was very unique about the man's deep set, sapphire-blue eyes. Her eyes moved over his face. It was agonizingly perfect. His olive-toned complexion was flawless; a feint shadow highlighted his high cheekbones and gave a perfect definition to his chiseled jawline. The stunning beauty of the man was overwhelming. For one who never really judged people by their appearance, Reece found herself judging him. There was something not so entirely normal about his appearance. Something…not so human. Her emotions had never once played victim to a man's appearance before. It was bothering her that this was happening with him, and happening at a time when she needed to remain undistracted.

"So," she continued studying his face, "the Ciatron are aliens? So what does that make you?"

He smiled wryly. "Given that we are not native to Earth, we, too, can be considered extra-terrestrial beings."

Reece shook her head, and Levi laughed. "Reece, we are flesh and blood, just as you are. The only difference between a human being and a Pemdai being is the way our minds work. We have complete control over our minds, and we utilize it to our advantage. For example, if faced with pain, I can shut off the pain receptors in my body so I can no longer feel that pain. Our talents go far beyond that, but for now I think that is a fair enough explanation." He looked at her hopefully.

Reece smiled and shrugged her shoulders with disbelief and amusement. "Oh, yes, fair enough. So—you're all just a race of super-humans. That's no big deal."

Levi tilted his head and grinned at her. "If that is what helps you to understand us, then yes, super-humans."

"And the telepathic thing, part of the super-human stuff?"

"Yes."

Reece bit her lip in concentration, trying to think of more things he could be capable of, when Levi stood abruptly and reached his arm out to her.

He smiled sympathetically at her. "I'm sure I have probably given you more than enough information for you to absorb for now. I know this has been quite a stressful day for you, and I would be happy to answer any further questions you might have, but for now I believe it would benefit you more to relax and freshen up. Allow me to escort you back to the Palace."

Reece, reminded of her appearance earlier in the bathroom, couldn't agree more. For the first time since she met the man, she truly did appreciate his concern for her. She placed her delicate hand in his sturdy palm and rose up. They began slowly toward the Palace.

"My mother has a special room prepared for you," said Levi. "She has already made plans to escort you down to dinner tonight. I hope this will be agreeable?"

Reece looked up and smiled back at him. She couldn't help but find his old-fashioned manners attractive. "I believe it will agree with me, and I thank you for your concern."

Levi smirked. "Then please allow me to escort you to your room."

Chapter 6

The room that was set aside for Reece was astounding. For one thing, it was enormous! And it had doors that seemed to lead to other rooms—a suite of rooms, probably, since this one was set up as a sitting room, not a bedroom.

Levi's features lightened with amusement at her surprise. He had guided her here himself, rather than ask a servant to do so. *Maybe so he could watch the country cousin's reaction,* she thought. She hated to admit it, but she felt intimidated. "Levi...um..."

"Reece, this room has been arranged and prepared for you by my mother. It may be, perhaps, more than one person requires. However, when accommodating guests, she spares no detail or comfort, and any attempt to dissuade her from this extravagance will fall upon deaf ears."

Reece could not help but smile back at his grin. She could tell he was restraining laughter. "Are all the rooms this big?"

"Most are, yes. Some are bigger. We have many close friends and relatives living throughout Pemdas. We enjoy providing them all of the comforts of their own home while they visit us, sometimes for months at a time."

Reece nodded her head. "Well...I suppose I can get used to this. Maybe too used to it. I mean, staying here is probably going to make it difficult when I have to go back to my two-bedroom apartment in Philadelphia." She laughed.

"You will also have one of my mother's maidens to attend to you. I suppose she will help you find your way around your chambers as well," he added. He pressed his lips together in a fine line, preventing them from turning up into a smile.

Reece squinted at him, feigning suspicion, and Levi laughed aloud.

She lifted her chin. "This is all very amusing for you."

Levi shook his head. "Please, forgive me. I in no way intended to make light of your situation amongst us. I believe my mother would punish me severely if she knew I had welcomed you to your room in this manner." As hard as he tried to pull all humor from his face, he did not succeed.

Reece laughed in return. "Don't worry about it; I'll be fine."

Levi became more serious. "Once you are ready, my mother will be here to escort you to dinner. I shall see you then. If there is anything extra that you require, the maiden will be able to assist you, or to fetch one of us if need be." He nodded respectfully to her and made his exit.

Reece watched him leave. She was finding him more and more interesting.

She turned back to the exceptional room that awaited her. Square columns framed the entry hall and the living room area. A warm, honey-toned color filled the walls, giving the room a more intimate feel. At first glance, Reece was truly overwhelmed by the sight of the room before her.

The furniture was lavish, as all the furniture she'd been witnessing in this palace was. However, it was the way the room was arranged that allowed for a more intimate feel, leaving Reece less intimidated to be in it. A long sofa with matching chairs had been arranged in front of a fireplace.

The sofa and matching elegant chairs were upholstered with silk-like fabric, cream in color, and outlined in a darkly-polished, ornately-carved wood. The furniture was so rich and exquisite, she was afraid to touch it.

Rich ornaments of vases and sculptures were subtly placed on free-standing marble-topped tables throughout. Four large arcaded windows were adorned with a rich silk fabric and pulled up on each side to give a subtle view of the Palace gardens and wooded hills that were situated at the backside of the Palace.

Reece was overwhelmed by the grandeur of the room and had forgotten she should be afraid to sit on the fine, rich furniture. So it was when she had turned to sit on the sofa that she heard a shy voice. "You must be Miss Bryant?"

A young maiden who, if Reece were to guess, was around the age of seventeen approached her, carrying a tea tray. She was a picture of flawless beauty, with soft, white skin and long, dark hair.

"Yes, I am. Thank you."

"My name is Jasmeen, and I am here for anything you may require." The young maiden set the tray on a small table next to the sofa. She poured steaming hot tea into a porcelain cup and handed the cup with a saucer to Reece. "First things first," Jasmeen smiled brightly, "I am under orders to make sure you are completely rejuvenated prior to dinner this evening."

"Thank you, I think."

Jasmeen narrowed her eyes, studying the clothing Reece wore. She spoke confidently. "I would love to take you on a tour of your rooms, but I believe there are more pressing issues to be handled before that. First I have arranged a nice warm bath, and then you need a change of clothes."

Reece looked down at the running ensemble she had thrown together earlier that day. "That may be a problem. I didn't have a chance to pack my bags for this little vacation. I'm afraid to admit, this is all I have to wear."

Jasmeen giggled in return. "Miss Bryant, as we prepared for your arrival, we took your wardrobe into consideration. I have a closet filled with fashionable garments that will fit you perfectly."

Reece chuckled. "Well then, I guess I can't argue."

Jasmeen smiled kindly at Reece. "Come, follow me. I have a bath already drawn for you."

Reece stood and followed the vibrant young maiden through a door, which opened into a small hallway.

"The water is a perfect temperature, and I believe you will feel much more rejuvenated when you are done," Jasmeen proclaimed while opening a door to their left.

Reece's jaw dropped open, not only at the size of this particular room, but at the objects in it. *Why am I surprised? Nothing should surprise me in this place anymore.* Claiming the entire length of the wall in front of them was a rectangular marble tub, sitting up on an elevated surface. Four marble steps led up to where candles were lit and placed in tall glass containers placed around the thick sides of the extravagant bath. She was thankful to find they had showers here as well, as a large enclosed area, surrounded by clear glass on three sides, was perfectly centered on the back wall to her right. The wall to her left had a decorative door, and further down a pedestal sink sat in front of a large oval mirror.

"Through that door, you will find the lavatory," Jasmeen advised as she led Reece toward the enormous tub. She reached down and picked up a porcelain container. "This solution will cleanse your hair, and soften it as well." She pointed toward four round soap-like objects. "Those will not only help to cleanse your body, but rejuvenate and eliminate any fatigue in it as well." She looked at Reece and smiled.

"Wow, thank you."

"You have plenty of time before dinner is served, so relax and indulge yourself." Jasmeen pointed down to where she had placed two neatly folded fluffy towels. "Use these to dry, and right here," she lifted the sleeve of a white matching bath robe, hanging next to the grand bathtub on a free standing rack, "this is your robe. Once you are done, exit to your left, and I will be waiting in the vanity room. Is there anything else I can get for you?"

Reece laughed. "I think this will do. Thanks, Jasmeen."

Jasmeen gave Reece a quick curtsey and made her exit.

Reece set her tea next to a candle on the edge of the bathtub. She slipped out of her clothes and relaxed into the warm water. The water was like silky fabric against her skin, and any previous tension her body carried prior to slipping into it was rapidly leaving.

Jasmine was correct about the rejuvenating effects of the soaps. When she washed her face, her eyes did not feel as tired as before, and she did not believe her skin had ever felt softer in all her life. *This is like a miracle bath or something.* She laughed inwardly.

Now completely refreshed, Reece sank back down into the tub and closed her eyes. She had no idea how long she sat like this before she finally decided to step out. Once she dried off her body, she twisted her hair up in a towel on top of her head, slipped into the robe that was set out for her, and started out to where the young maiden said she would be waiting.

Upon her exit of the bathroom, Reece turned left and followed the small hallway. It led her into another brightly lit room, where the young maiden was waiting to attend to her. This room alone was the size of her apartment in Philadelphia. She stood in amazement, staring at a tall mirror that nearly encompassed the entire wall before her. A long marble table stood in front of it, with an array of beauty supplies laid out in an orderly fashion.

Jasmeen motioned for Reece to have a seat in a chair in front of the table. "Please, have a seat. Let me get started on your hair."

Reece laughed. "Are you kidding me? This is beyond every woman's dream. This is a makeup room?"

Jasmeen smiled and nodded. "I suppose you could call it that. Now please, come and sit."

Reece stared at the young maiden with concern. "I really don't need you to go through all of this trouble to help me get ready. I'm sure you have better things to do?"

The maiden smiled. "Miss Bryant, I will hardly be putting myself out. I understand you are not accustomed to having someone to attend you, but in time you will learn to embrace it. Now please, come and sit."

Reece did as the young girl asked and relaxed back into the chair. She watched as Jasmeen took the towel from her hair and quickly ran a brush through it. She watched as each stroke of the brush through her hair made it drier. *Now that's weird.* "Is that brush, like, a blow dryer, too?"

Jasmeen continued running the brush through Reece's rapidly-drying hair. "A blow dryer? I am unsure as to what that is?"

Reece laughed. "Oh, well, it's what we use on Earth; it blows hot air into your hair and dries it."

Jasmeen smiled. "And that is healthy for your hair? It's not damaging to heat it in such a way?"

Reece's lips twisted. "Well, yeah, I guess it does damage it. So, that brush doesn't conduct heat in any way or anything like that?"

"No, there is an energy force that is expelled through the fine bristles. It evaporates the water with every stroke. I suppose you could say the energy works the same way that heat would. It's also the same energy we use for our illumination," she answered while continuing her long brush strokes through Reece's now almost completely dried hair.

Reece reached up and ran her fingers through her hair so she could study its transformation. She stared in amazement, as she could not remember her hair ever looking so shiny and healthy. *I need to make sure I take that brush and the shampoo back to Philadelphia when I leave. This is fabulous.*

Still uncomfortable with the young girl styling her hair, she tried to convince her, once again, that she could take care of it on her own. "You really don't have to go through all this trouble. I can do the rest from here."

Jasmeen giggled again. "Don't fret over such nonsense. You have extremely beautiful hair, and I shall enjoy being the one to style it!" She set the brush on the counter and stared at Reece in the mirror. "Blue eyes. Good."

Reece smiled as Jasmeen muttered to herself.

Jasmeen turned to Reece and started applying powder across the surface of her face. She worked quickly on her cheeks, eyes, and lips. As quickly as she had started, she had finished. She put her supplies away and grabbed a tiny, round rod. *Great, here comes the curling iron.* As Jasmeen began making tiny ringlets in her hair, Reece noticed that there was no power cord, and from what she could tell, no heat to create the curl.

"Does that use the same energy as that brush to make the curls?"

Jasmeen laughed softly as she continued focusing on her work. "Yes, it does."

Reece looked at her reflection in the mirror and was quite impressed with the makeover. Her complexion looked flawless; her wide eyes sparkled with a pearlescent color. Her cheekbones had more definition than Reece believed was possible. Her lips had a natural gloss upon them, enhancing their natural color and fullness. The strangest part was that she felt as if she wore no makeup at all.

Once Jasmeen finished, she set the curling iron on the counter and smiled. "There, now you are ready to dress."

Most of her hair had been pulled to the top of her head, falling in small, intertwining ringlets, strewn with tiny, cream-colored roses. A few larger curls cascaded over her left shoulder.

Reece swallowed hard, gazing into the mirror. "Um…wow. I really don't know what to say. Thank you, Jasmeen."

Jasmeen laughed. "Thank you, Miss Bryant. Now, in order to complete the look, we must have you get dressed. Follow me; your closet is just over here, around this corner."

Reece followed her farther into the room, where another door was. As they stood at the entrance to the room, Reece gawked at its contents. "All of these clothes are for me? Are they all gowns?"

Jasmeen laughed. "Indeed, they are." She walked over, pulled a dress out, and turned to hand it to Reece. "Now, here is what you will wear for dinner tonight."

Reece reached out and took the shimmering, pale blue dress that Jasmeen had offered her. "Jasmeen, exactly what kind of dinner is this? I think you may have me completely overdone."

Jasmeen laughed. "When the Empress arrives, you will most likely feel underdressed."

Reece studied the extravagant gown, knowing that a corset would likely accompany it, and she hoped that there was another option. There was no way she was about to wear this. It was too much. "Jasmeen, I'm not trying to insult you here, but do you remember what I was wearing when I first walked in the room?"

"Miss Bryant—"

Reece shook her head. "Please, I can't wear this. Is there something a bit simpler? I'm not really a fancy person like that—not even on Earth."

Jasmine grinned. "Well, I can't say I didn't try. The Empress did take into consideration our differences in fashion when she had your wardrobe tailored. Give me a moment." She took the dress from Reece's hands and turned to walk deeper into the closet.

Reece sighed with relief. She really didn't want to make the sweet girl feel bad, but there was no way Reece was going to wear that gown.

Jasmine returned with another dress. *Great, these are the options? Seventeenth Century queen, or red carpet premiere?*

Reece exhaled. "Jasmeen? I'm not sure that this is any better than the other one."

She scrutinized the dress. The shiny, satin-type material was a brilliant scarlet color. Reece noticed its daring neckline and the capped sleeves that were designed to hang off the shoulders. The hopeful look in Jasmeen's eyes forced her to give in. "Well...I guess this will have to work."

Jasmeen giggled with delight. "You will look ravishing in this gown. Now, over there are your undergarments. Once you have them on, I will help you with the gown."

Reece restrained the urge to roll her eyes in response to the young maiden's excitement.

"Jasmeen?" she called out once she was ready.

"Yes, Miss Bryant. I have the dress here, now raise your arms and—"

"Jasmeen," Reece turned and stared at the excited girl, "how did you all know my size? Please do not tell me that Levi and his cousin...what was his name?"

"Master Harrison?"

Reece's eyes narrowed down at Jasmeen's cheerful smile. "Yes, of course, *Master* Harrison. They didn't go through my clothes in order to give you my measurements, did they?"

Jasmeen stared reassuringly at Reece's irritated expression. "Miss Bryant, they simply informed us that you are very close in shape and size to Master Levi's younger sister, Princess Elizabeth. The Empress took this into consideration for the tailoring of your garments."

Reece let out a breath of relief. "That's good to know. Now, let's get this dress on."

Jasmeen helped Reece slip the dress over her head. Reece stared in shock at her reflection in the mirror. Her hand absently brushed over her stomach as she twisted to the side to view the back of the dress.

Reece gasped in awe at the webbed pattern of what appeared to be red rubies and diamonds, which were strung throughout the open back. The satin material of the dress fell from her shoulders and drooped down to the small of her back, just below the stringed jewels. Her back felt exposed and bare; however, the jewels were so many, and webbed in such a unique pattern, that her skin was hardly visible. She was at a loss for words.

"Miss Bryant, you look absolutely stunning."

"Thank you, Jasmeen," she replied softly, still taking in the beauty of the gown.

Jasmeen chuckled. "If you are intended to stay for long, I hope you will be willing to try some of the other gowns that are of our fashion?" she asked hopefully. "I believe you will look breathtaking in them."

Reece cocked her head. "Jasmeen, let's just take this one day at a time, okay?"

Jasmeen nodded and smiled. "Anything you wish, Miss Bryant. Let us complete the dress, shall we?"

Jasmeen reached around Reece's neck and clasped a necklace. It was a brilliant red ruby, oval-shaped and framed with tiny shimmering diamonds.

Reece gently caressed the necklace. "I feel like a queen."

Jasmeen smiled while placing matching earrings in her ears and finished by clasping a bracelet of rubies on her wrist. "Well, you're the guest of honor."

"Jasmeen, please tell me that I won't walk out there into a room full of people and be the only one dressed like this? I mean, it's beautiful, but it seems a little too elaborate. Are you absolutely sure this is how I should be dressed?"

"You are dressed entirely appropriately. You will definitely feel more comfortable when the Empress arrives. Here are your shoes." She bent down to help Reece put on the matching strappy red heels. "Let us return to the sitting room, and I shall get you a refreshing, hot cup of tea while you await the Empress' arrival."

While Reece sat gently on the small sofa, sipping her tea with care and trying not to ruin her dress, she watched a sunset such as she'd never seen. The vivid green colors of the fields changed as the sun slid below the horizon until the sky was fully dark. They went from shining vividly with the light of the land's peculiar sun to glowing brightly and colorfully, with no apparent light to cause it. It was as if the landscape were lit with a black light. It was similar to what she witnessed in the dark forest, yet with the darkness of night, everything was glowing brighter now. There had to be some light source causing this. Their moon?

She stood up and walked over to the great windows, searching for the source of light that would create such an effect. She found nothing, only an iridescent, purple sky. She glanced down at the gardens she had walked through with Levi earlier and noticed the many different blooms on the bushes and trees were not their normal vibrant colors anymore. Instead, it seemed as if the trees and bushes had multicolored lights strung throughout. It was a rainbow of different colors—teals, fuchsias, lavenders, and many others—that were shimmering with this unique, illuminating quality. The darker it became, the brighter the colors became. *Amazing!*

"Miss Bryant, the Empress, Lady Allestaine, is here to meet you," Jasmeen announced and quietly made her exit.

Reece turned to find a tall, slender woman standing at the top of the steps. The woman was exquisite in every possible manner. The gown she wore was more elaborate than Reece thought possible, but it paled in comparison to her physical beauty, which alone was put in the shade by the kindness and good humor of her expression. A tiny smile appeared on her perfect lips. *This can't be the Empress; she's too young to be Levi's mother.* The brunette hair, the slender figure, all seemed to belong to a woman Reece's age. But the beauty of the face—that was Levi, feminized. And the smile—that, too, was his.

She glided down the steps to where Reece stood. She was taller than Reece, and close-up she had a few wrinkles around her brilliant, chestnut colored eyes. The dress she wore, with the exception of the front bodice and front skirt, was made of a rich, blue-green silken fabric. The front panel and bodice were lined in a dark green velvet material, with a black and silver embroidered sparkling lace overlay. A shimmering ribbon, fashioned out of thousands of tiny diamonds and emeralds, formed a narrow band, which edged over the top of her bodice and swept over her upper arms in three individual strands. She wore a sapphire choker and a tiara of diamonds, emeralds, and sapphires. The lavish jewels made Reece's jewelry look simple and modest.

"I am delighted to meet you, Miss Bryant. My name is Allestaine, and I believe you have already made my son and husband's acquaintance. I trust you were well taken care of by Jasmeen? Let us sit, we have a few moments before we must leave."

Reece smiled and took her seat next to the beautiful woman. "Thank you, should I call you Lady Allestaine?"

"You may call me whatever you like, Miss Bryant. I am accustomed to 'Lady Allestaine' by my closest friends and family; you are welcome to refer to me as such, but only if it is comfortable for you." She smiled.

"Okay, and if you don't mind, I would be more comfortable with you calling me Reece. 'Miss Bryant' isn't really something I'm used to."

Allestaine chuckled. "Very well, then. "Now, please tell me, Reece, are you happy with the arrangements I have made for you? Things can be changed, and other rooms are available, if you are not."

"I couldn't have dreamed of more fabulous accommodations! And Jasmeen has been very welcoming and helpful, thank you. She seems to be an artist; I feel like one of her creations."

"Jasmeen has a way of doing that; she is one of the best in the land. I am truly grateful that her work is to your liking. Tell me, Reece; was your journey to Pemdas pleasant? My husband told me of your distress."

"I am doing better now, thank you. Levi was able to explain more. It is all very difficult for me to try to absorb."

The lady laughed. "Perfectly understandable. I must apologize for being detained with my duties today; I would rather have been the one to help you with your adjustment. I would not like to envision how the men handled it." She shivered delicately. "That is why I am here now. I must have no doubt that you are truly comfortable."

The woman's smile was heartwarming, but Reece could not help but feel intimidated in her presence. Never had she felt so beneath another person, so uncertain of her own manners.

"Lady Allestaine, everything is more than I would dream of asking for. I'm beyond grateful for all of your concern, and all you have done."

"It's the least I could do. I understand you are aware that you will be staying with us for some time?"

"Well, I'm not sure how long, but yes, I am. The Emperor and Levi both mentioned that until things are settled, this is where I will have to stay, for my own safety, and the safety of Pemdas."

"I know they are working on different ways to return you as soon as possible. Until then, we must try to make you as comfortable as may be, living among us. I am aware that the cultures of Pemdas and Earth are different. I am sure you are already starting to gather that yourself?"

Reece laughed as she looked down at herself. "Yes, that will be something I'll have to get used to—dressing up like this, just to eat dinner."

Allestaine laughed with her. "I understand the clothing fashions differ greatly here than what you are familiar with on Earth. I did not expect that you would be thrilled to wear a corset or anything of that nature so quickly. I do hope the modifications I made with the seamstress will suit you for now."

"Yes, I think it will work just fine. I'm a little nervous to eat dinner in a dress so nice, though."

Allestaine stood, preparing to leave, and Reece followed. "Follow my lead at the table, Reece, and all will be perfectly well." The lady gave Reece a teasing wink, and then led her from the room.

Chapter 7

The dinner party awaited their Hostess and guest-of-honor's arrival in a large parlor. Upon entering the lavish room, Reece let out a breath of relief when she found that she and the Empress were not the only ones dressed for a formal affair. Her eyes were drawn to three young women, close to Reece's age, sitting off in a group of their own. The iridescent lighting of the room shimmered off a vast array of bright jewels adorning their extravagant dresses and beautifully arranged hair.

Her eyes were then drawn to the transformed appearances of Levi and Harrison.

Both men were standing next to a tall window at the front of the room, conversing easily, not yet aware of the women's entrance. Levi was a faultless picture of royalty. He wore all black, with the exception of a white shirt, silk waistcoat, and cravat. Harrison stood with his back facing them, and therefore Reece could only assume that under his dark blue tailcoat, he was wearing the same fine attire as Levi.

"Her Imperial Majesty, Lady Allestaine, and the guest-of-honor, Miss Reece Bryant," the footman announced. All conversation ceased, and those who were seated immediately stood. Reece was feeling good until the footman proclaimed their entrance. She felt a wave of anxiety come over her as all eyes fell upon her.

Navarre smiled proudly as he made his way to them. As he approached, he gazed adoringly at his beautiful wife's face as she stretched her hand out for his greeting.

He reached for it and gave a short bow while he kissed the back of her hand. He rose up and smiled. "My love. You look as enchanting as ever tonight." His eyes sparkled with his apparent love for her.

"Thank you, my husband." She gave a quick curtsey.

Navarre brought his attention to Reece. "Miss Bryant, may I affirm that you also look livelier than since I last saw you. I trust you feel more refreshed?"

"I do, thank you." Reece smiled and bit her bottom lip, wondering if she should give the man a curtsey as well. *Ugh, he's the Emperor, of course you have to.* Reece quickly offered the man the best curtsey she could muster and hoped it wasn't noticeable that she had no idea what she was doing.

Once Navarre gave Reece a pleasant nod of acceptance, she looked up to find everyone staring intently at her. Harrison appeared to be restraining himself from bursting into laughter, but Levi's countenance was quite the opposite. There was no trace of humor in his face, as his darkened eyes seemed to be scrutinizing her. *Glad I can amuse one of them at least,* she thought.

Allestaine took Navarre's arm, and he led both women down into the sitting area, where the guests were waiting to meet Reece.

Patiently awaiting introductions were the three young women Reece noticed when she first entered the room and a man who appeared to be close in age to the Emperor and his wife.

"Miss Bryant, allow me to introduce you to Samuel and his two daughters, Simone and Catherine."

Simone had pitch-black hair, more elaborately arranged than that of anyone else in the room. With features favoring her father's, she was as striking as she was attractive. Catherine had lighter hair, and less prominent features.

"Samuel is my chief advisor over the Pemdai Guardians. He and his family will be residing with us while we work on returning you safely home."

Samuel nodded. "My men and I are doing everything within our power to return you to your world. Until then, I hope that you will be comfortable here in Pemdas."

Reece smiled. "Thank you, Samuel."

Navarre acknowledged the young woman who was standing next to Harrison that she had not yet been introduced to.

"This is my niece, and Harrison's oldest sister, Lillian. She and Harrison are my brother Nathanial's children. Nathanial is king of Vinsmonth, one of the largest kingdoms in Pemdas, which is nearly a five-day journey from here."

Reece returned Lillian's pleasant expression with a kind smile. If not for the introduction, Reece would have never assumed this was Harrison's sister. The only likeness she shared with her brother was her blonde hair and light blue eyes. Her features were softer and more rounded than Harrison's.

"We need no introductions here," Navarre added as he rested his hand on Levi's sturdy shoulder, "however, I would like to mention in both Levi and Harrison's presence how proud I am of their efforts today for getting you here safely."

"It's nice to see you both again," Reece returned.

Levi's eyes penetrated through her as he gave her a simple nod. "Miss Bryant," he acknowledged in a deep voice.

She was starting to feel helpless with all of the formalities and traditions she knew nothing about, and she smiled with relief when she saw Harrison's not-so-serious expression.

"Miss Bryant, you appear to be feeling much better." He grinned. "I must say, I am amazed at how well you clean up; after the events you faced earlier, this is very impressive," he teased as he glanced down at her gown.

Allestaine immediately interjected, "Nephew, you know how much I enjoy your wit; however, this is not the time for it."

Reece looked at Allestaine's concerned expression, which was now directed at her. She decided it would be best to reassure the woman that she could take care of herself. "Lady Allestaine, if you saw what I was wearing earlier, I'll have to admit, you'd probably be saying the same thing." She laughed.

Appreciative of the young man's good humor, Reece turned to Harrison, who was watching with amusement. "Thank you, Harrison, I'll take that as a compliment. And I have to say—" she glanced at Harrison's silver and blue striped waistcoat, "you clean up almost as well as I do."

Harrison let out a soft laugh while Levi's lips tightened, stifling a laugh.

"Well, I see you may have finally met someone who can match your quick wit!" Navarre interjected with a laugh.

"Indeed," Harrison nodded in agreement, "I may have." He then smiled mischievously at Reece. "However, only time will tell," he finished with a wink.

Soft laughter filled the room; however, the only person who appeared to be un-amused with Harrison and Reece's banter was Simone. Her pleasing expression from moments ago had been replaced with a scrutinizing one, directed toward Reece.

Allestaine spoke and brought Reece's attention back to a much more pleasant face. "One person is absent this evening." She smiled playfully at her husband.

Navarre laughed. "Well, my lady, I must beg your forgiveness for my absentmindedness. Our daughter, Elizabeth, has been away visiting friends, but she will be arriving home within a day or two and will be excited to make your acquaintance."

Reece smiled. "I look forward to meeting her. Thank you."

Allestaine chuckled. "As you can see, Reece, there should be plenty of female companions to keep you occupied. I know you must have wondered earlier if my nephew and son would be your only source of friendship here."

Reece laughed softly. "It is nice, thank you; and it is very nice to meet you all." She hoped her response was adequate.

Once the introductions had concluded, Navarre offered his arm to Allestaine. "Let us make our way to the dining hall, shall we?"

Allestaine turned to Reece as she accepted her husband's arm. "Levi will escort you, Reece."

"Miss Bryant?" Levi politely requested while offering his arm.

"Thanks," she responded, nerves taking the place of her manners. *I really hope I can pull this dinner off without humiliating myself.* She anxiously speculated what awaited them.

The dinner party followed Navarre and Allestaine out of the room and down a long hallway that ended where two servants opened the double doors in front of them.

Most of the illumination in the dining hall came from the candelabras that were positioned upon the long oval table situated in the middle of the room. Chandeliers hung from the white paneled ceiling, dimmed to allow a more intimate atmosphere.

As they approached the candlelit table, she saw pewter place settings laid out in pristine fashion on top of a beautiful scarlet table cloth. *Well, at least it's darker in here; hopefully, no one will notice if I use the wrong fork,* she thought as she became overwhelmed at the different utensils placed around the table settings.

Navarre led Lady Allestaine to the chair placed to the right of the head of the table, and Levi showed Reece to her place, which was situated to the right of his mother. The guests filtered in around them. Navarre stood at the head of the table, Levi to his left, and Harrison next to him. Samuel stood at the opposite end of the table, with his daughters to his right and Lillian to his left.

The dinner guests stood behind their chairs, waiting to be seated. Before they sat, Reece glanced over at Levi, only to find that he was examining the dress she wore. In the moment his eyes met hers, he exhaled and his expression darkened. He quickly turned his attention to his father.

It seemed clear to Reece that he took issue with what she was wearing. *Oh! Well, looks like the Emperor's son doesn't approve of my wardrobe this evening. Perhaps I should go and change back into my tracksuit; he didn't seem to have a problem with that outfit earlier,* she thought as she laughed inwardly.

Once the Empress was seated, all of the guests followed her example.

"Miss Bryant, I can't help but notice that something seems to have amused you? Is there anything you care to share with the rest of us?" Harrison asked.

Of all the people that would notice Reece laughing at her private joke. "Oh—I was just admiring how well dressed everyone is," she smoothly lied.

Before Harrison could answer her, the staff came out with a variety of foods. Reece stared in awe as each decorated platter filled the dining table before them. Meats, small, game-like birds, and fish were placed in orderly fashion around different soups and breads.

How are we supposed to eat all of this? No wonder they need an obscene amount of flatware, she thought as the servants placed a prepared plate of food down in front of her. Reece looked at the plate of food, then the table in amazement; she could not imagine this small group consuming the entire meal.

A soft laugh came from across the table. "Are you impressed with the meal, Reece, or are you that hungry? If your appetite is as large as your eyes are right now, we may have to order the staff back to the kitchen to bring the second course out this instant."

Reece lifted her eyes from the feast before her and responded with a challenging grin, "I think this should be enough for me, but if not, I will let you know."

Allestaine smoothly cut in, "Nephew, please tell me you have not treated Reece in this manner for the entire day. I am afraid to wonder what her true opinion of us will be."

"Aunt, when have you ever known me to jest? Of course, I was completely formal while introducing Reece to Pemdas." He winked at Reece and grinned.

"What will I do with you, Harrison?" said Allestaine as she reached for her glass of wine. "Although, I must say that I am grateful to both you and Levi today." She looked at her son, who nodded back. "Levi, I understand you helped Reece come to a better understanding of her situation this afternoon?"

Levi looked quickly toward Reece, who smiled. He didn't smile back. "Thank you, Mother," he said unenthusiastically. "I am pleased to hear the information was well-received."

The Lady's eyes narrowed. "As was I, Son. I explained to Reece my concern for not being available upon her arrival. However, with your explanations, she was not as distressed, as I had feared."

"Your gratitude is greatly appreciated; however, there is no need for such accolades." He stared somberly at his mother. "I believe we have only served as our duties have commanded us."

Wow! This guy seems to be in a foul mood. Or maybe he just hates to be in the spotlight. Reece was a little shocked by the response he had given his mother.

"Levi, you must learn to receive gratitude in the spirit in which it is given. I fear you will get little thanks if this is how you receive it."

Harrison joined in. "My lady, I will gladly accept your appreciation for what we have done today. It appears that I must now speak for myself, as my cousin's modesty is sparing me the gratitude I believe I so deserve." He looked toward Levi, laughing. Levi only stared back at him in response, and then brought his attention back to his meal.

What's his problem? He's acting as if he's been abducted from his home, thrust into an alternate reality, and forced into a monkey suit for dinner with strangers, she thought as she took a bite.

The food was delicious, and Reece became so engrossed in the meal before her that she barely noticed Levi engaging her in conversation. "Are you finding your living quarters and arrangements comfortable, Miss Bryant?"

Of course, he waits until I have a mouth full of food. She hurriedly swallowed her bite and answered, "I am, thank you."

Levi didn't have a chance to respond before Simone interrupted. "Miss Bryant, I am not sure what is arranged for you tomorrow, but the other women and I would love to show you around one of the towns we enjoy shopping in." She smiled sweetly toward Reece.

"If there are no plans for me, I'd be happy to go with you."

Allestaine gently placed her delicate hand on Reece's arm. "Reece, you are free to do whatever you wish. Tomorrow will be a lovely opportunity for you get to know the young ladies better."

Reece smiled in confirmation. The dining atmosphere remained mostly subdued after that, and Reece was grateful. Harrison and Levi engaged in minor conversation with each other, and every once in a while Navarre and Samuel would interject on subjects that the ladies didn't seem to know much about; they listened intently, though, and offered encouraging smiles if one of the men glanced in their direction.

Once finished, Reece was pleasantly filled by the delicious meal. One by one, the dinner guests finished their meals as well.

After dinner, Navarre and Allestaine walked arm in arm, leading the group from the dining hall and into the sitting room where she had first met Navarre. The room was pretty much the same, except that more furniture had been added and placed throughout. Musicians sat in the far corner of the room, playing instruments, adding to the relaxed environment the family chose to retreat to.

They walked down toward the large sofas, where everyone found a comfortable seat. Simone asked Reece to join her and her friends in a more secluded seating area, which was situated in the front corner of the room.

Allestaine and Navarre took up seating on the large couches next to Samuel and remained in conversation with him. Levi and Harrison made their way to the large fireplace and remained standing, involved in their own conversation.

From where Reece sat, she had a perfect view of the illuminated lands on the other side of the large windows. She also had an excellent view of the rest of the occupants of the room.

As the room filled with separate conversations, Reece noticed Allestaine keeping a watchful eye on her. When their gazes met, she smiled sweetly at Reece.

As her eyes wandered throughout the room, she couldn't help but notice Harrison and Levi, in their own conversation. Harrison stood casually, his back to Reece and one arm resting on the mantel. In the other hand, he held the glass of wine he had brought with him from the dining hall.

Levi was the exact opposite. He stood tall and straight, as if still in the odd mood he'd been in at dinner, but the conversation with Harrison brought a tiny smile to his lips every now and then. Then he turned a bit, and his eyes met Reece's. She gave him a slight, formal smile and was pleased to see his lips turn up in a faint smile in return. *Nice to see him in a better mood.*

"Levi has mentioned that Earth is full of big cities," Simone spoke, pulling Reece's gaze away from Levi's.

"That's true," Reece answered.

"And there's something about the colors?" Simone continued.

"The colors? Oh, well, yeah, the colors—let me tell you, the nights at home are nothing like this! This is so beautiful!"

Simone smiled charmingly. "Indeed! The beauty of Pemdas is profound. Levi and Harrison have also told us that there is no other dimension out there that displays such beauty—night or day."

I bet they have, Reece thought before responding, "Well, I can't tell you about other dimensions, but in comparison to Earth, Levi and Harrison are correct in saying that it is much more beautiful here."

Reece smiled faintly in return to Simone's proud grin before her interest was drawn to the glowing scenery outside the windows. Reece was starting to develop a mild irritation with the woman. It was in the way she held herself, along with the arrogance of her tone while speaking to Reece. Her negative opinion of the woman was quickly replaced while staring out the window. *Well, I guess the woman does have every right to be proud of living in this place. I really shouldn't fault her for it.* She became so involved in the electric blues, and vivid pinks and reds, that she was startled when Simone addressed her again. "Miss Bryant, how do you pass the evenings on Earth?"

"Well, if my friends and I are not studying, we'll watch television or something."

"Watch television? Is it entertaining?" Lillian asked.

"It is. Although I suppose that would depend on what you would classify as 'entertaining'. Sometimes, I see it as a waste of time and would rather read a book or get out of the house."

"I enjoy the entertainment of having fine conversations with my closest friends," Simone replied. "Hopefully, you will in time, too."

Reece laughed in return as the three women went on talking about people and things she didn't know. As it became obvious the young women were now intentionally ignoring her, Reece returned her attention to the windows.

"Miss Bryant." The deep voice startled her, and the young women immediately silenced, seemingly stunned by the interruption.

Levi and Harrison had made their way to where the young women sat. "I'm curious," Levi continued. "Is there something special that you see in the gardens? I notice that most of your attention has been directed toward them."

He was still extremely reserved, without any humor in his expression, while Harrison's face was lit up with amusement. Had she been rude to look out the window? The other women didn't look upset; they only waited for Reece's response.

"Yes, Miss Bryant," Simone added, "I'm curious as well."

The 'Miss Bryant' thing was getting old and making Reece uncomfortable, so she figured she should just address the issue now. "Please," she looked at the group around her, "call me Reece."

Levi grinned, "Very well then, Reece, is there something in particular that has caught your attention outside?"

"I'm not really watching anything in particular. I'm just intrigued by the way the land lights up at night. I'm sorry if I was being impolite," she said to Simone. "I hope it didn't seem like I was ignoring anyone."

Harrison laughed. "Reece, these ladies would not know if they were being ignored or not. Am I correct, Simone?"

"Harrison, you do go on about nothing! You'll never understand how ladies interact." She looked at Reece. "The beauties of Pemdas can fascinate any one of us at any time, night or day."

Levi cleared his throat. "It's a lovely evening to be outdoors. Would you ladies care to join us for a walk? I believe Reece would have a much improved view of the gardens that she seems so enchanted with."

Simone stood. She was very tall, only a few inches shorter than the men. "That's a wonderful idea, Levi.

Ladies, we should take advantage of the mild evenings while we still have them."

Reece and the other ladies stood in unison and went to bid goodnight to Allestaine. "It's a fine night," the lady said. "Enjoy your walk. I will see you all tomorrow."

Simone led the group gracefully from the room, with the exception of Levi and Harrison, who were detained by Samuel. Reece followed slowly behind the other women. They all walked so elegantly that they appeared to float through the hallway. By comparison, she felt clumsy and loutish. She turned to see if the men were close behind, but only found an empty hallway.

"Reece, dear, please keep up. I don't want to be held responsible for your becoming lost in the hallways." Simone laughed in her soprano voice.

They went through the atrium Levi had showed Reece earlier and out the doors and down the steps to the Palace gardens. Simone, Catherine, and Lillian stopped by a fountain surrounded by concrete benches, took their seats, and smiled up at Reece, who was looking longingly into the greenery.

Catherine laughed. "Reece, you may walk the gardens if you wish. We will be here, relaxing beside the fountain."

Gee, thanks for giving me permission to do something, Reece thought, as she was starting to become irritated with the way these women were talking down to her. Now they were being obvious about trying to get rid of her? Reece did need some time away, as she knew she would likely say something to them in regard to their rude behavior soon enough. "Actually, I think I will. Thanks."

Simone responded with a charming smile. "Enjoy yourself; the gardens are more enchanting when traveled alone and no distractions are present."

Reece followed a path toward plants with glowing, iridescent flowers. They seemed to change color as she moved past them—now purple, now red, now green. As she stepped carefully along the path, farther and farther away, the laughter of the young women began to fade. She was still in the Palace gardens, though, and she was pretty sure she could find her way back. Although she knew it was obvious the women were trying to get rid of her, she appreciated this time alone. The events of the day were starting to catch up with her, and she needed some down time.

Something fluttered its glowing blue wings in front of her. She slowly reached out to it, and it came to rest on her outstretched finger. It was as small as a butterfly and colored like one, but it had only two broad wings, and they were brighter than any butterfly's. She stood still, not moving a muscle as it explored its place of rest on her finger. She felt the weary, stressed energy leaving her body, which was being replaced with a calm peace, as if she'd had a sound sleep.

A soft chuckle from behind made her jump, and the glowing insect fluttered away swiftly. She turned and saw Levi, who was biting his lip to conceal a smile. The good humor that had returned to his face had brightened his deep blue eyes. Pleased that he seemed to be in a much better mood, she decided to smile in return instead of reprimanding him for startling her.

He allowed his lips to curve up at one corner as he spoke softly, "Those are the Tenillian. They are an interesting species in our land. They give their unique energy to objects they touch."

"That little thing that was on my hand? It's what made me feel so rested?"

He smiled down in response to her amazed expression.

"That's amazing! How do they do that?"

He tilted his head, smiling. "They have a unique way of gathering and storing energy from our vegetation; it's simply a transfer of that energy, from them to you."

Her eyes followed him as he approached her. "Nice to see you're in a better mood. Does it take scaring me half to death to put a smile on your face?"

He walked up to her, eyes searching hers. "I'm sorry I startled you. I'm surprised the ladies allowed you to wander off alone, as unfamiliar as you are with the gardens. I decided it would be best to find you before you became lost and were forced to spend your first night in Pemdas outdoors." He laughed. "Harrison is still back with the women, enjoying the opportunity to make them feel ashamed of themselves. Since I am here now, allow me to escort you to another section of the gardens. I believe you will find it even more intriguing."

Reece nodded in acceptance. She followed him quietly as he led her past topiary bushes, glowing vividly green. A miniature bridge over a tiny valley led them to an open area with stone benches. Another small pond, which was surrounded by ferns, shone silver; when she looked, she saw that the shine came from hundreds of small fish, or whatever fish equivalents there were in this place, swimming beneath its surface. In the center, a stone boy played with a stone ball. The ball seemed balanced on a column of water that rose up and spilled into the pond.

Levi led the way to a bench. Insect-like creatures fluttered around them, twinkling like Christmas lights. Large groups of them flew back and forth in the canopy of tall trees over the benches.

"Why does everything glow like this?"

"It is due to the distinctive qualities of our atmosphere. It creates a unique energy that surrounds the lands, allowing the things that feed from it a natural way of glowing." He looked up into the trees. "Even though I've lived here my entire life, I'm still astounded by the beauty of Pemdas at night. I can only imagine how it seems to you."

"I am truly amazed. It's good to hear you admit that you're not used to it either, but then again, you do go to Earth a lot. I can't understand how you would ever want to leave this place."

A voice answered from behind them. "Speaking of Earth…how am I doing with my earlier predictions,

Reece?" Harrison stepped over the bridge and took a seat on an empty bench.

Reece looked at him, confused. "Predictions?"

"I believe I mentioned something along the lines of, 'You will never want to return to Earth.'"

Reece laughed. "Oh. Well, I'm not sure I'm at that point yet. Speaking of returning to Earth, how long do you think it will take until I can go back?"

"It all depends on when the Ciatron lose interest in you. Our hopes are that they'll investigate your stand-in and come to the conclusion that you are not the one they seek. Obviously, the clone does not possess the information that you possess, and we're hopeful that their interest will wane," Levi said.

"What exactly is a 'stand-in' anyway? Obviously, it's something that looks and acts like me, but is it a real living being?"

"No—it's more like a humanoid robot. An android. The exact image of you, and programmed with all of your memories and knowledge."

"What? How does your world make something like that?"

Harrison laughed. "We have inventors and scientists in Pemdas, too, Reece!"

Reece shook her head. "That's really hard for me to believe, I guess."

Harrison chuckled. "Oh? How's that?"

"Um, well, it just feels like I've time traveled or something coming here. You know, like you all wouldn't be so advanced with your technology." She looked over at Harrison's attire. "For example, a little over an hour ago, I was expected to wear a dress with a corset, then I see you two, changed into tailcoats, trousers, and waistcoats." She smiled at Harrison's amused grin. "I think it's pretty obvious that the last time everyone on Earth dressed like this, it was back in the eighteenth century. And Earth's scientists and inventors weren't creating robots and things of that nature."

Levi chuckled. "Reece, it is perfectly understandable for you to view Pemdas in such a way. You will find as you are with us that it is not only the way we dress that will remind you of the earlier cultures of Earth, but you will also see that we do not rely on technology as Earth does either."

"I guess that explains why we came here on horseback, then. That's the only way everyone gets around here?"

"I believe you will find a ride in a horse and carriage in Pemdas is just as relaxing, if not more, than driving in a vehicle on the paved roads of Earth, especially the luxurious carriages of Pasidian Palace," Harrison added with a grin.

Reece was amazed at the fact that horseback was their preferred method of transportation. "But why is it like that here? I really don't get it. It seems that Pemdas would be more technologically advanced, given the car we left the park in. And the object that was in your hand that you were looking at in the car–" she directed at Levi, "that was like a cell phone or computer, wasn't it?" She looked at the fountain. "I guess that's what is confusing to me."

"You are correct in your assumptions about our technology. It is far greater than Earth's. The device in my hand was what we use to communicate with Pasidian's command center. We communicate with it telepathically," Levi responded.

Reece remembered the way Levi had seemed to be ignoring her in the car earlier and how he was staring so intently at the transparent object in his hand. "Well, I guess that explains why you were constantly staring at it in the car. You were using it to have a conversation through your mind?"

Harrison laughed. "Yes. That is why you had the privilege of conversation with me in the car. Levi wasn't ignoring you; he was informing Samuel about the success of our mission."

"Then why wouldn't you use your cars and stuff like that here?"

"We only use things of a technical nature when we visit other worlds. The use of vehicles helps us blend in with certain cultures, when necessary. And those communication devices are essential for our communication with Pemdas while we are on any given mission."

Reece frowned in confusion.

Levi leaned forward and rested his elbows on his knees. "Reece, I believe the best way for me to simplify the cultures and customs of Pemdas is this: you see, all cultures change over time, they change with the leadership. Pemdas has lived for thousands of years without civil war and unrest; therefore, our leaders have remained in power for longer periods of time. As a result, our change came slower. However, it was mainly due to that fact we have been able to witness how too much change can have very negative effects on a culture, and more importantly its environment. For example, we witnessed this as we watched Earth evolve into what she is today. After seeing the negative effects these 'advances' brought to the planet, the Pemdai chose not to embrace that sort of change and to remain in a time prior to the Industrial Revolution on Earth. It is not only the Pemdai rulers who have chosen this way of life, but it is also a mandate of the Pemdai people as well. No one here is eager to compromise our environment, or our health, for a 'convenience' that is unnecessary."

"The difference between your culture and ours," Harrison added, "is not that we do not understand technology, or even that we don't use technology; it's that we refuse to allow a selfish compulsion for unnecessary conveniences to govern the quality of our lives, the lives of our children, and the future of Pemdas."

Reece leaned back. "Well, that makes sense. Come to think of it, there are still many cultures on Earth today that don't drive cars; most of them have fewer conveniences than you."

Harrison smiled. "Exactly."

The sound of the young women joining them interrupted their conversation.

"Oh, please, help us," Harrison muttered, resting his face on his hand. Reece could not help but laugh. He stared speculatively past her to the sounds of giggling from the women as they approached them.

Harrison spoke, clearly annoyed, "I'm surprised you ladies have found a sudden interest in this location. The walk alone seems as though it would be very trying to your delicate frames." Levi sat up straight and said nothing.

"Harrison, I believe we have heard enough from you this evening," Lillian snapped.

Harrison suddenly took on the same stiff air as Levi. "I hope the reason you have come all this way is to offer Reece an apology. I am sure Lady Allestaine will not be pleased when she finds that you all have been so rude to allow a guest to wander off alone." He laughed. "Or perhaps," he started with a voice of sarcasm, "she will be under the impression that you brushed her off and will be grateful that you are taking her into some small village alone tomorrow. I am sure she will have no reason to distress herself about leaving Reece in your care," he finished while giving all three women a challenging expression.

Simone looked unconcerned. "Harrison, you treat Reece as if she were a puppy, lost and never to find her way home. Reece, dear, please forgive us. We would never have let you run off alone had we imagined you would get lost."

~~I swear, if this broad calls me 'dear' ONE more time.~~ "I wasn't lost, and it's okay. Don't worry about it," Reece answered.

"So you agree that these men are overreacting? I believe men can be more dramatic than ladies at times!"

Her high-pitched laughter was cut off when Levi stood up. "I believe you are missing Harrison's point," he said in his deep voice. "We understand perfectly that Reece is not a lost puppy. We are simply making sure that our guest is properly attended to. Your selfish behavior has me wondering whether or not we should trust her into your care." His stern gaze fell upon Simone. "Regardless of the severity you will face when the Empress hears of this, you, Madam, have proven to me that you have no interest in making an honored guest feel welcome in my home. I suggest all three of you remember that you, as well, are simply our guests. You will straightaway be asked to leave should you not treat Miss Bryant with the dignity and respect she deserves. I suggest you heed my warning, for you know very well how the Empress feels about Reece's uncertain situation. Do not force her to regret trusting you."

The women seemed at a loss for words until Simone found some. "Please forgive us for making light of the situation. We meant no disrespect. You're right; we should have kept closer company with Reece. We were selfishly caught up in our own conversation and took for granted that Reece would find her way around the grounds on her own. Reece, forgive us. I do hope you will still spend the day with us tomorrow."

Levi turned to Reece for her answer.

Oh, great! What am I supposed to say now? Reece faintly smiled. "Don't worry about it, I enjoyed the time alone anyway. It seemed to work out perfectly since Harrison and Levi answered a few more questions for me. If you ladies still want to do something tomorrow, I'll go with you."

"Well, ladies, this has been an eventful night," said Harrison. I believe we should retire and start fresh tomorrow." He stood.

"You make an excellent point, Harrison," Simone said. "Now, would you be a kind gentleman and escort us back to into the Palace?" She raised one hand slightly, as if to rest it on his.

Harrison looked at her with a mischievous grin. "Madam, I would happily offer you my arm; however, there are three lovely ladies and only one other man available to escort them. It would be discourteous of us both to offer any one lady an arm."

You have two arms, thought Reece before she realized that this was Harrison's way of dodging Simone's request. She had to turn her head away from the group to prevent them from seeing the amusement in her expression. *Poor thing, she probably should have seen that one coming.*

Simone stared incredulously at Harrison before she stormed off toward the palace. Lillian shot her brother a dark glance while Catherine scurried after her sister. "Reece, we shall see you for breakfast tomorrow. Rest well," said Lillian as she turned her back to Harrison and followed after the others.

Harrison and Levi waited, presumably until the women were out of earshot, and then burst into laughter. It was the first time Reece had witnessed them both laugh out loud. "I take it you and they don't get along too well?"

Harrison chuckled. "That would be an understatement. Those women know how to put on an act. They think they're the crème de la crème, and their fantasies are only fueled more by staying here at the Palace. Hopefully, your manners will rub off on them tomorrow."

Reece laughed. "You want the college student to tame the sophisticates? Not going to happen, Harrison."

Levi looked toward Reece. "In all seriousness, are you sure you'll be comfortable joining them tomorrow? Different arrangements can be made."

"I'll be fine. I'm sure after following me for the last couple of years," she shot both men a knowing glance, "you should both know by now that I can handle myself. If I get lost or left in a village, I'll hail a horse-drawn cab and tell the driver to take me to the Emperor!"

Both men laughed.

"We are sure that you can handle being around them, Reece. We are just giving you an excellent opportunity to get out of it if you want," Harrison said.

"It wouldn't matter either way. I'll just be making a scene if I back out now."

"Reece—" Levi started.

Before Levi could say anymore, Reece interrupted him. "No, seriously, I've got this. They really didn't bother me that much tonight. I can handle it."

Harrison studied her. "Well then, let's get you back to the palace. I believe you'll need all the rest you can get if you plan to spend an entire day with them. Don't say we didn't warn you." He offered her an arm. "It seems as though I can finally be a gentleman, now that the clucking hens have left us. Allow me, Reece."

She accepted Harrison's arm, and the three of them turned to leave the garden.

Chapter 8

That night, Reece was more exhausted than she had ever remembered being in her entire life. Enveloped in a white, silk, lavender-scented nightgown, she made her way to her bed. The massive four-poster bed was isolated in a room of its own. She wasted no time getting up into it, and once she slipped under the soft and silky comforter, she very quickly fell into a deep, peaceful sleep.

Reece woke the next morning to sounds coming from the next room. She pushed the soft covers back and let her feet drop over the side of the bed. She wrapped herself in her robe and made her way out into the sitting room.

She walked over to the large windows, where the morning sun was shining through, and gazed out onto the lands. The sky was painted in blues and pinks, complementing the lush green grass on the rolling hills that lay before it.

She noticed a herd of black horses in a white-fenced pasture surrounded by the forest; they looked like the horses that Levi and Harrison had used to bring her into Pemdas. Foals frolicked while their dams attended to the business of grazing.

Reece smiled at the morning this magical land gave her and allowed herself to appreciate it. She began to feel a sense of gratitude for the new world she had been introduced to.

Two figures walked out to the horses—her two male companions from the previous day. Levi had a pleasant smile on his face and walked with purpose, taking long strides. Alongside him was his cousin, Harrison, laughing as usual. As they reached the fences, Harrison leaned against it and turned toward his cousin.

Levi didn't look back, but stared into the group of horses. One horse lifted his head and came to him. Levi patted his strong shoulder, and then directed his attention back toward Harrison. The men were still in conversation at the fence when Reece was interrupted from her peaceful reverie.

"Good morning, Miss Bryant." It was Jasmeen, carrying a tray of tea.

The Miss Bryant thing again, she thought as she dropped the curtains she had been hiding behind while watching the men. "Good morning, Jasmeen. Please call me Reece; 'Miss Bryant' is a little too formal for me."

Jasmeen smiled kindly. "Very well, Reece. It is a lovely morning, is it not?"

Reece grinned. "It is. I was wondering if you were here or not. I thought I heard someone out here when I first woke up, but I have to say, I had no idea you would be here already."

She laughed. "I've been in and out of this room. Your bed is made and your clothes laid out, all while you have been staring out the window."

Reece blinked. "How did I miss that? And Jasmeen, you don't have to make my bed, too. I can do some work as well. Honestly, I am not used to people caring for me. You'll spoil me, and when I go home to Earth, I'll be helpless."

Jasmeen smiled. "I suggest you should enjoy it as you would a fine vacation."

Reece reached for her cup. "I guess I will."

Jasmeen smiled as she left. Reece sipped her tea and turned back to the window. Now, different people dressed in servants clothes bustled around, scrubbing steps and pruning bushes.

Jasmeen returned to the room, ready to prepare Reece for the day. "Reece, as soon as you are ready, I have your outfit arranged for the day. I was told that you will be out shopping with Simone, Lillian, and Catherine. I must have you dressed properly if you plan to spend the day with them."

She smiled and walked into the next room. Reece set her tea down and followed behind. Jasmeen had everything, from make-up to shoes, laid out, and she was ready to go to work.

Please don't tell me we are back to corset dresses again. I'd hate to have to ruin Jasmeen's morning, but I couldn't really care less about how I look in front of those women, Reece thought as she followed Jasmeen into the vanity room. She walked over to the chair and sat down. "You really do not need to go to all this trouble. I can handle most of this myself."

Jasmeen went to work as if she hadn't heard a word, but she said, "Please—don't worry about troubling me. This is what I do."

Reece smiled. She couldn't argue; she really did enjoy this part of the new world she was forced to live in. "Thank you, Jasmeen. In that case, what did you pick out for me to wear for this momentous occasion, another ball gown?"

"Since you will be spending your day with the women, we must have you dressed impeccably." She dangled a curl and let it drop.

Reece shook her head and got her hair pulled. "Ouch!"

"I'm sorry. Hold still, please."

Reece was beginning to wonder about these young women. She remembered how Harrison and Levi felt about them, and she became curious as to what the day ahead of her might bring.

It was strange to realize that only a few days earlier, she'd been living a normal life. Life was so unpredictable. She thought back to the day her dad died, remembering how perfect life had seemed, and then a phone call changed everything.

It was happening again, but to a degree she never imagined possible. Who could predict their lives could change like this? She watched Jasmeen transform her appearance once again. Overwhelmed by the idea that she was truly in another world, she softly exhaled.

Jasmeen finished her make-up and looked at her sympathetically. "Reece, you don't have to spend the day with those young women. I'm certain that other arrangements can be made, if necessary."

"Oh, I'm not worried about spending the day with them. I was just thinking about how drastically my life has changed since yesterday morning."

She stood up and followed Jasmeen into the closet. Jasmeen selected a gown, draped it over her arm, and plucked two delicate, matching shoes off a floor-to-ceiling rack on the opposite wall.

"It's a lot to accept, Reece. But rest assured, your stay in Pemdas will be a pleasant one." She held out the clothes to Reece.

"Really…another gown? Aren't there any pants I can wear, or anything like that? I'm really not much of an extravagant dresser."

"I've been told that in your culture, women are free to wear whatever they wish. Here in Pemdas, ladies do not have any desire to dress as men do."

"Well, Jasmeen, I don't really see it that way."

Reece studied the dress. It was another fancy gown, tailored more to Earth's style; however, it was just as extravagant as the corseted dresses she had seen the ladies wearing to dinner the previous night. *Well, if I'm going out into public today, I might as well try to blend in,* she thought as she contemplated giving in and having Jasmeen go get her a dress that suited the Pemdai culture.

"Miss Bryant, is there something wrong with the gown?" Jasmeen asked with concern.

A tiny smile drew up on Reece's mouth. "Jasmeen, I'm not really in the mood to stand out in the crowd today. I think we'd better stick to your fashions. Is there another gown, possibly like whatever the other ladies will be wearing today?"

Jasmeen's expression radiated with excitement. "Are you absolutely sure? We do not want you to be uncomfortable in any way."

Reece laughed. "If I wasn't sure, I wouldn't have asked. Go get the dress, Jasmeen, and please try to keep it simple," Reece finished with a reproachful gaze.

Jasmeen returned with a pale gown. It was simple in such a way that it did not have rich colors, nor was it embellished with hundreds of jewels.

Once Jasmeen finished helping Reece into the dress, Reece was surprised to find that wearing a corset was not as horrible as she had expected. The gown was exquisite, with embroidered striped silk satin of champagne and coral. The square neckline and capped sleeves exposed Reece's soft, cream colored skin. As she studied herself in the mirror, Jasmeen brought a delicate strand of pearls around her neck. Whether Reece wanted to admit it or not, she was a perfect picture of nobility.

Well, I guess this is what you get when you live with the royal family and the Empress designs your wardrobe, she laughed to herself.

Jasmeen smiled. "It appears you like the dress, Reece. I'm delighted!"

Reece tilted her head. "Let's not get carried away just yet, Jasmeen. It's a lot more comfortable than I expected; however, I am only trying to make sure I blend in with the ladies when we go into town today. If I go with them in some different style, I'm afraid I might be attracting unneeded attention to myself."

Jasmeen chuckled. "You should not have to worry about that, Reece. Now, here are your shoes. They may appear uncomfortable, but I believe you will find they are quite the opposite."

Jasmeen bent down and helped Reece put on a pair of champagne colored heels. Comfortable or not, Reece did not really know if she would make it through an entire day wearing heels. This was definitely something she would have to get used to.

Jasmeen finished off the look with matching pearl earrings and dismissed herself to attend to Reece's tea, leaving Reece standing there, staring at this unimaginable image of herself.

She made her way over to the large room and found a concerned Jasmeen walking toward her.

"Is everything all right, Jasmeen?" she asked.

Jasmeen snapped out of her silent thoughts. "No. I mean, everything will be all right, I am sure. But the Princess Elizabeth was in an accident on her way home to the Palace." She walked toward Reece. "Lord Navarre, Lady Allestaine, and Masters Levi and Harrison are en route to her this very moment. I have been directed to give you this letter from Lady Allestaine." She handed the letter to Reece.

Reece unfolded the letter.

Dearest Reece,

I am sorry you must receive this news by letter. We received the news of our daughter's accident only moments ago and are leaving in haste. She is being cared for in a kingdom that is a little over a day's journey from Pasidian. We hope to find her recovering, but of course, nothing is certain.

Mistress Lillian, Harrison's sister, has volunteered to help keep you company in our absence. She and I have discussed how I wish for you to be attended to. She understands my concern over the importance of standing in my place to care for you.

I look forward to spending time together when we return. Until then, please enjoy your stay and the things the young women are looking forward to showing you.

Warm regards,

-Allestaine.

Reece looked at Jasmeen, concerned. "Does she need to be seen by someone on Earth?"

Jasmeen responded, "Reece, she will be attended to by the finest doctors in Pemdas; the Emperor and Empress, however, will not rest easy unless they are there in person to give comfort to the Princess."

Reece was reminded of her conversation with Levi about the intelligence of the Pemdai people and figured that Earth was probably in the Dark Ages as far as medical treatment went. "Well, that is good to know."

A few moments later, a knock at the door announced Lillian's arrival.

"Hello, Reece." Lillian gave a small, forced smile. "Miss Bryant, if you are ready, I shall bring you down for breakfast."

"I am, thanks. Will everything be okay with Elizabeth?"

Lillian's eyes narrowed. "The Princess will be fine." She looked down at the note in Reece's hand. "I wasn't aware that you had been the given news already."

Why wouldn't I have? What's her problem? "Yes, Jasmeen just told me and gave me this letter from Lady Allestaine."

Something seemed to bother Lillian about Reece being informed; however, she removed any evidence of it from her face and forced another smile upon it. "Shall we go, Reece? The ladies will meet us in the dining room."

Well, this day already seems to be promising, Reece thought as she followed the young woman from the room.

Two servants opened the large double doors to the dining hall, and Reece followed Lillian into the room where Simone and her sister Catherine were already seated at the far side of the table. Reece quickly found a seat across from Simone, and next to Catherine.

"Good morning, Ladies," she said, trying to engage them in conversation. Simone smiled brilliantly, then sobered. "It is good to see you up and feeling well this morning, Reece, but have you heard about our dearest Princess Elizabeth's accident?"

"Yes, Lady Allestaine wrote me a note before she left. I hope she's going to be okay?"

Simone's eyebrows shot up in shock, then she recovered and sent a charming smile to Reece. "That is interesting, indeed. Perhaps, girls, Lady Allestaine is still concerned about yesterday evening? She must have not trusted us enough to give us the news ourselves."

Hurt feelings about a note, just what we need today. Reece thought it would be wise to salvage whatever rapport she had with them. The family was gone, and she had no other companions. She reached for some fruit. "It didn't seem that way at all, Simone. She only wrote about how sorry she felt for having to leave and mentioned that I would be in good hands with all of you."

Reece knew she was embellishing the letter's contents slightly, but it wouldn't hurt to allow the women to believe what she said. She was determined to keep the peace while the family was away.

"I'm sure that is exactly what she said," Lillian muttered.

Catherine finally spoke up while buttering her toast, "Oh, let's move forward, shall we? Reece, are you still in the mood to shop in town with us today?"

"It sounds like fun," Reece said.

"Oh, indeed! It will be marvelous."

Chapter 9

Half an hour later, Reece was being helped into a carriage by a footman. "I'm curious about something?" she questioned when they were on their way.

Simone furrowed her eyebrows. "Yes, and what exactly are you curious about?"

"If Princess Elizabeth is in a kingdom at least a day away, are there a lot of different kingdoms like that around here?"

"Reece, unfortunately I am unable to give you an accurate answer about exactly how big Pemdas is. You probably should have asked the men last night when you had them to yourself." She glanced quickly at the other two women in the carriage, and then back to Reece. "However, if you must know, there are roughly a hundred kingdoms in the diverse areas that Lord Navarre oversees."

"Oversees? Aren't there kings, or something like that? How does that work? It's not like that on Earth; and from what you are saying, Pemdas seems to be almost as large, but there isn't one man who stands rule over everything."

Lillian let out an exhale. "Reece, if you must know, Lord Navarre rules over the entire realm of Pemdas. Yes, there are many different kingdoms throughout our world that are run individually by their appointed kings. The kings ultimately answer to Lord Navarre, their Emperor. For example, my father rules the Kingdom of Vinsmonth and sets the standards for the kingdom; however, if there are problems with his leadership or corruption in his government, the Emperor will step in and see that it is corrected."

Now that's interesting. Simone must have seen the look of disbelief on Reece's face, and therefore she quickly added, "Reece, I do hope you understand the importance of the family that has decided to take you in. Pasidian Palace is an honorable place to be, even for a servant. You could probably understand now, when I tell you how astonished I was to find that someone from Earth would be allowed to reside there."

"Well, Simone, maybe you can trust the judgment of the family you admire so much, since it was their decision for me to stay there with them."

Simone stared speculatively at Reece's gown. "It is truly admirable for you to decide upon our fashion style today, Reece. The gown you wore to dinner last evening had me wondering who was attending to you, or if you were being attending to at all."

Simone giggled as she glanced over to her two friends, who were trying to suppress their laughs.

Reece felt the heat rushing to her face, angered by the comment. She would not let Simone degrade her. She quickly stifled her rage and replied, "Well, if you think you were distressed by my choice of dress last night, you should have seen my attendant's reaction." Reece laughed.

Simone's expression at first was that of utter repulsion, then it quickly softened and she laughed. "Reece, dear, forgive me. I must have forgotten about your delicate position. I believe my scolding from the Empress would be dreadful if she knew I had caused you any distress."

Reece could go back and forth with Simone all day, but she knew that in the end it would all be pointless. She decided it was best to change the subject. Even though it had seemed longer, it had only been about ten minutes since they left the Palace and were now in the village in the valley below it. It was the same village she had ridden through with Harrison and Levi the previous day.

"Is this the place where you shop?" She looked at Catherine, who seemed to be the only young woman that was attempting politeness in the group. Unfortunately, it was Simone who felt she needed to inform the ignorant Earth girl about everything.

"Reece, darling," Simone giggled, "of course we do not shop in this village. This is where all of the produce, meat, and all other necessities the Palace might require come from. For the most part, the people here are bakers, butchers, farmers, and their families."

"Oh, well that's interesting. So, where is it that we're going, then? I didn't see any other towns but this one yesterday."

"The town we are taking you to is about a thirty-minute journey from the Palace. It is very large, and I believe you shall enjoy it," Catherine replied.

Simone rolled her eyes and let out an exasperated exhale. "So, Reece, what was it like to ride a horse with a man? I am curious as to whom you rode with upon your arrival into Pemdas yesterday?" Her eyes stared darkly at Reece, awaiting a response.

Whoa! Where did that come from? "I'm not sure what you are getting at, Simone?" *And I'm not sure why we are having this conversation.*

Simone laughed. "Now don't you dare avoid the question, Reece. We ladies want to know what it was like."

"Riding a horse? Um, a little uncomfortable. I'd rather…"

"Reece," Simone interrupted, "You must not be getting my point. Yesterday, you rode horseback with the two most sought after men in all of Pemdas. I don't know of any woman that would not be envious of that. What was it like?" She giggled.

Oh, please! Is she serious? Reece didn't know how to answer the question. Simone had definitely made it clear that she had some bizarre obsession with Levi and Harrison. This was probably half the reason Simone had been acting so rude to her.

"If you must know, I rode with Harrison; and given the fact that I had much more important things on my mind at the time and I didn't know who either man was, I couldn't say that it was an enjoyable experience. But now that you have made me aware of who they are, I'll be sure to report back to you next time."

Lillian laughed. "See, Simone, you have nothing to worry about; she was nowhere near your precious Levi."

Reece closed her eyes in sheer annoyance; she was reaching her limits of being able to tolerate them and their odd personalities.

"Lillian," Simone spoke in astonishment, "you know I was not concerned about that! We all know neither Levi nor Harrison would choose anyone outside of royalty for their bride; Levi has already made that perfectly clear. So for any of you to believe he would choose someone from outside of the realms of Pemdas…" She stared at Reece with a mischievous grin. "Well, let's just say it would never happen. Levi is far too superior for that."

Bride!? Is this what these women worry about all day? Who's going to marry Prince Charming? What a joke! Simone's gaze didn't leave Reece's face. "Well, now that that's all cleared up, can we talk about something else?" Reece asked.

Simone's dark eyes appeared wicked when she responded, "Oh, well of course we can talk about something else; this is probably making you uncomfortable."

Reece exhaled. She was strongly considering feigning an illness and going back to the Palace alone. The three women went on and on for the entire trip. Listening to the superficial girls talk had her ready to jump from the carriage. She sighed with relief when large buildings finally lined the horizon before them. *I either ditch them now or figure out how to deal with them,* she thought as the horses made their way into the large town.

As soon as the coach stopped in front of a large building, a footman was opening the carriage door and lending a supporting hand to help the women out of it. As she stepped out of the coach, she immediately understood why the young women did their shopping here. Tall stone buildings stood side by side. Each building was unique in its own way; some were covered in ivy, while others had elaborate designs carved into their polished stone surfaces. Elaborate windows showcased everything from clothing to household furnishings, and many other trinkets.

It seemed as though the merchandise that was offered for sale was similar to that being sold at any other boutique shopping area on Earth.

She was enjoying taking in the sight of the magnificent shopping street, which was filled with the scent of freshly baked goods, when a high-pitched voice cut through her quiet moment. "Reece, quit dragging behind! I will not be scolded again by her ladyship for your lack of attention."

The women laughed and waited for Reece to catch up. They all turned into a large building, filled with various fine objects—from saddles to sapphires, dresses to diamonds. The young women went ahead; Reece became so caught up with displays of porcelain and silver that she almost forgot about them.

They went through dozens of shops like the first. They had lunch on the balcony of a large inn in the middle of the village. So intrigued with being in such a unique town, Reece was finding it easier to deal with the women. She had given up trying to answer the women's rude comments, and without a target, they gradually ceased. They did continue to point out the beauties of the scenery, and Reece was glad to agree, to nod, and to be impressed. It was the truth; the town was beautiful, and agreeing with them made a more peaceful afternoon for Reece.

On the way back, Reece learned, to her dismay, that this shopping adventure would not be her last with the women. Shopping was pronounced to be their favorite pastime, and they were determined to drag Reece along in order to show Lady Allestaine their care for her guest.

Upon reaching the Palace, they retired to their rooms to freshen up for dinner. Jasmeen's high spirits amused Reece and strengthened her for dinner with the other three women.

At dinner, the four young women were alone at the table. Simone entertained them with underhanded comments about Earth, and about Reece. Catherine and Lillian laughed, encouraging Simone further, while Reece kept resolutely silent.

Reece had hardly ever been as relieved as she was when dinner was over. She opted out of joining them in the sitting room. Their looks of surprise made her think perhaps she should have offered an excuse, but she didn't really care. She'd spent enough time with them. She knew she would have to build some form of acquaintance with them, or her days here would be miserable. As much as she didn't want to, she had to face these women and deal with them.

"You know," she said to Jasmeen before getting in bed, "I think I want to start the morning off with a run, and maybe a little exploring. Get me up early, will you?" Jasmeen looked dubious, but Reece was determined.

"All right, if that's what you want. Will you wear your Earth clothes?"

"If they are clean, then yes. It may horrify the good Pemdai people, but I can't run in a long skirt."

"As you wish," Jasmeen responded as Reece settled into bed. "Sleep well." Reece nodded tiredly, and as her eyes closed, she drifted off to sleep.

Chapter 10

Reece was up the next morning and slipped into her running clothes before Jasmeen appeared. Still annoyed about the previous day with the young women, she wondered how she would make it through this one.

She found her way easily from her room to the back of the palace and set off in the direction from which Levi had brought her on the first day. A vigorous run was exactly what she needed; she looked forward to getting back into some semblance of her familiar routine.

When she returned to the palace, she showered and allowed Jasmeen to dress her for the day, even continuing to agree on the Pemdai fashions. Fortunately, she was in a much better mood; she felt refreshed, more like herself, and ready to face what might come.

Breakfast was surprisingly enjoyable, as Reece managed to ignore most of what Simone rambled on about. The fact that the young women did not include her in most of their conversations made it easy for Reece to ignore them without seeming rude. When Reece was addressed, she replied briefly, allowing them to move on with their discussions.

After breakfast, shopping was, again, the order of the day. Reece enjoyed getting out, despite the company. She found the town delightful, and the inhabitants welcoming and friendly. It amused her to watch the young women interact with the residents and the workers. They acted like they were royalty, gracing everyone with their presence, and the people seemed to good-naturedly go along. If anyone noticed Reece or found her interesting, Simone was the first to make them aware that she would not be staying long.

Three days of these shopping adventures had passed. The constant insult now coming from Simone was about how Earth was so entirely beneath Pemdas. Simone would slyly maneuver her way through insults, always subtly implying that Reece was equally as vulgar, being from such a place. Reece shook it off; Simone had no idea of the differences, and she knew it. Having experienced both places, Reece had concluded that both had their pros and cons; however, she would never get into that particular argument with Simone. As much as she would love to shut the woman down entirely, Reece was wise and learned in the beginning that it was always best to remain silent when Simone would start in with her insults. Reece inwardly knew the truth, and that was all that mattered.

It was on the third night after the family had left the Palace that word came they would be returning within a week, sooner than was expected. Elizabeth had been in a carriage accident; she was thrown and suffered a broken leg after a wheel had come off. She was to stay behind until she was fully healed. Allestaine would not have her travel until she was assured the ride home for her would be comfortable.

Apparently, they expected Elizabeth to be riding and dancing within a month. Lillian told a very curious Reece that they use a healing lotion that mends such injuries expediently.

Two days before the family's scheduled return, Reece had finally reached her limit with Simone.

Every evening after dinner, the young women settled in the sitting room. Reece enjoyed the soothing environment, and it usually helped her unwind from a long day with her companions. The weather had begun to cool, and so each evening Reece sat in a comfortable chair between the windows and the fire, curled up with a blanket, and found her serenity. On her lap, she usually had a book from the Palace's library, while the young women generally spent their evenings flipping through pages of various books on fashion.

Reece was perfectly content. She allowed her mind to drift from her book to gaze out the windows before her. Relaxed and comfortable, she closed the book and settled further into the chair.

Giggling and laughter brought her attention to the sofa where the three women were lounging in front of the fireplace. She smiled at their bond. Their personalities might not match hers, but they seemed very close. She found herself missing her friends back home. She faintly smiled, and then returned her gaze to the window, watching the moonlight sparkle in the grass and waters below it.

"Reece? Reece, I must know this instant what it is that you are staring at!" Simone demanded in her soprano voice.

Reece snapped out of her relaxed state and looked up to find Simone coming toward her. "Every night that we have come in here, you end up sitting here, reading one of our books. And now, here you are staring out of the windows…at what? Absolutely nothing!"

Reece sat up in her chair, slightly stunned. "I didn't know that what I do, or don't do, with my time concerned you so much, Simone. I'm flattered that you've taken the time to question what I'm doing." She smiled gently and waited for an answer.

"I'll take that as a compliment," Simone said as she brushed the hair lying on her shoulder to her back. "I simply find it amazing that one would consume her time gazing out of a window into darkness after hearing the news that in only two more days, a certain family is to return to the Palace." She winked at Reece, and Reece stared at her in confusion.

Simone laughed her usual high-pitched trill, which would have been contagious had there been no malice behind it. "We all know Levi and Harrison will return with them. I will admit that it has been rather…well…rather boring and dull without them around, wouldn't you?" She cocked a brow and giggled.

Oh, please. Here we go…the Levi and Harrison thing again, Reece thought once she understood what Simone was trying to imply. "Are you asking me if I find it boring around here without two men I hardly know?"

Simone took a chair opposite Reece, blocking the window. She cleared her throat, as if preparing to lecture her. "Don't you find it stimulating to hear of their return? Why, I've never met a woman who wouldn't be excited about the return of two exceptionally handsome men. After all, I'm sure you know they will be giving you their undivided attention."

Lillian stood and came over to the conversation. In the last few days, Lillian and Catherine had both seemed to change their attitudes toward Reece. They weren't friendly, but their insulting comments had ceased and they no longer seemed disgusted by her presence. Now, Lillian looked questioningly at Simone, but her friend willfully ignored her, pursuing an agenda that Reece was unsure about.

"I have no idea what you are trying to imply," she stated as she set her book aside. "I have put up with your rudeness long enough, and therefore I'm not going to answer your ridiculous question."

She stood up. Simone also stood and used her tall, slender figure to tower over Reece. Her face flushed with rage as she squeezed her lips into a fine line. For the first time since she met her, Reece found no beauty in the woman.

Then Simone smiled, with what seemed to be a great effort of will, and her features softened. "Reece, I was speaking in jest, trying to lighten the evening."

Reece didn't say anything.

"You did not think I was accusing you of anything?" Simone said, almost crooning the words.

Reece looked at her in disbelief.

"I hope I have not upset you, Reece. We've enjoyed entertaining you for this past week or so." She giggled—a combination of amusement, malice, and perhaps a touch of nerves.

"Entertaining me? Well, I guess that would be one way to put it. And I have been entertained—or at least educated—by your pathetic spite. I've spent these last few days listening to your ignorant contempt of me and my home. I think that if I hear the words 'our beautiful Pemdas' one more time, I'll lose my mind. You have done nothing but treat me like a desperate fool from some other miserable land. Then you insult me further by insinuating that I would sit here and daydream of your men?"

Simone was expressionless while Reece finished, "I've had all I can take. It's a big palace; I don't have to stay here with you women." She turned to leave, and then stopped, looking back to find all three women staring at her in shock. "Don't forget, I didn't choose to come to here. I was kidnapped and forced to live here by your marvelous Pemdas warriors, who are interested in Earth only as it serves to keep 'your beautiful Pemdas' safe. Believe me when I say I would far rather be home with my friends."

It was Simone who made the first effort and walked toward Reece. She laid a hand gently on Reece's arm. Reece shook the hand off with a shudder, as if it were a spider.

"Reece," said Lillian, "I'm sorry. Simone has finally crossed a line, and she knows better. Please, don't leave; we've truly enjoyed your company."

Reece stared into Lillian's eyes. What a coward. She was afraid Reece would tell the Empress. "Allow me to make this perfectly clear: I don't need anyone's sympathy, especially any of yours." Her tone was smooth and deadly. "I'm glad you enjoy my company. I, on the other hand, have had better conversations with the silversmith in the village than I've had with any of you. Fine clothes obviously don't make either fine manners or interesting minds."

Simone's eyes narrowed while Reece continued. "Your idea of keeping someone company seems to be a mixture of ill-will and showing off, but without the courage to do either one openly. You've pretended to befriend me while stifling laughter whenever I speak and belittling my home from morning until night. Why? Because you're all too self-absorbed to make the effort to know someone new or learn about a different place. Then you feign astonishment about having alienated me! Well, I thank you for showing me what your 'lovely land' of Pemdas is really like."

Reece nodded formally. "Ladies, I bid you goodnight." She spun on her heels and walked briskly away. Her heart was beating fast, but she felt cleansed and free.

In her dimly-lit room, a fire had been lit and her nightclothes laid out. Jasmeen's attention to her needs comforted her more than she thought possible. She fell asleep with a smile on her lips, thinking about how the maid was a better companion, and a better person, than any of the ladies.

The following morning, she woke earlier than usual. After her run and shower, Jasmeen was ready to make her up for the day. This was becoming Reece's favorite part of the day. Jasmeen was always full of energy and life. Reece wished she could spend all of her time with her until Samuel decided she could safely return to Earth.

"Maybe more of a natural look today, Jasmeen? Will I shock anyone if I don't have my hair up?"

"Not in the daytime, on the Palace grounds." Jasmeen smiled. "You wouldn't want to go into the shopping areas that way, though." She arranged Reece's hair to flow freely down her back before fetching a blue silk gown. "There's a matching coat as well; the weather is growing chilly. Winter is upon us now, and we may see snow."

"Thank you, Jasmeen." Reece smiled at her. "Thank you for everything."

Sending word that she wouldn't be at breakfast, Reece grabbed a warm muffin from the kitchen and set out for a walk. She'd found a secluded trail while out running one morning; it was one of her favorite routes to walk. She watched small creatures hopping or darting through the green shrubbery. Reece laughed, as the area seemed to be filled with small rabbits and squirrels throughout. It was intriguing to see how the nature was identical to Earth's. It was probably why she loved these walks; it was where she felt closest to her home. The trail led along the creek, the same creek that seemed to surround the Palace, and opened into a meadow that was like its own world. Tall lavender flowers blanketed the ground like purple snow. Dark green trees with low-hanging, mossy branches made a backdrop against the sky. This was serenity, and she found, as she had since she first discovered this place, that peace seeped into her bones.

A white fence with a stile over it led to the horse pasture. She stared in awe at the black horses as they grazed and drank from the creek bordering the meadow. After a moment of hesitation, she climbed the stile and sat down in the pasture, on a long tree that had fallen on its side.

This was new to her, to be so close to the horses without a fence between them. Even so, she found herself completely relaxed. With serenity all about her, she closed her eyes and listened to the insects, the creek, and the shuffling of the horses, letting the sounds fill her heart and soothe her spirit.

Eventually, she started to feel the cold. Jasmeen had been correct, and Reece was grateful for the long coat she had been given. It was probably time to head back; she didn't want anyone out looking for her. Feeling rejuvenated, Reece stood, stretched, and started back toward the path.

She was distracted by a foal, which frolicked away from the herd toward her. Amazed, she stopped and turned, trying not to startle it.

It slowed to a walk, lowered its head, and came nearer. Reece held out her hand, and the black foal came closer, investigating her by smelling the air around her. When its nose was within her reach, she touched it gently. It seemed to trust her; perhaps it trusted humans in general. She ran her hands through its short mane—silky smooth, like the rest of its coat. It leaned against her. Then it stood up again, looking at something behind Reece. She turned to see what had the foal's attention.

A familiar figure stood on the other side of the fence. Levi, wearing a long black overcoat, was leaning against a tree; feet and arms crossed and eyes glowing with amusement. How long had he been there? Reece had thought they weren't due home for two more days.

He looked tired, but his smile almost erased any evidence of his journey home. It was plain to her that he must have arrived back to the Palace this morning, as his hair was not as neatly kept as she had seen it before.

Reece strolled in his direction, the foal frisking alongside her. "Do you enjoy sneaking up on people in the middle of nowhere?"

He chuckled as he started toward her. "I see you've found yourself a little hiding place." A stunning smile lit his face.

"Not such a good one; you found me right away," Reece said. Levi's presence did something to her voice, but she hoped he didn't notice that. "I was actually on my way back to the palace. I didn't want to have anyone looking for me and risk giving away my secret little place."

Levi laughed. "Your secret little place, is it? I believe the horses had it first." He reached out to the foal, who was nudging Reece for more attention, and scratched behind its ears. "Although it appears to have served you well—at least, I can see you've made a friend." He rubbed under the colt's chin.

"I guess I have," Reece said. Watching him pet the foal was having a weird effect on her heart rate. She was baffled by her reaction. In the small amount of time he'd been gone, she hadn't once thought about him. She had forgotten how stunning the man was. Now it was coming back as a rushing wave, making it difficult to concentrate in his presence. "I was amazed when he decided to come over to me." She laughed, looking at the colt, which was now nuzzling under Levi's coat.

Levi laughed as well and stepped over the stile into the pasture. "I also was shocked when I saw him approach you. These horses do not give their attention to just anyone. This fellow's breeding should make him a far cry from outgoing and friendly. His sire is my horse, and Areion will make you work very hard for acceptance. These horses are our most valuable possessions. I believe we told you that they are the only ones who can leap through the boundaries and bring individuals into Pemdas."

Reece nodded. "So, these are the only horses that can do that? Not any other kind?"

"Only these. They have minds of their own, and a kind of rudimentary emotional antennae. They know whether or not anyone will bring us problems. In battle, they are as good as a human warrior. They're not naturally this friendly to anyone, but once you gain their trust, they're loyal to the death."

Was something wrong with the foal that was now nibbling on her sleeve? "I hope I didn't get the little guy in trouble," Reece said, tugging on her coat. "He just seemed friendly. I'm sure he'll still make a great horse for you guys." She looked at Levi, unsure about how stupid she sounded.

He shook his head. "You think you soured my horse, do you?" His playful eyes waited for a response.

"Your horse? Great, now I've ruined the future horse of the king's son…um, I mean, Emperor's son…even worse!"

He laughed. "I'm teasing you, Reece! This colt is just fine, and I think he'll be an even fiercer warrior than his father is. I merely find it interesting that he chose to approach you. He shows me daily that I have yet to earn his trust, and then in one small moment he gives himself to you completely and seems to include me in his overtures. I believe I should just let you have him."

Reece smiled wryly at him. "I might take you up on that. At least, until I go back to my home on Earth. I think it will be fun to have a little friend like this."

"He seems to think so, too. You know, now that he's bonded to you, he needs a name. Perhaps you could name him for me?"

"Oh—I don't know. I don't think I could come up with one. Nothing like the names you use here." She turned away and stroked the foal's soft back.

"His name will come to you," said Levi. "Spend time with him, and I am sure something will come. It will help you pass the days here." He offered his arm. "Come. Let us go back to the Palace, where it's warm." Reece patted the foal's rump. "Go on, little guy. Go and find your mama. I'll come back tomorrow, maybe with a treat for you." The baby horse ran off, and she laid her hand on Levi's inviting arm and permitted herself to be helped over the stile.

"Maybe I spoke too soon," he said. "I think you may ruin that horse, indeed."

She looked up, meeting his teasing eyes. "Oh? How's that?"

"Well, if I was him and a beautiful woman was petting me, talking to me, and promising treats, I'd be spoiled. I'd be good for nothing but lounging around pastures all day, waiting for attention."

"Well, I must remember not to bring you apples, then." She enjoyed this playful side of Levi. "Can I ask you something ridiculous?"

"Ridiculous?" he laughed. "I'd be delighted to hear a ridiculous question after the week I've had. Please ask." He held up a low-hanging branch for her, and then ducked it.

"Well, I am curious—is this how men always escort women here? I mean, it seems old-fashioned. Is it customary at the Palace? In the village, I saw plenty of women walking with men, but not all were arm-in-arm."

He stopped walking and turned to her, forcing her to withdraw her hand from his arm. Suddenly, she questioned herself. It was more an awkward than a ridiculous question; perhaps Jasmeen would have been a better person to ask.

Levi looked down at her with confusion in his eyes. "Does it bother you? I had not considered that it could make you uncomfortable. In your part of Earth, I know contact such as this isn't usual among relative strangers. Forgive me for not thinking of that."

"It was a silly question, Levi. Of course it doesn't make me feel awkward. I actually enjoy it. I kind of wish the men on Earth would respect women the same way."

His smile widened, and he offered his arm dramatically. "Well, Miss Bryant, shall we, then?"

She looked up at him and delicately placed her arm back in his. "Mr. Oxley, I thought you'd never ask."

They walked together toward the palace. After a few moments of walking, Levi's deep, smooth voice broke through the silence. "I've heard that you have been out alone on these walks for the last few days or so? Have you been enjoying your stay here? My mother was quite worried when we left you so quickly after hearing of my sister's accident."

Reece snapped out of her cheerful bliss. "I'm sorry! I didn't even ask you how your sister was! Is she recovering well? I wish your mother hadn't felt bad; I was only worried for you guys."

Levi smiled. "Elizabeth is very well, thank you. She was rather annoyed that we all traveled that far, simply because she broke her leg."

They were now out of the tree-covered path and in the gardens at the back of the Palace. Reece sighed softly.

Levi looked down at her questioningly. "Is something wrong?"

"No, I'm fine, thanks.

Reece stared ahead. Was there to be no respite from the "women" who should have been her friends?

"Something's wrong. Has something happened that I should be aware of?"

"It's nothing. I guess I would just rather enjoy being outdoors today." She smiled as brightly as she could.

Levi studied her face with a doubtful look. "You are free to do whatever you like; you are not a prisoner." He smiled slightly. "However, the weather has cooled quite drastically, and I would be surprised if you wished to stay outdoors for much longer."

A familiar voice interrupted. "Levi?" Harrison called out from top of the steps at the rear doors. "Where have you been?" Harrison asked as he ran down the steps. He wore an expression of mock-sternness. "You've been acting strange ever since you demanded we ride home last night. It is not that I mind getting away from the watchful eyes of your parents, but you didn't even have breakfast this morning when we returned. What's going on?" He looked down at Reece. "Good morning, Reece. It's easy to see that you are well." He looked down at her dress. "I might also add, you complement the Pemdai style of dressing very well. Until now, I was sure you would order Levi and me to return to Earth and fetch your usual attire." He winked. "Have you been enjoying your stay, without us here to entertain you?"

Reece smiled. "I have, thanks, and don't tempt me with the idea that you two could go back and pack up some normal clothes for me either; I hadn't considered that idea yet." She laughed. "As for enjoying my stay here without you, you should know that I've been entertained pretty well by the lovely 'Ladies of Pemdas'." She chuckled to herself at her inside joke. Harrison's eyes brightened, and he grinned, but Levi's posture became rigid. He looked at Reece with eyes from which all humor had fled.

Harrison clapped his hand onto Levi's stiffened shoulder. "Pretty well, eh? I might have to disagree with you, Reece. From word at the breakfast table this morning, I believe that it was you who entertained our fine 'Ladies of Pemdas'." He smiled admiringly.

Levi's expression was unreadable. Reece's face grew hot, and she swallowed hard, wondering exactly what had been said and who had said it.

"Well, I don't think anyone would refer to it as entertainment but—"

"I definitely view it as entertainment!" said Harrison. "I'm just sorry that Levi waited until last night to have us race back to the Palace in record-breaking time. Cousin, if we had only left yesterday morning, I believe we would have arrived in time to watch Reece have quite the conversation with the lovely Simone!"

Reece managed an uncertain smile, but Levi showed no interest in Harrison's lighthearted joke. "I only wished we *had* left earlier." He stared darkly up at the Palace.

Harrison changed the subject. "But that is not the pressing issue here. What happened to you at breakfast? You rode back to the Palace as if you hadn't eaten in weeks, then you vanish as we're walking in to eat! What are you two doing out in this cold?" He shook his head. "I would have appreciated the option of joining you and Reece instead of being left with the three bickering hens. I thought you were more compassionate, Levi."

"I went to find the horses," Levi said. "With the weather coming in and the young foals among them, we must move them from the big pasture, bring them closer to the stables. I came across Reece where the creeks divide." Though he answered Harrison, it was obvious that his thoughts were elsewhere.

"Quite the little wanderer, aren't we?" said Harrison. "That's a substantial walk. Not that I blame you. I probably would do the same if I was forced to be around those women all day, every day." He addressed his cousin. "I'll send for Javian to bring the herd to closer grounds. Samuel is expecting us to report for training."

Levi nodded. "Very well. Let us escort Reece inside." He offered her his arm.

"Let us," Harrison agreed with a laugh, gesturing dramatically toward the door.

"Go be trained, guys. You don't need to walk me in. I've managed alone pretty well for the last couple of days."

"It's no burden," said Levi. "In any case, I intend to have a discussion with the women who had you in their care."

Reece didn't argue, but her stomach knotted. After Simone's accusations the previous night, she really didn't want to risk being found with both men in tow.

As they reached the top of the stairs, she stopped. "Levi, would it be okay if I went in alone? Please don't ask me to explain, it's just something that I would be more comfortable doing." She raised her eyebrows and tried to smile, hoping he would not question her request. But it was Harrison who looked down at her in confusion. "Are you serious? Reece, if this is about—"

Levi cut off his cousin in a soft voice. "Certainly, Reece, if that is what you prefer. We will see you tonight at dinner." Unsmiling, he gently removed her arm and motioned for her to enter.

She walked back into the palace alone, but her caution was wasted. She saw no sign of the young women as she made her way quickly to her rooms.

Chapter 11

eece was glad she'd taken her walk early. The weather became extremely cold outside, and she spent most of the day in her sitting room, curled up before a crackling fire with a blanket and a couple of books from the library. She lunched in her room, rather than with the young women. Her annoyance with them was subsiding, but even so, she was not in the mood to be in their presence. She wished she could pass on dinner as well, but that would be too public a slight, and it might cause Levi and Harrison concern.

The day passed pleasantly, and dinner time came too soon. When she entered the dining room, the young women had just sat down at the table. Their conversation halted as soon as she walked through the doors and took her usual seat.

"Good evening, Reece," Catherine managed after a few moments of tense silence.

Reece looked at the three women sitting across the table from her and forced a smile. "Good evening, ladies. It's nice to see you all again," she lied.

Simone shot Reece a stern look. "It is, is it? With the way you have avoided us all day, and after our conversation last night, I felt we would never see you again."

You hoped, Reece thought. "It wasn't that at all, Simone. After I returned to my room, I realized how tired I was." She smiled with false sweetness. "I guess I'm not in the same shape as all of you. Trying to keep up with all your exciting adventures finally got the best of me. I spent the day relaxing, and I'm feeling much better now." She reached for her wine glass.

Simone arched her eyebrow. "Oh? I wasn't aware we had pushed you beyond your limits; next time, we will keep your frailty in mind."

"I am happy you are feeling better and are able to join us," Lillian said in a flat voice that gave the lie to her artificial smile.

Reece was thankful when the doors swung open to admit Levi and Harrison.

"Ladies!" said Harrison, grinning. "Forgive us! We are late, and fully aware of the inconvenience we have caused. You all are beautiful, lovely, and charming this evening…and I am starved." He relaxed into the chair at Reece's left.

"Ladies," said Levi, nodding briefly, and took his seat at the head of the table. Once Levi found his seat, the staff entered, bringing in the first course.

Simone, who was seated to Levi's left, sipped her wine delicately. She looked at Harrison, who sat directly across from her. "Harrison, must you burst loudly into every room? Perhaps if you spent less time on Earth, your manners would improve. And sit up—you look like an unruly child at the table."

Levi never looked up from his plate, but a tiny smile played in the corners of his mouth.

Harrison leaned back in his chair and rested his arm on the top of Reece's chair. He stretched his other arm lazily on the table. "Simone, what do you know of Earth manners? You don't show any interest in the place. You cast your judgments prematurely and make yourself into more of a fool than I."

Reece stifled a smile, but thought it best to focus on her plate, as Levi was doing.

Simone smiled widely at Harrison. "Well, you certainly didn't learn such obnoxious habits in Pemdas. How do you expect to find a wife among the women in your land with such obnoxious behavior?" She laughed in her soprano trill. "Unless, of course, you wish to go against duty and family by taking an Earthling for your wife. Your boorish manners are unlikely to attract anyone better." With pretentious delicacy, she placed a bite of meat into her mouth.

Harrison's smile died. He leaned forward and addressed Simone directly. "Madam, you have forgotten yourself most profoundly. Whatever ill manners you feel I possess, I assure you, they are nothing in comparison to what you have just displayed by crudely insulting two of your fellow guests."

Reece looked up, startled; she hadn't seen this side of Harrison before. "Such behavior," he continued, "will not find you a husband either in Pemdas or on Earth."

He reached for his glass, sat back in his chair, and continued to stare at the rising red tide on Simone's angry face. He took a sip and seemed to revert to his usual good-humored self. "I can assure you of this, my lady: there are plenty of women in Pemdas who would grant me their hand this instant, should I ask for it. However, unlike you, I have much more important things to think about than marriage." He waved his hand dismissively in Simone's direction, and then applied himself to his dinner.

Reece restrained herself from bursting into laughter and noticed Levi was having difficulty with that as well.

The three women, obviously annoyed, now talked of trivialities among themselves while Levi, Harrison, and Reece ate in silence. As Reece silently studied the women while she ate her meal, a thought came to her and she softly laughed.

Simone gazed at her with curiosity while Harrison turned to Reece and grinned. "Miss Bryant? Anything you care to share with us? I believe we could use a little humor tonight."

Reece looked up to find all three women staring at her in disgust. Levi sat back, clearly amused. He took a sip of his wine and waited for Reece's response.

"Well, I'm not really sure if it's funny or not, but I just realized that Simone was correct last night."

Simone's eyes became fierce.

"Please, enlighten us," Harrison said.

"You see, I didn't agree with her when she asked me if I thought it was dull and boring without you men around. It turns out, I was wrong." She laughed, and then smiled at Simone's heated gaze. "You were right, Simone; having Harrison and Levi back has definitely served to make our dinner more exciting than it has been lately. Wouldn't you agree?" Reece finished with an innocent smile.

A sharp arch of Simone's brow challenged Reece's humored expression. "Reece, I am having difficulty understanding what you are trying to imply? Could it be that you are trying to find a way to embarrass me in front the gentlemen?"

"I was speaking in jest, Simone; you know, trying to lighten the evening." Reece smiled as she used Simone's exact words from the previous night against her. "Actually, it's quite a compliment, Simone; I've never been one to openly admit when I was wrong."

"Well, Miss Bryant, while you have paid Simone a compliment, you must know you have managed to deeply offend me," Harrison teased.

Levi let out a soft laugh. "How's that, Harrison? I believe Reece has paid us both a fine compliment."

"Indeed, Levi; however, it took her until tonight to realize it was dull and boring without us around?" He shook his head. "What a pity, I'd hoped she was better impressed with us before we left." He brought his attention to Simone's deadly gaze and smiled wryly. "Turns out, it was only Simone who had been longing for our return."

Reece bit down on her bottom lip as the horror and shock that touched Simone's crimson red face gave her an overwhelming desire to burst into laughter at that moment. She forced herself to study the food on her plate.

"Harrison, do not flatter yourself," Simone snapped.

"I am not flattering myself, Simone. I am only seeking an apology from Reece. Unfortunately, at this time she is more interested in her plate of food than she is for my wounded feelings."

Reece lowered her head as she tried to maintain her composure. The table grew silent, and she could feel Harrison's gaze on her, waiting for her to respond.

She swallowed hard and cleared her throat, but remained focused on the plate before her. "Harrison, I'm sorry if I offended you in any way." She gained the courage to look at him. "I think it came out wrong, I was only—"

Harrison smirked and smoothly cut her off. "Speaking in *jest?* I believe that is a new word in your vernacular, Reece."

Reece closed her eyes, trying with all her power to keep a straight face. She didn't know how she did it, but she opened her eyes, met Harrison's grin, and kept her composure enough to answer, "Indeed, Harrison, it is a word I learned from Simone last evening."

Harrison and Levi both laughed aloud, and fortunately for Reece, Harrison couldn't respond as they were interrupted by the staff bringing in the second course.

The guests remained silent as they were served, but Simone could not avoid discord for long. "How was your visit to Sandari, Levi? I am curious, how is the lovely Isabelle?" She smirked and glanced toward Reece.

The other two women's heads snapped up, looking at Simone with apparent shock. Harrison whistled softly. Levi's jaw tightened, and his expression became dark. Simone seemed a bit startled by his reaction.

"Isabelle? It is unclear to me why you have taken a sudden interest in the Duchess of Sandari, but I am sure she is well. She is to be married before year's end."

Simone recovered and put on a sorrowful expression like a mask. "Married? Are you certain? This is astounding, indeed. How did you take the news? You must have been devastated; I can't even imagine. Ladies, did you hear what our Levi has just announced?"

Lillian and Catherine appeared as shocked as their friend. Levi ignored the dramatic question. To Reece's surprise, it was Harrison who answered. "Why the sudden concern for the Duchess? I am amazed that you care enough to inquire about her." He looked toward Levi. "Forgive me for this, cousin." Then he returned his gaze to Simone. "You're implying that she broke Levi's heart, when it was Levi who decided they should not suit—and Miss Hamilton seems to have borne up well, as she's planning her trousseau now. No broken hearts in the tale. And if there were, they are hardly any of your business, or your concern." He sat back in his chair, frustration and disgust apparent in his features. "I do hope you haven't entertained Reece with your nonsensical fantasies in our absence. At least you have fulfilled your promise not to let her become lost in some village. I must commend you all for that." He looked at the three women. "Nevertheless, I have lost my desire to sit in your presence any longer. I think I speak for Reece and Levi when I say I believe we are finished with your presence here, and we shall happily retire elsewhere."

He stood and offered Reece his hand. She accepted and prepared to leave with him. As Levi stood, he announced, "Ladies, after tonight's events, rest assured, we will finish the conversation at a later time. Until then." He spun on his heels and followed Harrison and Reece out of the room.

As the door closed behind him, Levi quickly came up beside Harrison. They strode down the hallway, turning down a corridor that Reece had never explored. Harrison exhaled. "Excuse me for this, Reece, but what in all of hell has gotten into that woman?" he demanded, looking at Levi.

Levi's face softened, and his mouth quirked. "Perhaps she was right in her accusations about you, my friend; it seems your mouth has become as foul as your manners are shocking!" He laughed, and Reece joined in. The cousins seemed to have changed places; now it was Levi's turn to lighten the mood.

Harrison looked at Reece. "I will say, I am impressed with how you handled yourself tonight."

She smiled up at him. "I've had quite a few days of practice." She laughed.

The room they entered was unquestionably a man's domain, complete with deep burgundy leather sofas surrounding a fireplace. The room had dark wood paneling throughout, dark green curtains covering the windows, and a large billiard table, which sat off in a corner on its own. "Allow me to offer you a more comfortable place to relax," said Harrison.

The soft leather engulfed Reece luxuriously. Levi sat across from her as Harrison busied himself with glasses at a small cabinet in the front corner of the room. When he offered to pour drinks, Reece requested a glass of wine.

Harrison and Levi both had snifter glasses filled with an amber liquid.

Harrison sat down in a tall-backed chair. His shoulders relaxed, and he seemed to be melting into his seat. "We should have taken our dinner with Samuel in the command center," Harrison announced, still utterly annoyed.

Levi took a sip of his drink and laughed at his cousin. "You look as if you came from a battle, Harrison."

Harrison took a large gulp, and with wide eyes he gestured back at the dining room with his glass. "You feel that was far from one? I believe we should send Simone in to battle the Ciatron; she may be the greatest weapon we have ever had, and we didn't know it." He took another big gulp of his drink.

Levi looked at his cousin as if he were seriously considering the idea. "That is an alternative. Though I fear the horses would sense Simone's character and not allow her to ride them. She would never make it across the borders."

Everyone laughed and relaxed even more. Reece found comfort in having both men around again. It was the first peaceful evening she'd had since the older members of the palace had gone.

Chapter 12

The next week passed without any trouble for Reece. By the time Navarre and Allestaine arrived back at the Palace, Harrison and Levi were being dispatched to resume their duties on Earth.

Upon their return, Navarre was rarely around, and Allestaine made a special effort to entertain Reece. Her first discussion with Reece when she returned was in regard to a conversation she had with Levi before he returned to Earth. She told Reece that he informed her about the young women's detestable behavior in their absence. Allestaine expressed her embarrassment for the way Reece had been treated by Lillian, Simone, and Catherine. Without going into detail, she assured Reece that the three women understood they were fortunate to remain in her home after displaying such behavior.

In the days following Navarre and Allestaine's return, the weather became bitterly cold. For the next three days, Reece was unable to venture outside, take her usual morning run, or visit her new friend, the colt. A storm made its way into the area, bringing snowfall and dropping the temperatures even farther. The snow accumulation was not much; however, it was the bitterly cold winds that forced Reece to remain indoors. *Is it possible to get cabin fever in a palace?* Sure, the Palace was large and there was plenty to do, but Reece had always found her solace outdoors.

Fortunately, Allestaine kept her occupied; they gardened together in the greenhouse, and every once in a while Allestaine took Reece into the kitchen with her to make a special dish—usually a favorite of Navarre's.

Reece was grateful for Allestaine's efforts, but she grew tired of remaining inside all day. Every morning, she would wake up to find the sun covered with thick clouds, daring to snow again. She would make her way out onto the balcony, only to find the temperatures were still stinging cold.

After the long week of glacial temperatures, Reece finally woke up to the sun peeking through her bedroom curtains. She breathed a sigh of relief and quickly made her way over to the windows. When she drew the curtains back, she was exhilarated at the site of the brilliant blue sky, and not one cloud in sight. After she went through her normal routine of preparing for the day, she grabbed a thick wool coat and made her way out onto the second floor balcony. The air was not as bitterly cold with the sun out; however, it was still too cold for her to go trudging through the snow. She hoped by the afternoon the temperatures would warm more and she could take a walk, even if it was down to the stables where the colt was.

That afternoon, she was in the greenhouse with Allestaine, picking flowers for the vases in various rooms. She forced herself to concentrate on the aromas of the indoor garden while arranging the vases, but it was difficult. All she wanted was to be outside. Once they were finished, she planned to do just that. Whether or not the temperatures had warmed since that morning, she planned to get out of the Palace.

As Reece silently planned her day out, Allestaine looked up and smiled lovingly over Reece's shoulder. She turned to see who was there and saw Levi standing in the doorway.

"Levi, it is nice to see that you and Harrison have returned safely. It is good to have you home. Are you on your way to meet with Samuel?" Allestaine said as she brought her son into a loving embrace.

Levi greeted his mother and smiled over her shoulder at Reece, whose eyes had locked onto his. "Good afternoon, Mother. No, Harrison opted to confer with Samuel in my place this time. He owes me, and I figured this was the perfect time for him to pay me back, as I was in no mood to sit in meetings this afternoon."

"Ah. And instead you have decided to help us ladies fill the vases—how kind!" Allestaine's smile was as mischievous as Reece had ever seen it.

Levi laughed. "I think I'd rather sit in meetings with Samuel than report for flower-arranging duty. I'm here for Reece. From what Father has told Harrison and me about everyone at Pasidian being forced indoors for a week, I believe she could use some time outside the house."

Reece looked up as startled as a prisoner suddenly offered freedom. Levi's eyes warmed as he approached her, ignoring the shocked expression on his mother's face.

The way he looked at Reece, his smile igniting the blue of his eyes, her heart raced and her stomach reacted like she was on a roller coaster. She closed her eyes and tried to get a grip on herself. Was it the prospect of going out that excited her, or was it Levi?

She did what she always did when her emotions reacted to the sight of him such as they were doing now—and pushed the unneeded sentiment away. It was the only way she could think rationally in his presence.

"Reece, would you join me outdoors for the afternoon?" he asked politely.

I bet I look like a kid on the first day of summer vacation. "That sounds wonderful, Levi, but I was helping your mother..."

Allestaine cut her off. "Go, Reece. But Levi will hear from me if you are too chilled and become ill."

Levi offered his arm, and Reece accepted. When she looked back, Allestaine's sweet smile had been replaced with a more serious and concerned expression.

As they left the room, Levi mentioned that Jasmeen had an outfit arranged for Reece so that she would not become so chilled outdoors. Levi waited patiently in Reece's sitting room while Jasmeen went to work, helping Reece into an entirely different style of dress than Reece had worn before.

Once completely dressed, Reece looked at herself in the mirror and laughed. The outfit she was dressed in was tailored in more of a masculine style. It was still lavish in its appearance, being rich navy blue, with silver embroidered trim and buttons. Even still, the fitted wool jacket that she was wearing over a long matching skirt was nothing like the gowns she had been wearing lately. Underneath the wool tailcoat, Reece wore a white silk shirt with a black velvet waistcoat over it. Her legs would also be kept warm with black velvet breeches, something she definitely hadn't worn since she'd been in Pemdas.

Jasmeen finished the ensemble when she tied a white silk cravat around her neck, covering the last of her exposed skin. After Jasmine ensured that all of the buttons on her jacket were buttoned, she stepped back to admire the outfit, and Reece laughed again.

"Jasmeen, I'm shocked that you would allow me to wear this. This outfit is nothing like the gowns you have been insisting I wear lately." Reece chuckled. "I guess what I'm trying to say is, this is the first time you haven't dressed me up like a princess."

Jasmeen smiled. "Master Levi has requested that you wear this outfit outdoors with him today. With what he has in mind, you will appreciate the habit."

"Habit?" Reece asked.

Jasmeen giggled. "Oh dear, I almost ruined it. Master Levi has requested I say nothing in regard to his plans for you—he looks forward to surprising you with an outdoor adventure today. Now, let us put on these boots so that your feet will stay dry and warm." Jasmeen helped Reece into fur-lined boots, and then handed her a pair of black leather gloves.

Once her ensemble was completed, Reece met Levi, who was patiently waiting in her sitting room. Levi stood as soon as Reece entered. She teased him by twirling dramatically. "Well...what do you think?" she asked.

Levi laughed, and his crystal eyes sparkled. "I think it will work perfectly for what I have planned." He approached her and offered his arm. "Shall we, then?"

Reece placed her hand on the inside of his arm, and they were soon walking through the Palace. She had no idea what Levi had planned, and she could barely contain her excitement. She didn't know why he'd have her dress in such an interesting outfit just to walk the grounds, but also she didn't want to take the fun out of it by asking too many questions. Imagining the freedom of getting out of the palace exhilarated her so much that she gripped his arm tighter.

"Are you that excited, Reece? I'm not sure what I have planned will live up to your expectations."

Reece couldn't stop smiling. "I'm overjoyed to be going out. I really appreciate your doing this for me."

Finally, they reached their usual exit at the back of the palace. As they exited, Reece stared down past the snow-shoveled steps and saw that a groom with a black horse stood at the foot of the steps. Reece stared at the horse, filled with sudden doubt. Levi softly laughed and led them toward the steps.

"Are you up for a horseback ride today?"

Reece did not know how to respond. She wanted to be outside, but a horseback ride? She feared how it would turn out.

Her expression must have shown her trepidation because Levi laughed aloud. "You have nothing to fear, Reece. Areion loves to travel through the snow, and he is very steady upon it. He has been neglected while I have been on Earth. I felt you both could use some time away."

They approached the large black stallion. He appeared interested by his new visitor, and Reece admired his beauty up close for the first time. He seemed to be the essence of power—living power, not the dead power of an automobile. His eyes followed her as she slowly reached her hand to him, just as she had to the young colt in the meadow. He nosed her hand and grunted, then turned his attention forward.

"He likes you," said Levi. "That's quite a compliment." He patted the horse on his muscular shoulder. Reece laughed nervously and stared up at the tall horse, wondering how she would get on without making a fool of herself.

Levi laughed. He grabbed the thick black velvet cloak, which had been draped over the horse's saddle, wrapped it around her, and secured the clasp at her neck.

"This will help to keep you warm as we ride. The riding habit you are wearing will not be warm enough," he added as his lips curved up into a tiny grin.

Reece was too nervous trying to figure out how she would get on the horse to thank him for the gesture. The saddle was different from what she remembered seeing on Harrison's horse.

Levi reached up. "This is a saddle that you will be more comfortable on while wearing a gown. Our ride will be different from the first ride you took with Harrison. These saddle horns," he gripped one of the leather posts, "are what you'll rest your legs on, and they will keep you balanced on the horse."

Reece stared at Levi in confusion. "I have to ride sideways? Are you sure I won't fall off?" She looked up at the long saddle, and by studying it she could tell it had been custom made to fit two riders.

Levi chuckled. "I will be riding behind you, and with my arms surrounding you while I rein the horse, there is no way you will fall. It may feel a little uneasy at the start, but you will find it is more comfortable riding this way in your habit than riding astride, as you did with Harrison."

Reece exhaled. "Well, I'm not going to make you any promises, but I really don't think this is going to work."

Levi grinned. "It will work. You will be fine, or else I wouldn't have considered taking you on a horseback ride with me. Now, if you'll allow me."

Levi reached down, gripped her at her waist, and effortlessly placed her up into the saddle. *Man, this guy is strong,* Reece thought as she wrapped her right leg around the upper saddle horn. Levi stood at the horse's side and helped position her left leg between the upper and lower saddle horns. He finished by guiding her left foot and helping her place it into a stirrup just below. It was not as uncomfortable as she imagined, and with her left foot in the stirrup, it helped even more for her to maintain her balance. The horse remained perfectly still while she sat waiting for Levi to join her. The saddle had more cushion than she imagined, and the leather ridge separating where Levi would sit behind her lent enough support for her to be comfortable.

Once Levi was assured she was settled into the saddle, he turned to the groomsman, who handed him his long black greatcoat. He pulled on the coat, two leather gloves, and walked over to mount the horse.

He grabbed the reins, a handful of mane, stepped his foot into his stirrup, and in one swift, powerful motion he hoisted himself up onto the horse and positioned himself behind Reece.

Her heart reacted for a short moment, being in such close proximity to him.

Levi tapped his heels to the horse's side, and they began to move forward. "You may hold onto Areion's mane for added support, if you wish," he said as the horse began to pick up his pace.

Levi guided the horse out of the gardens at the back of the Palace and onto a trail that led them into the forest that surrounded the Palace. Reece was slightly uncomfortable riding this close to him, and it wasn't because of anything he was doing. Levi's face was serious and focused; he had done nothing for her to believe that this was anything more than a usual horseback ride for him. What Reece was having difficulty with was the fact that every time she inhaled the scent of his rich, masculine cologne, it gave her an overwhelming desire to lean into him, bringing her face in closer to where his black silk cravat covered his neck. It was ridiculous, and she knew it. She decided to ignore the irrational desire and bring her mind to other things, like the scenery around them.

"Well, I guess you were right; this ride is a little more comfortable, and I can see everything so much better than when I rode on the back of Harrison's horse," she said.

Levi grinned, yet maintained his focus on guiding Areion through the forest. "That is good to know. Once we get through the forest, the countryside will open up and there will be more sights for you to see."

Once they were through the hillside forest, Levi allowed the horse to gain speed. With one hand gripping Areion's mane and the other securely gripping the top saddle horn, Reece found herself thoroughly enjoying the ride.

They rode past creeks, along the shore of the ice-bound lake, and headed toward a steep mountain. She looked at the thick trees at the base of the mountain, wondering if they were going there. As quickly as she pondered it, the horse entered the trees and slowed to a walk.

Levi leaned into Reece and squeezed his arms tightly around her, bracing her as they started up the steep mountain trail.

Reece instinctively leaned into Levi's strong chest and closed her eyes, not wanting to see what was before or behind them until Areion stopped. When he did, they were at the upper end of a large clearing. They dismounted, and Areion wandered over to nibble at a patch of green, where sun or wind had uncovered some grass.

Reece turned away from him to look at the clearing and found she was looking out over the whole mountainside and the land below it. She hadn't known how high they were. It appeared that all of Pemdas was before her eyes, and the entire land was blanketed with snow. Forests made dark patches, and rivers and lakes shimmered like silver on white velvet.

She was speechless. She turned, and Levi stood behind her, his eyes sparkling like the rivers and lakes below them. "Well, what do you think? Is this a better view than the inside of the Palace?"

He smiled down at her, cocking a brow. Impulsively, she stood on her toes, reached up, and threw her arms around his neck to hug him. "Thank you so much!"

"I'll take that as a yes, then."

She was acting like a child, but she didn't care. Wherever she looked, she saw beauty; clean, white snow, and cold, fresh air.

Levi stood tall by her side. "This is my hiding spot."

She smiled up at him, remembering their conversation on the day when the foal had adopted her. "Well, I can say I would never have been able to find you, as you did me."

His mouth quirked up into a grin so attractive, Reece felt a momentary urge to place her lips on his, just to feel their softness. As suddenly as this unexplainable desire came over her, she conquered it and brought her attention back to the scenery before them.

"So, is that the Palace over there?" she asked as she started taking notice of the structures off in the distance.

"Yes, it is." He pointed to the forest of trees that surrounded it. "Those were the trees we came through, and we followed along the Pasidian River, which led us up to this location."

"The women brought me into a town, and after visiting it for three days in a row," she cocked her brow and added dryly, "I figured it must be where you all do your shopping. Can we see it from where we are now?"

Levi laughed as he watched her animated expressions. "You will not be able to view it from here; that town is farther west from the Palace. He looked out and pointed to a hillside in the distance. "Out beyond those trees is where that town sits."

"Ah." Reece crossed her arms and took in more of the countryside.

"Reece, I must say, I am very sorry that you had to endure so many day trips with those women. After their display of rudeness upon our return, I can hardly imagine how miserable you must have been to be out in their company, not to mention being at the Palace in their company."

Reece felt his eyes on her, but the concern in his low, smooth voice told her she shouldn't dare look at him. For fear of her emotions overruling her logic, she continued to gaze at the scenery. "It wasn't that bad, really. I tuned them out for the most part after the first carriage ride into town. Once we were going through the shops in town, they went ahead and left me to take my time browsing the stores on my own, in peace." She looked at Levi and saw him staring off into the distance, jaw clenched. "Levi?"

He looked at her; his eyes seemed darker now, and his brow creased. Reece realized that the women's poor hospitality had upset him once again. "Levi, you seem upset, but you shouldn't be. I really did enjoy myself. The people in the town were very kind to me, and the local silversmith, Allan, I think was his name, was one of the nicest men I've ever met."

Levi's face softened, and he laughed softly. "If that truly is the case, I will be sure to thank that particular silversmith personally." He let out a soft exhale. "Well, I have to say that I am embarrassed to learn that the merchants in town have proven to be more respectable than our friends and family."

"It really is fine, Levi." She smiled.

His lips twisted up into the smile that Reece was starting to find irresistible. *Does he always have to smile at me like that?* she thought as she managed to keep her emotions intact.

"Reece, did you want to return to the Palace from here, or would you like to remain outdoors for a little longer?"

Reece's eyes narrowed as she studied his face; there was something behind his grin, but she couldn't figure out what it was.

Levi laughed. "Reece?"

She lifted her chin. "Well, since we just got here and I haven't seen the outdoors in almost a week, I was hoping we wouldn't have to go straight back." She continued to study his amused expression. "What did you have in mind, Levi?"

"I plan to introduce you to a city in my world the proper way. Would you care to join me for lunch?"

"Are you asking me out on a date?" She laughed. "The Emperor's son? The most sought after man in all of Pemdas…having lunch with the girl from Earth?" she teased.

"Is that what those thoughtless women talk about all day long?"

Reece raised her eyebrows. "That and marriage. I figured that's pretty much the life of the young women here in Pemdas. All the ladies dress up with the expectation that the Emperor's son will notice them and want to marry them one day."

Levi shook his head disbelievingly. "I don't think I want to know anymore. With what I have already heard, I only hope I can redeem any good opinion you may have had of me before those women destroyed it."

Chapter 13

They rode for close to twenty minutes into a town seemingly the same size, if not larger, than the one the three young women had brought her to. However, this place seemed much more affluent in its appearance than the other one.

Levi rode through the cobblestone streets, between the tall, elaborate buildings. The individuals walking down the streets, and the many different carriages they were passing were all exquisite. Reece was thankful they were on their way to lunch, as the aromas now filling the air were that of freshly baked breads, cinnamons, and other spices.

The town seemed to be getting larger before her eyes as Levi turned down a different road—the buildings seemed to go on forever. For the first time, excluding the horses, she felt as though she were back on Earth. This town was definitely larger than the one that Simone, Lillian, and Catherine had taken her to.

Areion appeared to stand out in the crowd of horses and carriages passing them on the street. Some people stopped and stared, some pointed, and some waved. It wasn't until Levi stopped in front of a cottage-style building covered in ivy and he was formally addressed that Reece realized why they had attracted so much attention riding through the village.

The attendant took the reins, and Levi dismounted Areion. The attendant bowed. "Your Imperial Highness, our city is once again honored by your presence."

Levi nodded. "It is my pleasure, sir." He turned back to Reece and assisted her dismount from the horse before offering his arm. "Miss Bryant?"

Reece took his arm, and he led her into the building. When they entered, Levi helped her to remove her cloak, and after he removed his own, he handed them to the waiting attendant. An older woman, well-dressed with gray hair pulled up into a loose bun, made her way over to them. A pleasant smiled spread across her face when she curtsied before Levi. "Your Imperial Highness, it is an honor to serve you and your guest today."

Levi acknowledged her greeting with a nod. "Good afternoon, Mrs. Anders. Allow me to introduce to you Miss Bryant, our most honored guest from Earth." Levi smiled at Reece.

Reece felt the heat in her face as the lady smiled and curtsied before her as well. Reece didn't know how to react; no one had acknowledged her in such a way, and she didn't want to appear rude. She thought it would be best to follow Levi for now.

"Miss Bryant, it is a great honor to meet you." The lady looked up at Levi. "Shall I show you to your usual table, Your Highness?"

"That sounds perfect, thank you." The table was situated out and away from view of the restaurant's other guests. The dining area was simple, and not very large from what Reece had experienced in the land thus far. She was thankful for the privacy of their table, as more than one person took interest in them as they passed. The table sat in a nook of its own, surrounded by three floor-to-ceiling windows. The view from the windows displayed an enclosed garden area, complete with a white stone fountain and pebbled walkways.

Levi pulled Reece's chair out for her, and then smoothly pushed it back closer to the table once she was seated. He took his seat across from her, but Reece didn't engage him in any conversation; her attention was taken by the uniquely crafted gardens just outside the windows to her right.

Levi helped ease her curiosity. "The vegetables and fruits they serve here are all grown in those gardens. It has always astonished me how The Anders are able to sculpt their vegetable gardens and orchards so magnificently. I believe they are as impressive as the gardens of Pasidian Palace."

Reece looked back at Levi. "It's very beautiful."

Before they could say anymore, the staff arrived, filling glasses with water and placing a loaf of hot bread on the table in front of them. Wine was offered, yet both declined and opted for hot tea instead.

Reece placed her napkin in her lap. "So, Your Imperial Highness, what's for lunch today?"

Levi grinned while a hint of red touched his cheeks. "Well, Miss Bryant," his eyes sparkled as he laughed softly, "that would depend on what you are in the mood to eat this afternoon."

She smiled mischievously. "Ah! They serve hamburgers here?"

Levi's brilliant blue eyes danced with humor. "Unfortunately, they do not. However, I can bring you to a location where they would be able to accommodate that, if that is what you prefer," he finished becoming more serious.

Reece laughed. "You would get up, leave this restaurant, and cause a scene, all so I could have a hamburger?"

Levi took a sip of his water. "Miss Bryant, you must understand, at the moment I have only your best interest in mind. As I told you earlier, I plan to introduce you to one of our cities the proper way."

Reece let out a soft laugh. "Well, this could get interesting." She stared at him, studying his amused expression. She exhaled and decided she should probably stop giving him a hard time. "Well, you're in luck; this bread smells delicious, and I don't really like hamburgers. So, Your Royal Majesty, there's no need to cause a scene."

Levi nearly choked on his water and coughed out a laugh.

Reece couldn't help but laugh in return. "I really didn't think it was that funny." She watched him as he regained his composure.

"Miss Bryant—"

"Reece," she demanded.

Levi's eyebrow arched. "Levi."

"Fine." She smiled. "Levi it is! Now, since we have reached an understanding with our names, when are you going to cut into that bread?"

Levi laughed, took the knife, and sliced into the warm bread. She took the piece he handed her, buttered it, and took a bite. It was a bit sweeter than the breads that were served at the Palace; however, it was equally delicious.

"This is my favorite place to dine in the city. Not only for the privacy, but their soups and toasted sandwiches are my favorite in all of Pemdas."

"And all the other dimensions you've visited, of course."

Levi chuckled. "Of course."

"Well, then, I grant you permission to order for me. Soup sounds like it would hit the spot. Do you have a favorite?"

"Yes. I prefer the tomato basil soup above any other they serve here."

"Tomato basil it is."

Levi motioned for the staff and gave them their order. Along with their soups came a variety of fruit and vegetable salads, grown from the garden outside their window. The intensity of the food's flavors was similar to the Palace's, but there was a unique richness in every bite she took, and she was starting to become full a lot sooner than she would have expected.

While they ate, the conversation was kept light. Levi mostly informed Reece about the specifics of Casititor, the city they were in, and how it was one of the most populated cities in Pemdas. When Reece inquired as to why the women hadn't taken her to this city, Levi simply grinned and let her know that in order to get into the city by carriage, they would have to travel five more hours outside of the small town they had taken her shopping in. Fortunately, by horseback they were able to come into the southernmost part of the city. By horseback, the journey back to the Palace from this location was only an hour away.

Once Reece had finished eating, she took a sip of her freshly refilled tea and sat back in her chair, watching Levi as he finished the last of his soup. She smiled as he sipped it silently from the side of his spoon. *Poor guy, that soup has got to be ice cold by now.* He was so attractive, watching him do something as simple as eating his soup sent butterflies swarming throughout her stomach. He must have noticed her studying him, as he looked up and grinned at her innocently.

"Forgive me, I believe I have talked the entire time, and now I am keeping you while I eat," he said.

The sympathetic look on his face sent her heart racing. "It's fine. If I didn't have fifty million questions for you all of the time, you probably would have been able to eat your soup while it was warm." She laughed. "I should be the one apologizing."

Levi shook his head. "If I were in your position, I would not have let anyone out of the room until all of my questions were answered. It's perfectly understandable, Reece."

"Well, good; maybe you can answer something else for me, then?"

Levi laughed as he took a sip of his water and leaned back in his chair. "Ask away."

"This dimension," Reece began, "where exactly is it? I mean, like, in the universe?"

"Well, we are simply in a different dimension on the planet Earth. Where we are in the dimension of Pemdas is actually in the same location as what you would refer to as Western Europe."

"So we are still on Earth, but not *really* on Earth?"

Levi grinned. "That's one way to think of it, yes."

"I guess that must be why, even though it's obvious I'm in a very foreign place, I see so many similarities between here and home. It does seem very 'seventeenth-century Europe' here."

"We do have many similarities to that time period on Earth and its culture. There was a time when the Pemdai and those on Earth were very close, and we shared many different ideas with each other."

She set her tea down and crossed her arms. "That is truly amazing...more than amazing...mindboggling. Well, I've always wanted to go to Europe. I guess I can cross that off my bucket list."

Levi chuckled. "Well, Pemdas is not really Europe...but hopefully it is close enough to satisfy that desire."

Reece smiled in response. Levi's lips curved up into that stunning grin again, and his eyes smoldered as he gazed at her. *A few more of those smiles, and this guy isn't going to know what hit him when the Earth girl impulsively kisses him for no apparent reason.*

"If you don't mind my asking, why do you and Harrison choose to serve on Earth, or whatever it is you do? You're both royalty, and given that his father is a king and yours the Emperor, you're seemingly next in line for the thrones here, right?"

"Being a Guardian on Earth is the one of the highest honors a Pemdai can receive. We are honored to serve."

"Wow, you really are passionate about protecting Earth, aren't you?"

"The Pemdai are very passionate about our love for Earth. It is why you may see so many similarities between Pemdas and Earth. In Earth's earlier days, as I just mentioned, our people were very close with a select few there."

Reece smiled. "That's pretty cool."

Levi laughed. "Yes, it is very *cool.*"

Reece grinned. "Are you making fun of me?"

"I would never consider doing such a thing." He tossed his napkin on the table. "Now, Miss Bryant—" Levi stopped to correct himself. "Forgive me...Reece; I would like to take you on a tour through the shops. Would you care to join me for a walk?"

She sat up. "I'm ready whenever you are."

As they walked down the streets that had been recently cleared of snow, they were stopped more than once by townspeople wishing to meet the Emperor's son. The people seemed elated to see Levi; even more than that, they seemed starstruck by him. Levi must have sensed Reece's uncertainty about how she should act when they were approached. He kindly introduced her and told the people that she was an honored guest, esteemed above all others at Pasidian Palace. She was shocked to see how he held her in such high regard, considering how Simone and the other women treated her in public.

She watched how patient and generous Levi was to the people who were interrupting the tour he was attempting to give Reece. His humbleness and kindness were delightful to witness. He had every right to brush off the people who were disrupting him if he wanted to; however, he did not. He was compassionate and genuine to each person that approached them, and there were many.

As they were about to enter a silversmith's shop, they were stopped by a silver-haired gentleman with two young women at his side.

"Your Imperial Highness! What a great honor to have you visiting us today," the man proclaimed loudly, forcing Levi to stop and turn to acknowledge him.

Levi's entire demeanor changed in the instant he turned to answer the man. His body was rigid, his jaw tightly set, and for the first time since walking through the city, Reece noticed Levi's appearance had changed dramatically. He now held himself with an air of utmost superiority while interacting with the man.

A crowd had gathered around as Levi spoke, "Mr. Sterlington, it is always my pleasure to visit Casititor. Allow me to introduce our highest guest of honor, Miss Reece Bryant, from Earth."

The man smiled faintly and nodded to acknowledge Reece, yet he seemed to be analyzing her carefully with his gaze more than anything else. The two women on either side of him did the same. They appeared to be Reece's age; they were beautiful, and dressed to display their wealth. Reece felt their scrutinizing glares even when she wasn't looking in their direction.

Looks like I'm about to meet the women who are after the most sought after man in Pemdas. This should be interesting.

The man nodded his head toward Reece somewhat dismissively. "Miss Bryant," he managed.

Reece didn't know much about formalities in this land, but from want she had witnessed thus far, never once had she been introduced to someone by Levi and received only a curt nod in return. The reaction by whomever she was being introduced to was not of importance to Reece; however, after feeling awkward by all of the bows and curtsies that came with every introduction, the man's forced gesture made it plain to her that he was not so enthusiastic about making her acquaintance.

"Your Highness, I am sure you remember my daughters, Annalisa and Susanna?"

Both women dropped their heads as they gave Levi a dramatic curtsey.

Levi nodded. "Ladies."

One of the women spoke, "Your Highness, it is lovely to see you again." She looked speculatively at Reece with eyes so mysterious that Reece became curious about who she was. The woman returned her gaze to Levi. "Forgive me if I am intruding on his privacy, but...is His Grace, the Duke of Vinsmonth, also visiting the city today?"

Reece felt Levi's arm tense. She quickly did the math; since Harrison's father was the King of Vinsmonth, she assumed that would make Harrison the Duke.

"His Grace is currently in meetings with our commander, as we have just returned from Earth this morning," Levi responded curtly.

The young woman smiled and bowed her head in response.

Mr. Sterlington approached Levi and spoke in a whisper close to Levi's left ear. Since Reece was still holding onto Levi's right arm, she was able to hear every word.

"Your Highness, I do hope I am not out of line, but I must declare, I am a bit surprised to see His Imperial Majesty's son escorting a woman from Earth on his arm. I only ask out of concern because I believe questions will—"

Levi backed swiftly away from the man, forcing Reece to as well. He stood rigid and tall, towering over the man. His voice was low and purposeful when he responded.

"Mr. Sterlington, I can appreciate your concern; however, you must have forgotten that Miss Bryant is an honored guest of my family. Moreover, His Imperial

Majesty holds her in the highest regard, more than any other in all of his acquaintance. I suggest you keep that in mind as you search for the proper words to apologize to Miss Bryant this instant."

The man appeared as though he would faint at any moment. His face was ashen gray when he looked at her. He gave an exaggerated bow to Levi and spoke, "Your Highness, I must beg your forgiv—"

"I'm not the one who is in need of an apology, sir. Your imprudent question did not insult me."

The man's cheeks flushed red while the two women at his side stepped back and tried to disappear into the crowd surrounding them.

The man bowed. "Miss Bryant, please forgive my foolishness; Pemdas is indeed honored to have you."

Reece didn't know what to say or do. Fortunately, she didn't have to do anything. Levi responded before she had the chance.

"Now, if all of you will excuse us, it is getting late and we must return to Pasidian soon."

With that, he turned and led Reece into the silversmith shop.

As they walked into the shop, they were greeted warmly by the owners. Reece was grateful that Levi seemed to relax as soon as he turned his back on the disagreeable man outside. They seemed to pick back up from where they left off, before Mr. Sterlington's rude interruption. Reece didn't ask questions, and she instead turned her attention to the beautiful items on display.

The shop carried many different items, ranging from cutlery, tea, and coffee services, soup tureens, candelabras, and jewelry. Reece stood in awe, not only at the beauty of the silver, but at the unique shapes and details of each item.

When they made their way over to the jewelry displays, Levi requested to see a certain piece closer. He turned to Reece and explained the uniqueness of the thin bracelet he held in his hands. It was a slim, silver arrow, designed to wrap around one's wrist snuggly. He explained to her that the arrow was the most sacred symbol to the Guardians.

"The Pemdai believe that an arrow represents courage and protection," he said as he took her hand gently and clasped the bracelet around her wrist.

Reece gasped, her heart raced, and she couldn't think straight. Her skin seemed to burn in response to his tender touch. She managed to think well enough to know that she could not accept such a gift. She shook her head. "Levi, I can't accept this." She found the courage to look at him.

His lips curved up on one side, and his icy blue eyes stared into hers. Reece's heart was beating so rapidly, she thought she might hyperventilate. Never in her life had she reacted to any man like this. She had never found herself in a position where a man had this kind of effect on her emotions.

"Reece, I want to give you this gift as a reminder of Pemdas so that when you do return to Earth, you will remember the Guardians who protect you." He brought her hand back into his, to examine the bracelet wrapped delicately around her wrist. "It suits you perfectly," he politely added.

She gently withdrew her hand from Levi's so that she could examine the bracelet. "Levi, this is really beautiful; I love it. Thank you."

"It's my pleasure."

Reece watched as Levi paid the man; the thin paper he handed him was the size and shape of a dollar bill, but with more of a foiled appearance.

They exited the shop and were only a few feet away when a young boy called out to Levi. He was around the age of ten or eleven and dressed in ragged clothes.

"Are you the Emperor's son?" the boy asked.

Levi stopped and gave the young boy his undivided attention. "I am."

The boy stared up at Levi in awe, then looked at Reece, and back to Levi. "Your wife is beautiful, sir."

Reece couldn't help but giggle, and he felt Levi laugh softly at her side. "This is Miss Reece Bryant; she is the Emperor's honored guest from Earth. Forgive my lack of manners for not introducing her properly." He leaned down and spoke softly, "However, I believe I have only put myself in an awkward position at the moment."

The boy laughed.

Levi rose back up. "Young man, what is your name?"

"Christopher Jared, sir."

"Tell me, Christopher, do you live in the city?"

"Yes, sir. I live with my momma and sisters. Momma works in a bakery down that street," he said as he pointed behind Levi and Reece.

"Ah! That is a very commendable job. I will tell you, the next time I come into town, I will make sure to visit her bakery."

"My momma would likely pass out if you do, sir."

Levi smiled, yet studied the young boy. The expression on Levi's face made Reece wonder what it was he was contemplating.

"Christopher, would you be willing to do a job for me?" Levi asked.

"Yes, sir. I can do almost anything but help Momma cook."

"Well, it appears you and I may have some things in common then, young man." Levi laughed. "Tell me, how are you with handling horses?"

"Sir, before my Papa died last year, I used to tend to his horse all the time."

"Then I believe you are qualified for the job I intend to offer you. You see, Miss Bryant and I have traveled quite a distance from where my horse is currently. Will you retrieve him for me?"

The boy's eyes widened and sparkled with excitement. "Oh sir, yes, sir!" he said as he turned to leave and run down the street.

"Christopher?" Levi called, and the boy stopped and turned. "You may need to know where he is," Levi said with amusement. "He is in the private stables at Carnsworth Inn." He pulled another foiled bill out from his coat and handed it to the boy. "Hand this to the stableman, and he will know that I have sent you for my horse, Areion."

The boy looked at the money Levi handed him and swallowed hard before turning to run down the street to retrieve the horse.

While they waited for the boy's return, Levi pulled Reece over to a more private area.

"Reece, I wanted to take a quick opportunity to apologize to you for Mr. Sterlington's impudence earlier." He looked at her somberly.

"Levi, don't worry about it. I wasn't offended; I really thought the guy was kind of weird, given how everyone else had been treating you. Something didn't seem right about him."

Levi laughed. "You're a very intuitive person, Miss Bryant. Yes, the man is strange indeed. He is the official who runs this city, and he is a bizarre man. Every time I am in town, word travels to him and he will track me down so he can re-introduce his daughters to Harrison and me."

"Oh! That's kind of creepy," she added.

"It repulses me; it's obvious that he is trying to use his daughters to make his way into our family in order to advance his social and political agenda."

Reece laughed. "Ah, trying to marry them into the royal family?"

"It sounds pretentious, I know; but that is exactly what he is trying to do, and to gain his riches in that manner." Levi shook his head. "The woman who inquired about Harrison seems to have a bizarre obsession with him. She sends him odd correspondence, and sometimes she will send him gifts." Levi laughed. "I believe she is the only woman that Harrison seems to be frightened of."

Reece laughed. "So, she's a stalker?"

"That would be one way to look at it."

Just then, their attention was brought to the magnificent stallion being led by the boy down the street. Reece watched Areion, intrigued by the way he trotted so gallantly behind the young man. With his shiny black coat, large hooves, long, flowing tail and mane, coupled with his muscular build, Areion made the other horses in the town look scrawny in comparison.

The boy approached, and Areion halted behind him. The boy handed the reins to Levi. "Sir, I didn't know you rode a Guardian horse. I have never seen one up close until now. Are you really a Guardian, too?"

"Yes, I am. That is another reason why Miss Bryant is with me. I served to protect her while she was on Earth."

"Wow. I hope to be a Guardian one day when I grow up."

Levi smiled. "As long as you remain as courageous as you have shown me that you are today, I believe that one day you will make a fine Pemdai warrior."

"Thank you, sir."

"Thank you for retrieving my horse. I trust Areion gave you no trouble?" Levi asked while Areion grunted in return.

Did the horse understand that? Reece let out a laugh.

"He was real good for me," the boy answered.

"Good." Levi handed the boy three bills. "Thank you for your service today, young man."

The boy stared at the money in his hand as if he'd just been handed a winning lottery ticket. Reece watched tears fill his eyes as he looked back up at Levi. "Sir, this is more money than I think my momma has ever made in her whole life."

Reece fought back the tears that were filling her eyes, as well as the desire to reach out and hug the young child.

Levi chuckled. "Well, I'm not sure it's that much. However, take it to your mother and let her know that the Emperor's family is sorry for the loss of her husband."

"Thank you, sir."

"Now hurry along and go bring it straight to her. Miss Bryant and I must be getting back now."

"Yes, sir." The boy turned and ran off through the buildings. Reece looked toward Levi, marveling at his benevolence. He looked back at her and offered a shy smile in return. *I think I'm in love with you...* she thought, while having an overwhelming desire to hug him and tell him that he may very well be the perfect man. She opted for a less dramatic response instead. "That was so wonderful for you to do that for him and his family," she said.

Levi's cheeks colored lightly. "There was no way I was going to let him go without taking an opportunity to help him. Now he and his family will be able to afford new clothes and food. It is the least I could do. The welfare of all of Pemdas' citizens is my family's responsibility."

Reece smiled and approached him at the mounting block. "Well, I think it was beautiful." *I think you're beautiful,* she thought as she smiled, and this time her eyes didn't waver as they stared deeply into his.

Once they mounted the horse, they were both soon off and away, making their way out from the village and back to the Palace before the sunset. As they rode, Reece was starting to become weary. More than once, she was tempted by the cold, chilled weather to lean into Levi and allow him to warm her. She battled with this desire, but her muscles had become so tense while trying to stay warm that fatigue was setting in, and she was miserable trying to sit up in the saddle. With the sun setting, the temperatures were cooling drastically. Levi didn't say much; he seemed more intent on getting them back to the Palace, where it was warm.

"How much longer?" Reece asked through her chattering teeth.

"Forgive me, Reece, I know it is cold. However, I am keeping Areion at a slower pace so that the winds will not chill you further. If you are comfortable doing so, you may lean into me for warmth, and I will bring Areion to a faster speed. We are about thirty minutes from the Palace."

Reece contemplated for a moment, and without another thought she leaned into his chest. He gathered the reins into his left hand and wrapped his other arm tightly around her. Reece melted into his strong embrace, absorbing the warmth radiating from him.

"I am sorry, I lost track of the time. I should have been more vigilant, knowing the weather is still bitterly cold," Levi said in a low voice.

Reece laughed softly. "Well, thankfully I'm starting to warm up, so I won't hold it against you. I really had a great time today, Levi. Thank you again."

"It was my pleasure, Reece."

As she relaxed further into Levi's sturdy embrace, she looked down and touched the bracelet he purchased for her. *Why does he have to be from another world?* As the horse gained speed, Levi tightened his arm around her. She deeply inhaled the rich fragrance of him, closed her eyes, and realized that if she wasn't careful—she could easily fall in love with this man.

As she lay in bed that night, Reece struggled with the new feelings she was having for Levi. She couldn't forget his bright eyes, his passion while talking about his country, and the places he had taken her to. She recalled the people of the small village and their reaction to him, showing her his true character. She tossed in her bed. *Ugh, Reece! Why are you doing this to yourself? He's from another dimension!*

As sleep was beginning to overpower her, she realized she was losing the battle against her attraction to him. She had to admit the truth of what she feared the most—she was falling in love with a man who could not love her in return.

Chapter 14

The next morning, Reece was still in high spirits from the previous day's outing with Levi. She walked to the windows and let out a sigh of contentment when she saw the sun again. Soon, the snow would be completely melted and she could spend her time outdoors again.

After Jasmeen finished applying the finishing touches to Reece's wardrobe for the day, she left to prepare Reece a cup of tea. Reece made a few small adjustments to her hair before making her way out to the sitting room. As she walked into the room, she found a familiar figure standing in front of the fireplace.

It was Levi, wearing a deep blue button down shirt, tucked neatly into his crisp dark trousers. Reece had not seen him in clothes like this since the day he and Harrison brought her into Pemdas. She felt a sudden pang of anxiety overcome her. *Is he here to take me back to Earth? He has to be; there's no other reason he'd show up here dressed like this.*

Levi lips pulled up into his usual stunning smile.

I bet that smile could cure cancer.

"Good morning, Reece."

"Good morning to you, too, Levi. So, have you come to give me the good news?"

Levi chuckled as Reece made her way over to him. "The good news?"

"By the way you're dressed, I'm assuming that you're here to let me know I'm going back to Earth."

Levi's brow creased. "Forgive me, Reece, but no. Samuel is still not comfortable with your return at this time."

Reece exhaled; strangely, she was relieved. "Well then, what brings you here so early, and dressed like a stockbroker no less?" She laughed.

Levi half-smiled. "My mother has requested that I escort you to a private breakfast with her this morning. And you were partially right; Harrison and I are to return to Earth this morning."

"A private breakfast, huh?" Reece asked.

"Yes, she wishes to converse with you without distractions in regard to your day in the city yesterday. She took a great interest when I informed her about the boy, Christopher, we met. I believe she would like to invite you on a journey back to the city with her. My mother is very involved with the impoverished areas throughout Pemdas, and she would like to ensure that the city is doing everything in its power to adequately provide for its citizens."

Reece's eyebrows rose. "Wow. I think it would be great to watch your mother in action."

Levi offered his arm. "I believe you will enjoy it. Now, if you are ready, my mother awaits you in the sunroom."

Reece placed her arm in his, and he led her out from the room.

"Levi?"

"Yes."

"Do you think I will be going back to Earth soon?"

"Samuel is fairly confident that within a month or so, when he is assured the Ciatron have lost all interest in your stand-in, you should be able to return."

Reece's lips twisted up in thought. "I'm not ready to go back, Levi; I mean, I'm not prepared."

Levi stopped walking and turned to face her. "Reece, we will still be protecting you either way."

"No, you don't understand. I seem to have gotten caught up in your world here and forgotten about the world I am from. Right now, during my semester break, I would be studying for my third year in med school. It's going to be my hardest year, with rotations and all, and I'm not ready for it." She trailed off.

"Reece, I understand you are sacrificing a lot right now."

She looked back up at him, ignoring his response. "I have to find a way to study. I can't forget about my responsibilities on Earth. I can't forget who I really am, and my 'real life' responsibilities."

Levi offered his arm again and resumed their walk. "Reece, you are a very intelligent young woman. I have no doubt that when you get back, you will pick back up where you left off without any trouble."

Easy for you to say. "Yeah, I guess. But I think I'll feel better if I took a couple of hours out of my day to study and stay on top of things."

Their conversation was cut short as Simone, Lillian, and Catherine approached them in the corridor.

"Levi—Reece—well, this is a surprise," Simone announced, forcing Levi and Reece to stop and greet them.

Reece was surprised to see the three women. She had rarely seen them around the Palace since Allestaine and Navarre's return; the three women had made great efforts to avoid her. Her body tensed under Simone's scrutinizing gaze. It was obvious the woman was not happy to find Reece with Levi.

"Ladies," Levi acknowledged them.

"Good morning," Reece managed.

Simone smiled at Reece. "It is a *good* morning, Reece. We were just on our way to your room to give you our farewells."

"Farewells?" Reece questioned.

"Well, yes. You see, we will be traveling to a friend's estate for a short vacation. It is quite a distance from the Palace, and we may be gone for close to a month. So," she smiled, "if we do not see you before you return to Earth, we wanted to use this opportunity to wish you well."

"How very considerate of you, Ladies. Now—if you'll excuse us, my mother is awaiting Reece for a private breakfast," Levi answered with irritation in his voice.

Reece was grateful that Levi politely interrupted before she had a chance to answer. Simone was unceasingly proving to Reece what a strange person she was. *Yeah, I'm sure you wouldn't be able to rest if you knew you didn't say goodbye to me, Simone.*

Reece smiled at the three women. "Thank you. I hope you all enjoy your vacation."

Lillian and Catherine both smiled and offered their farewells. Simone's eyes narrowed as she took notice of the arrow bracelet on Reece's wrist. Reece watched as a hint of red touched the woman's cheeks; she could feel the anger radiating from her.

"Enjoy your breakfast, Reece. As I said, if you should return to Earth and we don't see you again, it was a pleasure to know you."

Before Reece could respond, Simone and her friends hastily made their exit.

Reece looked up at Levi, who had a grin playing in the corner of his mouth. "I'd like to say it would be lonely around the Palace without them; however, I believe you'll finally find yourself at peace amongst us now."

Reece shook her head. "Well, I'm glad Simone reiterated why I need to be studying."

"As I said earlier, Reece, you should not worry over your schooling. When you return to Earth, we will help to make it a smooth transition for you."

Reece forced a smile upon her face. "I really don't know how you're going to do that, but okay."

Once they were in the sunroom, Levi led Reece to her seat and walked over to his mother. She stood to give him a heartfelt hug. "I suppose you and Harrison are prepared to leave?"

"All ready. It should only be a short visit—two or three days." He looked at Reece and grinned. "Reece, everything will be fine." He then addressed both women, "I will leave you two ladies to enjoy your breakfast. Enjoy your day."

"Be safe, Son. We'll see you soon. Thank you for bringing Reece this morning."

Levi nodded. "It's always my pleasure." He gave a quick bow, turned, and exited the room.

Allestaine looked at Reece with concern. "Is there something troubling you, Reece?"

Reece smiled, hoping it would ease Allestaine's concern. "No, I'm fine. I was just worrying about my third semester in medical school this year. But like Levi said, it's all going to be fine."

Allestaine smiled. "Yes, it will."

Two servants brought out various breakfast items and set them on the table. They filled the ladies' tea cups and made their way from the room.

As the women ate their breakfast, they spoke about Reece's visit to the city the day before. Reece's animated account of the day's events delighted the Empress.

"Reece, it appears that you enjoyed your visit to the city, and I am thrilled to hear it. Levi and I had a brief discussion about the young boy, Christopher, that you met yesterday."

"Yes, what Levi did for his family was so kind," Reece replied.

Allestaine smiled. "That is what I wanted to talk to you about. You see, after Levi informed me about his family's loss, I feel obligated to pay them a visit. Would you care to join me?"

"Oh, I'd love to. When are you planning to go?"

Allestaine smiled. "Well, my daughter will be home within the week, and I have made plans to go after that.

Elizabeth is excited to meet you, and I believe this will be an excellent opportunity for you and her to get acquainted."

"I really do look forward to meeting her."

"She will be much more enjoyable company for you than Simone, Lillian, and Catherine." She laughed. "Now, regarding our visit to the city, we will be staying for close to three days and will be visiting the areas where the less fortunate live. I have amassed clothing and other items that have been donated for those who might be in need of them."

Reece smiled; this family's interest in those less fortunate was very endearing, to say the least.

"Is there anything I can do to help you prepare?"

"Well, if you'd like, once we finish breakfast you can accompany me to the collections room, where I have been organizing the donated items."

Reece nodded; the last of her concern for school was waning and being replaced with the excitement of helping Allestaine with her charity work.

The rest of the afternoon passed fairly quickly. Reece was amazed at all of the items Allestaine had accumulated. Excitement washed over the lady as she would show Reece the different outfits and pieces of furniture that were to be distributed to the needy.

"Reece, to see the expressions on their faces...it delights me more than anything." She laughed. "Excited as they are, I am equally as thrilled."

"I have never been a part of anything like this, Lady Allestaine, but considering Christopher's response to Levi yesterday, I can only imagine what it will be like to go and donate all of this," Reece said as she looked around the room filled with furniture.

Allestaine smiled. "I truly believe you will enjoy this; I am happy you are coming with us."

The two women passed most of the day going through all of the items and arranging them. Reece became more excited about the trip and the opportunity to witness the happiness this would bring the people that were to receive the items.

After breakfast the next morning, Lady Allestaine dismissed herself to attend to her duties. Reece used this opportunity to go into the Palace's vast library in search of a book containing medical reference material.

She walked along the many different books, not knowing where to start. *I'm never going to find anything in here.* Her attention was drawn to an area of books that might resemble what she was looking for. She pulled one off the shelf that seemed like it would relate somewhat to medical science. She opened it and glanced through its pages. None of the terms they used made any sense to her, and she knew it was pointless to try to read it. As she reached to put the book back on the shelf, another caught her attention.

It was a history book about the Pemdai people, and it instantly sparked her interest. She pulled it off the shelf and took a seat in a chair by the window. So involved with the interesting writings within the book, she barely caught the image of the tall figure standing in the doorway. She looked up, slightly startled, and noticed Levi—dressed as if he had just stepped off Wall Street—staring at her with an amused expression on his face.

At first glance, the impeccably tailored black suit he wore gave the impression of power and wealth. Was it the suit? Maybe it was just Levi. Everything about him exuded nobility and inexorable power. If it weren't for the stunning grin he wore, she would have been somewhat intimidated to be in his presence at the moment.

"Forgive me if I am interrupting you," he said as he crossed the room to where she sat.

He took a seat in a chair across from her, holding three textbooks in his hands.

Trying to keep a level head in response to this exquisite man sitting in front of her, she responded, "This is a surprise, Levi. You're back from Earth already?"

"Yes, we handled the assignment much sooner than we expected." He looked at the book she held in her hands. "Catching up on Pemdai history, are we?"

Reece fanned the pages with her fingers. "You could call it that. Actually, I came in here hoping to find a book that would relate to medical science." She laughed. "That was kind of an absurd idea. I couldn't even understand the terminology you use here. But hey, I tried," she finished with a smile.

Levi softly laughed, stood up, and handed her the books he brought in with him. "Maybe you could relate better to these terms."

Reece stared in disbelief at the books Levi placed into her hands. She looked up at him. "Levi? These are my books from school."

He grinned. "Indeed, they are."

She placed the books over on the side table and stood up. Any childish attraction she had toward him earlier had vanished. She was absolutely speechless by what he had done. The consideration he had taken for her with this gesture had overwhelmed her with admiration for him. "How did you manage to get these?"

"Well, Harrison and I took a little detour on our way back to Pemdas. We have ways of doing things on Earth without being noticed…we've had a lot of practice," he finished with a wink.

She smiled widely and resisted the urge to reach her arms up and around him to thank him with a heartfelt hug. The generosity of this man outshined any faultless quality he carried in his physical appearance. "Levi, I really don't know what to say. Thank you so much," she managed.

"It was my pleasure, Reece. Now if you will excuse me, we just returned from Earth, and I need to get cleaned up before Harrison and I report to Samuel."

She smiled. "Okay. Thank you again."

He grinned and gave her a quick bow before he turned to leave the room.

Reece laughed inwardly as she watched him walking confidently across the room in his pristine suit. *The guy looks like a million bucks right now, and he thinks he needs to clean up?* She shook her head and turned with excitement toward where her books awaited her.

Reece sat back down in the chair and felt more motivated than ever to start going through them. She had no idea how long she sat before she realized she wasn't getting anywhere with her studying. She didn't know where to start, or what she needed to study. Unable to engage herself into her books, she decided that a change of location might help.

She walked over to a sitting area just outside of the library, which overlooked the main entrance to the Palace. It was perfect. The sofas were inviting, and the views of the Palace gardens behind them were magnificent. Feeling more confident now, she walked over to a plush sofa and sat down. She flipped one of her books back open and began to read. The change of location didn't seem to help her either, as now she was distracted with the scenery around her. If she wasn't staring at the chandelier that hung over the entryway, her eyes were drawn to the grand staircase in front of her. Why was this happening? Levi goes out of his way to bring her these books, and now she has no desire to study? Reece was determined to get something out of these books. She brought her attention back to the paragraph that she must have read at least hundred times and started to read it again. As soon as she started reading, the front doors to the Palace opened and two tall men walked through them. Levi and his father were impressive in their appearance, dressed in white muslin shirts, complemented with their cravats and lavish silk waistcoats. Even though this was casual dress for these men, Reece still marveled at their attire. The men went their separate ways, and Reece returned her attention to the book in her lap. However, instead of reading the words on the pages, she was envisioning Levi in his pale blue waist coat, crisp white shirt, and dark trousers. *I can remember every detail of Levi's outfit, but I can't manage to remember the sentence I've read a hundred times.* She didn't want to study anymore—she'd never felt so distracted before, so disengaged. But now, because Levi went out of his way to bring her books to her, she felt obligated to.

She laid her head on the back of the sofa, closed her eyes, and softly exhaled. What time was it anyway?

"Reece?" A low and smooth voice called out.

Levi. What am I supposed to tell him when he asks what I've learned so far?

She opened her eyes to find him staring down at her with that ridiculously handsome grin.

"Hey, Levi," she responded.

"Everything okay?" he asked.

"No, not really. I don't know what my problem is; I can't focus. I haven't even been able to read a whole paragraph without my mind wandering off, and then I'm staring at the lights or whatever. I don't get it; I can't concentrate on any of this."

Levi laughed. "Well, maybe I can help."

Reece exhaled. "I doubt it," she answered, knowing very well that he would only magnify her inability to concentrate.

Levi arched his brow at her. "I believe I can. Give me a moment."

He turned and disappeared down the grand steps before her. She shook her head, realizing this was going to be a waste of both their time. *Oh well, I'm not in a position to turn down help.*

Levi was soon up the steps and approaching her. He extended his arm out to her. "Come with me. I have sent for some trays of food to be brought out onto the balcony. We can start going over your books there."

"Oh." Reece stood up abruptly. "I forgot, I was supposed to meet your mother for lunch."

Levi laughed. "As soon as I noticed your absence in the dining room, I realized you were probably up here engrossed in your studies. I explained as much to my mother as I dismissed myself to find you."

"Well, shouldn't we have lunch with your family then?"

Levi shook his head. "With Harrison out for the afternoon and you and me taking our lunch on the balcony, my mother and father are currently enjoying a quiet lunch alone. A luxury they rarely enjoy." He walked over and picked her books up from where they lay scattered on the sofa. He tucked them under one arm and offered Reece his other arm. "Shall we?"

There was no backing out now. She had to admit, this was kind of neat; maybe studying with Levi would be helpful after all.

Chapter 15

The temperature outside was much warmer than it had been in days, making lunch on the balcony an excellent idea. While they ate, Levi read through one of her textbooks. It was his calm, yet assertive demeanor, combined with the lovely weather and scenery, that seemed to help Reece relax. Thankfully, she could finally concentrate on the material she had been struggling with earlier.

She hadn't realized just how famished she was until she started eating. With nourishment her body obviously required, she was more alert and focused. As it turned out, Levi wasn't the distraction she thought he'd be. Having his help was more useful to her than she initially imagined.

He easily proved to Reece how intelligent he was. She was awed at his ability to take the difficult material and make it interesting to her in a way it never had been before. By the time they finished their lunch, Reece had gained more knowledge from her books than she believed she could have learned in a week.

As they were relaxing with their tea, a servant walked up to the table. "Master Levi, Mr. Howard is here to see you, sir."

"Thank you," Levi answered the servant and brought his attention back to Reece. "Please excuse me for a moment." He politely excused himself and made his way up the short staircase to speak with the young man who waited there.

Reece used this opportunity to admire the physique of the tall and noble man. Even with his back to her, she could sense the command and authority he always carried himself with. Strength and power always seemed to radiate from him. *There's nothing wrong with admiring him,* Reece thought innocently.

After a short conversation with Mr. Howard, Levi returned to his chair. "Forgive me for that interruption. That was Mr. Howard, one of the Guardian instructors."

"Oh. Are you leaving again?"

Levi grinned. "No, we won't be returning to Earth for at least two weeks. Harrison and I were asked to instruct a new group of Guardian recruits. Mr. Howard was here inquiring after Harrison."

"Where is Harrison anyway?" Reece asked.

Levi sipped his tea. "He has been planning the training curriculum we will be using in our combat sessions next week. By the time he has finished, I believe the new recruits will hate us both." He laughed and returned his attention to the textbook he had been reading.

"I think that's enough studying for one day. I don't know about you, but I'm pretty much done going through this stuff."

Levi laughed. "That is understandable. I am sure you have been at this since I returned this morning, anyway."

Reece grinned. "Pretty much. This was really nice, though, Levi. Thank you for everything you did to help me today."

Levi smiled. "It was nothing. I must say, I enjoyed going through the information in your books."

After they finished their desserts and tea, Levi told Reece that he and Harrison would be traveling to Sandari the next day to escort Elizabeth back to the Palace. He offered to assist her further with her studies during his free time upon their return, and Reece accepted the offer without hesitation.

Over the next two days, Reece was engrossed either with studying her books or helping Allestaine organize items in the collection room. Even though she had stayed busy, she had to admit that she missed Levi. He and Harrison were due back at any moment with Elizabeth, and the thought of seeing him again brought a wave of excitement through her. She knew she probably wouldn't encounter any of them until dinner, as it was a long journey from Sandari Kingdom to Pasidian Palace. With that in mind, she tried to remain focused on her reading.

She sat on the sofa just outside the library, which was turning out to be her favorite place to study. Sitting out on the landing gave her a perfect view of the Palace's main entry; however, Levi and his family rarely used this area to enter the Palace. So it came as a surprise that, while she was enveloped in a lengthy chapter of her book, the front doors of the Palace swung open and a young woman walked through the doors holding Levi's arm. She secretly watched the two make their way into the entryway. Levi's smile was radiant as he escorted the beautiful woman into the Palace. Reece grinned; this must be Elizabeth.

Appearing to be close to the age of seventeen, Elizabeth was polished and lovely. She was dressed superbly, even for someone who had been traveling in a carriage for most of the day. Her beautifully-styled hair was a lighter hue of blond than Reece's, and from what Reece could determine from this distance, she seemed to resemble her mother, just as Levi did his father.

Reece assumed they were on their way to meet Allestaine, and she brought her attention back to the book in her lap.

A few moments later, she was politely interrupted from her reading.

"I hope we are not intruding on your studies, Miss Bryant?" Levi questioned formally, surprising Reece.

Her head snapped up to find Levi and Elizabeth standing in front of her, both wearing brilliant smiles. Up close, Elizabeth was more beautiful than Reece had initially thought. *This family couldn't possibly be any more attractive.*

Reece stood up. "Absolutely not, Levi." She looked over at Elizabeth and smiled.

"Elizabeth, this is Miss Reece Bryant. Reece, please allow me to introduce you to my sister, Elizabeth," Levi announced proudly.

Levi's face was glowing as he stared down at Elizabeth. Reece could easily see the love and admiration he carried for his younger sister.

Elizabeth spoke softly. "Miss Bryant, it is truly an honor to meet you. I have heard so much about you. I hope you have been comfortable living here with us in Pemdas?"

Reece instantly felt the purity and properness Elizabeth carried within her. Reece smiled at her. "Elizabeth, please call me Reece. And yes, Pemdas is wonderful; I have been extremely comfortable while I've been here."

Harrison made his way up the steps and over to the group. "Reece, I see you have finally met a young woman who is actually a pleasure to be in the same room with," he proclaimed upon his approach.

Elizabeth's cheeks colored lightly.

"Yes, Harrison, I think I have." Reece smiled at Elizabeth.

Harrison laughed and brought his arm around Elizabeth. "Lizzy, you must know, Reece has had quite the impossible challenge of dealing with Simone, Lillian, and Catherine. It is good to have you among us all again at Pasidian."

Elizabeth smiled up at Harrison. "Yes, it is good to be home. I am looking forward to accompanying Reece and mother to Casititor as well."

"Elizabeth, your mother has been showing me all of the items already donated," Reece added with excitement. "I think this will be an incredible trip. I'm really looking forward to joining you both."

Levi politely interrupted the ladies' conversation. "Reece, forgive me, but I was just bringing Elizabeth to meet with my mother. I fear if I delay any longer—"

Reece laughed. "Yes, your mother has been anxiously awaiting all of you." She looked at Elizabeth. "It was very nice meeting you."

"The pleasure was mine, Reece," Elizabeth returned with a gentle smile.

Reece sat back down as Levi, Elizabeth, and Harrison walked down the corridor together. She gazed intently at Levi as he escorted his sister, walking with his usual air of grandeur and nobility. He was incomparable to any man she had ever met. Yes, she was very excited he was home. *What woman wouldn't be thrilled to be around him again?* Denying any attraction for Levi was beginning to seem futile at this point; it seemed that her heart had its own ideas.

Chapter 16

ver the next couple of days, the three women spent the majority of their time preparing for their trip. Elizabeth was proving to be a very humble and intelligent woman. It didn't take Reece long to see the admirable similarities between Elizabeth and her mother, and she enjoyed her company a great deal.

The morning of their set departure, Navarre and Levi escorted the ladies to their carriage. They said their farewells and were off to the city of Casititor.

The Pasidian Imperial Guards escorted them to the town. In front of their carriage, six men rode on white horses, carrying flags with the Emperor's crest. Following behind the carriage were ten men riding in the same fashion.

They arrived late that evening and were shown to an exquisite apartment where they would stay for the next three days. Dinner was prepared and awaiting their arrival. As they ate, Allestaine shared her plans with Reece and Elizabeth for the neighborhoods they would be visiting in the city.

After breakfast the next day, Allestaine informed the guards that the first place they intended to visit was the bakery where Christopher's mother was employed. As they began to get closer to the bakery's location, Reece noticed a considerable change in the conditions of this part of the town. The two-story buildings that lined the streets were utterly dilapidated. The second stories of the businesses seemed to house the less fortunate living in the area. Reece noticed that tenants had put everything from towels to boards in the windows where glass had once been. Everything about this part of town was oppressive; it was all in disrepair.

Reece was taken aback by the scene before her. Sure, she had seen impoverished communities before; however, she didn't expect this in Pemdas. The places she had seen thus far would never have led her to believe these conditions existed in this world. Allestaine's expression mirrored Reece's disbelief. The look on the lady's face was severe. It was obvious she was extremely displeased with the dire state of this part of the town.

Once they reached their destination, Allestaine requested that Reece and Elizabeth stay outside with the guards so that she could have a private audience with Christopher's mother.

"It's as if the government of the city has turned a blind eye to this part of city. It breaks my heart," Elizabeth said to Reece as they waited for Allestaine to return from inside the small bakery.

"I agree. These conditions are depressing."

"It's extremely disheartening, Reece. Most of the money my mother raises is donated to this city because it is one of the largest in its kingdom. I believe my mother will not rest easy until she has spoken with Mr. Sterlington about this," Elizabeth said.

As the women continued discussing their disbelief about the situation, a small group of barefoot children wearing ragged clothes approached where they stood.

"You are both from the Emperor's Palace, aren't you?" a young girl asked.

Elizabeth knelt down, bringing herself to the child's level. "Yes, we are, and we have brought you children lots of goodies, too." She reached down and tapped the little girl on her bare foot. "We have plenty of shoes for you as well, sweet one."

The girl leaped and wrapped her arms around Elizabeth's neck, almost causing her to fall over. "Miss, if there was anything I could ask for, it would be shoes."

Reece restrained her tears and held her arm out. "How would you children like to see all the gifts we've brought for you?"

The children shrieked with delight, causing Elizabeth and Reece to laugh in return.

Allestaine spent the majority of her time meeting with the adults in the area, learning more about their living conditions. She, Elizabeth, and Reece also toured the many different businesses and gave them supplies they needed. She notified each business owner that the Palace would be funding all of the repairs that were required to return buildings back to their once excellent condition.

Each day while visiting this part of the city, people from all around would make their way to this location to meet the Empress. Most would thank her for taking interest in the less fortunate and would donate either personal items or money in an effort to help.

On the final day, Allestaine, Reece, and Elizabeth were at the bakery early. They sat at a small table inside, eating their breakfast.

"I find it interesting that Mr. Sterlington has not shown himself yet. He knows very well that I've been in town these last few days. I know he is avoiding me; this is the first time that I have ever had to send word to him that I am visiting his city. He expects me to believe that he had no idea I was visiting town?" Allestaine asked as she arched her brow at both women sitting across from her. "It only makes him guiltier for what he has done."

"Well, Mother, from what Reece and I have learned from many of the townspeople, most of the citizens have unfavorable things to say about his practices," Elizabeth responded.

"As well as they should."

When they finished their breakfast, there was already a crowd of people outside the small building. The three women stood and went out front to greet the townspeople who were waiting to meet them.

Mr. Sterlington appeared within the hour of Lady Allestaine's arrival to the location. He waited patiently as she finished a conversation with one of the townspeople. Elizabeth and Reece were occupied by a group of children; however, they became distracted by the scene before them.

"Your Imperial Majesty, forgive me for not arriving sooner to accept you properly into the city," Sterlington said.

Allestaine turned to face Sterlington, offering the silver-haired man a stern, icy glare.

"Do not presume that I require your greetings to feel comfortable in this city."

"Majesty, allow me to humbly beg your—"

"Hold your tongue, man. I am in no mood to hear any of your senseless words or excuses for the dreadful conditions I have been witnessing over the last three days in this part of the city." Her eyes were like flint, staring at him with utter repulsion. "I work very hard to make sure that those who are struggling are having their needs met. I believe you should know very well that most of my efforts have gone towards Casititor because the population is great, and therein the poverty levels are high."

Mr. Sterlington was expressionless, yet guilt radiated from his pale blue eyes. "Allow me to—"

Her eyes blazed with fury at his interruption. "Mr. Sterlington," her voice was low and steely, "I have nothing further to say to you. I have more important things to do than to talk to you right now. You're excused."

Allestaine spun on her heels and walked into the bakery. Mr. Sterlington slowly turned to leave. When he did, his eyes darkened when he noticed Reece staring at him. He frowned at her with a look of utter disgust. Reece felt an odd chill run through her and immediately turned her attention back to the children, who were playing a handball game in the street.

There was something about the silver-haired man that bothered her; she just couldn't place it. As she contemplated the man's character, one of the children overthrew the ball and it began to roll down the street. Reece turned to run after it and caught up to it almost a block from where she had been standing. She knelt to pick it up, and as she stood again her heart raced when she noticed Levi walking up the sidewalk with Harrison. She laughed when she saw the crowds gather around, forcing them to halt and interact with them.

Reece turned to bring the ball back to the children, but was suddenly face-to-face with an irate Mr. Sterlington. She gasped with shock, wondering where the tall, angry man had come from. Reece was instantly uncomfortable and hoped the guards that stood outside of the bakery were watching her. She was relieved when she saw the three guards staring intently in her direction and starting to make their way to where she stood.

"Reece Bryant!" Mr. Sterlington growled.

"Mr. Sterlington," Reece returned in a stern, yet calm voice.

"I will have you know that I blame your presence in Pemdas for all of this," he rumbled.

The man was obviously delusional as he spat his words violently out at her. Reece was startled by the unexpected confrontation and had difficulty finding words in response to the man's accusations. "I have no idea what you are talking about. Please excuse me." She tried to walk past him.

The man gripped her arm tightly, causing Reece to gasp in pain. "I can see to it that your life is destroyed, madam. Whether they say that you are the Key or not, you are nothing but scum to me." He smiled darkly, searching

Reece's confused expression. "I can have you removed from Pemdas, you know?"

Reece tried to jerk her arm free. "Get your hand off me," she said harshly.

The man captured her other arm and brought her face close to his. "You listen to me—"

"Sterlington! Remove your hands from Miss Bryant this instant!" Levi commanded in a deadly voice.

The man removed his grips from Reece, and his face paled as he turned to find Levi and Harrison standing tall and unyielding in front of him. Both men wore dangerous expressions, mirroring the Imperial guards that now surrounded all of them.

"Your Imperial—"

"Not another word," Levi snapped.

The guards stood a few feet away, giving Levi his space and waiting for his command. Elizabeth quickly rushed to Reece's side as Harrison stood in-between both of the women protectively.

"Magnus Sterlington," Levi addressed the man with superior command, "I demand to know why you have threatened Miss Bryant in such a way. You should know I have heard every threatening word you have said."

The man swallowed hard and looked up into Levi's fiery gaze. "I was only upset about—"

"Your threats are treasonous!" Levi interrupted him.

The man laughed nervously. "Come now, Your Highness, let us not overreact."

Levi's jaw tightened, and his eyes became fierce. "You forget who you are speaking to! I suggest you guard your words in my presence, Sterlington!" Levi nodded to the guards standing in the distance, and they approached immediately. "Gentlemen, take him to the prison chambers; the Emperor will decide his fate for the threats he has made against Miss Bryant. I will not waste another word on this man."

Reece didn't have a chance to see the man's reaction before the guards swiftly gripped him and led him out and away from the street.

Levi turned to face Reece, his form still dangerous and stiff. "Miss Bryant, are you okay?" he asked solemnly.

She smiled faintly, mildly intimidated by his current disposition. "I'm fine, Levi, thank you."

Levi nodded and offered his arm. "Let us get you back to where my mother is."

Reece took his arm. "Can he really get rid of me?" she asked as Levi escorted her back toward the bakery.

Harrison laughed, breaking through the tension. "HA! Not likely, Reece."

"Reece, you have nothing to fear. Do you think I would let anything happen to you? It is Harrison's and my duty to protect you, whether on Earth or in Pemdas." Levi added in a serious voice, "Do not concern yourself over him; he will be dealt with accordingly."

They were in the city for less than an hour before they said their farewells to everyone. Allestaine promised a return visit in the coming months to check on the progress of the restorations, much to the delight of the townspeople.

Levi escorted Lady Allestaine to their awaiting carriages, walking ahead of Harrison, Reece, and Elizabeth. He still seemed upset over the confrontation with Mr. Sterlington, and it seemed as though he and his mother were sharing their own private conversation about the incident.

"So, my ladies; other than dealing with Sterlington, how was your visit?" Harrison asked.

"It was a wonderful experience, as it always is when helping my mother with her charity work," Elizabeth responded.

"It was really extraordinary to be able to take part in this. I have to admit, before Levi brought me here and we ran into Christopher, Pemdas was starting to freak me out a little."

Elizabeth softly laughed as Harrison looked at Reece. "Starting to freak you out a little? If this is such a frightening world for you to experience, maybe Levi and I should take you into a few other dimensions out there."

"That came out wrong," Reece responded with a laugh. "It's just that I was starting to believe that Pemdas was some strange and perfect world; a place that didn't experience poverty."

"I must say, I am shocked to hear you say that you thought Pemdas was perfect," Harrison answered.

"Well, I was getting that impression, yes. But given that I had been staying exclusively around the Palace, I guess that's why I would come to that conclusion."

Harrison laughed. "Even after being in the company of my sister, Simone, and Catherine—*at the Palace*—you still imagined Pemdas was perfect?"

Reece and Elizabeth both laughed. "That's a good point," Elizabeth said.

"Hmm, you got me there, Harrison."

When they returned to the Inn, they had lunch while the luggage and carriages were being prepared. Harrison and Levi rode along side of the convoy, assisting the escort home.

As they rode home, Reece stared out of the carriage window, secretly admiring Levi as he rode alongside. He sat tall and authoritatively in his saddle, and she inwardly marveled to herself that Levi was the epitome of the perfect man. She realized now, as she watched him ride gallantly alongside their carriage, that this was the type of man she could truly love.

For the first time since her father's passing, she felt contentment in her life; happiness that only Levi seemed to ignite in her. It was as if he filled a void she never knew existed. Was there a possibility that she could be falling in love with him? She couldn't deny it anymore; it was obvious she already had. But would he ever love her in return? The idea of that possibility brought a shiver of excitement through her. Against her better judgment, she closed her eyes and imagined herself in his arms.

Chapter 17

In the weeks following their return from Casititor, Reece spent most of her time with Elizabeth. Both women began studying together, as Elizabeth had to prepare for her new tutor that was arriving within the week.

When they weren't studying in the library, they would take strolls through the gardens. Elizabeth loved hearing about Earth and what the world was like. The days seemed to pass quickly now that Reece had an excellent companion to spend her time with.

With Samuel's trepidation about Reece's return to Earth, he kept Harrison and Levi busy on assignment in Philadelphia, hoping to expedite the process. However, it was nice when they were home, as they offered to help Reece and Elizabeth with their studies. Even though the men were an excellent help to both women, they were a distraction as well.

So, it was on a warm and sunny afternoon that Reece and Elizabeth were caught up in a lively conversation with both men in the library. All four had completely gotten off the subject of their studies, and Reece realized it was time for a break. Getting out every morning for a jog and taking walks with Elizabeth was enjoyable, but she wanted to do something exciting.

"I think I want to learn how to ride a horse. What do you guys think?" she asked enthusiastically.

The room fell silent until Harrison laughed and answered her, "Well, Reece, we thought you'd never ask. Fortunately, Samuel has given Levi and me the next couple of days leave to relax in Pemdas, and we would happily oblige you. This, my friend, shall be interesting."

Levi grinned. "We can arrange a riding session for you tomorrow, Reece."

The next afternoon, Levi escorted Reece out to the stables. As they neared the intimidating stallions, Reece began to wonder if this idea was more than she bargained for. When they reached the stables, she noticed Areion standing next to a horse unlike the other Guardian horses. It was black, with patches of white painted throughout its coat. This horse had a long, flowing mane, and its hooves were covered with long, feather-like hair.

"I have arranged for this horse to be brought up for you to ride," Levi announced as they approached.

"Okay, so I guess I don't get to learn to ride on a Guardian horse, then?"

Levi chuckled. "Reece, it would be better to start you out on a more docile horse. This horse comes from a breed that is very similar to the Gypsy Vanner horses on Earth. They are very patient creatures and are excellent to learn to ride on. They are the only horses that my mother and sister will ride."

Levi went through the basic instructions of how to control and maneuver the horse. He informed Reece that the horse would be able to feel her energy, and therein it would easily try to get away with certain things if it could. If Reece was timid in leading the horse in a certain direction, the horse would likely protest. She had to remain confident while riding, and most of all she had to know she was in control.

It all seemed rather easy to Reece. Levi promised that he and Areion would ride close to her, in case she had difficulty guiding the horse. He also mentioned that they would take it slow until she felt comfortable enough to bring the horse up to faster speeds, letting Reece gain more confidence while on horseback.

"Do you have any questions, or are you ready to give it a try? I want to be sure you are feeling confident. The horse may be docile, but horses are very stubborn in their own way. You must understand, riding horses can be dangerous, and I don't want you hurt or—"

"Levi," Reece interrupted, hoping he wouldn't change his mind. "I'm ready." She smiled confidently at him.

Levi helped her onto the horse. Reece's heart jumped when the horse's weight shifted beneath her. She gripped tight onto the saddle horn, wondering if she could do this.

Levi looked up, the humor in his sparkling eyes captivated Reece, taking her mind off her sudden fear. "You okay?" he asked.

She smiled, trying to maintain confidence. "Yes. Just trying to make sure I'm doing everything right."

Levi handed the reins to her and showed her again how she would guide the horse. "Areion and I will pace the horse at a slow walk, so do not worry about holding a tight rein. Just stay relaxed, calm, and—"

"Confident. Right," she finished his sentence. "Got it." She was quite nervous, but didn't want Levi to see it.

Levi's lips curved up slightly. "Not too confident, Miss Bryant."

As Levi turned to walk toward Areion, three things happened at once. As Harrison and Elizabeth made their way down to them, Harrison called out, announcing their arrival. Reece startled, pulled back hard on the reins, and absently kicked her heel into the horse's side as she turned to look back in their direction.

The horse sprang forward into an immediate gallop, taking Reece out and away from the stables, toward the woods.

Reece's heart was racing, but she felt exhilarated all at the same time. She maintained her focus and tried pulling hard on the reins to stop the horse. The horse jerked its head out in protest and gained more speed. She felt panic setting in, but tried to remain calm and think her way through the dangerous situation. As the forest was enclosing all around her, she heard thundering hooves over the sound of the horse's she was on. The next thing she knew, Levi was sitting behind her on the horse. He grabbed the reins, pulled back gently, and called out for the horse to stop.

The horse responded by slowing its stride, and soon after that it halted completely. Reece collapsed back into Levi's chest and looked up into his worried face. When he looked down, Reece couldn't restrain her laughter in response to the expression on his face. It was the first time she had seen him look scared.

Levi's eyes studied hers for a brief moment, and then he shook his head. "Reece, I do not understand how you can laugh right now."

Reece laughed again; she could feel his heart pounding against his chest. "Levi, I have no idea what happened, but that was actually kind of fun."

Levi stared at her incredulously. "Fun? Reece, you could have been seriously injured. The horse would not stop for you, and if I—"

Their eyes locked, and Reece fought the urge to run the tips of her fingers along the creased lines of his brow. "Well, Levi, you did stop him, and I suppose this marks the second time that you have saved my life."

Levi dismounted the horse, but would not let its reins loose.

Reece arched her eyebrow sharply in an attempt to challenge him. "I think I can handle the horse on my own now."

"I am only making sure you and the horse do not startle again." He looked back in the direction they had come from. "Harrison and Elizabeth are approaching on their horses."

Levi looked back at Reece with a smug grin, and Reece laughed in return.

"Well, I'll say that pretty much does it for riding lessons, Reece! Looks like you're ready to take on a Guardian horse now, maybe even leap over Pemdas' barriers!" Harrison called out as he and Elizabeth approached.

"Reece, are you okay?" Elizabeth asked with concern.

Reece smiled in return, but before she could answer them, Levi did.

"It seems Reece enjoys living on the edge of life every now and then." He looked up at her with amusement, and then back to Harrison and Elizabeth. "Once I was able to stop the horse, her only response was that 'it was fun.' I believe I was more concerned for her safety than she was."

Harrison and Elizabeth laughed.

"That's the spirit!" Harrison said. "I knew there was some love for adventure buried deep inside you; we just had to get your head out of your books to find it."

Reece lifted her chin. "I've always loved a good adventure, Harrison," she responded proudly.

Harrison's lips quirked in humor. "Really? Because all I've known of Reece Bryant is that she was the young lady who frequents coffee shops, studies, goes to school, and…well, um—"

Reece's eyes narrowed as Elizabeth tried stifling a laugh. "I also run, and I've taken dancing lessons, too. I don't just sit in coffee shops and study all the time."

Dancing Lessons? Really, Reece? She knew that it was a ridiculous response and wished she had let Harrison win this argument. So, it did appear that she was quite the college nerd after all.

Harrison laughed. "Oh—indeed, please forgive me, Miss Bryant; I don't know how I could've overlooked all of those other thrilling escapades. I stand corrected; the thrill of being on a horse's back as it runs away, wildly out of control, is very similar to the daring adventures of dancing and running."

Fortunately, Levi saved her by responding, "We could stand here all day and listen to you two go back and forth; however, I believe our plans were to teach Reece to ride." He looked up at Reece and grinned. "If you should choose to show us a little bit more of your adventurous side today, you need to recall my instructions for stopping the horse."

Reece laughed. "Yes, next time I won't pull back so hard on the reins."

"Excellent! Riding lessons are over; now let's go have some fun," Harrison added.

The four set off out through the woods and into the open fields behind the Palace grounds. Reece was becoming more comfortable riding the horse and found it enjoyable. They spent the next few hours riding alongside the Pasidian River and touring a few of Harrison and Levi's favorite places to play when they were children. It seemed like it was too soon when they had to return back to the Palace.

Once the horses were handed over to the stable men, Reece and Elizabeth made their way to the side gates of the Palace while both men remained in conversation with Javian.

As Reece and Elizabeth were laughing and giggling together, recalling the day's events, Simone, Catherine, and Lillian finished their descent from the Palace steps into the garden. Simone stopped and stared at both young women with a look of disgust.

"Ladies, it is a beautiful afternoon. It's lovely to see you all out and enjoying a walk in the gardens, I presume?" Elizabeth said in her usual sweet tone.

Simone stared at them and offered a tiny grin. "You two have been out riding horses?" she questioned, while the other young women laughed. "How lady-like."

"Yes, we have, and we had a great time," Reece said, ignoring Simone's seemingly rude remark.

"Well, you won't catch me with the stench of horse on my clothing, and you will never see me–" she eyed both women's dresses, "in a riding habit either."

"Simone, Lillian, and Catherine. What a delight," Harrison said as he approached. "I haven't seen your lovely faces around the Palace in a while."

Simone stared darkly at Harrison. "It's because we left for a while, Harrison. We have been gone for over two weeks."

Harrison chuckled. "Wow, I didn't even notice. Hmm, actually, there was something I did notice. And I suppose now I know what may have enticed the lovely Simone away from the grand Palace."

"Harrison, must you always insist on playing games with me?"

"Games? Ah, Simone, I would never play games with a woman like you. But am I curious—why would you take a sudden interest in an old friend of mine and Levi's? You know, that strapping young lad that goes by the name of Michael Visor."

Simone's face turned bright red while Harrison laughed aloud.

"Harrison, that is enough. You have crossed a line; you would do wise to find your manners immediately," Lillian interjected with a sharp tone.

Harrison stifled a laugh. "I was only engaging the lady in conversation. I am always about my manners, sister."

At that moment, Levi approached. "Ladies," he greeted them.

The three women gave him a quick curtsy.

"Good afternoon, Levi, we were just speaking about Reece and Elizabeth's horseback riding," Simone said as she gave Harrison a deadly look.

"Well, I believe Reece and my sister would feel much better talking with you about their day out after they have freshened up. Now, if you will excuse us."

Reece quietly sighed with relief at how smoothly and quickly Levi was able to remove them from the presence of the ladies.

"I had forgotten they'd left the Palace. Do you think that's what Simone was upset about?" Elizabeth asked as she held onto her brother's arm.

"Do not be ridiculous, Lizzy. You know those women better than that. They are upset that they were not invited to enjoy the day out with us," Harrison answered.

"Very true," Elizabeth said.

"Now, let us all get cleaned up and make sure we give them every detail about our excellent new riding student here," Harrison said as he winked at Reece, who was walking by his side.

The four entered through the back doors of the Palace, still laughing over the events of Reece's first horseback ride. Their conversations were abruptly halted when they saw Navarre, Allestaine, and Samuel standing in the foyer waiting for them.

Navarre smiled. "I know you all probably want to freshen up from your horseback ride; however, Samuel wishes to have a short meeting with all of us."

Without another word, the group followed them into a meeting room and took their seats around the table. The broad smile on Samuel's face gave Reece a sinking feeling as to what this short meeting would be about.

Chapter 18

Navarre stared at his commanding officer, who was the only one left standing in the room. Navarre smiled faintly at Samuel's odd behavior. "Samuel? Please sit and tell us the reason for this meeting. I, for one, haven't seen you smile in weeks—I am very interested to hear the reasons for this unexpected meeting."

Samuel sat as ordered and cleared his throat. "The stand-in has been successful, my Lord."

Navarre's features lightened. "Go on, Samuel."

"The Ciatron have entirely lost interest in it. After studying it for the last month, they have decided that Reece Bryant does not carry the information they seek."

The moment had finally arrived. *I'm going home.*

Levi's expression grew dark, and he broke in before Navarre could comment, "How can you be sure?"

"They have left Earth altogether. There are still a few of them among the people of Earth, but no more than before. We all know very well they will never stop searching for the Key. However," he said with a broadening smile, "we have thrown them completely off. They will no longer think Reece is a person of importance. Reece can return and possibly live out the rest of her life on Earth without any interference from them."

"Does this mean it's over?" asked Reece. "I can go back to my life, with everything normal again?"

Samuel looked toward the men at the table before turning to her with his answer. "For the most part, yes. We must continue to guard you to ensure your safety, but we will not interfere with you. Unless you become a person of interest again, of course." He laughed. "Even if you do, and we need to send a stand-in in your place again, I am sure it would be easier for you to adjust to Pemdas this time." He smiled reassuringly at her.

Everyone at the table looked relieved, except Levi. His gaze was locked on Samuel's face. When he turned to look at Reece, his face showed no emotion.

Navarre interrupted the silence with a booming laugh. "Well! That's the news we have longed to hear. I believe I speak for everyone," he looked at Reece, "when I say that you will be missed among us, but to take you back safely is a great accomplishment. I am very proud of everyone who made this happen." He reached for his wife's hand and held it.

Samuel agreed. "I have arranged for the stand-in to return to Pemdas tomorrow. Reece is free to go home at any time after that."

Navarre nodded. "Harrison and Levi will leave early in the morning to retrieve it. I want them to make sure everything is confirmed to be safe for Reece's return." He looked toward the young men, and then back to Samuel. "It's not that I do not trust your word, Samuel, but the men will make sure the transition goes as smoothly as possible. They know Reece, and she's comfortable with them." He smiled back at Reece.

Levi sat silently in his chair as the other men discussed how they would bring her home. His expression was blank, yet she still felt her breath catch at the sight of him. As she subtly watched him, she realized that she had fallen in love with this man. Her heart had betrayed her, and now it wrenched at the thought that she must leave his world now, possibly never to see him again. She felt sick to her stomach.

The men discussed having Harrison and Levi leave early the next morning, and Navarre suggested they stay for a minimum of three days in order to confirm the safety of Earth for Reece. He sent concerned glances in his son's direction more than once. It was obvious that Levi's mind was somewhere else. Questions directed at him had to be repeated before he answered.

Voices were faint in the background, and Reece hardly heard when Navarre addressed her, "When Harrison and Levi have confirmed that the reports are true and you will be safe, we will return you to your home on Earth."

The men were still making plans for Reece's return when she slowly stood up. In that moment, all the men at the table stood as well. She forced a smile and addressed the group. "I can't thank each of you enough for everything you have done to make this happen for me." She felt her voice crack. She had to make this exit quick, and without causing a scene. "But if you all will please excuse me, I think the horseback riding must be catching up with me, and I might need to lie down for a little bit."

Allestaine smiled at Reece with concern. "Allow me and Elizabeth to escort you back to your room, Reece."

Reece had to find a way out of the polite request. She needed to be alone. Her stomach was in knots, and she felt as though she would burst into tears at any moment. She wouldn't take the risk of letting that happen in front of any of them.

"I really appreciate the offer, Lady Allestaine, but I'm fine." She smiled reassuringly. "I will see you all at dinner tonight." She looked at Samuel and smiled. "Thank you, again, Samuel. It is wonderful news, and I know you have been working very hard to make this moment happen for me."

With that, she turned, avoided eye contact with everyone, and made her exit from the room. She turned down the corridor, and for some strange reason she felt like she couldn't breathe. She needed to get outside. She turned and walked toward the doors that led out to the Palace gardens.

She quickly made her way away from the Palace and struck off in a direction she hadn't taken before. She followed a fence, which led up into a thick forest. Without hesitation, she trekked into the unexplored area. The thickness of the dense forest had covered most of the sunlight, only allowing small patches through.

When she came up to a small creek, she heard a noise from deeper in the forest, and then saw the horses on the other side of the fence she had followed in. She leaned against it, looking for the colt. As the horses started to move farther into the forest, she saw him standing still and watching her. She held out her hand, and he trotted over to her.

Reece petted his nose and ran her hand along his neck. "Well, it looks as though I have to say goodbye to you, little guy."

"Have you chosen a name for him yet?" a deep voice asked from behind.

Reece spun around. "Levi?" She flattened a hand over her racing heart. "You need to clear your throat or something before you come up on me like that." The colt shied away from the fence.

Levi's eyes didn't have their usual brightness. "I'm sorry I startled you. It wasn't my intent."

She didn't know what to say to him. He wasn't acting like the Levi she had come to know. His features were darker, and even his smile was formal, with nothing behind it. He looked intimidating.

She looked back at the colt, which was edging closer now. "I haven't spent much time with him…you don't have to use the name I picked."

Levi rested his arms on the top rail of the fence and one foot on the bottom rail. "So, you have named him, then?"

"Sort of. It's not very special, though; it's just what I call him in my thoughts."

He smiled, and this time his smile looked genuine. "Would you care to share the name with me, or must I guess?"

She looked meekly back at him. "Arrow. Like the bracelet you bought for me." She shrugged and smiled back at him.

"Arrow will be his name, then." He returned his attention to the colt, which had lost interest in them and was heading back to the herd. Levi watched the horses make their way through the thick bushes, moving farther up into the forest.

"How did you know I was here?"

He pushed himself up from the fence and turned to face her. His eyes were darker and more mysterious than she had ever seen them, and a small smile pulled up one corner of his mouth. "After I saw you exit the Palace gardens, I decided to follow you." His eyes never pulled away from hers. "I must confess something to you, Reece, although I don't wish to startle you."

Unsure about what he could say to startle her, she responded, "I'm sure I won't be as startled as I was when you appeared out of nowhere. What is it? Is something bothering you?"

He looked at her as if he were begging her to read his mind. "I don't know how to approach this, but I feel I must. Harrison and I will leave in the morning, and I may not have another opportunity to speak with you." He stared deeply into her confused eyes. "Reece, I came to ask you not to return to Earth."

She frowned, trying to understand why he would ask that question. "Levi, I have to go back."

His face became troubled as he searched for more words. "You really do not. You may stay for as long as you like." He looked at her hopefully.

"Levi, I don't belong here. You know that. You shouldn't tempt me." She was beginning to be annoyed. If he meant what she hoped, he was going to have to be a lot more forthright. "I'm not sure why you would ask me this."

Levi's eye's penetrated through her. "Reece, I believe you know exactly why I would ask you to stay," he said quietly. He lifted her chin gently with his finger so her eyes would meet his.

Reece stared into his eyes and swallowed hard. Her head was spinning, and her heart was racing. Was this moment really happening? "I do?" she managed in a soft, nervous voice.

He tilted his head to the side, his eyes still intently studying hers. "Yes, you do." He smiled briefly. He then softly spoke, "Reece, can't you see? I am in love with you." He grinned. "I could not leave tomorrow without knowing if you might be able to love me in return."

Chapter 19

"Please, say something." He looked down to her, his eyes bright and hopeful.

She stared up at him. "You...love me?"

"More than you could ever know." He smiled at her, his eyes glowing in his anticipative face. "I was inquiring about whether or not you could possibly feel the same," he said teasingly.

Reece knew she had given herself away completely. "Levi, I can't...I can't let myself do this."

He looked confused, all trace of humor gone. She tried to walk past him, but he stopped her by gently holding her arm. "Please explain. Why can't you?" Reece looked down and away from him. "Reece, please look at me." When she did, he went on. "I could understand if you did not return my feelings, and I would respect that. But I will not stand here and listen to you tell me that you *cannot.*"

Of course she loved him, and she wanted to stay in Pemdas more than anything. But in reality, she knew a relationship with Levi could never work.

"It's not—it's not right. It's been made very clear to me that we are from separate worlds. And not only are we from separate worlds, but you will be the Emperor of this place one day. I've been told your people won't accept anyone from outside of Pemdas at your side, especially someone from Earth." She closed her eyes, unwilling to watch his reaction to the truths she reminded him of.

Of course, everything she learned about this situation was from Simone and her friends, but Reece wasn't ignorant either. Simone was only one small voice in an entire dimension. Reece understood very well that this would only cause problems for Levi in his world. He needed to find the right woman for him, and Reece knew she was not that woman.

Levi gently put his index finger under her chin. When she opened her eyes, he said, "Reece, those are ridiculous excuses. Do you think I care about other people's opinions? The only opinion I care about is yours. I will ask you again, will there ever be a chance for you to return my love?"

His eyes danced with amusement.

She couldn't tell him no. "You know the answer. I've already fallen in love with you. But it's against everything that's right for you. It's against everything that's right for me—"

His lips silenced her. At first, his kiss was soft, his hands gently cupping her face. There was no way she could, or would, fight this. She had longed for this moment, his lips on hers, and it was more intoxicating than she had ever imagined it would be. To taste the sweetness of his kiss, to feel the softness, yet power, in his smooth lips…made her yearn for more. She stood on her toes and reached under his arms to pull him closer. She spread her hands over the thick wool of the back of his greatcoat, feeling the impressiveness of his muscular frame for the first time. She marveled at the power she felt in him as her hands continued to trace along the steely contours of his broad back. He was perfect, and she hungered for more of his kiss. He answered her desire and responded by kissing her more urgently and passionately than she had ever been kissed before. Not a fun kiss. Not an experienced kiss. If she had to put a word to it, this was a devoted kiss. A kiss that seemed to mean something, perhaps far more than she knew. It sent shivers through her body, and her head became light. She slowly pulled away from him, and he finished by kissing her softly on her nose.

As she leaned into him, he pulled her close into his chest and rested his chin on the top of her head. "I should say I'm sorry for that, but it would be a lie." She could hear the smile in his voice. He lowered it to a whisper. "I have so longed to hold you like this. I have been waiting for you." She felt his chin move away from her head, and something soft—a kiss?—replaced it.

She pulled herself together, stepped back, and looked into his bright blue eyes. She reached up to caress his cheek. "I think we've made our lives pretty difficult."

He brought his hand up and placed it over hers, then closed his eyes and slowly turned his lips into the palm of her hand. When his eyes opened, they were darker, almost smoldering. "Reece, you must believe me when I tell you that I love you, and I will not allow anyone, or anything, to stand in our way." He brought his strong hands to her face, cradling it, while his thumbs gently caressed her cheekbones. A tiny smirk played on his lips, and then he became serious. "You must promise that you will trust what I say. There hasn't been much time for me to prove myself to you, but I beg you, for now, to trust me."

She could not help but laugh in response to the memory of the first day he had spoken to her. He had made the same request then.

He smiled back, in what seemed to be perfect comprehension. "There will be more than one opinion of me and you, but it will not affect my love for you. I am prepared for it."

Doubt must have been apparent on her face. "Come with me," he said as he reached for her hand. He led them away from the fences and upward to where they could see past the trees, down to the enormous Palace and the gardens surrounding it. She stared at it and immediately felt as if it stared back, reminding her that a relationship with this man was impossible. The Palace was beautiful, but she wasn't part of it.

She stood there, defeated, and slowly shook her head, searching for words to explain that this love could never work. He, too, stared at the view in front of them. Reece wondered if he realized what she did.

"It is beautiful, is it not?" he asked.

"Yes, it is." *But it's not for me.*

"I have battled with my feelings for you, and I have already questioned the issues you have brought to my attention. I am no stranger to the reasons why I should not love you." He slowly turned to her, his face serious. "When Harrison and I were instructed to guard you, I had to force myself to view you strictly as our assignment. It was difficult, but possible, until the day your eyes met mine in the airport. Then I began to see everything differently. I found myself longing to be in your presence, though I didn't know why."

He took her hand. "Then we brought you to Pemdas. And having you here, in my home, was almost more than I could bear. I found myself battling my emotions. I knew what was expected of me; I could not allow myself to have feelings for you. But I constantly found reasons to be in your presence. I told myself it was only to make sure you were properly taken care of, and I assured myself that there was nothing wrong with enjoying the company of a new person. But I found myself needing to watch you smile, or to hear you laugh. Your smile—"

She looked up at him in wonder and smiled.

His breath stopped for a moment. "Yes, that smile. What it does to me—I can't explain."

His own smile—open, unsought, reaching eyes as well as lips, did something to Reece also. He lightly stroked her jaw with the back of his hand. She leaned into the caress, and he laughed softly. "I have more than anyone in my world could ask for. But what I want, Reece, is you."

His thumb tenderly caressed her neck as he bent to kiss her. Her heart was beating rapidly, and each stroke of his thumb sent shivers through her. She didn't know how she did it, but she managed to pull her lips from his and exhaled. She wanted to taste the sweetness of his lips again. She had to make it clear to him. "But Levi—"

"I know. I know better than you," he interrupted her. "When others find out, most will be intent upon destroying our feelings for each other. I will not be inclined to tolerate any of it. I will leave this place with you, if that is what is required. If you do not wish to live in these lands, then we will live together where you will be most comfortable."

She hadn't thought of that. This was a whole new set of issues. "Another part of Pemdas? Or—you would live on Earth with me?"

He nodded once. "If that is what you are most comfortable with."

She looked at him quizzically, with more challenging questions lining up one-by-one in her mind.

He shook his head and laughed. "You don't have to decide anything this instant. We'll have plenty of time to discuss it when I return. Now," he offered his arm, "let's head back to the Palace."

As they walked back to the Palace, they decided jointly that they would tell no one of their feelings for each other until Levi returned. If there were to be hurtful comments, they would face them together.

Once they arrived at the palace, they parted ways. Levi would probably not be at dinner that evening, but he promised to try and see her before he departed the next morning.

The rest of the afternoon dragged. Reece missed him the moment they parted. She became frustrated by her new weakness, knowing this would only make his time away seem like forever. *At least I'll have Elizabeth,* she told herself.

After dinner, they spent the evening in the sitting room. Reece was hoping to see Levi, and she forced her eyes to stay open to read. After reading the same sentence a dozen times, she pulled herself from the large chair she sat in and placed her book on the table. It was pointless to keep fighting sleep, so she stood and said her goodnights. There was no sound of the men anywhere in the palace.

She was halfway up the stairs when a deep voice softly called, "Retiring so soon, Miss Bryant?"

Levi stood at the bottom of the staircase with one hand on the banister and one foot on the bottom step.

Her heart immediately reacted. "Oh! I thought I wasn't going to get to see you tonight!"

He started up the steps to where she stood. "Our meetings went longer than expected. We were waiting for reports from a couple of our men, but we seem to have lost communication with them."

"Is everything okay?"

"Everything is fine. It happens every now and then. Although having to make plans without their information was an inconvenience. It took more time to make arrangements, and frankly, I was in no mood to be away from you." He offered his arm. "Would you care to join me on an evening walk in the gardens?"

"I would love to. Let me get a jacket." No longer sleepy, she raced to her room and returned wearing a warm wool coat. They strolled together leisurely on the small path where they had walked on her first evening in Pemdas.

It was Levi who opened up their conversation. "It is odd, is it not?"

"Odd?"

A smile played in the corner of his mouth as he looked down to her. "The last time that we walked this location together, you were about to become helplessly lost. That is, until I came to your rescue."

She narrowed her eyes. "My rescue, was it? I was never lost, Levi. Maybe you just wanted a reason to follow me," she teased him.

Levi guided her to a bench near the small pond he had shown her on her first evening in Pemdas. He sat beside her with his arm around her shoulders and brought his other hand to her cheek. Reece's head spun wildly as he kissed her lips. Then he pulled back and studied her. "You're right, of course. Angry as I was with Simone, Catherine, and Lillian for allowing you to wander off, I was actually much happier for it. While Harrison stayed to scold them, I stole a few moments alone with you. At the time, though, I did not admit it, even to myself."

She chuckled. "I remember thinking that you looked really upset about something at dinner that night."

"What? Why?"

She laughed. "Well, I don't know. You seemed like you had a bad day or something, I didn't know what your problem was."

"Reece, I was completely taken by you. I had never believed anyone's presence could be so…intoxicating." His eyes sparkled reminiscently. "Did you realize how astonishing you looked?"

"Really? Because I noticed you checking out my dress, and you seemed to have had a problem with it." She laughed. "You're lucky I didn't change back into my tracksuit!"

"Is that what you were laughing to yourself about?"

Reece smiled. "Oh, you noticed that, too?"

He smiled. "Reece, you have always fascinated me, though I never believed there would come a day when we would ever speak. In the few short years that we watched over you on Earth, I saw your beautiful eyes sparkle with excitement toward so many other people. I learned to decipher your moods, to tell whether you were happy, sad, nervous, upset, or excited. I can discern your many smiles, the ones you give your close friends, the smile you display when you are embarrassed, and the ones when you are thrilled...and recently, I learned of the particular one for me. I watched your excitement illuminate every room you were in. I have watched you entertain those around you with the charming personality that only you possess."

She smiled at him. "I would have never believed that you felt that way about me. I have to say—you did a really good job of covering up your feelings."

Levi smiled mischievously. "I did, did I? You never questioned my constant concern for helping you study? Or finding an excuse to take you on a horseback ride in order to get you out of the palace, alone with me?" he finished with a soft laugh.

She shrugged. "I thought you were being a gentleman. You all are very courteous here."

Levi gazed at her with amusement. "Reece, if that had been the case, Harrison and I would have shared those duties."

Reece laughed. "Well, you had me fooled."

He grinned at her, with the stunning grin that always took her breath away. She traced his lips with her fingertips and studied his eyes. "This smile…"

Levi pressed his lips into her fingers, giving them a small kiss. "Yes?" His eyes shimmered as he remained staring at her.

Reece inhaled as she brought her other hand up to cradle his face within her hands. Levi's grin disappeared as Reece leaned in and softly kissed his perfect lips. She withdrew and smiled. "I have been tempted to do that more than once, every time you have smiled at me that way." She tilted her head to the side and laughed softly.

Levi slowly reopened his eyes. "Do you have any idea what you do to me?" He brushed the back of his hands along her jawline and down her neck. Her body shuddered at his tender touch. "No woman has ever amused or charmed me in such a way. In all of my life, I have never believed that any woman could ever have this much control over me." He tapped his index finger to her chin and smirked. "No woman but you. You must know that I am profoundly in love with you."

Levi brought his lips down onto hers again, and this time he deepened their kiss with more desire than before. His embrace tightened as he drew her closer into him.

Reece's head started to spin, and her heart skipped several beats. She managed to politely end the kiss so that she could catch her breath.

"It seems as though I'm just as helpless against you. I can't even think straight," she managed to respond.

Reece studied his humored expression. As she brought her hand to his face, he closed his eyes and exhaled quietly in response to her tender touch. Reece giggled in return. "I have waited so long for a moment such as this," he whispered. "I fear I will wake up in the morning, and find this was only another dream."

Reece cocked her head to the side and stared at him speculatively. "Another dream?"

Levi smiled. "Indeed, I could not escape you, even as I slept." Levi smiled. He cupped the back of her neck in his hand, and his eyes darkened with desire. "I love you, Reece Bryant."

She swallowed as her heart picked up its rapid pace once again. "I love you, Levi," she whispered.

Gently, Levi claimed her lips. When Reece deepened the kiss, he responded enthusiastically. They indulged themselves in their adoration for each other for quite some time before they pulled back, breathing hard. Levi tilted his head, looking at her. He kissed her cheek. Then her forehead. In a leisurely fashion, he covered her face with kisses, finishing with a light kiss to the tip of her nose.

She opened her eyes to see his, shining like sapphires. "Levi, how will I survive your leaving tomorrow?"

His mouth quirked. "The question is, how will Harrison survive? I'm going to drive him insane on this visit, rushing everything to get back to you."

Reece laughed and felt calmer. "I'm sure Harrison will be fine."

"My cousin has already suffered quite a bit since I found that I could not bear to be out of your presence."

Reece's eyes narrowed. "Has he now? I didn't realize Harrison was suffering around me."

"Don't get me wrong, Harrison thinks you're great, but he doesn't always appreciate my transparent excuses to be with you. I believe the worst for him was when I could no longer endure being away from you while visiting my sister. I convinced everyone that Harrison and I had to return for training. I believe he may have thought I had completely lost my mind." He chuckled. "I demanded we leave that very night and pushed Areion harder than I ever had so that your eyes would be the first thing I saw the next morning. Then I abandoned Harrison in the breakfast room, when we did not find you there with the other ladies. Do you remember?"

Reece laughed. "That's why you two returned before the rest of your family?"

He smiled and nodded. "That's when I realized I was helplessly in love with you."

Reece looked at him with concern. "Levi, what are people going to say? What will they all think of you for loving someone from Earth? Aren't you a little frightened?"

"Only one thing frightens me, and that is how much I need you in my life. I'll be miserable these next few days, longing to be with you again. And your opinion of me is the only one that matters. I wish to put off the announcement of our attachment until I return, simply because I want to be at your side. I will not tolerate your being victim to anyone's opinion, without me to defend you."

Reece shuddered internally. It was going to be bad, then. "Promise to come back quickly?"

"My love, it is my only desire." He stared intently into her eyes.

She returned his gaze as he slowly slid his hand through her hair and rested it on the back of her neck, drawing her closer to him, as his other arm wrapped around her waist. He began with a soft kiss upon her lips, and then traced her jaw with kisses.

Reece inhaled deeply, trying to keep her breathing as calm as his, but her heart was beating rapidly. She felt his lips turn up in a smile against her skin in response to her obvious reactions. He continued to place small, tender kisses along her neckline, forcing her to sigh with contentment.

One more kiss on the lips, and Levi pulled back with a sigh of his own. "I believe I should be escorting you back to the palace now. As much as I desire to remain here with you, I fear my emotions are about to overrule my judgment as a gentleman..." he smiled as he once more kissed her lips, letting his linger on hers for a short moment, then exhaled, "...and I cannot allow that to happen," he answered as he withdrew and gazed warmly into her eyes.

The next morning, Reece was awake before sun up. She found Harrison and Levi checking tack and mounting up. She stood at the top of the steps and watched with amusement as they joked with each other like mischievous little boys. As they turned their horses away, she called, "Levi?"

Levi turned Areion back toward the palace and was off the horse and up the steps before she could take a breath. Then she was in his arms, and he kissed her as if he were memorizing her. She was instantly lost in the sweet flavor of his delicious kiss. She inhaled the masculine aroma of him, letting it consume her entirely.

It was when Harrison cleared his throat dramatically that Reece felt the blood rush to her cheeks. She tried to pull back, but Levi held her tighter. He smiled and kissed her softly one more time before he turned to face his cousin.

"Now *that* is going to complicate things!" Harrison grinned.

Levi turned to Reece and kissed her gently on the forehead. "I will return to you as soon as may be, my sweet love." He touched the tip of her nose with his index finger and turned back to his horse.

Harrison smiled widely at her. "This will be an interesting ride, Reece; thank you for my entertainment. I guess this is the part where I promise to return him to you safely?" He laughed.

In one swift, powerful motion, Levi mounted Areion and looked back at Reece. He grinned and winked at her. Her heart halted in response to the smile that always took her breath away. Then, with a clatter of hooves on the courtyard, they were gone.

Chapter 20

Reece turned back into the palace as first light had begun to color the sky. She smiled at the rich scent of Levi's cologne lingering on her hands and coat. Her heart continued to respond to images of their last few moments together. All of these feelings and emotions were so new. Her breath caught, remembering the way he looked at her, the way his eyes reflected his love. She'd seen that love in his eyes many times before but hadn't allowed herself to believe it was for her.

She was rudely pulled away from her enjoyment of the moment when she was suddenly standing face-to-face with Simone. *Did she see us saying goodbye?* If there was one person she did not want to know about them, it was Simone. Why couldn't she and her friends have waited at least three more days to return from their vacation? She sighed with irritation and met the woman's speculative gaze head-on.

Reece managed a smile. "Good morning, Simone."

As Reece tried to walk past, Simone stepped in front of her, forcing her to halt.

"Reece Bryant. Do not think that you can walk past me after what I have just witnessed between you and Levi." Simone motioned to a side door. "It would be wise of you to join me, as I am sure Levi doesn't want this disturbing secret known to anyone," Simone said with disgust.

Reece inhaled, trying to remain calm, and followed Simone into the empty sitting room.

Simone motioned for Reece to sit on a small sofa, but Reece remained standing and stared at her sternly. "Just say what you need to say to me, Simone."

Simone's eyebrow arched sharply as she stared maliciously down at Reece. "Do not dare order me around. You are at my mercy now," she finished with a wicked laugh. "Now, I suggest you sit down and listen to me.

Reece sat on the sofa and stared up at Simone. "Go ahead, I'm listening," she said firmly.

Simone glared down at Reece. "I have hated you from the first moment I saw you. You and your kind on Earth repulse me. I've never understood why our men risk their lives to protect Earth's inhabitants from the other dimensions. It has never made any sense to me."

"Simone—"

"I have not asked you to speak," Simone snapped.

Reece stood up. "I don't know who you think you are, but I don't have to listen to this. I'm not at your mercy, and the only reason I chose to come in here was to let you know that what happened between Levi and I was not that big of a deal. I really—"

"Not that big of a deal? Is *that* how you view a relationship with one of the most powerful men in Pemdas? I should expect nothing less from a foolish girl from Earth!"

Reece exhaled in frustration. "That's not what I meant. There is no need to—"

Simone's features grew hostile. "Who do you think you are anyway, Reece?" Simone shouted. "What makes you think you can come into my world and act like you belong here? To watch you walk these palace halls as if this were your home utterly disgusts me. And that, Earth dweller, is why I was forced to extreme measures to have you removed from Pemdas!"

Reece stared intently into Simone's darkened expression. "What are you talking about?" she questioned in a firm voice.

Simone grinned. "You know exactly what I am talking about. My father and Emperor Navarre were obviously getting nowhere with your return, so I had to take matters into my own hands."

Reece's eyes narrowed. "What?"

Simone smiled sinisterly. "An arrangement has been made. Harrison and Levi will learn of it as soon as they return to Earth. In trade for you, the Ciatron will no longer be an enemy to Pemdas. We will finally have the peace that even our ancient Guardians could not create."

"That is not true, Simone, and you know it. The Ciatron have left Earth, and it's because they know I'm not the one they were searching for—"

"That's what they wanted the Guardians on Earth to believe. And therefore, that is exactly what the Guardians reported to my father," Simone answered. "It was the only way to draw you out of our land without being questioned."

Reece stared at Simone in disbelief; there was no way this woman would find a way to meet with the Ciatron. This was a lie and a threat, brought about by Simone's anger over seeing Reece with Levi. The woman was delusional.

Reece gazed intensely into her eyes. "Simone, if this is true, how were you able to meet with them? The Guardians are the only ones who—"

"Reece, have you forgotten that I am the daughter of their commander? I have my ways of learning how to have you removed. My father, obviously, wasn't getting the job done, and therefore I did it myself. I met with the people who were willing to have you removed from Pemdas, no matter the cost."

"Your father and the Emperor don't know about this?" Reece asked in a soft voice.

"Of course not. They will not believe in the Ciatron's peaceful efforts until after you are traded. And now, your beloved, Levi Oxley, must deliver you in order to have eternal peace with his father's greatest enemy. And I will finally be rid of you!"

"Simone!" Reece snapped harshly. "Do you realize what you have done?"

"I know exactly what I have done," Simone growled. "I've found a way to have you removed from our lands, and yet keep peace with our enemy!"

Before she knew it, Reece's hand lashed out and slapped Simone's face hard enough to jolt her head sideways. Simone's eyes flashed with fury, even as tears welled up in them.

"Have you lost your mind? Levi and Harrison will be lucky if they ever return! You've done nothing but condemn everyone! It seems to me that the Ciatron don't make deals—at least, they don't keep them. Haven't you paid attention to any of the reasons why I was brought here to begin with? All anyone can do now is hope that, for once, they will keep their word. And the only way we'll know that is when, or if, Harrison and Levi return."

"When Harrison and Levi return, dear Reece, which should be in a few hours, you will wish you had never laid your hand upon my face."

Reece shook her head in disbelief and turned to leave.

Simone called to her. "I do hope you have enjoyed your time with Levi. I'll make this promise to you: your kiss with him this morning will have been your last."

Reece stopped in the doorway. "Emperor Navarre and your father need to know about your secret arrangements with the Ciatron right away. You'll either go with me to tell them of it, or I will tell them on my own."

Simone's face darkened as she approached Reece. She wove her arm through Reece's. Reece violently jerked her arm free. "Do not touch me!"

Simone giggled. "Ah! Reece, you must relax. You wouldn't be foolish enough to try to disrupt my plans, now would you? You see, the friend who helped me wanted you dead, and I can easily arrange that as well!" She brought her arm back through Reece's. "It would be wise for you to keep this conversation between you and me." She laughed. "Now, my Empress is waiting on us for breakfast. Let us go."

Simone led Reece from the room. Reece continued to walk by her side, disillusioned at the thought of the events that Simone had set into action. Could Levi and Harrison be heading into a trap set by the Ciatron? There was no way the Ciatron would take the news of Navarre keeping Reece in Pemdas lightly. Levi and Harrison could be in grave danger. Reece felt sick, but she had to stay focused. Navarre would know best; she had to get away from Simone quickly and notify him somehow. They walked into the dining hall where Allestaine, Elizabeth, Lillian, and Catherine were seated.

"Good morning, ladies," Allestaine greeted them.

Reece offered a faint smile as she quickly made her way to a seat next to Elizabeth.

"Good morning, Lady Allestaine," Simone said enthusiastically.

As the staff brought out their breakfast plates, Reece sat silently contemplating how she would get away from Simone and get a message to Navarre. The longer she sat at this table, the longer Levi and Harrison would be on their own. She stood abruptly.

"Reece? Is everything okay?" Allestaine said as she looked at Reece in confusion.

Reece cleared her throat. "Everything is fine. If you'll excuse me, I left something back in my room. I'll only be a minute."

Simone stood. "Reece, darling, allow me to go with you."

Reece felt the blood boiling beneath the surface of her skin.

"Simone, Reece can manage her way around the Palace without someone at her side. There is no need for you to dismiss yourself as well," Allestaine said with a reproachful look at Simone.

Reece smiled at Allestaine. "I'll only be a moment."

"Take your time, Reece," Allestaine responded.

Without looking back at the table, Reece quickly made her way from the room. Fortunately, just outside of the dining hall, a servant was walking by.

"Excuse me, sir? Where can I find a pen and piece of paper, quickly?"

"Right this way, Miss Bryant," the servant responded as he led her into a room across the way. He pulled a paper and pen from a cabinet drawer and handed it to her. "Is there anything—"

"Yes, wait just a moment, please," Reece said as she sat down at a nearby table to write. When she finished writing about her confrontation with Simone, she stood and handed the note to the servant. "Take this message to the Emperor immediately. Let him know I said it is imperative that he reads this as soon as you place it into his hands."

"Yes, Miss Bryant." The servant gave her a quick bow and turned hastily to make his way out of the room.

Reece remained in the room, trying to gather herself. She closed her eyes and exhaled; her nerves felt as though they were on fire. There was nothing more she could do now, and she hoped she wasn't too late, for Levi and Harrison's sake. After a few minutes, Reece was finally able to return to the dining room.

She avoided looking at Simone and instead returned to her chair without a word. She looked at the food on her plate and forced herself to begin eating it.

"Reece, you seem unwell? Are you sure you are okay?" Allestaine asked.

Reece forced a smile. "I'm fine, Lady Allestaine. It's just been a rough morning for me."

Before Allestaine could respond, Navarre and Samuel stormed into the room. Navarre still carried Reece's note in his hand. Reece had never seen Navarre look so hostile, and her heart reacted with fear at the anger apparent on his face.

"My Lord—"

"Simone!" Navarre growled, interrupting his wife. "Simone, is it true that you have made contact with the Ciatron?"

Simone stared at Navarre in shock.

"IS IT TRUE?" Navarre roared, causing Reece to startle in response.

"My Lord, yes, it is true." She dropped her head. "But I never believed—"

"Have you any idea what this means?" Navarre turned to his commanding officer. "How was she able to make contact with them? Am I to believe that you are behind this betrayal as well?" He squared up to his highest in command.

Samuel flinched and reflexively stepped back. "My Lord, I am only aware of this now, along with you. I cannot tell you how she has come into contact with them." He turned to his daughter as if she were an enemy. "You will tell us at once how this has happened, Simone, or you will suffer the consequence of high treason!" he demanded.

Simone burst into tears.

Navarre looked at her and brought a deadly gaze back to Samuel. Samuel looked back at his Emperor sternly. "My Lord, you must believe me."

Navarre stared intently into Samuel's eyes before he exhaled and nodded. "Quickly, Samuel, dispatch a troop of Guardians to the Philadelphia vortex." Before Samuel could take a breath, Navarre demanded, "Go now! We may already be too late."

Samuel's expression was as dangerous as Navarre's when he swiftly turned to leave the room.

As Navarre approached the table, Simone tried to remain calm. "Your Majesty, allow me to inform you privately—"

"I have no time for private conversations, Simone!"

Simone swallowed loudly. "My Lord, I beg of you, what I am to tell you, you would only want to hear in private."

His gaze darkened, and she shivered in response. "Simone! Do not argue with me. My son and Harrison could be in grave danger—you will tell me everything you know immediately!"

All eyes at the table stared intently at Simone as she dropped her head into her hands and began to sob. Navarre walked over to Simone and towered over her. "Stand up." His voice was even and deadly.

Allestaine was immediately at his side. Simone stood and managed to speak through her sobs. "I meant no harm, your Majesty, you must believe me. I thought the Ciatron..." She paused as her increased sobbing was preventing her from being able to speak.

Navarre grabbed her arms. "What—Simone—what did they tell you?" he growled.

Simone went into hysterics, unable to respond.

Allestaine put her hand over her husband's. "Please, my Lord, release her and allow her to collect herself, or I fear she will be incapable of telling us what we need to know."

Allestaine led her over to a seating area near the large dining room windows, and Navarre followed. Allestaine sat and embraced the broken woman, rubbing her back soothingly.

With the lady's encouragement, Simone looked up at Navarre. "I was only trying to help us reach peace with our enemy."

Navarre's fists clenched, and his body turned rigid. Reece couldn't see his face, but she saw the quelling look Allestaine gave him.

"Please understand," said Simone, "there was no malice intended."

Reece contained her rage at the lie. She stared at the hateful woman with repulsion.

Simone, calmer now, began to speak more clearly. "I arranged a meeting with the Ciatron, with the hope that they would accept Reece as payment for an alliance with our world. They assured me they would. I knew we never had any chance against them and that an arrangement such as this could be our only way out of a war—a war, I believe, we could never win." She dropped her head into her hands, sobbing.

Navarre's knuckles turned white as Allestaine's expression became dark. "You know nothing of military alliances and war! Do you understand that your deceitful plan would not only result in Reece's demise, but also the destruction, and likely enslavement, of our world and others?" Navarre questioned in a low growl. "Of course you do not, because you have not a clue about who Miss Bryant really is! What gives you the power to go behind my back and make an agreement with our enemy? If Harrison, or my son—" he took a breath, "—or anyone else meets his death due to this *treason*, then I assure you, your fate will be the same as theirs."

Simone nearly fainted after hearing Navarre's threat.

"How were you able to come into contact with them?"

Simone opened her mouth, but no words came out. Navarre seemed to be growing more impatient by the second. "Answer me, now!" he shouted.

Allestaine looked up at her husband. "My Lord, allow me a few moments with Simone. Please, go with Samuel and see if we are having success with the troop he has dispatched. I will be there shortly."

She looked at him confidently, and Reece watched Navarre relax in that moment. "Very well." He looked down at Simone, who was crying hysterically. "Simone, your fate has yet to be decided." He spun on his heels and turned to leave the room.

As Navarre left, the young women still seated at the table were enveloped by their various emotions—shock, grief, possibly remorse. Reece wasn't sure what Simone felt. It might be mere chagrin that made her cry.

Elizabeth had broken into silent tears, and Reece sat with her arm around her. "Levi is the most determined man I've ever met, Elizabeth. We can't forget this is what they're trained to do. I am sure they will be okay," she whispered, and Elizabeth tried to smile.

"You're right. I hope the men sent to save them will help them in time," she said.

Reece hugged her. "Me, too," she answered softly as she returned her attention to those around her.

Lillian was comforting Catherine, who stared at Simone as if her sister were a stranger, shocked that she would do such a thing.

Allestaine continued to pursue answers. "Simone, the only way you can make this right with everyone, and I know that is what you desire, is to tell me every detail of what you have done."

Simone stared down at her hands. "I was given an opportunity to speak with one of the Ciatron guards. I foolishly thought that there might be a way to help Reece to return to the life she was most comfortable with, and also to help the stressful situation of our—"

Allestaine calmly interrupted her. "Reasons will not help us now. I need you to explain to me how you got the information to approach our most powerful adversary, and how you succeeded in meeting with them? How can a young woman from Pemdas not only disappear unnoticed, but find her way into the company of our greatest enemy?"

Simone stared at her with apparent regret. "I was motivated to seek them out myself, my lady. I—I went through the notes in my father's office. He had written in great detail about the particular ways that our warriors would confront the Ciatron, and it motivated me to make plans of my own." She sniffed.

Allestaine's eyes narrowed. "I fail to understand why a lady of Pemdas would feel it is in her interest to meddle with battle plans. Perhaps it was the fact that you are a child of our greatest Pemdai commander that inspired this interest? However, I am not so ignorant to believe that." She sighed.

"Simone, I don't believe you came up with this idea alone. I believe you have been betrayed, not only by the Ciatron, but by another who helped encourage your ideas."

Simone said nothing, but Reece could almost see her teeth clench.

Allestaine's eyes narrowed. "You will tell me, Simone. Who helped you cross the vortices? Who led you into the Ciatron's domain?"

"I was not helped. I did this alone. Please believe me."

Allestaine seemed to grow tall and terrible as she sat there, rapidly losing her patience. "My son could be in grave danger. If he is still alive, that is. I will not sit here and be played by a foolish woman whose wicked plans may have put lives in danger. You cannot have gone alone; the Guardian horses would not carry you. Who rode you through the vortex, Simone?"

Simone paled. "It was Michael Visor. He doesn't live in Pemdas anymore. He brought me home and left. I have not seen him since," she said sadly.

"What? Michael Visor? Why would he consider something of this nature? Levi always spoke highly of him." She put her hands on Simone's shoulders and held her captive. "Why, Simone? Why would he do this and not return to Pemdas?"

Simone stared meekly at the lady. "He didn't say, but he's always been envious of Levi."

Allestaine dropped her hands from Simone's shoulders. Her expression was deadly. Her voice lowered. "Of course, and now it makes perfect sense. Michael is Magnus Sterlington's nephew." She looked intensely at Simone. "Is that wretched man involved as well, Simone? You will tell me!"

Simone's expression was unreadable. "I'm not sure; Michael never said anyone else was involved. You must understand, my lady, I believed Michael when he said no one would be harmed. I never believed for one second that the Ciatron would hurt Reece or destroy Pemdas...I only—"

"Enough!" Lady Allestaine snapped. "The Emperor, his Commander, and I will discuss your reasons at a later time." Allestaine rose up from the sofa. "This entire situation seems to spring from hatred and jealousy, and not only Sterlington's and Michael's. There is more to your story than you have told us. Fortunately for myself, I have no need to ask you any further questions. But know this: if lives are lost due to your ignorance, jealousy, and stupidity, you will spend the rest of your life atoning for the blood on your hands." The lady looked toward the doorway. "Charles."

A servant who was standing by the door quickly approached and bowed. "Your Majesty?"

"Escort Simone to her room and place a guard at her door until the Emperor has decided what is to be done with her."

The servant bowed again at Allestaine's orders. "Majesty," he said as he turned to escort Simone from the room.

Elizabeth stood and embraced her mother. Allestaine looked calm, showing no fear or grief. Reece was sure Allestaine was terrified, but she showed no weakness in public. Simone rejoined her sister and Lillian, broken and in tears. She did not look in Reece's direction once, and Reece was grateful for it.

The three young women walked quickly out of the room. Allestaine remained with her daughter and Reece, who stood staring numbly at the doors that had closed behind the women.

"Ladies, if you will excuse me, I must give Navarre this new information," Allestaine said.

"Yes, of course," Reece responded. "I think Elizabeth and I will head outdoors and get some fresh air."

Allestaine nodded. "Very well. We must all be strong now and know that Navarre and Samuel will bring Levi, Harrison, and the rest of our men back to us safely."

With that, Allestaine quickly made her exit from the room.

Chapter 21

It was close to an hour after Elizabeth and Reece headed out to the Palace gardens that Allestaine rejoined them.

"Elizabeth, darling, I am going to need a moment alone with Reece," Allestaine said as she approached where Reece and Elizabeth were sitting.

Elizabeth stood and smiled. "Yes, Mother. Has father learned any more news?"

Allestaine brought her daughter into a loving embrace and stood back and stared confidently into her eyes. "Your father is planning with Samuel and the other warriors to help your brother and Harrison. We have no new information at this time; however, there is no reason not to be hopeful. Harrison and Levi would expect nothing less of us."

Elizabeth nodded, and Reece felt a wave of anxiety rush through her. *Still no answers?*

Elizabeth thanked Reece for her support and turned to walk back to the Palace.

Allestaine sat next to Reece and looked at her with concern. "Reece, I really cannot find the proper words to express my and Navarre's sincerest apologies in regard to the confrontation you experienced with Simone this morning."

Reece stared at Allestaine in disbelief. "Lady Allestaine, please don't apologize. I only hoped that I got the information to the Emperor in time. Does he know what could've happened to Harrison and Levi when they returned to Earth?"

Allestaine exhaled. "Not at this time. Right now, he and Samuel can only speculate. Once Navarre received your letter, he immediately tried to contact Harrison and Levi to see if Simone's words to you could be validated. When they did not respond, Navarre knew that the reason the Ciatron had left Earth, as Samuel reported, must have been a trap. We don't know what Levi and Harrison have faced upon their return, and that is why Navarre is assiduously sending men back to Earth to help them. We know very well that the Ciatron will be extremely hostile with our warriors since they have learned that we have had the Key residing in Pemdas. All we can do is hope that the Guardians being deployed to recover Levi and Harrison will be successful."

Reece's heart began to race. What were they really up against? All of this was happening because of Simone's jealousy and hatred of Reece?

"I can't believe this is happening," Reece said softly.

Allestaine looked at her sympathetically. "We are as astonished as you are. Reece, if I may ask, how is it that Simone would come to disclose such information to you? Please understand, Navarre and I are extremely grateful she did."

Reece cleared her throat. "I don't think she planned to. But this morning, she saw me outside saying goodbye to Levi—" Reece knew she had to tell Allestaine about her and Levi. She hoped the Empress would receive the information well. "Lady Allestaine, there is something I have to tell you, and I'm not sure how you will take the information. I know you have all been through so much already. You see, Levi and I –"

Allestaine placed her hand gently on Reece's. "Reece," a faint smile lifted in the corner of her mouth, "I already know."

Reece swallowed hard. "You know?" she asked, unsure of what to say.

Allestaine nodded, and then her countenance grew somber. "Reece, this may be the reason for Simone's betrayal; however, it will also be the reason I believe my son will return to us." Allestaine stood and extended her arm to Reece.

When Reece stood up, Allestaine embraced her. "Reece, you must understand, Levi will be doing everything in his power to return to you. Stay strong for him, and trust that he will," she said softly. She withdrew from Reece and smiled.

Reece had no idea how the lady could have known about her and Levi, but she was a very intuitive woman, and Reece had no doubt that Allestaine could have picked up on this long before Levi told her he loved her.

Before Reece could say anything more, Allestaine spoke, "Now, I must go speak with Simone, and I am sure Elizabeth would love your company."

Over the next three days, the atmosphere in the Palace was extremely tense. Everyone wore somber expressions, and if Reece encountered Navarre or Allestaine, it was usually while walking through the corridors. Allestaine would stop and give greetings to Reece and Elizabeth, but her mind was obviously elsewhere. She would offer assurances to Reece and Elizabeth that even though there were still no answers, they must know that no one was giving up. On the rare occurrence that they saw Navarre, his expression was grave. His acknowledgement consisted of no more than a subdued nod. The noble man appeared not to have slept since the night before Harrison and Levi went missing. The distress was apparent on his face, yet he seemed determined all the same.

Reece saw that the tension in the Palace was troubling Elizabeth. Therefore, instead of worrying for herself, Reece put all of her energy into comforting her. Even though the weather grew cold again and light snow would fall, Reece encouraged Elizabeth to get outside of the Palace with her.

Eventually, Lady Allestaine consented to allow Simone to join the other women at meal times. The Emperor and Allestaine made it clear to the woman that she was not to be trusted; however, the only reason she wasn't treated as a common traitor was because of who her father was, Navarre and Pemdas' most loyal subject. It was clear that Simone was not only victim to the Ciatron, but to Michael Visor's motives as well. He had led Simone to believe that it would be a simple trade and no one would be harmed. Simone, driven by jealousy, agreed to help. She might not have been treated as a criminal, but life as she knew it would never be the same. A guard was to remain at her door each night, and she was heavily watched throughout the day, due to the threats she made towards Reece.

Simone was a different woman since the morning she threatened Reece. She seemed feeble and broken now. It made Reece wonder if Simone actually did believe that the Ciatron would make a simple trade with the Pemdai.

Apparently, she was ignorant about Pemdas' greatest enemy, and of how important a person Reece was to their way of life.

Despite her grief, Reece did her best to remain strong; however, comfort only came to her when she curled up with the coat that she wore the morning Levi left. With the fragrance of his cologne still lingering on it, she would close her eyes and it would seem as though he was there, lying next to her. She would imagine his face, his vivid blue eyes, and the breathtaking grin he displayed that showed his love for her.

Reece knew Levi would return to her; he had to. It was only a matter of time. Navarre had men searching throughout all of the dimensions, trying to find Harrison and Levi, and she knew he would find them.

On the fifth day of Harrison and Levi's disappearance, Reece walked into the sitting room and stared out into the valley below. She gazed down at the village and silently begged for Levi to return to her.

She had no idea how long she stood staring out of the window before she heard a group of men talking in the hallway. *Levi?* Could he have returned without her notice? There were other roads beside this one that led back to the Palace; maybe he had returned. Her heart raced as she turned in hopes to find him standing in the doorway. She quickly walked toward the door, but when she looked out into the corridor, she realized that the voice she heard was Navarre's.

She listened as Navarre and Samuel approached a group of about fifty Guardians.

"Gentlemen, as you are all well aware, this is an extremely dangerous mission. Every Guardian we have sent out has not returned to us yet. But I ask you to remember who you are, and who the Pemdai are. We will not stop until all of our men are recovered. Pemdas is depending on you to help us bring our men home."

All of our men—what is going on?

"We are changing our approach about how we are returning through the various vortices," Samuel added. "This should help make this mission a successful one."

"Give us our orders, Emperor. We are ready and await your command," one man said.

"Very well, gentlemen. Let us go to the command center, where Samuel will show you the strategy that he has planned for this mission," Navarre said as he and Samuel led the way into another room.

Reece felt a sharp pain spasm in her stomach, yet the determination and confidence in Navarre's voice kept her from believing that she may never see Levi again. She exited the room; she needed to get outside. With every step she took, she lost hope that Levi would ever return. It had been five days now. They were sending men, and now it seemed as though all of the other men were going missing as well. What was going on?

That night was the first evening that Navarre had joined the women in the sitting room. He seemed confident, but Reece knew something wasn't right.

She pretended to read a book of poetry. Elizabeth sat close to Reece, reading a book of her own. They stayed close together, lending each other unspoken support. Simone, Lillian, and Catherine sat in their usual corner in quiet conversation. Allestaine was writing in a journal of some sort, and even though Navarre had joined them in the room, he remained withdrawn from everyone. He stood alone near the sofa Reece and Elizabeth were on, staring out the enormous windows.

Allestaine walked up to him, wrapped her arms around his waist, and he held her in his arms. "Navarre, what has happened?"

Navarre kissed her briefly on the head and exhaled. "We lost contact with the men we sent to Earth today as well. We can no longer send any more men. Allestaine, only thirty Guardians remain in Pemdas. All of our warriors have simply vanished. I must send word out and let all of Pemdas know I have failed them. I have never felt so lost. I know I have a purpose and a duty as a father and Emperor to all who depend on me. It is who I am, or so I thought. I am slowly being made aware that I am only a helpless victim, as the ones who depend on me have become. Tell me who I am now, my beautiful wife, for I can no longer answer this question." He stared out of the window.

Allestaine looked up at her broken husband. "You are who you have always been, Navarre: a man who places himself with his people, and never above them. It is why you are admired greatly and loved by all. You have not failed anyone, as I know you have not slept in nearly a week trying to strategize with Samuel and recover all of the men who have disappeared. Right now, you are only finding your fear, my darling. In this situation, you are as helpless as the rest of us. There is no shame in that."

He sighed. "I must disagree. There is a profusion of shame when you cannot rise to meet your duty for those who depend on you. My son, my nephew, and our loyal warriors fell into a trap; I know not where they are, what they are facing, or what they are thinking. Do they wait for me to bring them out? If so, how do I achieve this, when I have not a clue where to start? They depend on me, Allestaine, and I must bring them home. I must bring all the men safely back to their families. However, I have no way of doing so anymore. I have done all I can do."

Allestaine pulled back, bringing his focus down to her. "You will listen to me, Emperor Navarre. I will not stand here and be reminded of the one dangerous trait our son inherited from you—to believe there is no hope in situations you personally have no control over. At this point, there is nothing more that can be done. It is now time that you trust everything our warriors have been trained to do. They will find a way home, and we will get through this. We solve nothing by worrying over things we cannot help."

He did not answer; he only returned his gaze to the windows.

Reece was frozen. The group of men she saw earlier that day had not returned. Now she understood that they were Navarre's last attempt to find the men. It was as if the life had drained from her. She looked over at Elizabeth, who was intently reading her book.

"Lizzy—I think I'm going to go to bed for the evening."

Elizabeth nodded and stood with Reece. "I believe I will, too."

After Reece returned to her room, she collapsed onto her bed in tears. The same emotions of losing her father ripped through her, and emptiness consumed her. She started to take deep, calming breaths. She had to remain calm. She had to see Levi's face, to feel his closeness, to smell the fragrance of him. She had to believe he would return to her. She curled up on her side and brought her coat up to her face. The fragrance of Levi's cologne was no longer present. She closed her eyes tightly, but no image of Levi came. It was as if everything of him had disappeared. Panic, like poison, worked its way through her. She had to get out of this room, out of this Palace.

She pulled her coat on and quickly walked out to the spot where they had spent their last evening alone together.

She sat there, gazing up into the glowing nature all around her. She let the peaceful beauty of the different colors illuminating in the trees calm her and began to think more clearly.

She had no idea where Levi was, but she would not accept that he would never return. She couldn't give up hope. "Come back to me, Levi," she murmured.

Chapter 22

The next afternoon, they all sat together in the room that overlooked the valley below. Navarre was in a corner having a discussion with Samuel. In the opposite corner, near the windows, Elizabeth played the piano softly. Lady Allestaine and Reece sat together on a sofa, reading quietly, as the other woman talked in low voices at a table across the room.

It was how every day had passed since the disappearances, and no matter how many walks Reece had taken with Elizabeth to help clear her mind, she still felt empty inside.

She tried not to look out the window because it always disappointed her. It had snowed the previous night, yet the beauty of new fallen snow couldn't make up for the emptiness outside and the lack of hope that Levi would ever ride up that hill again.

Suddenly, the piano music stopped. Elizabeth stood up and peered out the windows. "Father? Someone rides to Pasidian...it looks like...one of the Guardian horses."

Navarre was at the window in an instant, but everyone else froze, waiting. Reece's stomach tightened into a knot as she tried to force hope away.

Navarre stood watching as the black horse made its way closer to the Palace. He brought his hand up over his mouth, concentrating deeply as the horse made its way into an identifiable range. "It is Areion," he said finally. "But who is his rider?" He strained his eyes to see.

At that moment, everyone in the room stood. Reece darted to the windows, followed by Lady Allestaine, who clutched her husband's arm while they watched the horse approach. Reece's heart was pounding in her chest as she watched the horse in the distance thundering toward the Palace.

Elizabeth reached for her father's free hand and held it. "Father, Levi is the only one Areion will allow upon his back; you know this. It must be Levi."

Suddenly, the horse lunged into full view—not on the usual road to the Palace, but on a direct line to the front of the palace, being ridden at an aggressive speed.

Levi! Reece covered her mouth with her hands in disbelief. She didn't know if she wanted to laugh or cry at the great relief she felt knowing he was alive. It was as if life returned to her again.

Areion cleared a hedge, and she could see that Levi wore the same clothes as the day he left. The expression on his face was dangerous, hostile. He bellowed for his groom and turned Areion over to him. "Slow his heart before it fails him…NOW!" he called out violently before heading to the Palace entrance.

Before anyone had a chance to move, everyone heard Levi's enraged voice as he stormed in through the front door.

"Simone! Where is SHE? Where is Simone?" Hearing the fury in Levi's voice, Reece almost felt frightened for Simone.

Levi paused at the door to the sitting room, found his target with his eyes, and strode straight to her. Navarre moved closer to his wife, and everyone else waited for the storm to break. Simone stood; her face reflected the fear from Levi's fury.

"WHAT HAVE YOU DONE TO US?"

Simone stepped back, and Levi pursued, paying no attention to the rest of the room. His shirt was filthy and torn, his face was bruised, and his hair was tangled and dirty. What had he been through? He looked as though he hadn't slept the entire time he was gone.

Samuel moved in front of his daughter. "Levi...there is no need for hostility at this time." He put his arm out toward Levi's chest.

Levi grabbed it and used it to lay Samuel out on the rug in front of him. Navarre stepped swiftly to his son and pulled him away. "Son, you are a better man than this." He waited.

Levi, his father gripping his arm, turned toward the woman standing stunned against the wall. "Simone—" he growled.

"Levi...we know," said Navarre as he turned his son to face him. Levi's face was black with anger. "Son, what happened? We need to know what you know."

The fire in Levi's eyes faded slowly. His gaze roamed the room, from one shocked woman to another. When he saw Reece, he exhaled, closed his eyes, and his posture softened.

Samuel lay motionless on the rug. Levi looked down at him, and Samuel's eyes widened. Levi stretched out his hand. "Commander, forgive me."

Samuel nodded and accepted Levi's hand. "Levi, where are they keeping the rest of our men?" he asked.

Levi's eyes became enraged again. "I will not speak of anything in front of that woman." Simone dropped her head into her hands, sobbing.

It was as if the fire of rage had been reignited in Levi as his eyes narrowed dangerously and his face grew darker.

She flinched away from him.

"Look at me!" Levi ordered her. "Or can you not face the consequence of your spite?" he asked in a tone of disgust.

Navarre placed a hand on his son's shoulder. "Son, can you tell us what's become of Harrison? Your uncle will arrive at any moment."

Levi's body went rigid again as his fists clenched white. "How am I to know Harrison's condition, Father? Because of this filthy object in front of me, I will not know until Reece has been traded for him and the rest of our men!"

Navarre looked at Lillian. "Take Simone to her room at once."

As Lillian escorted a sobbing Simone from the room, Navarre looked back at Levi. "We must get all the information we can from you, but first let us get your wounds attended to. Your return has restored the hope I almost lost. We will bring our men home," he stepped back and locked Levi's gaze on his own, "and we will finish this together."

Levi nodded.

"As soon as you are ready, we need to talk with Samuel to set our plans. Afterwards, we will have a quiet dinner—just family and Reece."

At Reece's name, life appeared in Levi's shadowy eyes. He turned toward her as a thirsty man turns toward water, and all his muscles seemed to relax. She took a step toward him, and the next minute he was in her arms. "Forgive me, my love," he whispered.

Lady Allestaine and Elizabeth approached Levi, hugged him, and told him how relieved they were that he was home. As the energy in the room started to unwind, Levi took Reece's hand in his. "Allow me a few moments to make myself presentable, and then I will return for you. When I speak with my father and Samuel, I want you to be there."

Reece nodded. She wanted so badly to ask him what he had been through, but now was not the time. Levi's eyes brightened. "I love you," he mouthed silently before turning to his father.

"Father, I will return shortly for Reece. There are some matters I wish to discuss with her alone, before we meet with you and Samuel in your office to discuss the situations we are to face. I would rather discuss these issues sooner than later."

Navarre nodded in agreement. "As you wish. Samuel and I will await you in my study. An hour?"

"Fine. We'll join you in an hour."

After Levi left, Navarre embraced his wife and followed Samuel out of the room. Allestaine and Elizabeth approached Reece, embracing her with happiness and relief before Reece made her way back to an empty couch to wait for Levi. Allestaine and Elizabeth walked toward Simone's sister, Catherine, who was sobbing and in hysterics. As bad as Reece felt for the girl, she couldn't bring herself to support her at the moment.

Reece brought her attention to the view outside of the windows. It was snowing again, and as she watched the light flakes dance in the wind, she felt relief completely wash over her. Reece watched the snowfall until Elizabeth came over to her. "Do you mind if I sit with you?"

Reece smiled and moved to one side. "Certainly not. How is Catherine doing?"

Elizabeth took the offered seat. "A little better, I suppose. How are you feeling?"

Reece grinned. "A lot better now that Levi's back. Although I'm still concerned about Harrison and the others, and I am a little worried about what happens now."

Elizabeth placed her hand over Reece's and smiled brightly at her. "I am certain that with Levi's knowledge of the circumstances, they will be able to come to a swift resolution. Please do not fear."

Reece smiled back. "I'm sorry I haven't been myself lately. It's like, nothing mattered but whether or not the men would ever come back."

"We've all been distraught. I haven't been myself either; no one has."

"Ladies," Levi greeted them from behind. He had wasted no time in returning. His deep voice made Reece's heart leap, and she turned around.

The bruises and scrapes on his face were still there, but he looked much more like himself. "Elizabeth, I must steal your friend for a while."

Elizabeth stood and hugged her brother. Levi wrapped his arms tightly around her and bestowed a soft kiss on the top of her head.

"I am so happy to see you again, Levi."

"Likewise, sweet one. It is good to be home."

"I know you must go see Father, so I will not detain you."

Allestaine, still in conversation with Catherine, gave him a reassuring nod, and he reached for Reece's hand to lead her from the room.

They walked together in silence down the hallways. Countless times, Reece had imagined what she would say to him if and when he returned to her. And here he was, by some miracle, holding her hand tightly, yet she had no idea how to approach him. She was worried for him and what he had gone through, but from his display earlier in the room, she felt it best not to approach the subject with him for fear of upsetting him again.

He opened the door to a dimly-lit room and stood back for Reece to enter. Before she could look around, he closed the door and seized her in a tight embrace. She rested her head against his chest, inhaling deeply the rich, masculine scent she had so desperately missed. As he gently touched her face, the tears brimming in her eyes overflowed and spilled down her cheeks.

"Reece, what's wrong?"

"I'm so thankful you're safe."

His piercing eyes were still concerned. He gently brought his hand to her cheek, tenderly sweeping away a stray tear. He then slowly brought up his other hand, cradling her face. His thumbs absently stroked her cheeks. "You're so beautiful. I have longed to stare into your eyes and to feel your skin against my own. We'll attend to matters with my father, but first I must have this moment alone with you." Fixing his eyes intently upon hers, he slowly drew his face in closer. Only when his lips were pressed against hers did he allow his eyes to close.

After the brief kiss, he rested his forehead against hers. "This—this is what gave me strength to endure. I had to get back to you. I yearned for your presence." He tilted her chin up and stared somberly into her eyes. "I needed to hear your voice, to feel your touch, and to simply see your face again." He traced her jawline with one finger. "My only, one love."

Reece wrapped her arms around him. "Levi, I'm so sorry for what you have been through. I wish I had words—"

"There's no need for words. We're together now."

Reece studied his face and brought her hand up to trace the bruise above his eyebrow. He closed his eyes and sighed. She cupped his face as he had hers and stood on her toes to kiss each fading bruise.

"I love you," she whispered, finishing with a kiss to his chin.

Levi's eyes opened, more brilliant than ever. He smiled the special smile he seemed to keep only for her. "And I love you, more than I can say."

Reece relaxed into his gentle grip, offering her lips, and without hesitation Levi accepted the invitation.

Chapter 23

L evi slowly ended their heated kiss. He smiled, his eyes showing concern, yet he didn't let go of her. "My love, I must request something of you before we meet with my father."

Reece stared at him. "Anything."

"I am about to present my father and Samuel with a plan that will seemingly put you at risk. I hope you know that I would never willingly allow your safety to be endangered, but we're at a complete disadvantage right now. I have an idea, but it depends on returning you to Earth for a while. Harrison is arranging a safe way for your return. If I did not have him, I wouldn't consider taking you back."

"Harrison is alive?"

Levi smiled brilliantly. "Yes, though I wouldn't say it in front of Simone. About my plan—"

She looked up at him and smiled warmly. "Levi, I understand you all have a lot to decide. I've watched your father walk around here hopeless and distraught for days on end. If there is a way to retrieve your men and the plans involve me, I want to be a part of them. I may not understand everything you all are talking about, but I do trust you."

He smiled down with admiration in his eyes. "You, my love...intrigue me." He bent down to kiss her briefly. "Harrison wanted me to point out that he's made good on the promise he made to you the morning we left."

Reece cocked her head. "Promise?"

"Yes, don't you remember? He promised to return me to you safely."

Reece closed her eyes and hugged Levi tightly. "I owe him, big time."

Levi pressed a kiss to the top of her head. "Now, let us go meet with my father."

Navarre's office was large and luxurious, but also clearly a working space. Situated in front of the Palace's imposing windows was a large, polished mahogany desk with a deep red leather chair behind it. Swords and other various pieces of weaponry hung on the walls by a fireplace in the front corner of the room.

Reece was immediately drawn to the paintings on the walls. The one that interested her most showed a dozen men dressed in black standing alongside their horses. Both the men and the horses were armored, as if for battle.

As she looked closer, she could see more detail. The men wore swords on leather belts. Their capes were folded back on one side, displaying black polished pads on their uncovered shoulders. Black boots went up to their knees; black gloves went up to their elbows. The only color they wore was the red lining of their capes. The men looked as fierce as their warhorses.

"These are men from the time of my grandfather's reign," said Navarre, coming up behind her. "This," he pointed to a man who was the spitting image of Levi, "is my father. Levi resembles him, does he not? It is intriguing to see my father, in my own son." He smiled down at her. "Shall we have you sit over here?" He pointed toward the desk. "I suppose Levi prepared you for what we will be discussing?" He offered his arm and led her over to one of the empty chairs situated around his desk. Levi, who had been having a discussion with Samuel since their arrival in the study, walked over to where Reece sat and took the chair next to her.

Navarre walked over to his seat. "Where's Harrison?" he asked as he sat in his chair.

"Harrison is safe—"

"Where are our men—what has happened? What information do you have?" Navarre interjected.

"Our men have been imprisoned at Castle Ruin. It is where they have arranged a council for you to attend, to present Reece."

Navarre gazed somberly toward Samuel, and then back to Levi. "Scotland? So they have remained on Earth? You have been on Earth this entire time?"

"Yes."

"How were they able to capture you and Harrison?"

"They were waiting for us outside the vortex with an army of Ciatron defenders. They used a mechanism to shut down our car, but when we got out and tried to fight, they overtook us." He shrugged apologetically. "They brought us to a holding area, where we found other Guardians. We had no idea, at the time, what was happening. More and more Guardians joined us; they were hunting them down throughout Earth. Then, without notice, they took Harrison and me away from the others. When we protested our being separated from the rest of the men, they told us they were relocating them to Castle Ruin. They told us that because we were the closest relations to Emperor Navarre, we would receive 'proper treatment' and would join our men in Scotland soon enough." Levi's face grew distant. His tone of disgust implied that there was much detail about their treatment that he was not mentioning. "It was at this time that Movac sent for me. He was in a room with six other Ciatron defenders."

"Movac is on Earth?" Navarre asked, surprised. "The leader of the Ciatron has left his protected domain? Their leaders have always been cowards—Movac must be very confident about whatever plan he has formed against us. Tell me, what did Movac have to say to you?"

"He knows that we have the Key with us in Pemdas. He has contacted all the leaders of the other dimensions and led them to believe that our reason for taking Reece into Pemdas is to gain ultimate control over all of them." Disgust was apparent on Levi's face.

"But they can't believe that!" Samuel said. Until now, he had remained quiet throughout the entire conversation, listening and a few times scribbling on a pad of paper.

"I wouldn't have thought so, but they brought me into a council chamber with most of the leaders. They do believe it, Samuel. I tried to dispute it; I reminded them of our services to them, but—"

"Reece," said Navarre.

"Yes. I couldn't deny that we had Reece in Pemdas and that we'd replaced her with a stand-in. With Movac's persuasion, they regarded that as proof of our bad intentions. They instructed me to return and bring you their terms."

Navarre sat back in his chair and stared at Levi. Resting his elbow on the arm of his chair, he leaned his chin on his fist and sat quietly. "It astounds me," he said finally, "that these leaders, who know of our cause to protect the Key, should so quickly allow their minds to be changed. It is as if they have longed for an excuse to make us their enemy. But there is no purpose to try to analyze the foolishness of other worlds. I must protect our own. What is this negotiation they present?"

"It's really Movac's requirement, but all the leaders agreed. They want you to return Reece to Earth and present her to the council there. They have given you three days to make your decision. If you choose to return Reece, they will decide at that time whether or not the Pemdai are to be trusted again. If trust is restored, they will release our men in trade for Reece."

Navarre stared at his son. "And if we do not?"

Levi looked at his father darkly. "First, they will take action against those of our men whom they hold. Second, they will attempt to prevent our ever leaving Pemdas again by heavily guarding our vortices into all dimensions." Levi leaned forward. "Father, the Ciatron are no longer our only enemy; they have turned all worlds against us."

Navarre inhaled deeply and leaned back into his chair. "So it would seem. Now we have the reason for Movac's presence on Earth. That coward would never leave Ciatris unless he was confident he had other worlds defending him against us."

Navarre looked over at his commander. "Samuel, what are your opinions?"

Samuel looked at Reece, and then at Navarre. He seemed uncomfortable with her in the room, but he answered calmly enough. "We are at a disadvantage. There is no way we can retrieve our armies from Castle Ruin with the few warriors we have left. Either we keep Reece amongst us, ignore these demands, and hope that they will return our men," Samuel inhaled deeply, "or we consider their demands."

Levi scowled at Samuel.

"I can see that this information has taken you off-guard," Navarre said. "I am equally surprised by this turn of events. Let us not forget that the Pemdai, under no circumstances, accede to coercion. We never have, and so long as I stand as Emperor, we never will. Reece will not be traded. We are not cowards, and we will not stay behind our secure borders and hide in the hope that our men will be returned. Our brave warriors are depending upon us to take action on their behalf. We must remember the soldiers we are, form a plan, and develop a strategy."

Levi addressed the two men. "Samuel...Father, allow me to provide you with an option to consider, as I believe it may be our only alternative. Harrison and I have formulated a plan. I am confident it will work, and with your approval we can bring Reece and present her before the council as a distraction."

"Harrison? How is he? Where is he?" Navarre quickly asked.

"He is well. He brought me through the vortex and returned to Earth. If we agree to bring Reece back to Earth with us, we will need a distraction at the vortex that she will be returning through. As I sit here with you now, he is in the process of arranging this."

Light had returned to Navarre's eyes. "Son, please enlighten me. How is Harrison running freely around Earth, and what is this plan you have come up with?"

Levi remained serious. "Forgive me for misleading you earlier, but I would not speak in front of Simone. Harrison and I have been free since early this morning. After they released me to return to Pemdas, I used that opportunity to free Harrison. They probably should have guarded him more heavily, as I was easily able to take their defenders down and retrieve him."

"Are you still in communication with him?"

"Yes. They returned my communication device to me, along with the car. Harrison drove me back through the vortex so that he could keep the car and device with him. It served us well that you allowed Areion to stay down at the gates." Levi shifted in his seat and looked at Samuel. "I couldn't contact anyone; I didn't have anyone I could trust. I was still struggling to understand how Simone could have contacted the Ciatron by herself."

Samuel nodded heavily. He seemed to have aged ten years since he'd found out about Simone's transgressions. "I have offered my resignation—"

"And I have refused it," Navarre said. "Samuel and Catherine have suffered enough. Levi, are you aware that Michael Visor, and possibly Magnus Sterlington, was involved as well?"

Levi's expression was steely as he stared intently at Navarre. "How was Sterlington able to plan something like this? I thought he had been removed from Pemdas?"

Navarre returned Levi's stern expression. "Believe me when I say that we are trying to solve that mystery as well. I should have never granted that man's passage to leave our land! I should have handled his abominable behavior differently. However, Simone has still not admitted that he was involved. She only told of us Michael's involvement, and we could only assume Sterlington is behind his nephew's scheming."

Levi exhaled and stared out of the window behind his father. "Why would Michael consider plotting something like this? Sterlington's motives are transparent, but Michael's?" He shook his head as he muttered to himself. It was clear that Levi was hurt that an old friend would be capable of such treason.

"Your father and I have relentlessly questioned Michael's motives. Regardless of whether Sterlington was involved or not, we cannot understand why either Michael or Simone would have wanted to go into the Ciatron dimension. It is all inexplicable to us."

"Utter hatred," Levi responded with a dark expression. He looked at Samuel. "I'm sorry to say it, Samuel, but I've seen it in Simone before. Everyone knows the Ciatron do not negotiate, especially with a Pemdai. If there was no malice involved, either Simone or Michael would have told us what they had done to 'resolve our problems' right away. Instead, not a word was mentioned, and Michael is still missing. Michael has always had a streak of envy in him, but I thought he'd grown out of it. Could that be a reason for his betrayal—to outdo me? But why Simone? Why would she—" Levi's face became fierce, and he turned toward Reece. She immediately knew that he understood Simone's motive.

He didn't say it, though, and Reece was thankful.

"But," he said, "we waste our time by sitting here and deliberating why we were delivered into the hands of our greatest enemy. We must decide what to do. You say Michael is missing. Was he questioned before he disappeared?"

"No," Samuel said. "Simone claims he went back to Earth. We certainly haven't been able to find him in Pemdas."

Levi's eyes were fierce, and with filled purpose. "Then that settles any idea of remaining here with Reece, hoping they return our men to us. If Michael Visor and Sterlington are among the Ciatron, they must be retrieved and brought back to Pemdas. I am fearful of the knowledge they may have obtained already if those traitors are amongst them. Even though I didn't encounter either of them while we were being detained, we can't be sure, so we must assume they are. We are forced to initiate the plan Harrison and I developed to return with Reece."

"If we return with Reece," Samuel said, "they'll expect us to trade her. There's no point in bringing her, unless that's what we intend to do."

A tiny smile drew up the corner of Levi's mouth. "That is precisely my point." He leaned forward, resting his elbows on his knees. "On no account would I consider trading Reece, but we will make it appear as though that is what we are doing. We are defeated in every way and are forced to bring her back, but if we can release our captive men and regain our armies while she is being presented to the council…we will reject their demands and return home with our men and Reece. In bringing Reece back to Earth, the hardest part will be getting her through the vortex without the Ciatron overpowering us; it is where all the guards will be waiting. This is why Harrison is arranging a distraction at the vortex, to give me a chance to get her through.

Navarre looked at Levi with concern. "They have guards positioned at all of our vortices?"

"Not currently, but when Harrison and I came through the Philadelphia vortex, they were in the process of deploying them. That's why Harrison had to return immediately after bringing me here, before they noticed him. Right now, the Ciatron will stop at nothing to intercept Reece. They know we are outnumbered, and they have no intention of letting us make it to the council with her. They plan to intercept us at the Bonnybridge vortex in Scotland, and that's where the heaviest guard will be. So, of course, Reece can't be brought through that one, and we can't use it.

"Instead, Harrison and I plan to return Reece through the Philadelphia vortex. Even with Harrison's distraction, we know they will pursue, but with enough of a diversion we can get her to Washington, where our aircraft is. After that, we'll have her safely in the air until we land in Scotland and bring her to the council."

Navarre's eyebrows drew together. "Son, I can appreciate this plan…but I am not convinced it is wise to bring Reece back to Earth. If we do, as I believe it is our only chance at getting our men back, we must be certain this will work."

Levi nodded. "I would not entertain any idea of returning her to Earth if I was uncertain of the outcome. Either way, we must force ourselves to realize we have no other option at this time. As Samuel has mentioned, we do not have enough men left to be successful in any attempts made to retrieve our men. As you have declared, we cannot sit here and be cowards. We must trick them into believing that we will trade Reece. You must present her before the council, Father, as if you were adhering to their demands.

This plan will require us to be careful in every way because there is an enormous risk involved. Samuel *must* be successful with the release of our men."

Samuel looked at Levi. "This will be complicated, but with Reece as a distraction, we should be able to manage it. If she *is* a distraction, that is—how confident are you that they will be distracted?"

"Once Reece is at the castle, I promise you the Ciatron will focus on her. Given that their dearest goal is to take her, they'll be relentlessly trying to prevent her from walking into that meeting." Levi looked at Navarre. "As long as they are trying to capture Reece, they will not think that we might come through their back doors to recover our men."

"Levi, this may work," said Samuel, "but I will need every last Pemdai guard with me. You and Reece will be on your own going into the castle. Are you prepared to handle that?"

Levi gazed out of the window and exhaled. He turned back to Samuel. "I will need at least one other Guardian with us. I need to have someone else protecting her, if I become distracted by an unexpected attack."

Navarre exhaled. "Do you believe that you will be that easily overtaken, Levi?"

"Navarre," Reece spoke for the first time, "is there a possibility that someone could possibly help to prepare me, so that Levi is more confident about bringing me through the castle alone? I mean—I don't know if I can really defend myself against anyone, but—"

Levi immediately interjected, "Reece, I will not put you under that kind of pressure. The training you would have to undergo will be demanding, and I'm not sure—"

Reece stared intently at Levi. "I want to help. If Samuel needs all his men, then it's the least I can do. If there is some way you can prepare me, I may be able to do this."

Levi exhaled as Samuel spoke, "Levi, I will need all of my men. As it stands now, I may not have enough. If Reece is willing to undergo some training, it will help us."

Levi's features darkened. "No! I will not put her in a position to protect herself if I am unable to do so."

"Levi, I am stronger than you are giving me credit for, at least let me try."

Levi looked over to Reece, studying her. After a moment, he looked back to Samuel. "All right, but I'll be the one to prepare Reece for whatever we may encounter. If I'm confident that she's ready, I'll be fine to bring her through the castle alone. It will not be easy, but as long as she is prepared, I can protect her on my own. If, for any reason, I am not confident that she's ready, I will need Harrison, or at least one other warrior, to go with me. I understand that you need every man available, and it is vital that we free our captive men. However, we must make sure there are no weak areas in this plan, or we will fail, and possibly lose Reece."

Navarre looked to Levi. "Levi, do you have any idea about how many are being used to guard our men at Castle Ruin?"

"That is unclear to me, Father, but I would presume that they are being heavily guarded. We must remember their collective minds will all be preoccupied with Movac's thoughts about Reece. They will never consider that we have our guards on the way to attack them and retrieve our men."

Navarre nodded. "This may indeed work. You must understand, though, that I will be forced into a holding area until Reece arrives. I assure you that the very moment I set foot in Scotland, I will be their prisoner, especially if Reece is not with me. There will be nothing that I can do to help any of you."

"Then we will plan for no less than six of your personal Imperial Guards to go through the Scotland vortex with you," said Samuel. "The warriors and I will enter separately to secure the airport where Harrison and Levi will be landing. If anything is done in haste, the Imperial Guards will protect you. They may not be trained the same as the Guardian warriors, but they are highly trained to remove you from hostile situations."

Navarre laughed in return. "The Ciatron will not harm me, Samuel; if they did, they'd lose their hold on all the other worlds. I'm only concerned because I won't be able to help Levi if he's having trouble coming through the castle."

"If Levi is unsure about bringing Reece alone, I'll arrange for a Guardian to go with him. I'll need Harrison," Samuel said to Levi. "He is superb at tactical planning, and I will require his skill. Be sure you tell him that."

Levi nodded.

Navarre spoke again, "We must not forget that Reece is our highest priority. We cannot allow her into the hands of the Ciatron." He looked at Levi with pride. "Son, you and Harrison have proven yourselves to be Pemdas' finest warriors. For that reason only, I approve of this plan of action." Navarre leaned back into his chair and exhaled loudly. "Indeed, I believe this will work. We already have the advantage, being at a disadvantage." He let out a soft laugh. "They will not expect us to try and fight with the thirty Guardian warriors we have left, and therein we will take them by surprise."

Before another word was spoken on the subject, a servant entered the room and announced, "Emperor, King Nathanial awaits."

"Thank you, James; please show him in."

Chapter 24

large, angry man erupted into the meeting room. Levi and Samuel stood. Navarre came around the desk, making his way to King Nathanial.

"Navarre, is there any new information—anything from Harrison or Levi?"

Navarre reached for his brother's hand and clapped him on the back. "Nathaniel, Harrison is well! Please sit; Levi returned to us nearly an hour ago and has been informing us of the situation."

Nathaniel relaxed somewhat as his gaze fell upon Levi. "Nephew, you're back!" He approached him and brought him into an embrace. "Good to see you, even if you're looking a bit battered! Please tell me, what has become of Harrison?"

"Harrison is in the process of helping us in a strategy to recover our men, my Lord," Levi answered.

"Come, sit, and I will explain," Navarre said as he directed Nathaniel to an empty chair.

After explanations were given to King Nathaniel, he seemed somewhat reassured and thanked Reece for her willingness to help put this plan into action.

Not long after the King had been caught up to speed, Levi took the opportunity to dismiss Reece so that she did not have to sit through any more of the men's strategic discussions.

As he and Reece strolled down the corridor, she felt the exhaustion of the past week set in. While she had feared for Levi's safety, her nights had been disturbed and her days had been a battle to maintain a presentable appearance. Now that he was safely at her side, she felt her mind and body beginning to fade and found it hard to concentrate. She smothered a yawn.

Levi chuckled and brought his arm around her. "You are tired, my love. Allow me to escort you to your room so that you may rest before dinner."

Reece tried to protest, but another yawn betrayed her. She shook her head with frustration. "I am fine. If there is anyone who needs rest, it's you."

"Reece, I could not rest if I wanted to. There is still much to discuss with my father, and I must arrange some things in order to prepare you for our return to Earth. I'll go over all of the details with you later this evening."

Reece shook her head again. "Levi, I'm fine. I'd feel guilty lying down to rest, knowing that you all are working. It was my idea to make sure no other Guardians went with us into the castle—"

"That is why I need you to rest," Levi interrupted her. "You have your work cut out for you now," he teased.

"Exactly my point. I volunteer myself for a military mission, and now I'm going to go lie down and take a nap? I don't think so. I think I need to start—"

"My love, I will hear no more. You will rest. I have plans after dinner tonight, and they include only you and me. It will be much more enjoyable for me if you are awake."

Reece arched her eyebrow, staring up at him. "Are you giving me orders, Levi?"

"If that is what is required for you to rest, then yes, my love, I believe that is exactly what I am doing."

Oh, well... There was no point in arguing with him when she couldn't even fight her own exhaustion.

As soon as they arrived to her room, Levi bent down and kissed her softly. "Get some rest; I'll see you at dinner tonight." He tucked a loose strand of hair behind her ear. "I love you."

"Love you," she said while fighting another yawn.

Levi's mouth quirked, and he laughed. Then he turned and walked away.

Reece lay down, but her mind would not stop ruminating about Levi and the meeting with Navarre and Samuel. After what seemed to be an hour, she pulled herself up from her bed.

She opted to take a hot bath to help rejuvenate her. Once she finished and was dressed, she dismissed Jasmeen for the evening. She had an hour until the family would be gathering for dinner, so she decided to have a cup of hot tea and pass the time quietly.

She sat on the comfortable sofa and gazed out of the window. When she finished her tea, she set the cup aside and rested her head on the arm of the sofa. Before she knew it, she was dreaming.

She was walking through an open, grassy field, and everything felt so peaceful. A crisp, fresh breeze bent the tall grass while butterflies danced throughout the field as far as she could see. She stood there inhaling the fresh air. In the distance, she noticed a tall, slender figure approaching. *You've come back to me.* She watched, smiling and comforted, as he walked toward her. His long strides picked up as he realized it was she who waited for him. As he approached her, he smiled vibrantly. His eyes glowed radiantly with love. He pulled her close to him as she stood on her toes, deeply inhaling the rich fragrance of him that she had longed for. "I love you, Levi…"

"And I love you."

Her eyes snapped open to find Levi on one knee in front of her. He brought the back of his fingers to caress her cheek. "My beautiful Reece, I hope I did not startle you?"

"Um, no. I think I must have dozed off. What time is it? Am I late for dinner?" Reece pulled herself up into a proper sitting position.

Levi chuckled in response. "No, love. But it is close to time. Are you feeling rested enough to join all of us? My Aunt Madeleine is looking forward to meeting you. My mother has done nothing but boast of the special young woman you are." He smiled proudly to her. "Elizabeth has been talking about you nonstop as well."

Reece cocked her head to the side. "I hope I can live up to all of this."

Levi laughed and rose up. He extended his hand out to her. "You need do nothing more than walk into that room, and everyone will be eating out of your hand."

Reece smiled and placed her hand into his.

When they arrived at dinner, Reece found herself at ease in the Palace for the first time in many days.

At dinner, Reece was introduced to Harrison's mother, Madeleine; she was a striking woman, with black hair and green eyes. Though her coloring was so different from Lillian's, their features were similar. Madeleine held herself very upright and didn't speak much, but whether that was just her way or she was worried about Harrison, Reece couldn't tell. She could not form an honest opinion of her, as Madeleine remained mostly quiet throughout the entire meal. When addressed directly, she would give short, though polite answers.

Dinner went smoothly, and Reece remained comfortable as she discretely watched Levi from across the table. Her heart was overwhelmed with love as she sat there admiring every stunning quality he possessed. She watched as he ate his meal and answered inquiries from his father and uncle. Levi's voice was cultured and smooth, but with a slight rasp that always seemed to make Reece's heart flutter. Her heart raced in anticipation of when they would finally be alone together.

Reece was not the only one stealing glances at the table; on more than one occasion, she noticed Levi look in her direction. His face would become radiant as he grinned at her before bringing his attention back to his plate. It was obvious that Levi was having the same difficulty getting through dinner as she was, as both now only wanted to be alone and in each other's arms again.

After dinner, Elizabeth played the piano for her aunt and uncle. Levi quietly excused himself, saying he needed to speak with Reece, and led her out to the benches where they had sat the night before he went to Earth.

Before Levi could motion for her to sit, Reece turned toward him and wound her arms around his neck, bringing him into a tight embrace.

She fought back tears, but was unsuccessful. Levi leaned down, wrapping his arms around her waist. "My love, please don't shed any more tears. I know this has been difficult for you, but I am home now, and we are together again," he whispered in her ear.

Reece sniffed and laughed softly at her unexpected response to being with him again. She pulled away and gazed up into the face she believed she'd never see again. Levi subtly grinned as he tenderly brushed away her tears.

"I'm sorry, it's just that last night was the first time that I believed I might never see you again." Tears returned to her eyes, and she quickly wiped them away. "I think it's all starting to hit me now, and I'm probably going to ruin our evening together by being an emotional wreck," she said as she smiled up at him.

"After what you have been through, it is perfectly understandable," he answered.

Levi guided her to sit, yet did not join her on the bench. His face was somber as he knelt down and took her hands into his. Reece stared at him in confusion as he slowly rubbed his thumbs over the back of her hands. His focus was intently on her hands as he exhaled.

"Levi?"

His darkened eyes met hers. "Reece, my father informed me of your confrontation with Simone and how you dealt with the distressing position she placed you in." He inhaled deeply. "I want to personally apologize to you for that. I should have been better aware—"

"Levi, no. Please don't blame yourself for any of this. How was anyone supposed to know Simone would do something like that—and all because of jealousy? At first I thought she was making it all up to scare me. But the more she talked, the more I wondered if the woman was truly that insane. And that's when, regardless of what she said, I knew I had to get a message to your father immediately. I knew your father would know how to deal with the situation, and whether or not what Simone said was true." She stared at Levi as she added, "I really think that woman is insane."

Levi's expression grew dark. "I have already paid her a visit regarding the threat she made you. She is fully aware that if she as much as looks at you, she will have to answer to me. After my discussion with her, I want you to know that you have nothing to fear from that despicable woman."

"Who is this Michael Visor guy that she planned all of this with anyway?" Reece asked.

"Michael was one of my and Harrison's friends. We formed a close friendship while we were in Guardian training together; however, once Harrison and I were assigned to guard you, he started to distance himself from us."

Reece shook her head. "It doesn't make sense to me. Any of it. Why would he be involved? He's a Guardian."

Levi exhaled. "True; however, as I said in the meeting, he has always been envious of me. And now it makes perfect sense—as Guardian, protecting 'the Key' is the highest honor one can receive. I'm sure now, Michael was not happy when he wasn't selected for that duty. Maybe that's what this is all about—trying to sabotage my and Harrison's duties of protecting you?"

"Levi—let's not talk about this anymore. Trying to analyze all of the motives of why Michael would betray Pemdas will frustrate you more. Our time is better spent making sure we can bring the rest of the Guardian's home. I can't imagine what their families are going through right now."

Reece ran her fingers along the concerned lines on his face, and his expression softened at her touch. He took her hand and brought it to his lips. His eyes closed as he let his mouth linger against the palm of her hand.

"How is it that I can love you more now than I did before?" His eyes were smoldering when he returned them to hers. "Thank you for the strength and support you offered my sister, and for being as courageous as you were in my absence. I am sorry that you had to deal with this alone and that I was not here to protect you from Simone's detestable behavior."

"Please don't apologize. You came back to me—that's all I needed and wanted from you." Reece smiled, and Levi studied her.

He stood and sat next to her. Without saying another word, he brought one arm around her and used the other to gently cradle her legs, bringing her effortlessly onto his lap.

He stared intently into her eyes. "As strong as I was enduring the torment we went through, there was a moment when I believed I would never hold you in my arms again. To believe I would never feel your closeness again," he exhaled, "that was the only time I felt as though I would die." The back of his fingers traced along her jawline and down her neck. "That was the only pain I suffered. And now, you are with me again, and in my arms. All I want is what I yearned for while I was imprisoned by those vile creatures. He grew more serious, and then carefully and studiously his lips softly savored her skin as they ran along her neck, to the base of her throat. Reece's body shivered at his warm breath against her skin.

"Your fragrance intoxicates me in ways that I can't explain," he whispered hoarsely. "To taste the sweet flavor of your soft skin—is almost more than I can bear. I have longed for this moment since the morning I left you."

He brought his eyes back to meet hers. Reece's heart beat erratically as she saw the hunger and passion in his eyes. She inhaled deeply as she watched him studying her.

His grip around her waist tightened, and his other hand brushed softly up and along her arm.

"I love you, Levi." She sighed.

He answered by cradling her head in his sturdy hand. Before she could take another breath, his mouth seized hers with a kiss so urgent and powerful, it consumed Reece entirely.

She ran her hands through his hair, wanting more from him. Levi answered this request by pulling her closer into him and deepening their ardent kiss further. The pain of their separation was now lost in their passion for each other. Reece could not have asked for more than to be here now, in this moment, with the man she loved.

After some time of relishing in each other's love, Levi withdrew and Reece leaned into him. She listened as his rapidly beating heart found its normal rhythm again. She stared out at the glistening fountain with contentment while Levi placed dozens of soft kisses throughout her hair.

"As much as I desire to sit in silence and appreciate our time together again," Levi said softly, "I must go over some of the details of our training tomorrow with you."

Reece chuckled and turned to look at him. "You're probably right. I volunteered myself, so I should know what I'm going to be up against."

Levi became serious. "Are you sure you are still feeling confident enough to return to Earth alone with me? Samuel and I have discussed this in more detail, and he believes he will be okay if he sacrifices one of the Guardian warriors he needs."

Reece shook her head. "I'll be fine. You just need to let me know what I have to do to help."

Levi stared intently into her eyes. "Reece, you heard me say I'd need to prepare you if I couldn't have another Guardian with me?"

"Yes."

"We must prepare you the best way we can to defend yourself, in case we come upon a situation where I am unable to." His eyes grew dark, and he inhaled deeply. "This goes against everything I am, to accept that I may not be able to protect you. If Harrison can arrange a sufficient distraction, you should have no need to defend yourself. However, we need to prepare for the worst." He exhaled softly. "We need to use tomorrow to train you as quickly as possible for this. It will be a grueling exercise. Are you positive this is something you are willing to go through?"

"Grueling? Don't you think what we are about to go through back on Earth will be hard enough in and of itself? Levi, you aren't going to scare me out of this; I hope I can learn as quickly as you guys might think I can. Hopefully, the self-defense class I took in my first year of college will help."

Levi showed a hint of a smile. "I must have you understand, Reece, this is not your average self-defense class. It is more of a mental training, and one that will be much harder on your nerves."

Reece smiled confidently. "Hey, I'll get to learn a little about what the Guardians do! It should be interesting."

He smiled mischievously in return. "That, my love, we shall see."

Conversation behind them, they spent the remainder of the evening sitting comfortably in each other's arms. Reece positioned herself to lie back against Levi and rested her head against his chest. They both remained quiet, enjoying the comfort of each other while watching the water glisten as it poured from the fountain into the pond in front of them.

Chapter 25

Jasmeen had Reece up before the sun. When she was dressed in her track suit and ready for the day's workout, she sat quietly on the sofa and waited for Levi to come retrieve her. As she waited, she recalled the previous night's events in her mind. The last things she remembered were the soothing sounds of the fountain and Levi running his fingers gently through her hair. She must have fallen asleep. *Wow, that's awkward.* Had he called a servant to carry her to bed? Or carried her himself?

When Jasmeen answered the knock at her bedroom door, Reece was a bit surprised to see that it was not Levi who stood there. Instead, he had sent a servant to escort her to the area where they would meet to go over the training he had planned for her.

They walked out beyond the barns, toward a group of long, windowless buildings that she had seen before, but never entered. Inside was something like a martial arts gym from Earth. Red pads covered the floors and lined the walls, and there were large punching bags placed throughout.

As the servant left her standing alone in the room, she was intimidated by what it represented. This was where the Guardians did their training, and now she was having second thoughts about whether or not she was up for this. She sighed. *Way to go, Reece. Trying to play everyone's hero, and you're probably going to make an idiot out of yourself.*

Levi, Samuel, and two other men entered from a door across the room. They wore loose, black pants and tight, long-sleeved black shirts that accentuated their muscles. Samuel and the two other men seemed to be pursuing another interest. They greeted her on their way out through the door Reece had entered by. Levi stopped in front of her, and she smiled confidently at him.

His answering smile was not as bright. "Did you rest well?"

"I did. Thank you for bringing me back to my room; sorry I fell asleep on you."

"There is no need to apologize. You needed the rest." His mood seemed odd. This wasn't the loving, compassionate Levi she had grown used to. This was an instructor, and taking his instruction lightly was not going to be an option.

He led her over to the middle of the room.

"Reece, the purpose of the training today is to prepare your mind to never surrender, no matter the situation. Tomorrow, we may come into a situation where it feels that I cannot help you. It will be imperative that you do not panic under such circumstances. I will need you to be fearless until I can get to you. You must understand; you will not have the physical strength to overpower your captors. Therefore, our focus today is to teach you to rely on your mental strength instead. You must want to fight, even though you know you are not strong enough physically. Your mind is the most powerful thing you have, and until we can teach you how to use its power properly, your body's natural tendency will most likely be either to freeze or to run. Either one will put your captors at a great advantage. If you can resist the natural urge to panic and instead put forth your best fight, it will give me time to get to you."

With that, he started the training.

After what seemed to be about an hour of jumping rope, running in place, and other various calisthenics to bring up her heart rate and stretch and warm her muscles, Levi picked up a pair of strike pads, much like the ones she remembered from her self-defense class. "Let us work on your form with a few strikes against these."

"I think I throw a pretty good punch, so be prepared. I don't want to hurt you," she teased.

He reacted with a look of annoyance. "Just strike the pads, Reece. I will adjust your form if I see need for improvement."

Not in the mood for joking, then. All right. She threw a couple of punches, got into her rhythm, and Levi stopped her to adjust her form. It happened over and over. Annoyingly, his face gave no indication of whether she was doing better or worse.

After the striking drills, he brought her over to a large punching bag in the corner of the room. First he showed her the kicking form he wanted her to use on the bag, then he allowed her to begin throwing her kicks against it.

She was tiring, and fatigue made her irritable. Levi was not helping. He began raising his voice and constantly stopping her to correct her approach to the bag. She never lashed back at him, although she wanted to. Instead, she pushed harder.

Levi never once stopped to allow her to rest. When she thought he actually would, he pushed her into a more rigorous drill. The only rest she got was the short time it took to take a sip of water before he brought her back to the center of the room.

"We will go through a series of motions that I want you to defend yourself against. I want you to give yourself over to your mind. Let the element of surprise take you, and then see how you can react with it."

They practiced many different self-defense moves. Levi taught her how to avoid being attacked and how to escape from various holds. He taught her how to twist away from someone coming up from behind; actually, she had trouble with that one. Over and over she tried, but Levi corrected her every time. When she finally mastered it, she felt triumphant.

Levi showed no reaction. She decided to give him an opportunity to give her the positive input she deserved. "Wow! I finally got it! I didn't know I could do that!"

He stared at her sternly. "The only way to know if you can actually do the move is to be in a situation in which you are forced to use it."

She looked at him incredulously. Her voice began to rise with frustration. "What are you talking about? You showed me the move, we ran the drill, and I got away from the bad guy. All I'm saying is that I learned something new."

His eyes narrowed, staring down at her. He looked annoyed. Well, she could do annoyed, too. "Whatever," she said. "What are we doing next anyway? Let's just move on."

"Stay here," he answered her flatly.

Reece stood and waited. She closed her eyes, trying to enjoy the break. Gradually, the dark behind her eyelids seemed to deepen and she felt calmer. She thought about sitting down.

Suddenly, she was grabbed and trapped. She knew immediately it was Levi. Now was her chance to show him what she'd learned. Using the moves he had taught her, she began to twist out of his grip. Her eyes flew open—to total darkness. She could see nothing. Panic set in, darkness consumed her, and she couldn't remember the steps she needed. Her heart beat loudly in her ears. She had to—had to!—prove to Levi that she could do this.

The angrier and more frustrated she became, the less skill she seemed to have. She began to cry out of frustration and anger. Levi had been right; she really hadn't learned the move thoroughly. They had worked for hours, and she thought she had learned something, but she really hadn't. The thought sapped her will to fight and her ability to think.

She tried to focus and fight against her tired body's screaming that she had reached her limits. Levi growled instructions in her ear, and his arms tightened around her more. She fought to try and listen to his commands, but she felt herself weakening further. Completely drained, she stopped fighting his strength.

Levi held her tighter. "Are you going to give up, Reece? Fight back!"

"Stop. You win."

"NO!" he shouted. "You must find your way out of this!"

She started to panic. She was afraid of this new Levi. She searched for air, but couldn't find it. "Levi, STOP! I can't breathe!"

He released her, and she collapsed to the ground, taking deep breaths. *All of this work was for nothing*, she thought, defeated. She lay there, her body weak and trembling from exhaustion. She knew she could not pull herself to her legs to stand if she wanted to. She was extremely fatigued, with nothing left. She became angry that she panicked and forced her body to recover itself.

When the lights to the room came back on, she saw Levi's back as he exited the building. She closed her eyes again, more upset with herself than ever. She could only imagine what he was thinking. She sat up and tried not to think. A short rest, and then she would pull herself to her feet and head to the palace, alone.

A few minutes later, Levi returned with Samuel by his side. Samuel gave Reece a concerned look and went to stand in the back of the room.

Levi went to Reece and knelt down, bringing himself to her level. "Reece, let us get you back to the Palace. You've pushed yourself beyond exhaustion. This will not work. Forgive me; I pushed you hard for nothing."

His words were not what she wanted to hear. "What? That's it?"

He answered her firmly, "We will have to find another way. I will have a Pemdai warrior travel with us tomorrow. This was too much, and too fast, for you. You are from Earth, and your mind is not capable of handling the stress that we Pemdai can. I am sorry."

She felt her body become instantly numb in response to the insult. Then the numbness was replaced by adrenaline, giving her a second wind. She stared angrily at Levi and spoke slowly and firmly, "I am not finished, Levi. I just needed a break."

If she hadn't been so angry, she would have flinched at his dark expression. "Reece, you cannot do this. It's over."

Heat rushed through her. Her anger took over and brought fuel to every muscle in her body. She used this newfound strength to restrain herself from slapping Levi's rigid face. She glared at him, but his expression didn't change. It only made her angrier. "Do not tell me what I can or can't do," she growled in a voice she hadn't known she owned.

Levi stood up, not taking his eyes from hers. "Get up." He squared himself back into a position she recognized. She squared up to him, her body begging for a chance to counter whatever he came at her with. When he advanced her, she countered the approach perfectly, without even thinking.

From out of nowhere, Samuel captured her from the side. She spun away. As soon as she escaped that attack, another came from the other side. She couldn't break free from this one, but she never stopped fighting. The attacker released her, and she was instantly attacked from another direction. Her mind stayed focused and intent.

With every hit, she fought with everything she had in her until the attacker pulled back or she was able to remove him. She wasn't perfectly successful; the men were too strong, and more than once she found herself helpless. She did not master the skills Levi had taught her, but she did exactly what he wanted her to do: she fought without considering to surrender. She could not make out the faces of her attackers, not even Levi's. She only knew that her life was in danger, and she fully gave herself over to the fighting instincts she had not known she possessed. She never gave up, and she never once panicked.

Reece did not know how long this went on. Amazingly, she did not feel tired. Adrenaline pumped through her body, and she felt nothing, only power. Finally, there were no more attacks. She stood in the middle of the room, out of breath, waiting, just in case. Her legs weren't shaking as they had earlier; she enjoyed the power she felt running through her.

When her eyes focused, she found Levi standing across from her, smiling broadly. Samuel stood at his side, and two other men walked over to join them. She let out a breath as Levi came to her and wrapped his arms around her.

Feeling her muscles begin to loosen and relax, she collapsed happily against him. Her heartbeat and breathing slowed.

"I believe we may have just unleashed our next greatest Pemdai warrior. It's over, my love; now, let us calm you down a bit."

She pulled back, looking up at him. "You planned that all along, didn't you?"

He smiled apologetically. "I will tell you, it was a lot harder than I expected to watch you transform into a raging lioness. Any attacker coming at you unexpectedly will be shocked when they meet with your newfound talents. I am beyond impressed. You have done extremely well today."

She smiled up at him. Samuel and the two other men walked over to them and expressed their opinions about how well she did before leaving the room.

"Who were those men with Samuel?" she asked Levi.

"They are Guardians; they were here today to assist in your training. I needed a couple of other men to add to the chaos while you were being attacked."

Levi was a completely different man from earlier; his expression was more pleasant.

He looked down at her. "Let us get you cleaned up and attended to so you'll be able to walk in the morning. We have a special drink for recovery; it will keep the soreness away from your muscles."

Reece laughed. "I didn't even think about that."

As they left the building, Reece noticed the skies had darkened. She looked up at Levi, amazed. "How long have we been training?"

He glanced down at her with a proud smile. "You were able to withstand all of that for twelve hours."

"What? Wow!"

"But," he said, "I need you to understand what you really accomplished today."

"Okay?"

He smiled. "It is for your protection that I say this to you, so please do not take this the wrong way. You did exceedingly well for someone who has spent only one day in training. This training was to help you stay calm in the event you are overpowered and I cannot get to you in time. The men who were helping with this exercise were given limits and told what Samuel and I needed to achieve. You did impress me, but you cannot take on a skilled Ciatron guard and hope to defeat him." He stopped just before ascending the steps up to the Palace and turned to face her. He reached down and caressed her cheek with the back of his hand. "Do you understand?"

"Levi, I'm not going to do anything crazy. I saw the way you fought those men in the park that day you saved me, and I watched how quickly you move. I know if I practiced every day for the rest of my life, I wouldn't come close to that. I'm not going to try and be your sidekick tomorrow, I promise."

He laughed. "Thank you, love. I don't need anything else to worry about."

"Well, quit worrying. I'm not that crazy. What I am, is starving; I really need to get cleaned up."

His eyes sparkled, and he bent to kiss her. "Let's get you to your room, and I will return in an hour to escort you to dinner."

Chapter 26

inner that night seemed to be another test of Reece's abilities; although this time, the test was how long she could manage to stay awake. She did extremely well up until the point that she was seated at the table and everyone began talking. Reece struggled to respond to the conversation. Levi looked at her more than once with concern, but when he saw her cover up a yawn, his face relaxed and he grinned. *Glad I'm amusing him,* Reece thought. She couldn't blame him, though; she knew she must have looked like a half-conscious zombie. If she closed her eyes, she'd probably wake up with her face in her plate.

After dinner, Reece said her goodnights, then she placed her arm in Levi's and he escorted her to her room.

"I feel as though I should carry you to your room, as I did the other night." He chuckled.

Reece mumbled a response. She couldn't remember ever being this tired. After he left, she collapsed into bed after quickly slipping into her long, silky night gown.

The next afternoon, Reece was making final preparations for her return to Earth. Levi had secretly retrieved a comfortable pair of jeans and a warm hooded sweatshirt from her apartment for their return. Jasmeen handed her the outfit and arched her eyebrow with reproach.

Reece laughed and embraced her. "Oh, Jasmeen, don't worry; if everything goes as planned, I'll be back and in an extravagant gown sooner than you think!"

Jasmeen returned the hug. "You're right, and I'd be worried, but I know you're in excellent care."

Reece had just finished changing into her jeans and sweatshirt when Allestaine and Elizabeth arrived to escort her outside to where the men were waiting. She quickly pulled her shoes on and went to her sitting room. Allestaine and Elizabeth looked as beautiful as always—a pictorial reminder of the life Reece could not wait to return to, if she would return at all. *Will we be successful?* She felt her nerves beginning to take over and fear setting in from everything they were about to face. Reece exhaled and hoped Allestaine did not see the anxiety that she was currently battling.

Allestaine smiled sympathetically, and she embraced Reece. "Let us not be so distressed. You will return to us safe and sound. Our brave men will not allow anything to happen to you, Reece."

She withdrew and placed her hands on Reece's shoulders. She stared directly into her eyes as she spoke confidently. "There are no goodbyes today." She smiled brightly. "You must know that my husband and son will take care of you. I have no doubt of that. All our love goes with you."

Reece could say nothing; she nodded in return.

"Reece, my mother is correct. You must trust that Levi and my father would never let anything happen to you, or you would not be returning to Earth with them," Elizabeth softly added. She walked over and embraced Reece. "You will be back with all of us before you know it."

Reece smiled at Elizabeth. Seeing the strength and confidence in her eyes, she felt somewhat relieved. Therefore, she drew her strength from Allestaine and Elizabeth as they walked down the halls and out to the courtyard.

When they stepped outside, Reece caught her breath at the size of the crowd. Family and servants, some of whom Reece had never seen before, stood waiting; among them were Nathanial and Madeleine. Nathanial was to remain at the Palace to stand in Navarre's place, serving as a symbol of strength until their Emperor returned.

Beyond family and servants, there were close to thirty men with horses; some mounted, and some still bidding their loved ones goodbye. The horses were dressed as if for a parade, in red blankets embroidered with gold arrows on them. She touched her bracelet, which bore the same arrow in the patterns. The horses also had matching fabrics that covered their faces, with three red billowy feathers that stood out from the top of the horses' heads. It was a magnificent sight to behold.

All the men were dressed in black. She searched for Levi and found him talking with Navarre and Samuel. Like the others, he wore all black, the same attire she had seen in the picture in Navarre's office. He wore the tall black boots, the leather gloves, and the red-lined cloak, with as comfortable an air as he had worn a business suit on Earth. He looked tall and imposing, and then he looked over at her and smiled.

Levi and Navarre walked toward Lady Allestaine and Reece. Navarre's clothes were identical, but with silver arrows instead of gold. Braided ribbons of silver draped down along one shoulder, matching the silver lining and trim of his cape.

For the first time, Reece wished that Jasmeen would have dressed her for whatever occasion this was. She felt completely ridiculous standing there in jeans.

Levi approached his mother, and she kissed his cheek. "I'm proud of you. Do well."

Reece followed Levi out through the lined-up horses. "Levi," she whispered, "I feel like an idiot. Why is everyone, including the horses, more dressed up than I am?"

He looked at her and grinned. "Of all the questions you could ask...but indeed, you look like quite the little Earth dweller, now don't you?" He unfastened his cloak and took it off to wrap it around her. "It will keep you warm on the journey."

The importance of this departure began to sink in. "Levi?" she asked as he was checking Areion's girth. "What's with all the dress up? Are we having a parade?"

He smoothed the blanket and turned to her. "It's a gesture. The people of Pemdas are sending their Emperor away in the hope that he will return home with their husbands and sons. We're in a bad way, Reece. My father is leading the last of the Guardian's army out to free the captives, avenge the dead, and restore hope. All this," Areion lowered his head to nuzzle him, and Levi flicked the plumes on his headstall, "brings confidence to the people."

Reece hadn't considered the significance of the Emperor's departure for the Pemdai; the emotions from the crowd were palpable. Their way of life was hanging in the balance, and although pride, confidence, and steadfastness emanated from them, it was obvious that there was some apprehension about this mission.

He picked up Areion's front hoof, checked it carefully, and then reached for the hind one. As he walked around Areion, hand on the horse's hindquarters, the stallion stamped the inspected hoof. Levi chuckled. "Areion feels the same as you," he said, reaching down for the other hind hoof. "The first part of this ride will be trying for him. He's not much for show, and he's not patient." Levi bent over the fourth hoof. "I expect he'll battle me until we're past the crowds and are able to speed up."

"So, it's going to be a bumpy ride, then?"

He shook his head and laughed. "That's one way to put it. You'll be riding astride, sitting behind me this time. You'll need to hold on tight to me, my love. I would put you on with another rider, but we are going through a different vortex than the others."

Reece laughed. "Liar. You would not."

"No, you're right, I would not." He smiled as the men began to mount their horses.

Navarre approached them. "Levi. Reece. We'll see you both in Scotland." He shook his son's hand and then, to Reece's surprise, gently embraced her. "Be safe, stay close to Levi, and we will await your arrival." He turned and mounted his horse.

Areion grunted and began raising his legs one by one, appearing to dance in place. Levi exhaled and spoke deeply to his stallion. "Areion, settle. If you plan on going with them, you might allow us upon your back." The horse restrained himself for Levi and Reece to mount him.

Immediately upon settling herself in behind Levi, Reece felt the tension in the massive horse. They hadn't moved, and already it felt as if they were trotting down the road. Levi directed Areion toward Navarre's horse while the rest of the riders lined up in pairs behind them. Navarre's horse stepped out at a gentle canter, and Levi tightened his hold on Areion. He was correct in assuming that Areion would be miserable. He shook his head and whinnied in protest. Reece noticed that the rest of the horses were in step; Areion seemed to be the only one who was marching to the beat of his own drum.

Reece was surprised by how uncomfortable the ride was compared to riding him previously. Areion constantly tried to go faster. When refused permission, he threw his head up and whinnied. "Calm down, you're making a fool of yourself," Levi grumbled as they approached the village below the Palace.

Navarre looked at them with an amused expression. "Hang in there, old man, it's almost over."

Levi shook his head, and Reece held tighter. The horse stopped fighting for more speed; instead, he forced all of his energy into the ground in protest, exaggerating his movements boldly. He stamped hard onto the ground with his hooves while bringing them up just as aggressively. Fearful of being jolted off, Reece focused on the waving villagers and tried not to laugh at the insults Levi was now throwing at Areion.

After they passed the village, Navarre turned his horse toward them. He reached over and shook his son's hand. "Son, we'll see you in Scotland. Give Harrison our best, and remind him of the plans Samuel has for him."

With that, he, Samuel, and the other riders spun their horses and headed off toward the hills in the horizon. Areion began dancing in place again as Levi turned back toward Reece and managed an awkward kiss. "Hold on to me tight, love. We are taking a shorter, yet more demanding route. Are you ready?"

Areion was fighting the reins again. "I don't think it matters either way; let's just get this horse moving before he hurts himself."

Levi laughed and loosened the reins, heading Areion away from the main road toward an open meadow. Areion responded joyfully to the loosened reins, finding his stride and his speed. Reece enjoyed this part of him, feeling his power and craving to dominate the ground beneath him. She laughed inwardly as they approached a mountain range, knowing they would be heading up it. She prepared herself, holding tighter to Levi's waist.

Areion's hindquarters gathered under Reece, and he seemed to leap up the mountainside. Reece marveled at the energy and strength the horse possessed. At the top, he found a new burst of speed. The next thing she knew, they were in the air, with the gray mist beneath them. She turned back one last time to see the beautiful land she hoped to one day return to. When the mist swallowed the mountain, she turned forward just as Areion's hooves found the other side of the chasm. They were now riding through the forest of the trees with red leaves.

In front of her she saw the gates, and for the first time since understanding about her return, she felt nervous. Levi dismounted, lifted Reece off, and led Areion to the left of a large stone structure, behind where Reece remembered them parking the cars.

Two men retrieved Areion and wished Levi and Reece well.

"So, this is where you keep the horses while you're on Earth?"

"For very short visits, yes. They stay here and are attended by the stablemen." He led her through the gates. "Wait here. I'm going to bring out the car, and I must change." He grinned. "Camouflage," he said and headed for the cave that was the garage.

Reece turned around and looked back down the path; it didn't feel like it was that long ago that she'd seen it for the first time. She remembered the way she felt the last time she was in this place as she looked at the majesty of this world through astonished eyes. Her life changed forever on that day, in every way. And now, coming full circle, she admitted to herself what had been weighing in her heart for a long time: she didn't want to go back to Earth. Ever.

Pemdas was her home now, and wherever Levi was, there was no other place she would rather be.

She turned when she heard the deep purr of the black car pulling out of the garage. Levi stepped out of the car, staring down at his communication device. He looked as much at home in jeans and a T-shirt as he had in his regalia. The man complemented everything he wore.

He looked up at her inquisitively, but she only smiled in return. He shoved his device into his back pocket with a casual ease that made Reece chuckle. It was as if his body and mind, as well as his clothes, were on Earth time now.

He approached her and pulled her into a tight embrace. "Harrison is waiting for us. Apparently, my good cousin, who finds excitement in everything, has planned a little street race as our distraction."

"Nice clothes," said Reece.

He stood back and held out his arms. "You like them? I have a nice leather jacket to go with it, and a matching one for you."

Wow! was all Reece thought as she took in the perfection of the strong man standing in front of her. The simple black T-shirt he wore left nothing to the imagination of the sculpted muscles underneath it. Yet, Reece's eyes were drawn to his solid, muscular arms and the beautiful olive tone of his skin.

"Mmm, you may not blend in as well as you think," she said with a meaningful sideways look. His cheeks reddened, and she laughed. "Okay, what has Harrison planned?"

"We will be coming in through the vortex as secretly as possible. Harrison has arranged to have as many cars there as possible to distract the Ciatron. Our vortex will open up to a wooded location, the same location we were at when we left from the park. It's on these secluded highways that Harrison has planned the distraction. The forest in this location will help keep our entering and leaving concealed. He has spent the last three days in your friend Jack's company, and Jack has offered to let us use his car. Harrison felt it best to put you in a car from Earth as quickly as possible. If his plan succeeds, the Ciatron will follow the Pemdai car, and not Jack's."

Reece answered him, shocked. "Jack is with him? Will he be okay? Will anyone be hurt by the Ciatron?"

"No one will be harmed. The Ciatron, like us, need to blend in with the crowd. They will have no interest in harming anyone, except us. Now Reece, the events that are about to transpire are going to be very intense, and it is vital that you follow my instructions without hesitation. Currently, the Ciatron are more interested in the street race than the vortex. Once our car comes through, that will change. They will be immediately alerted and will pursue us."

"Then what do we do?"

"When we come out of the vortex, we will drive to where Harrison awaits us in Jack's car. He will then drive us down to the race and return for the Pemdai vehicle. The Ciatron, who are constantly scanning through people's minds, will most likely sense your presence by recognizing the barrier in your mind. Harrison will drive his car next to ours in the race. We believe the Ciatron will assume you're in the Pemdai car, and not Jack's. With the Pemdai car next to Jack's, they shouldn't question it. But in any case, Jack's car will not be fast enough for me to outrun them."

"Do they have special cars, too?"

"No, but once they see the Pemdai car, they will take a car that they believe will be fast enough to follow it. They will move very swiftly, and Harrison and I must stay ahead of their changing plans. I'll be reading their minds and finding ways to keep us ahead of them. Harrison and I will be coordinating with each other mentally as well. I need you to know in advance that I will seem extremely distant, mentally. I won't be able to talk much, or answer questions, after we start."

"I don't understand why we would go in Jack's car, though, if you just said it may not be fast enough? What happens if it's not?"

"Our plan is that Harrison will lead them away from us in the Pemdai vehicle. We have another vehicle, which you and I will be leaving Philadelphia in while the Ciatron chase Harrison. Harrison and I have to keep Jack's car ahead of them long enough to confuse them."

Reece shook her head. "I hope this works. Street racing…really? Will you be okay driving Jack's car?"

"After this afternoon, you will find that I can maneuver all sorts of vehicles quite efficiently." He kissed her softly and stared intently into her eyes. "We must leave now. Remember, I'll be in a different frame of mind from here. From this point on, I need you to follow my every move."

She nodded. "Okay."

He smiled and kissed her. "I love you. From here on, I'll be focusing on getting you safely on that plane."

"I'll be focused on not panicking."

"Good; then we each have our task." They turned toward the car, and she walked around to get in. He opened the door and smiled down at her. "You look beautiful, by the way." He winked. That would be the last personal response he gave her until they were out of harm's way.

Chapter 27

When Levi got into the car, his appearance reminded Reece of the day she met him in the park; extremely reserved. He drove them out onto the black highway toward the vortex. The car raced down the tree covered highway, and before she knew it there was a blinding flash of light and they were on Earth.

Levi turned the car sharply up a trail into a forest of trees, where they found Jack's Camaro waiting for them, with Harrison in the driver's seat. Reece was shocked to see how different Earth was to her now. The colors were extremely dull, leaving the vivid blue in Levi's eyes as the only reminder of Pemdas.

"Reece, move quickly. We have attracted the Ciatron; they are making their way here."

Hastily, they got out of the Pemdai car and into the Camaro. Harrison stepped out and helped her into the backseat. She was thankful he had the heater on; she had forgotten how cold it was in Philadelphia this time of year. She felt like she was going into shock with all the drastic changes. She could not understand how Levi, Harrison, and the rest of the Pemdai Guardians did this all the time.

She sat back in the seat, feeling the adrenaline rush through her body. She took deep breaths, but the air of Earth felt heavy and only made her anxiety worse. She closed her eyes, trying not to panic, and was thankful when Harrison teased her.

"Reece, it is nice to see you again! I believe you will enjoy the little welcome-back-to-Earth party I have arranged. We'll be joining them in about five minutes." He smiled at her in the rear view mirror.

She looked up at his playful eyes. "Nice to see you, too, Harrison. I should have known you would come up with something like this. Street racing? Lovely." She chuckled, but could not conceal the nervousness in her voice.

Harrison laughed in return.

"So after you drop us off, how do you plan to get back to the other car?" she asked, trying to figure it all out.

"Reece, I have my connections. I have a ride waiting for me even as we speak."

It seemed to be less than five minutes before they joined streets filled with hundreds of cars and crowds of people.

Reece sighed. "How did you manage to arrange this forbidden, turbo-charged competition anyway?"

He smiled back at her. "Have no worries, Reece, we won't be detained by law enforcement today." He looked over at Levi. "You know where to go from here, correct? We are only behind a couple of cars. Jack is arranging our race right now." Levi nodded as Harrison pulled the car in and parked it alongside others.

Reece understood now why this was the perfect distraction. There were so many people and cars everywhere that it was confusing to know what everyone was doing. She was glad Levi knew what to do, because everything seemed so chaotic. People stood around everywhere in groups, staring at cars, and then more gathered where the cars were racing.

Levi and Harrison opened their doors, and Harrison turned to help Reece out of the back seat. Like Levi, he wore jeans and a T-shirt.

Harrison grinned mischievously. "This is where it gets fun. If we are going to have to outrun an enemy, we might as well do it right, eh?"

Reece laughed nervously. "I guess so."

"Now, go get in the front seat; we need to get you out of here."

Reece quickly walked around the car, where Levi stood, holding her door open. Stopping to speak to Harrison for only a moment, he swiftly came around and got into the driver's seat. Reece could not help but smile at how excited Harrison was. She shook her head as a group of girls approached him and watched as he indulged himself in the attention for a few moments before disappearing through the crowds.

Levi revved the engine loudly. He pulled out into a small, open stretch of road and lined up behind two cars that were waiting to race. Reece looked over at him, wondering what the next move was and wondering if now would be the time to hold on.

He was extremely serious, and his eyes seemed to see more than just the cars in front of them. When those cars sped away like bullets, Levi pulled up to the front, where an annoyed-looking man stopped him at a certain point.

Must be mad because we have no one to race? Where is Harrison? This isn't going to work, Reece thought as she turned to see if he was anywhere around. There was no sight of the car.

Then, as if out of nowhere, the black Pemdai car slid into its place beside them. Levi's lips turned up into a tiny smile. The crowd around both cars enlarged quickly as people noticed the lustrous Pemdai car. The man in front of them was preparing to signal their start. Reece braced herself. Levi's attention shifted to his rear view mirror.

He spoke in a very low voice, almost to himself, "They are behind us. We need to leave now!"

With that, the man waved them on. Levi responded immediately, and Reece found her head pressed back against her head rest. She held tightly onto the door handle and closed her eyes. That turned out to be a bad decision; all it did was heighten the sounds of the roaring car, and as they took tight turns, almost threw her into Levi. She opened them instead and tried to focus on the road before them. Harrison's car paced the Camaro. Reece could tell he was holding his powerful car back and wished she was in the faster Pemdai car at the moment. Levi gripped the wheel tightly with one hand, and the other manipulated the speed of the car while shifting its gears. His eyes, brighter than ever, repetitively scanned the rearview mirror.

It was not long before he spoke—quiet and low, "They're with you, and we still have one with us. I'll do my best to lose them, but without enough speed, I may have to find another way."

The Camaro now tore through an empty highway. Reece felt her weight constantly shifting in the car as she tried to keep her balance. *I'm gonna be sore after this.* She hoped she would be able to walk when she got out of the car. They turned onto a private road that went up a hill. A car still followed them, and when Reece looked to Levi for reassurance, she found none reflected on his dark face.

He reached over, bracing her tightly, and turned the wheel hard. The car instantly spun around and stopped. They sat, unmoving, in the middle of the empty road, facing downhill, the way they just had come.

"Stay here," Levi ordered. "Remember what we talked about." He got out and locked the car doors. The oncoming car stopped about ten feet in front of him.

Reece's heart raced. Was Levi giving up? *Not possible.* The two front doors of the other car opened, and two very tall men got out and swiftly approached Levi.

In a matter of seconds, Levi had the first man on the ground. Then there was a bright flash, and that man disappeared. The other one leaped onto Levi, got his arm around Levi's neck, and held something against it. *What?* Reece sat on her hands to stop herself from jumping out of the car. But what could she do? She was a moment away from opening the car door to create a distraction when Levi freed himself. He swept one leg behind his captor, spun around, and held him down until another bright flash came and the man vanished.

Levi walked briskly to the car as Reece unlocked the door for him. He turned the car around in one fluid motion and sped up the hill.

"Are you okay?"

"Fine, thank you. Please reach into the back seat and put on the jacket. We are almost to our next point, and I need you to be ready to leave immediately. There are more Ciatron making their way to us. They have communicated and are no longer following Harrison. We must get away quickly."

She reached for the leather jacket and pulled it on. As she was about to ask the reason for the jacket, they pulled up to a black motorcycle. Levi parked in front of the bike and reached into the back seat for his jacket. Then he was out of the car, grabbing two helmets from the trunk and pulling Reece out of her seat.

"Now," he said, "it doesn't matter whether or not you've ever ridden a motorcycle. Just keep your feet on the pegs and hold tight so your weight shifts with mine."

Levi put the helmet over her head and fastened it. He tossed her a pair of black leather gloves and pulled her jacket zipper completely up, covering her exposed neck. "You'll freeze without the leather covering your skin."

When his own helmet and jacket were on, he sat astride the bike and started it with a roar. He pulled his gloves on and motioned for her to join him. Reece found the pegs for her feet and positioned herself on the small, uncomfortable back seat. She leaned over and wrapped her arms tightly around him. Levi shifted the bike up and off its stand and turned to head down the road. The bike responded loudly to the gears as he shifted.

As they accelerated, Levi leaned forward and then reached back and clutched around Reece's leg to pull her closer into him. She molded her body tightly against his. As soon as she did this, her stomach reacted when the bike engine roared even louder. The trees became a blur. She could not have countered if she had wanted to; she was completely frozen stiff from fear, squeezing tightly against Levi.

Her eyes shut tight. Her stomach told her the bike was turning back and forth; with each turn, gravity grabbed her stomach from the left or the right. When she found the courage to open her eyes, they were coming off a windy road and approaching a traffic jam on a highway. *At least he'll have to slow down.*

He didn't. He maneuvered the bike through the stopped cars, speeded on by unfriendly gestures from automobile drivers. Their speed increased, as did Reece's heart. It was not long before they were through the jam and the cars on the highway were moving at regular speeds again. Hesitantly, she opened her eyes. Levi left the main road and headed onto an older, two-lane highway. Reece held tight and wished for this all to be over. Turns came up; at each one, she felt as if they were lying sideways on the ground. Finally, Levi slowed and pulled into an old run-down gas station with only one car at the pumps.

He pulled up to a pump, kicked the stand down, and gave her his arm to help her off. For once, she really needed the arm; she would have fallen without it. Her legs had become completely numb, and she gripped him with both of her hands, trying to steady herself. In one swift motion, he was off the bike and still there, holding onto her. He reached down and unfastened her helmet. "My love, it's over for now. We lost them back in that traffic. I am taking a more secluded route from here to meet Harrison."

Ah! He's acting normal again, she thought. "I don't think I can walk, and I am completely serious when I say that." She took a step over to the gas pump and hung on for dear life as he took the nozzle down.

"You're doing extremely well. Have you ever ridden a motorcycle before, by chance?" he asked, teasing her.

She arched her eyebrow at him. "No, actually, I haven't. And for the first time in my entire life, I believe I was just scared stiff."

He laughed and bent down to kiss her. "My love, you enchant me." He then pulled back, looking amused. "We are almost at the location where we will meet Harrison. He is already at the airport and is preparing the plane for take-off."

She looked up at him, confused. "You're talking through your minds to each other?"

He smiled as the pump clicked off, and he hung up the nozzle. "No, love, my helmet has a phone. We can't read each other's minds if we are a great distance apart. You need to find your legs again." He winked at her, swung his leg over the bike, and rode it to the edge of the gas station parking lot.

Reece walked there with some difficulty. She glared at the offending motorcycle and wondered if she could get back on it. Levi's face was alight with amusement.

He pulled her into a tight embrace. "We only have about thirty more minutes left to ride. I will need you to get back on the bike, whether you feel you that you can or not." He stepped back and brought her helmet over her head and smiled. "Hold tightly; the faster we ride, the faster you'll be on that plane."

With that, they returned to the bike. Reece settled in close to Levi and squeezed tightly around him. He brought the deep-sounding engine to life and did not waste any time bringing the bike up to top speed.

The sun was starting to set when they pulled into a private airport. Levi rode through the entrance and stopped alongside what seemed to be their private aircraft. He set the stand down and lent his arm to Reece to help her get off the bike. Her legs were tired, but not as weak as before.

The stairs leading up into the plane had extended down to where she stood. Levi got off the bike and took off his helmet as well. His eyes seemed to be glowing again. Reece was beginning to understand now that his eyes did this whenever he was mentally communicating or reading someone's thoughts.

He walked her to the steps. "Head up the staircase. I need to park the bike."

At the top of the steps, Harrison waited. He smiled widely. "You two made perfect time!"

Reece reached out for Harrison's extended hand. "I'm beat. You guys own a private jet?"

"You'd be surprised at how we get around while we protect this world. Now, have a seat so we can get out of here."

Levi stepped into the plane. "They're only a few minutes away. Find out from the tower if we're clear to go."

Harrison walked quickly toward the cockpit.

Levi looked over at Reece. "I'll be back to sit with you once we are in the air."

He walked toward the cockpit, where Harrison was already positioning the aircraft to head out to the runway. Reece buckled into a comfortable leather seat that faced a table. Out the window, she could see three or four cars speeding into the gates of the small airport. She tensed. The airplane picked up ground speed as it followed the blinking lights toward its takeoff point.

As the plane slowed and turned, she saw people standing outside the fence, watching them. From Levi's recent report, it had to have been the Ciatron. Her heart rate began to pick up.

The next moment, the plane was speeding along the runway, and for the first time since they had come through the vortex, Reece felt truly safe. She let her head lean against the leather headrest as the plane's ascent pressed her into her seat. A glance out the window showed the land dropping away. She closed her eyes and tried to think of nothing but the peace she had been given.

Her eyes popped open after Levi unfastened her seatbelt and scooped her up. He placed her on a long leather sofa. "You need to rest, my love. The hardest part is over now, and you are safe."

"I guess I should thank you for not killing us on that motorcycle?"

She smiled as she sat up and curled her legs underneath her. She motioned for him to sit next to her, and he did. He brought his arm around her, and she snuggled into his tender embrace. Feeling the adrenaline still pumping through her veins, she knew she couldn't rest. Her mind became flooded with everything they had gone through to get to this point. "Levi—I'm curious about something."

She felt him laugh quietly as he ran his fingers through her hair. "After this afternoon, I am not surprised. What is it that you are curious about, love?"

"So, when those two Ciatron men disappeared today, they were being sent back to their dimension right?" She looked up for his response.

He stared down to her and smiled. "That is correct."

She sat up. "The Guardians can't kill them?"

"No. We are simply sending them back to their dimension. It is extremely frustrating to us, but we don't know how to completely destroy their kind."

She settled back into his embrace. "I'm just glad you are safe; it was terrifying to watch you fight them."

He squeezed her gently. "Do not ever allow yourself to worry over me like that, my love. This is what I have done for many years. I can handle myself."

"Hey!" she said. "I just thought—how's Jack supposed to get his car back?"

He laughed. "You won't stop, will you? We must find a way to calm your nerves so you can get some rest before tomorrow." He stood up. "You haven't eaten anything since breakfast; let me get you something." He turned and walked toward the front of the plane.

While he was gone, Reece found the bathroom. When she looked at her hair in the tiny mirror, she gasped. "Must be true love," she muttered as she tried to do something about the tangled mess.

When she got back, there were two plates on the table filled with fruits, vegetables, and a variety of meats and cheeses. Levi was walking over to the table with a bottle of wine. He smiled wryly at her. "Unfortunately, Harrison did not prepare us a fine dinner before our arrival." Then he laughed as he sat and poured her a glass of wine. "I believe this would probably agree with you better than Harrison trying his hand at cooking anyhow."

She reached for her glass, laughing. "And you? I was expecting a romantic meal this evening, and all I get is cold cuts and finger foods?"

Levi shot her a pitiful look. "My love, I must resolve to demonstrate my romance in some other form; I fear my culinary skills are minimal."

She laughed as she began to eat.

Levi swallowed a bite and took a sip of water. "About your friend Jack? He's probably retrieving his car now. He helped Harrison bring the motorcycle to that location. Once the little race party was over, he told Harrison he would have a friend bring him to it."

She shook her head. "I'm surprised he let you and Harrison drive his car."

Levi laughed. "Your friend Jack was only paying Harrison back for the privilege of driving our car."

Reece rolled her eyes. "Men are so ridiculous sometimes."

She leaned back in her seat and stared out of the window while Levi finished his meal. Her eyes became heavy, and she startled when Levi stood up. "Come, lie on the sofa. You look as if you could sleep."

She took his hand and followed him back to it. He brought over a pillow and blanket and wrapped it around her as she snuggled against his side.

"I'll wake you about an hour before we land, and we'll talk then. For now, just rest."

Her eyelids responded to his command, and she was asleep.

Chapter 28

Reece woke to Levi softly brushing her hair from her face. "I need you to wake, love."

She opened her eyes to find him kneeling next to her, smiling brilliantly. She grinned back to him and reached out to touch his handsome face while her eyes adjusted to the morning light on the airplane. He reached to her hand that caressed his face and gently kissed it. "I do not know what is more beautiful; watching you sleep, or the first smile of your day being intended for me."

She began to sit up. "Good morning," she managed.

"I made you some toast and attempted to make you some scrambled eggs. Hopefully, you'll like them; I'm not really one to cook."

She laughed as he led her over to the table. She looked down and smiled at the perfectly sliced oranges that Levi used to garnish the plate.

As he sat down to join her, she looked across the table at him and smiled. "This looks delicious, Levi. Thank you, but aren't you and Harrison going to eat, too?"

He nodded. "We already have. Fortunately, Harrison approved of my cooking, or else you would be having orange slices and toast for breakfast." He laughed.

Levi poured her some orange juice as she took a bite of the scrambled eggs. "Levi, they are delicious!"

He grinned. "I'm glad you approve." He then became more serious. "Reece, I fear today will be very demanding. We are facing a situation with an uncertain outcome. There is only one thing I *will* be sure about, and that is your safety. I will not allow you out of my sight, under any circumstance." He reached for her hand. "No matter what the outcome of this day, you will be leaving Castle Ruin by my side."

Reece nodded.

"My father has an enormous challenge awaiting him today as he faces the Council of Worlds. What Simone and Michael have done has not only put all of Pemdas at risk, but it has also destroyed our reputation and good faith with the other worlds. My father must restore their trust in us while ensuring that you are kept safe." His eyes grew dark, and he reached for her hand. "I am not trying to frighten you; I just need you to be prepared for whatever I may do at any given moment. I will remove you from any intended harm." His eyes were as sincere as his promise. "We are going into this situation at a disadvantage. We must trust that Samuel and Harrison will free the rest of the Guardians, because we will need them immensely."

Reece finished her breakfast and followed Levi as he stood from the small table. He brought her into a tight embrace. "I have my own plans, if their plans fail. I love you, Reece. I will protect you. Do you trust that I will?"

She looked up at him unquestioningly. "Of course, I do."

He kissed her head softly. "Freshen up, my love; there are clothes in the back room for you to change into. We will begin our descent into Scotland soon. We have contacted Samuel, and he is waiting to retrieve us from the airport."

When she was ready for the day, she found a seat on the plane as it began its descent into the beautiful country beneath them. Reece had always had a great desire to visit Scotland, and she laughed as she thought about the circumstances that she was finally able to do so. *This isn't exactly how I would've planned it.*

The airplane descended smoothly onto a private airport runway and followed the markers to its destination. Two black Pemdai cars waited, and the plane came to a stop next to them. As the engines shut down, Levi and Harrison exited the cockpit and came to her.

Levi led the way, dressed in a dark business suit. Harrison, in contrast, wore sniper attire—a tight-fitting, long-sleeved shirt with a high neck and black pants tucked into black, lace-up boots. He smiled at Reece. "Did you enjoy your breakfast? Levi only went through two cartons of eggs to make them." He laughed.

She grinned. It amazed her how the guy was always in a great mood, regardless of the circumstance. "Actually, I did. And scrambled eggs can be a challenge—nobody likes them slimy."

He laughed as he walked past Levi, who was stopping to help Reece up from her chair.

Harrison walked to the back room of the plane while the stairs were being brought down, giving Reece and Levi a moment alone.

Levi brought Reece into a tight embrace. "My love, stay close to me, and remember what you learned in your training. I need you to stay focused, as best you can." He bent to kiss her, letting his lips linger on hers.

When Harrison returned, he was pulling a black leather glove onto his left hand. "Ah! Practicing for the council today?" He arched his brow, teasing them both.

Reece's cheeks flushed, but Levi laughed. "I'm willing to give it a try. It may buy you some time if you have trouble freeing the men we need."

"When have I ever failed a mission? Give me a mission impossible, and I will shine!"

He wore black leather protective gear over his clothing. It formed to his body and covered his chest, arms, and the upper half of his legs. Knives and other weapons were sheathed and strapped to his legs and arms. Harrison shook Levi's hand and clapped him on the shoulder. "Be careful, Levi. I'll have your back when you least expect it."

"I know," said Levi. "You always do."

Harrison bent down to give Reece a hug. "Say 'hi' to Movac for me!" As he stepped back, his features became somber. "You're in good hands. Do not fear; this will all be over soon enough." He nodded, and then he was gone, down the steps to the ground.

"Are you ready?" Levi asked as he held out his arm for her.

She put her arm through his and let him lead her down the steps to where Harrison and Samuel stood in conversation.

Samuel, who was dressed in the same clothing as Harrison, extended his hand to Levi. "Excellent work yesterday, Levi." His expression became solemn. "Let us go bring our men home. Levi, follow Harrison and me. If all goes well, we'll have our men freed quickly and will join you in the council."

Harrison and Samuel got into the first black car while Levi led Reece to the one waiting behind it. They followed them out of the private airport, where ten other black cars joined them; half of them pulled in front of Samuel and Harrison, and the other half followed behind Levi and Reece. Levi remained calm, but was very quiet. His eyes were glowing brightly; Reece knew that he was listening in, mentally, on the conversation in Samuel and Harrison's car. He held her hand and absently rubbed it with his thumb.

As the cars sped through secluded mountain roads, Reece was awed by the breathtaking landscape. The bright green hills reminded her of Pemdas, though the colors were less vivid. After a while, she found she was clenching Levi's hand tightly.

"We are getting closer. Are you all right?"

She inhaled softly. "Yeah, I think so." But everything began to weigh on her. She did not know what to expect or how bad things were about to get. She rested her head back against the seat and tried to compose herself. She forced herself to take comfort in Levi's words. Of course she trusted him, but she was not sure if he could save them.

They traveled on a gravel road that cut through the soft green grass of the rolling hillside for about ten minutes before Harrison, Samuel, and the other vehicles veered off the road suddenly, cutting through the grass. Levi continued on the gravel road as it ascended up the hillside.

It wasn't until they crested the hill that Reece saw an enormous castle situated on the mountain top. *Castle Ruin.* It was obvious that this was a stately castle in its time; however, what seemed to be hundreds of years of neglect had left it in shambles.

As Levi maneuvered the car to the front steps of the building, two men descended the steps that led to the entrance. Levi was out of the car and opening Reece's door before they reached them. The men were very tall and very pale, and they smiled sinisterly at Reece and Levi as they approached them. Their eyes were vacant, seemingly lifeless.

Levi had his arm braced tightly around her. "Step aside," Levi commanded.

As Levi guided Reece past the men to begin their ascent up the stone staircase, one of the men put his arm out to stop him. Levi stopped and exhaled. "Remove your hand from me, now!" he growled.

The man stood face-to-face with Levi. "Guardian, you will serve me soon. I suggest you show me the respect a master deserves!"

Levi reached out and gripped the man's neck. In the same moment, he lurched forward and head-butted him. As he dropped to the ground, Levi half-guided, half-carried Reece up the steps toward the other man, who backed away and let them pass.

His grip on her was starting to become uncomfortable. She looked up at his angry face and touched his hand. The grip loosened, and he looked down toward her. "Stay focused," he commanded.

He marched them forward at an extremely fast pace through dark halls, lit by widely-spaced flickering candles. Her heart was pounding in her chest. Nothing seemed to calm her, not even him. Levi warned her, but she had not fully comprehended the danger they were in. Yesterday, adrenaline had shielded her; today, with an extremely angry and mentally detached Levi, she feared everything.

As panic began to filter its way into every rational thought she had, she started to fight Levi's grip. She felt claustrophobic, and she couldn't catch her breath.

Without warning, Levi turned into a darkened room. Reece's heart rate matched her breathing; she tried slowing them, but was unsuccessful.

Levi braced the back of her head with his hand and brought his mouth next to her ear. "Are you all right?" he whispered gruffly. "I know you are scared, but I need you to calm yourself down. This will be over soon, but we are currently in great danger. You must focus on what you learned in your training. I cannot be confident that I will get you to my father if you are panicking or fighting me."

"I don't know if I can do this," she whispered, still trying to catch her breath.

"You don't have an option anymore. You have to," he commanded. "It's imperative that you restrain your fear in order for me to protect you. Samuel and Harrison are facing the same dangers we are, and their plans depend upon our making it into that council. Ciatron defenders are scattered throughout, waiting for us to come through the castle. You must focus; I know you can do this."

It was exactly what she needed to hear. Even though she was frightened far beyond what she could have imagined, she needed to gain her composure. "Yes," she said as she took a breath. "Yes."

"Very well, we must go. Do not be afraid; I will protect you. This is what I am trained to do."

He took hold of her arm and led her from the dark room and back into the bleak hallway. The candles flickered eerily; shadows came and went where there seemed nothing to cast them.

A man jumped out of the shadows. As the man approached them, Levi thrust the heel of his hand into the man's chest. The moment his hand struck the man, there was a loud crack. Levi threw him up against the wall, turned back to Reece, and gripped her arm tightly. "Quickly. Move," he said in a deadly tone.

They marched on swiftly, hearing noises from behind. A grand staircase before them was lit by hundreds of candles. Levi led her up the steps. "We're close," he said distantly.

It seemed as though there was nothing left but empty hallways, and Reece began to gain confidence. Levi led them around a corner, and they began to walk down a narrow passageway. Then, it all happened in an instant. One moment Levi had her in his tightened grip, the next she was torn from it. She screamed as she was dragged backward into a dark room. Her heart felt as though it had stopped. She tried to scream again, but nothing came out. As she tried to fill her lungs with air in order to call out to Levi, a large hand clamped down over her mouth.

The door to the room was open, and Reece saw bright flashes of light coming from the hallway. The arm that was wrapped around her abdomen was squeezing her back into her captor's chest. "We've got you now!" a raspy voice snarled into her ear. She pushed against the arm with all her strength, but was unsuccessful in freeing herself.

The doorway was now completely dark. Where was Levi? What happened to him? Her body would not respond to anything she forced it to do. She was paralyzed with fear. She forgot how to inhale; her legs felt numb beneath her. Her heart pounded so loudly that she could hear nothing else. *Focus, Reece!*

She stared into the darkness for Levi, but didn't find him. She began to recall her training; she had to find a way out of this attack. She tried to spin out of the man's grip, but was not successful in releasing herself; he was too powerful. She was, however, successful in removing his hand from her mouth, and she managed to scream. "LEVI!"

No sooner had she screamed before the hand seized her mouth again, wrenching her head back. As she struggled to break free, she felt a sharp blow to her kidney so forceful that she buckled, yet the captor held her so tight that she never fell to the ground.

As the captor dragged her backwards, Reece continued to stare into the darkness, hoping to see any sign of Levi. Her heart nearly stopped when she noticed a faint blue glow out of the corner of her eye. Levi's eyes.

Her attacker stopped his backward motion. "Come any closer, and I will snap her neck!" His voice did not sound like the men they encountered at the entrance to the castle. It was normal, like Levi's.

Reece kept fighting him, searching for a way out. The eyes she thought she had seen were gone. She struggled to breathe as the man's large hand covered her mouth and nose.

"I know you're in here, Oxley. Why don't you show yourself? Are you the coward your father is? SHOW YOURSELF!" the man screamed in her ear. "You know I will rule over you, Levi. They have made me one of them! Once we take you captive, Pemdas will be mine to rule!" The man laughed darkly. "Once we get the map to the stone from the girl, we will control everything. Pemdas will be…"

Her captor's body jerked, and in that instant Reece was able to break loose and fall to the ground. As soon as she was on the ground, she twisted around, facing where the man was that she freed herself from, and scurried backward on her hands and feet until her back hit a wall. As fast as she could, she stood up against the wall.

She could hear nothing except for rustling and heavy breathing coming from the middle of the room. She struggled, without success, to see through the dark and interpret what she was hearing.

After hearing a loud, guttural moan, the room fell silent. Was it Levi who had ended the struggle? She couldn't tell and could not trust whoever was left in the room with her. She moved as quietly as she could, breathing slowly and shallowly, away from where she heard the scuffle.

"Reece?" It was Levi.

Relief flooded through her. "Levi!" She reached into the darkness and found him standing in front of her. His hands found hers, and he pulled her into his chest, holding her tightly for a brief moment. "We must leave at once. Come with me now," he said as he marched them briskly out of the room.

When two men advanced on them in the hallway, Levi reacted without hesitation. In one fluid motion, he lunged forward and struck the first man in his throat with a powerful blow; he planted his foot solidly on the ground and whipped his other leg around until it connected with the second man's knee with a loud, resonating crack. Before the man's body buckled to the ground, Levi followed up with his fist and struck him in the jaw. Both men seemed to hit the ground at the same time, unconscious. Reece was shocked by how quickly the entire exchange had taken place. Levi was back at her side in an instant, clutching her around the waist as they charged past the attackers.

They turned a corner and walked down a short hallway before stopping at a doorway. Levi shoved the heavy wooden doors open, and they stepped into a large room. Navarre and six other Pemdai men were waiting inside.

"Levi! Son, whose blood is on your shirt? The Ciatron do not bleed…are you injured?"

Levi responded, "It's Michael Visor's blood; he was part of their plan to intercept Reece."

Navarre's face became fierce. He reached his arm up around his son's neck and drew him in to meet his eyes. "Let us finish this, now! I will abide this no longer!"

The fury in Levi's face mirrored his father's when he nodded in response.

Navarre looked to his guards. "As soon as we enter the council chambers, go retrieve Michael. Take him directly to Pemdas." He looked at Levi. Father and son's eyes glowed fiercely.

Levi took Reece into his arms one last time. "Remember our conversation on the airplane this morning." He reached into his inner coat pocket and pulled out two tiny gold ovals with arrows engraved on them. He placed one on each side of her forehead, and they adhered to her skin.

She looked at him quizzically. "What are these?"

"There will be many different languages spoken in this council chamber today; these will interpret the languages so that you can understand what is being said. I want you to be able to hear it firsthand instead of waiting for me to interpret it for you."

"Oh, okay." Her heart was pounding again.

He stared confidently into her eyes, and then gave her hand to his waiting father. Navarre escorted her toward two large doors as Levi walked protectively at her other side. Their faces bore the gravest expressions she had ever seen.

The doors opened slowly, and Reece gasped at the scene before her.

Chapter 29

The faces that stared at her were not all human-like. *Aliens.* She had never considered the possibility that all of the stories—myths, legends, conspiracy theories—that she had heard about could actually be true. She supposed there was life out there, but the visual realization of it was shocking. Until now, her understanding of aliens went no further than the Pemdai, who were much like the people of Earth. The room was filled with over a hundred different strange entities, and it took Reece a moment to be able to comprehend the reality of the sight before her eyes.

There were beings in the crowd that resembled unfathomable creatures. Creatures that, despite Hollywood's best imaginations, were more frightening to look at than anything she'd ever seen; real or imaginary. One had a dragon-like face, with bone-like spikes throughout it. It had scales covering his body, claws for hands, and a serpent-like tongue slipped in and out from between its slender lips. Another had a shiny, brown, elongated head. It's large, round eyes glowed red and appeared to highlight its razor sharp teeth. These monsters looked like evil incarnate. As she looked away, she recalled the first time Navarre explained to her about the other dimensions and worlds apart from her own. He couldn't understand why Earth's leaders kept it all a secret from their people. At this moment, she understood why and was grateful that they did keep it a secret from everyone. Even as she stood between the two fearless men who protected Earth from these things, she wondered; if she were to survive this, would she have nightmares for the rest of her life? She pulled her eyes away from the horrifying beings and hoped she would easily forget what they looked like.

There were others that were more fascinating than they were frightening. One individual looked as though he, if it was a 'he', was transparent. His neighbor had an enormous sized head atop his tiny body. Another being's skin was colored such a bright red that it made her eyes water just by glancing at it.

Her heart almost stopped when her eyes fell upon a group of well-known men that she recognized from Earth. From the faces she recognized, she could easily discern that all of the major leaders from Earth were in attendance. They stared intently and somberly in her direction. They sat close to the front, where long wooden tables stretched the entire length of the enormous, open room. Three long tables were arranged in horseshoe shape, with the opening facing the door. Behind the closed end of the horseshoe, another table stood on an elevated platform. At this table sat six individuals; two of them human-looking, the other four were not. Two of them spoke to each other quietly, yet stared darkly at Reece.

Whether or not she felt safe with Levi and Navarre, she wanted out of this room. She hoped that Harrison and Samuel would arrive with their men quickly and this would all be over.

A voice spoke as if it were coming through loudspeakers, and the oddness of it startled her as the sound resonated through the dimly lit room. "Thank you for honoring our request, Navarre. Now, release the Key and let her come forward."

Reece clenched Navarre's arm tightly, and her other hand, of its own accord, reached for Levi's rigid arm. He brought his arm up to accept her gesture. She stood gripping the arms of the two tall men, staring into the crowd as a large, skinny creature stood up from his seat behind the table. His entire body was opaque gray, with long, slender arms and legs. His head was elongated with a narrow face and large black, oval eyes.

Navarre answered. "The woman will remain with us until this issue has been resolved. Then, she will leave with us." He turned his commanding face to those who sat around the tables staring at them. "We are not here to honor anyone's requests! We are simply here to demonstrate that the accusations against our kind are untrue. We also come to insist that all of our men, who you have unjustly imprisoned, be released immediately. We stand before you for no other reasons."

The gray creature walked out from behind the table on the platform. He stepped down to the floor and made his way through the center of the tables before he stopped. "Emperor Navarre, I see that you have come here today believing, in ignorance, that you hold a superior position to the rest of us. Could the child clinging to your arm be the source of that delusion?"

"Do not fool yourself into believing that I will stand here and tolerate your frivolous accusations, Movac," Navarre said sternly. "I demand an explanation for the imprisonment of my men."

Movac laughed and shook his head. "Emperor, you and your men are no longer to be trusted. Therefore, we took the necessary precautions." He stretched forth his long arm toward Reece. "Allow her to come forward, away from you, so that we may regain the trust we all once had. We need answers from her, as well."

Navarre growled back, "She is not here for the Council; I am! I suggest you find another way to regain your trust in us. Provoking me and dismissing my demands will not help this situation."

Movac stopped and turned his back to Navarre. "Interesting, isn't it, Navarre?" He turned back around with a hostile look on his face. His tone changed entirely. "You forget who you are speaking to, Guardian! Do you not understand what you face? All the dimensions demand answers, and until they receive them, you stand here as an enemy!" His wicked mouth turned up into a sneer. "I suggest you choose your words carefully, Emperor."

Navarre inhaled deeply, and Reece could feel him controlling his rage. "Very well, then. If there are questions of me, let them be asked. The woman will remain at my side."

A strange voice spoke, causing Reece to search the faces in the room to see who it came from. She could not place it until the transparent being stood. "Navarre, we have been close throughout all of our years serving as our lands' trusted leaders. These words are not so easily spoken by me, but unfortunately, I cannot apologize for my concerns." He paused before continuing. "Since ancient times, we have always trusted the Guardians to protect

Earth. Unfortunately, how can we trust anyone who holds the one thing in their possession that can give them supremacy over all of our worlds? I cannot believe that you would not be tempted in the least to unlock the information in this woman's mind; therefore, I am forced to question your motives."

Navarre turned a bit to face his accuser. "Before questioning my integrity, Misqualis, question your perspective. We. Are. Pemdai. 'Guardian' was not a self-imposed title; it was granted us by this very council, for our service of protecting all of you. Now you stand here and question those who have protected you? You fear being ruled by outside forces, and yet you are being ruled by fear itself. It is not now, nor has it ever been, the desire of the Pemdai to rule over other worlds; but simply to allow each its own autonomy, and to live in peace ourselves."

He gently removed Reece's arm from his, leaving her in Levi's care. He walked a couple of paces in front of them. "I will not stand here and be told that the Pemdai can't be trusted, after all our kind has done for every one of you. Have you all so quickly forgotten the battle that was fought many years ago, which necessitated the creation of this stone?" He waited for a response from the crowd.

The Ciatron leader stared at him fiercely. "Of course we have not forgotten what your ancient Guardians helped to create, Navarre! How could we? However, you speak of the past. Why must the Guardians believe that our kind still seek to control the Earth?"

"Movac, your kind has always sought power to rule over everything in its entirety. It is why the stone is hidden away, never to be found."

Movac smiled widely. "Is it hidden, Navarre? I believe you have the answer in the Earthling, and you will soon take your place over us all; using the powers of the stone to manipulate the Earth, and therein, the junctions by which we all travel."

Navarre spoke gravely in return. "Even if I sought such things, the map cannot be retrieved to locate the stone. It may be in her mind, but it is absolutely inaccessible."

Another voice echoed in the room. "So you admit to having tried to access the information, Emperor? What would be the reason for such an act? If you have taken the Key into your dimension for her protection alone, as you so claim, why would you have that knowledge?"

Before Navarre could answer, Movac spoke, "The reason is power. That's what the Pemdai are after. They say they serve all of us by keeping Earth unharmed—but from whom? From us—all of us—the other worlds that only seek to learn from the peculiar planet. We do not need anyone to police us!" he snapped. "I do not remember any world asking for the Guardians to protect Earth. We all rightfully have access to it."

Navarre faced him squarely. "We do not require anyone's approval to do what is necessary to protect the Earth. Your kind is not to be trusted."

He looked around, catching the eye of each being in the room. "I ask everyone here to remember the last confrontation with the Ciatron. They used their knowledge to manipulate the people of Earth into believing that they were their gods and creators. If it were not for the creation of the stone by this woman's ancestor, we would all have been enslaved or destroyed by this enemy who stands before us now. If you believe Movac would not attempt this again, you are greatly deceived."

Movac snarled viciously. "Those days are gone!" He stepped aggressively toward Navarre. "You stand there and resurrect the days that almost destroyed our entire world. You treat me as if I were a fool! Of course I remember the Battle of the Ancient Guardians; our world will never forget it."

Levi brought his arm up and embraced Reece, bringing her closer to him. Movac turned to look at them. He walked over and stood towering over Reece and Levi.

Reece felt strangely calm. In fact, as she stared into Movac's black, almond eyes, she felt an odd desire to withdraw from Levi's tightened embrace and walk to her enemy. He smiled down at her as Levi's arm tightened even more around Reece.

"Step away from her, now!" Levi commanded.

Movac smiled. "You love this human. Ah, this is all the more interesting."

Navarre interjected from behind him. "Movac! Leave the woman, and my son, now! If you are to be trusted, then why, may I ask, are you trying to persuade her to go with you?"

Movac turned to face Navarre, releasing the mental hold he had over Reece. As he did, she felt her panic return and clung closer to Levi. She shook her head, trying to figure out what had happened to her.

"You may ask nothing of me!" He turned to face the rest of the room. "Members of the Unification, may I ask what your final word is on Emperor Navarre and the rest of the Guardians who have controlled our well-being in their own way for all these years?"

Navarre stepped back to Levi and Reece. He exchanged a glance with his son. Reece felt as though they were losing any hope of coming to a resolution. There was no sign of Harrison and the rest of the men, and she stood ready for whatever Levi led them to do.

A young man who was seated at the elevated table, one of the few in the room that looked human, stood. "I see no reason to trust the Pemdai any longer. All these years, we have believed they were protecting us, when in reality they were limiting us. Emperor Navarre, I may speak only for myself and my land, but we do not need the Pemdai to have any say over what we seek out of Earth. You have used the power we have given the Guardians to break the treaty and bring the Key to the stone into your own world. I believe the woman should be taken from them and kept on Earth, where she belongs," he finished and resumed his seat.

408

Another stood. "I agree with Lucas! I, too, have underestimated the control we have given to one world by allowing them to rule over a land that is not theirs. The woman must be returned to Earth."

The one with the dragon-like face stood. "Let the Council know, and understand, that the removal of the woman from her place on Earth is a direct violation of the Xylander treaty, signed after the great battle. As such, this Council is justified in whatever retribution they so choose."

Others in the room eventually stood and agreed, leaving Navarre helpless.

Movac turned around and smiled. "I agree, as well. By breaking the treaty, these Pemdai have overstepped their boundaries as Guardians. I will insist upon a punishment for them, and for all of the inhabitants of Pemdas."

Navarre remained silent as the room proceeded to discuss the punishment. One stood. "There can be no greater punishment than to require them to stay upon their own soil, never to return to Earth." The room agreed in unison.

Reece realized it had all been decided before they even entered the room. She felt sick. Levi stood as still as a statue, and Navarre stepped forward to say, "You all have been gravely misled. I am sorry for your ignorance."

Movac looked back toward where Levi and Reece stood and nodded.

Instantly, Reece was removed from Levi's grip. Two beings held her, one on each side. They were not the

Ciatron, but very tall, slender, orange beings with elongated heads. Levi had three dragon-faced beings attempting to restrain him as he fought violently to free himself. It took another three combatants to finally overpower and restrain him.

Tears welled up in Reece's eyes as she watched him in this vulnerable state. She turned to see what had become of Navarre. She was surprised to see him standing there, unrestrained. His eyes began to brighten as he stared at his son, who was being held up against a wall. Levi's enraged expression began to fade, and his eyes became vivid as well.

Navarre turned and addressed Movac. "Release my son, now!"

Movac laughed. "Navarre, have you not been listening to anything? We will no longer live under the Pemdai Guardians. Your son will be released when you both are returned to your land for confinement."

Navarre turned back to Levi and continued to stare deeply into his eyes. Levi's eyes closed, and he exhaled. Were they defeated? Reece felt the room spinning around her. She could not remember how to breathe. A black blur came over her vision; the voices of the council members rang in her ears, and she began to lose consciousness. It was over. She no longer felt her heart beating and no longer felt her legs beneath her as she drifted off.

As she lost consciousness, her mind began to display comforting images of Levi and the safety he had provided for her...

All of her memories of their time together flashed rapidly through her mind—every moment they had shared, from her first sight of him in Philadelphia to the present day.

She remembered his words on the airplane from earlier that morning. *"I have my own plans, if theirs fail. I love you, Reece. I will protect you. Do you trust that I will?"* The words echoed in her head. *"Do you trust that I will?"*

Reece slowly came to, only to see Levi being dragged toward the front of the room as the Ciatron leader approached him. Navarre stood captive between two Ciatron beings.

She could not bear to witness this, but she knew that neither Levi nor Navarre would let it end like this. She knew they had the power and superior strength to free them somehow.

Just then, the two doors in the front and the two doors in the back of the council chamber opened simultaneously, and in charged countless Pemdai warriors.

The warriors parted as Samuel and Harrison entered, followed by even more Guardians. For the first time, Harrison looked fearsome and ready for war. When he looked at Reece, his face was rigid and dark with fury. "It would be wise to release this woman...now!" he demanded. He stepped forward and in a seemingly effortless array of movements put one of her captors on the floor and restrained the other. Harrison moved so rapidly that Reece couldn't figure out what he had done to send the second captor to the ground, writhing in pain. Harrison offered Reece his left arm, and she took it.

Everyone in the room appeared to be frozen, except for the Pemdai warriors who swiftly secured the room. Levi and Navarre were released. The room was silent. Their accusers were at a loss for words as they found themselves surrounded, their lives subject to Navarre's next command.

Navarre's voice broke the silence. "It is no mystery now that you all sit in this room at my mercy." He made his way to the center of the room. "If I were the untrustworthy man you believe me to be, answer me now: why should I not take action against all of you this instant?" He walked down through the tables. "Do I not have every right? All of you insult me with your foolish accusations and threaten to exile me and enslave my people to our land?"

The Ciatron leader stood silent as Navarre continued to question them. "I may forgive your ignorance, but I will not forget your foolishness! Everyone in this room has proven to me they can never be trusted!"

The same young, human-looking man that spoke earlier stood. "Emperor Navarre, you must be reasonable. Regardless of whether or not you allow us to live, or by your authority we perish, if you leave this room with anything less than an agreement with this Council, you will have signed a declaration of war and the subsequent extinction of your people."

Navarre turned with fury. "You speak of declarations of war, Lucas…after you enslaved thousands of my men? You speak of agreements with the Council after you lured me here by a plan of entrapment? Know this! Pemdai are ruled by no council. The Pemdai are ruled by honor and duty. We will defend our lives, the lives of those on Earth, and the lives represented by every member of this Council. If you view this as a declaration of war, then so be it! Let me remind you, the treaty was that the stone was to remain on Earth. It mentioned nothing of the Key. We leave this Council by the treaty, justified in our actions! I came here today only to gather what is mine and to return to my land with the Key, which was entrusted to us by your ancestors. We will defend her with our lives. If you seek her, be ready to exchange her life for your own, for that will be the cost. The Key will reside in Pemdas; if you seek to pursue it, then you shall bleed on our soil, as we have bled on yours for thousands of years while defending it. If you decide to question this plan of action, then maybe you should question the one who deceived you all to begin with." He glanced darkly at Movac.

Navarre turned to leave, then a voice of reason spoke out. "Emperor Navarre, if I may have one last word before you leave us on these terms."

Navarre stopped and turned back to face the council.

"Your Excellency," the voice continued. "You have reminded me of the legends told to me as a child. Legends that spoke of the bravery and sacrifice your people have endured for us all. It shames me greatly that this Council, in its lack of wisdom, has forgotten that history lesson. Trust is not given; trust is earned. And the Pemdai have earned the trust of all worlds, time and time again. Never before has this Council parted without a unified directive. Therefore, I ask that all members present stand in support of Emperor Navarre's declaration to return the Key to the protection of Pemdas. I ask not that you blindly give your trust to the Guardians, but that you simply remember who they are and respect their resolve."

As the Council stood in unison, Navarre acknowledged their concession with a nod. He sent silent command to Samuel. At Samuel's word, the Guardians stood down and fell into formation behind Emperor Navarre and Samuel as they exited the council chambers.

Chapter 30

As As the Guardians followed Navarre and Samuel out through the doors, Reece saw Levi quickly making his way over to them. Without hesitation, she walked briskly toward him, and they collided into a powerful embrace. Reece buried her face into Levi's neck and sighed with contentment.

Levi's lips brushed along the side of her cheek as he brought one hand up to tenderly caress the back of her neck. "It is over, my love," he said softly.

She closed her eyes and relaxed further into his sturdy embrace. She tightened her arms around his slender waist, grateful she was safely in his arms again. She felt Levi rest his chin on the top of her head as his hands tenderly caressed up her back.

He slowly withdrew and stared deeply into her eyes. "Let's get you out of here," he said as he drew her arm up into his.

Levi escorted Reece toward the doors, where they met Harrison. As the three of them followed the last of the warriors making their way out of the room, Levi reached over to Reece and plucked the translators from her temples.

Reece glanced back at the room. The council members were not speaking to one another, but were making their ways out of the front doors to the room. The entire atmosphere of the room had changed; instead of the thick, condemning pressure from earlier, humility reigned.

As they exited the castle, the Guardians filed down the countless stone steps while Levi led Reece and Harrison to the edge of the balcony, where Navarre and Samuel stood.

Reece could not believe her eyes when she saw what awaited them. The balcony overlooked acres upon acres of flat, neatly trimmed grass, surrounded by a stone wall. She stood in awe of all the spacecrafts that were being boarded by the council members, waiting to travel back to their own dimensions. Some of the crafts glowed, and then quickly disappeared, without ever moving. Four triangular ships rose simultaneously from the ground and sped off sideways before they vanished. One by one, she watched the different shaped vessels disappear.

She watched Movac, who was trailed by about twenty of his men as he walked up onto a platform and into a large, round spaceship.

"Have we lost any men?" Navarre asked while staring intently at Movac's ship.

"We were fortunate to not lose any of our men, Emperor. We have had only four wounded, and they have already been taken back to Pemdas," Samuel answered.

"I wonder," said Harrison, "is this the same triumphant feeling that the Ancient Guardians experienced after they defeated the Ciatron? Because I must say, there is nothing more enjoyable than watching Movac get up into that ridiculous craft with the knowledge that all of his scheming was for nothing. Now he must return to his lands and hope that the leaders in the Council today did not recognize his true motive!" He laughed. "Once again, The Pemdai have sent the Ciatron home wondering if all the worlds will choose to unite against them."

Navarre continued to stare straight ahead as he answered him, "Indeed, I believe that the feelings of victory felt by our ancestors were the same as what we are feeling at this moment."

He turned and addressed the four of them. "However, we all must understand that today Movac will return home with his men, only to begin plotting his next move. The

Ciatron never have, and never will, give up their pursuit of the Key, or the power that comes with the discovery of the stone. However, we shouldn't be prideful over this victory. We must never believe that we have ended their cause."

Navarre turned back to watch the departing vessel. "I suppose they will leave Earth today with heightened motivation for finding more creative ways of pursing Reece." His features softened. "For now, let us all enjoy the short reprieve we have been given."

The Ciatron were the last to leave the grounds, leaving only the Pemdai men below. Reece watched as the crowd of Guardians made their way to their cars and quickly sped away from the castle.

Navarre turned to Levi and clapped him on the arm. "Well done today, Levi. I know it was not an easy task. I am proud of you."

Harrison interjected, "And here I thought Samuel and I had a hand in saving the day, too."

Navarre chuckled. "Harrison, you and Samuel have made me, and all of Pemdas, proud today! No doubt your father will be honored by your achievements, as well." Navarre went on, teasing his nephew, "Although your timing could have been a little faster."

Harrison laughed. "I'll have to keep that in mind for the next time I'm ordered to ambush a hundred men with a company of thirty soldiers. Please excuse my tardiness."

"Here we go," Levi smiled mischievously at his cousin.

"Samuel will need to document the facts of their rescue mission because Harrison is sure to embellish this story each time he reminds us of it for the next sixty years."

Harrison laughed loudly. "I only repeat the stories of my victories because I know how much everyone loves to hear them."

Navarre broke through the jesting and said, "I am grateful to each one of you standing here with me, for if any of us were absent today, we would most likely not be standing here with each other now. Now, let us return home; I am certain the Empress impatiently awaits us. I should not like to be chided for taking my time returning home when she is so eager to see all of us safe and sound."

He looked at Reece. "As you heard in the council meeting, I have made it very clear to all that you will be living amongst us in Pemdas. I know this is your home, and we will never stop trying to find a way for you to return, if that is your wish. For now, I must insist that you to return with us. I know that my wife and daughter will be thrilled by the news," he glanced at Levi with a subtle grin, and looked back at Reece, "as well as the others in my family."

Reece smiled, unsure of how to respond.

Navarre then offered, "Harrison and Levi will escort you back to your apartment to retrieve anything you wish to bring with you. I would ask that you use this time to bid your farewells to any friends or family members that you have. This may not be easy, but it is not only for your safety, but for theirs as well."

He turned to Levi. "I am only comfortable with your remaining on Earth for three days, at most. I will have Samuel dispatch a Guardian unit to stand by, should you need backup during your stay. I know the Ciatron will not return, but I will not take any chances. Use every minute you have on Earth wisely. Our men will be waiting and watching from the minute your plane lands in Philadelphia until they have seen you back through to Pemdas. We will see you all then."

With that, he smiled widely, turned, and walked down the steps with Samuel toward their vehicle.

Harrison put his arm on Levi's shoulder, squeezing Reece where she stood between them. "Well kids, it's just us again! There is only one thing I must know before our departure…" He breathed in deeply and let out an exaggerated sigh. "Is Reece content with these arrangements? You realize you're going to have a love-struck fool chasing you around every day, don't you?"

Reece laughed. "I'm sure I'll manage."

"We'll see about that!" Harrison stepped back and ruffled Levi's hair. "I'll meet you two lovebirds at the car!" he said as he turned to hop down the steps toward the car.

Levi turned to face Reece. She stared deeply into his brilliant blue eyes as he smiled at her. "You did extremely well today, Reece." Relief and happiness were apparent in his voice.

She gazed into his eyes, eyes that reflected everything he felt for her. He was so unbelievably handsome when he smiled at her in this manner.

There was nothing she wanted more than Levi. She knew, if given the option, she could never choose living on Earth over living in Pemdas. She felt as though she didn't belong on Earth anymore. Since her father's death, she had no real attachment here. Her absence would go noticed only by her college friends, and that would easily be worked out.

She studied Levi's face, intrigued by the man she loved. He not only saved her life physically, he had saved her in many more ways than he would probably ever understand. He filled a void that she didn't know existed. She didn't know she was missing anything until she fell in love with him. She reached up and caressed his cheek. He caught her hand and brought it to his lips, never allowing his eyes to leave hers. "I love you," she whispered.

His eyes took on a deeper glow. "I love you."

"Well, are you ready?"

He softly laughed. "I am only waiting for you, love. My only wish is that you are happy on your return to live with us in Pemdas."

Reece wound her arms around his neck. She softly ran her fingers through his hair and smiled. "Levi, I love Pemdas—but more than that, I love you. I couldn't imagine living anywhere—"

She was silenced when his lips captured hers. He wrapped his strong arms around her waist, drawing her closer in to him. Reece molded her body tightly against his, savoring the rich taste of his kiss.

"Should I fly the plane to Philadelphia on my own?" Harrison shouted from the car below. "It looks like you two are ready to go straight to Pemdas from here!"

They both laughed.

"Shall we?" Levi said as he offered Reece his arm.

They arrived in Philadelphia in the early evening. Reece slept on the flight and woke up starving. Levi and Harrison thought dinner out would be safe for all of them, and they encouraged her to bring her friends along.

Dinner was an upbeat occasion, and Reece felt as though it was the perfect way to close this chapter of her life; saying goodbye to old friends while in the company of the people with whom she would spend the rest of her life.

Everyone took the news of Reece's departure well. Jack gave her a hard time for "ditching him," but was happy for her.

"Back to San Diego, huh?" Lori said with a sigh. "Are you absolutely certain you don't want to be my roommate for the rest of your life?"

Reece laughed and reached over to give her a hug. "I'm definitely going to miss you, Lori."

With promises to return to visit when she could, Reece was able to leave without any uncomfortable interrogation.

The three days spent on Earth went quickly; there was not much for her to prepare. She had only a few boxes that Levi carried down into the car. Lori was more than excited that Reece gave her the majority of her wardrobe, with the excuse of starting a new life and needing new clothes for it. Levi arranged the sale of her car, pricing it to sell the same day he had listed it. She was completely ready to leave. They could have left earlier, but Levi encouraged her to take the time with her friends.

The morning they left, Lori and Jack waited to see them off. They said their goodbyes with a few tears from Lori, but none from Reece, who felt as though she could not wait one minute longer to leave Earth.

As they came through the vortex, Levi pulled the car into the stone garage. Once they were out of the car, Levi walked Reece over to the gates. Before walking through them, Levi stopped and pulled her into a loving embrace. He held her tightly as he brought his lips down on hers.

Harrison approached from behind. "I think you two could use some time alone. I'm starting to feel uncomfortable." He laughed as he went through the gates before them.

Reece flushed and decided to change the subject. "What about the boxes from my apartment?"

Levi smiled down at her. "I notified the Palace to send servants to retrieve them."

When they walked through the gates to where Harrison stood, the sound of the horses thundering toward them made Reece's heart react with anticipation of their return to Pemdas. She gripped Levi's hand excitedly as she watched their magnificent approach. Levi looked down and smiled at her reaction.

Areion slowed and pranced over to where Levi stood. Once they were on Areion, Reece wrapped her arms tightly around Levi's waist. Areion began stamping his feet, eager to go.

Once Harrison was on Saracen, he turned to Levi and Reece. "Shall we race?"

"Not today. I believe I will be taking an alternate route this time. Go on without us; I know you're desperate to get home."

Harrison's eyes narrowed, studying his cousin. "Indeed?"

"Indeed."

Harrison chuckled, shaking his head. He spun his horse down the road and raced off.

Areion became instantly jealous and extremely impatient, but Levi held him back. "Would you care to take an alternate route?"

She shrugged. "Would it matter?"

He laughed as he answered. "No, my love, it would not."

Levi let slack fall in the reins, and the horse leapt forward toward Pemdas. Areion led them over the barrier, lunging over the gray mist. Reece held tightly onto Levi as he let the horse choose his own speed. Illogically, the faster he ran, the smoother the ride was.

It was before reaching the forest that Levi turned right, off the road and through a grassy meadow with a tall mountain range behind it. *This must be the scenic route,* Reece thought. They traveled alongside a large river, with tall trees outlining its banks. Areion slowed as he stepped them down a deep, narrow, stone road, cut like a canyon through rock. The stone walls dimmed the light of the sun, and the air chilled.

Once they were through it, Areion's pace increased. Levi covered Reece's hands, bracing her. "Hold on."

Areion sped up, digging at the ground beneath him as he began his ascent up a mountainside. This was Reece's longest climb yet on the horse; she felt it in her legs and back. Just as she was about to ask for a break, they reached the top. Even Areion seemed to feel relief to be finished with the climb. He did not fight his master as Levi walked him straight ahead, toward the edge of the mountain top. Reece squeezed Levi tightly and buried her face in his back.

She felt him laughing as Areion stopped moving. "I believe the view that Areion worked hard to show you is much better than the back of my shirt. Open your eyes, love."

As she looked over, she was rendered speechless. The trees on the top of the narrow mountain peak were minimal, and she was able to view everything around them. They stood overlooking Pemdas—hills, valleys, and farmland that seemed to go on forever. Far in the distance, past smaller mountains and hills, water glistened. "Is that an ocean?"

"It is. This is the best view of it. It is not necessarily my favorite ride, but the reward is worth it."

She stared ahead, amazed by the beautiful view. She leaned into his back, her eyes gazing out at the sparkling body of water.

"Wow," was all that she could manage.

Levi spoke softly, "I felt I should welcome you to your new home in this manner."

Reece squeezed her arms tightly around his waist. "It's breathtaking, Levi. Thank you."

"You are very welcome. Now, let us give Areion a break. I must share this view with you properly, anyway."

They dismounted and walked to a spot of scrub grass off to the side, which offered a better view of the ocean. Levi pulled her into his arms, and she let her body relax into his embrace while taking in the view. They said nothing for a few moments; she only felt the soft kisses he bestowed to the top of her head.

"The first time I was brought here was by my father; it was when he explained to me what would be expected of me when I became Emperor."

Levi stared intently out toward the glistening waters of the ocean. "My father compared the power and duty of an Emperor to an ocean. Just as the ocean is viewed as powerful, one day I would be viewed in the same manner.

He spoke of how unpredictable the ocean is. It can be peaceful one moment, and then with no warning it can become fierce, instantly humbling you. With that, he instructed that as long as I understood the gravity of the position I would hold, and yet remain humbled by it, I would be able to cope with the responsibility."

He pulled back to face her, his expression somber. "Reece, if given the option and you should choose to reside in Pemdas indefinitely, I must know your feelings about my chosen appointment. I cannot allow you to be misled into believing that a relationship with me would be like any other normal one."

Reece looked up at him, confused, unsure of where this was all going. Of course, she was not afraid to love someone of his importance. Yes, it was different, exciting, and demanding all at once. She knew that she would need to eventually find balance in all of it, and most importantly admit to herself that she was loved by a true prince. That was the hardest part for her, given she did not necessarily view him in that way. It was not his place in this world that she had fallen in love with. She fell in love…with him.

She tried to arrange her thoughts into words. "Levi, I understand that you will one day stand as ruler over…this entire world." She laughed at the thought and went on. "I know I don't have a firm understanding of what that will require of you day to day, but I want to do everything I can to make that responsibility easier for you. You don't need to worry about that scaring me. I love you so much…you should probably be more worried about that instead!" she teased.

Levi's eyes danced with amusement as they remained locked onto hers. He grinned down at her and softly called for Areion. *Leaving already? What did I say?* Levi continued to stare into her eyes, never once turning to look for the horse.

"Levi?"

He reached down to her face, tenderly letting his hand caress her cheek. "You are so beautiful," he said. She felt his gaze through her entire body. "You must know that I love you with my whole heart. I've loved you since I first saw you, and I want to spend the rest of my life loving you more the next day than I did the day before. I am unable to imagine my life without you, and I have no desire to do so."

Reece's eyes widened at the realization of what was happening. Her mind swam with the words he declared to her. Never did she imagine that love like this truly existed, and never did she imagine it would find her. Levi turned to the waiting horse behind him, reached into a pocket in the saddle, and quickly returned his eyes back to hers. He slowly led her away from the horse and stood with the magnificent view behind him. She could not speak, but it was the answer in her expression that encouraged him further.

Levi's eyes glistened as he reached slowly for her hand, his features showing his passion and love for her. He closed his eyes as he brought her delicate hand up to his mouth and softly kissed it before returning his adoring eyes to hers. "You are the only person my heart has ever desired, or will ever desire." His lips turned up into a tiny smile. "I'm afraid you have fallen in love with a man with very little patience. I usually waste no time in securing what I want; and that is you, Reece Bryant, more than anything. Would you please grant me the greatest honor I could ever receive by becoming my wife?"

Tears filled her eyes, tears of joy, and love, and utter happiness. His words echoed in her thoughts—*Would you please grant me the greatest honor I could ever receive, by becoming my wife?*—and she stared down, absently shaking her head from side to side.

Levi's eyes crinkled in laughter. "No?"

She laughed, too, reaching up to his bruised cheek, staring at him with more love than she ever knew she could feel. "Yes, Levi. Of course, yes."

He stepped forward, towering over her, smiling brilliantly. He went to kiss her, but stopped and took a step back. He reached for her left hand. "I almost forgot," he said as he laughed softly. "I arranged for my mother to slip this ring in Areion's saddle pouch. It was my grandmother's."

Reece looked down at the brilliant blue and silver-like stone, blurred and wavering by her tears. "Levi, this is the most beautiful…" Before she could finish, his lips were on hers.

He kissed her deeply and passionately, and she returned the kiss with just as much desire. They became lost in each other. Later—how much later, Reece didn't know—Levi jerked and suddenly pulled away. He stood back, eyes vivid in their color, as if he were seeing something invisible to her.

"What is it, Levi?"

He looked down toward her and grinned. "I know where the stone is."

Epilogue

Simone

Simone gracefully walked the halls of the Palace, trying to ease the frustration of being cooped up inside of it.

She had grown tired of the one woman she despised. She felt that if she had to spend another minute in that girl's presence, she would likely choke her.

What did everyone see in Reece Bryant anyway? Why didn't they treat her like the simpleton she was? The ignorant girl is so agreeable that it's annoying; and yet, everyone adores her for it. Watching her walk around the Palace, dressed formally as if she were a woman of Pemdas, is nauseating. She's an outsider from Earth, brought here for her protection. Earth! Of all places! Now she roams the halls of the Palace freely, as if it were her own; and why? Because Levi and Harrison need a pet project? Disgusting. Reece Bryant should be made to live among the residents of a simple village; possibly with a lonely family who is in need of some company. To have anyone from Earth residing in the Emperor's Palace is unacceptable.

Her smile? Nothing would please me more than to see it slapped off her pretty little face. Well, naturally she's wearing that senseless grin all of the time; she has the two most sought after men in the land catering to her every need. This entire scenario is infuriating, and now Lillian and Catherine agree that she isn't so bad after all. What do they know, anyway? The girl could charm her way into friendship with everyone else, but she will never befriend me.

Simone exhaled in frustration; all of these thoughts were consuming her like poison. Reece just needed to leave this place. *Soon enough*, she thought. *Father has been in meetings constantly, making great efforts to rid that pest from our land. Soon enough.*

As Simone was crossing through the foyer, the back door opened swiftly, revealing Levi's hasty entrance. Her heart skipped a beat.

A broad smile crossed Levi's face when he noticed her. Simone's breath immediately caught; he had never looked at her in this manner before. She could never recall a time where he had ever smiled so brilliantly. He was always so reserved, and yet commanding. It was what Simone loved about him, the opposite of his annoying and insufferable cousin, Harrison. Now, here Levi stood before her, and he was smiling so brightly, *for her?*

"Good afternoon, Simone," Levi greeted her politely.

Simone smiled widely back at him. "Good afternoon, Levi. This is a lovely surprise, and it's nice to see you have returned safely from Earth."

Levi's grin broadened, and Simone could barely contain herself. She never imagined him being any more attractive than he already was. Her cheeks flushed.

"Thank you. I am looking for my mother. Do you happen to know where she is?"

He was so appealing that Simone was having a difficult time comprehending what he was asking her.

Simone cleared her throat delicately. "Oh yes, of course, she is in the garden room. I believe she is trying to make Reece feel as if she were outdoors or something." She rolled her eyes. "You know, Levi, all of us wish the weather would—"

She was interrupted when Levi bowed curtly and thanked her. He spun on his heels swiftly and walked briskly down the corridor.

Simone thought it was odd of him to act in such a manner, but did not let it trouble her. The smile he meant for her was more than enough to give her the strength to endure Reece's visit. She smiled as she gracefully walked into the room where Lillian and Catherine were. Her heart beat rapidly every time she thought of his excitement to see her.

Upon entering the room, she was thankful Catherine and Lillian were occupied with fashion magazines. Simone had no desire to converse with anyone at the moment; she did not want to remove the image of Levi from her mind. She greeted the young women as she poured a hot cup of tea to help soothe her nerves. She walked over toward the windows, sipped her tea, and gazed out onto the snow covered gardens. Everything was beautiful again.

She looked down to see Areion patiently waiting for his master to return to him. Simone smiled. She knew Levi would return soon, and she would watch the man she loved ride off on his beautiful stallion. The man commanded his horse like none other. The way he controlled the ferocious steed, and the power and might he used in doing so, had always captivated her. He was perfect in every way.

She gazed around the snow covered grounds; it all seemed so marvelous now. It was amazing how a simple interaction with the handsome Levi Oxley could change her outlook on everything. She knew she must find a way to steal some time alone with him.

As thoughts of Levi danced around in Simone's head, she nearly choked when her attention was brought back to Areion. His master had indeed returned, but he was not alone. *Reece Bryant? Is he taking her out somewhere?* Rage flooded her veins, and she gasped with fury. Lillian and Catherine were too involved in their book to notice Simone's reaction.

She was nauseated as she watched him help Reece on his horse. She felt as if she would faint as she witnessed the man she loved lead his horse past her window and away from the palace. She gazed out the window, outraged as she took in the sight of Levi's arms wrapped around the girl.

*****

Simone woke in a state of panic. *These dreams will be the death of me!* She ran to her sink to splash cold water on her face. She gasped for air and tried to calm herself. "Rachael!" she demanded. "Where are you? I need you this instant!"

"My deepest apologies, Simone. I did not know you were awake. Allow me to get you some tea. Was it another nightmare, my lady?"

Simone glared at the young maiden. "Rachael, you forget yourself! It is none of your business why I am awake. Why are you not already attending my needs anyway? I will have you replaced this instant if you fail me one more time. I will be ready for my day clothes after this cup of tea, so have them ready. Now get out of my sight!"

"Simone?"

"What, child? You are bothering me."

"Simone, it is still three hours until daybreak. Are you certain you would prefer to begin your day already? If not, I can arrange for some tea so that you may return to a decent slumber."

Simone exhaled in defeat.

This was Simone's life now, tortured and haunted by the past. Living with the constant nightmares of why her life was ruined. This nightmare haunted her most, and she was frightened each time it returned to her. She thought she had completely removed this day from her heart and her mind. The dream served as a reminder of the reasons she went to such great lengths to remove Reece from Pemdas.

It was after watching Levi ride away with Reece and learning that he had taken her to Casititor that she arranged to leave the next morning on a vacation. However, it was not the vacation that Lillian, Catherine, and the others believed she was taking. Once Catherine and Lillian were distracted, she searched out an old friend, Michael Visor. She needed help coming up with a plan to remove Reece from Pemdas. Michael was perfect; he despised Levi as much as Simone hated Reece.

Ironically, when she met with Michael, she discovered that he had already made plans of his own to remove the woman. It seemed that Michael and a few others weren't as pleased to have this wretched girl from Earth among them either. Her only concern about the plan was that it required a Guardian horse to cross the barrier. She knew very well that a Guardian horse would never allow any of them on its back; not with the malice intended with their actions. Their senses were far too keen to accomplish the mission.

When she expressed this concern to Michael, he laughed in response. Then he showed her how he was able to manipulate his horse into doing whatever he commanded, be it good or bad. It was perfect; they had their way out of Pemdas, and now they could easily cross into Ciatris. Her plans to remove Reece were well underway, and Simone was prepared for success. She was still baffled about where it all went wrong.

She calmed herself and looked toward the concerned young girl. "Just make the tea, Rachael; I'll be out in a moment."

Simone stared at herself in the bathroom mirror as the maiden swiftly left the room. She was disgusted by her reflection in the mirror. She would not, however, allow herself to believe she was falling apart. The Oxley family had since forgiven her duplicity, but it was not coming without a price. There was not one person who treated her with the respect she deserved. Fortunately, they all believed the story she gave them as she feigned innocence, and her punishment was not as severe as Michael Visor's would be.

Michael, poor man. Luckily, Levi spared his life after their encounter at Castle Ruin, but that was the kind of man Levi was. Her heart wrenched with pain, recalling how much she loved him. And now he despised her. She tried with everything in her power to block the memory of the day he returned from being imprisoned on Earth. As irate as he was toward her, it did not compare to when he sought her out that afternoon to reprimand her for threatening his beloved Reece. She had never witnessed the man so hostile with his words. She believed she would die of heartbreak then and there. Levi was intimidating to be sure; however, she never gave much credence to the superiority of the man until he confronted her the night before he returned to Earth to bring Reece to the council meeting. Once again, he assured her that she would never have his forgiveness, and if the decisions of her fate were left up to him...

She shuttered at the horrid memory and walked into the next room for her tea. She promptly dismissed her maiden and attempted to unwind her frazzled nerves. She sat on her settee and began to sip her tea. This entire situation had gotten out of hand. She could no longer live among any of these people. Her constant, torturous dreams reminded her of the scorn she had to endure from everyone on a daily basis. She was not only haunted with these horrors in her dreams, but they followed her while she was awake as well. She could not escape any of it, no matter how hard she tried.

She was treated as a disease; everyone strayed away from her and treated her as if she were contagious. How did this happen? Until last night, she held on to the hope that everyone would move forward and forget what she had done. It was not an easy process, but she was managing. More than once, she considered leaving and trying to find a life somewhere else. The only thing that stopped her was the hope that when the men returned from Earth, Reece would not be among them. Reece would have been traded to the Ciatron, and it would be over.

Simone understood everyone's anger toward her, but in time that would all mend. Everyone would forget, move on with their lives, and everything would be the way it was before *she* came. She knew she could charm her way back into all of their good graces soon enough.

All of this actually seemed like it could work itself out until word came from Earth that the Council of Worlds had agreed to allow Navarre to bring Reece back into Pemdas, where she would remain…indefinitely.

She could not imagine that the Emperor would allow someone from Earth to take permanent residence in their world. She knew that once her father returned, they would prepare for their journey home, away from the Emperor and his family. For the first time in her life, Simone was never so happy to leave the grand Palace.

Hopefully, during her time away the nightmares would cease. More importantly, with any luck, Levi would lose interest in Reece, just as he did Isabelle, and she would have her opportunity to prove to him that she was a better person after all of this.

But it was last night that she was proven wrong.

After Harrison arrived and Levi and Reece were not with him, the fury within her ignited once again. She could not imagine why the two would not have ridden directly to the Palace together with Harrison.

The sun had disappeared, and Simone seemed to be the only one concerned by their absence. Lady Allestaine's mood was electrified; Simone had never seen her so excited. Simone wanted nothing more than to return to her room, but everyone was ordered to await their arrival.

Simone was miserable, or so she thought she was. Finally, an hour after the sun disappeared behind the horizon, Levi and Reece walked into the room.

Simone's eyes narrowed as they openly held hands in front of everyone in the room. She looked at Lady Allestaine, waiting for the disdainful response that was sure to follow; yet, she found the opposite. The lady held her hand over her heart while she brought the other one to rest in the bend of Navarre's arm. Navarre smiled enthusiastically toward the two as they entered the room, and Simone did not fail to notice Elizabeth wipe a stray tear from her cheek. Something was different. Why wasn't anyone upset that these two were off alone, until dark, together? Why was Harrison smiling so mischievously at them both? What was going on?

It was when Levi proudly announced that Reece accepted his offer of marriage that Simone nearly collapsed. She searched for air, but her lungs would not take it in. Her eyes burned with rage, and she was doing everything in her power to remain seated. Oh, how she hated this girl, with every fiber of her being. She could no longer live in this land, not with any of these people. As far as she was concerned, Navarre corrupted this land by allowing such an abomination to take place. Why would Levi disregard everything that was revered and sacred to the Pemdai by doing this?

She sat in shock as the room exploded into cheers and Lady Allestaine rushed to give both Reece and Levi her blessings. Reece smiled brilliantly as Levi stared at her adoringly. Simone's heart kept a rapid pace as fury and rage radiated from her. She remained quiet; no one noticed that she did not congratulate the two, nor did they seem to care.

She spent the rest of the evening trying to find an excuse to dismiss herself from the crowd. She couldn't leave too soon and risk appearing to be envious of Reece; she wouldn't give that girl the satisfaction. Reece could never know how much Simone loved Levi. She turned her attention to the captivating man who was in conversation with the men. She noted that although Levi smiled radiantly, his attention was focused on Reece, and not the men surrounding him. *Has he even noticed I am in the room?*

As she watched him gazing at the girl, she began to feel hatred for him as well. He was as ignorant as Reece. Pemdas was no longer a place she was proud to call her home. She would not live in a land where her future Empress would be a nonsensical, naïve girl from Earth. She had to find a way to leave, and soon. Michael's horse led her through the vortex once, and he *would* do it again.

She continued to sip her tea, recalling these horrid events from the previous night. It was supposed to have relaxed her; however, it did quite the opposite. She was wide awake and fully aware of why this nightmare resurfaced. What else would she expect after hearing about Levi's engagement the previous night? She had to leave, and it had to be now.

Simone looked around her room and realized Rachael was nowhere to be found. Quietly, she packed everything she would need to leave for Armedias. It was a world just as unique and beautiful as Pemdas, and she could easily find a home there. She knew that with her looks, charm, and close affiliation to the Pemdai royal family, the rulers of that world would welcome her with open arms.

Excitement flooded through her. She would not wait another moment. She would not spend one more day in this land, hearing of the future Mrs. Levi Oxley. As she hastily made her way from the Palace, she found her way down to where Michael's horse was stabled. Her heart startled when a man approached her.

"Michael?" Simone whispered. "What are you doing here? How can you ride? How did you escape from your prison cell?"

"You don't need to concern yourself with my ways of escaping." Michael whispered quietly back, "In regard to your questioning my abilities to ride a horse, I am compelled to ask the same of you, Simone. What brings you down to my horse's stable before sunrise? Are you planning to run away?" He laughed.

"I must leave this place at once. Have you heard of Levi's engagement?"

Michael brushed his hand over Simone's cheek. "I take it that you are not the lucky bride to be? Is your heart broken, along with every other girl in Pemdas?"

Simone batted his hand away from her cheek. "Michael, do not be absurd. You know I cannot stand Levi; it is why we worked together to destroy him." She then brought her hand to his rugged face. "Oh, Michael, you know I have always loved you. Levi is too proud; I detest his presence. Come away with me. You can no longer live here either; everyone despises us both. I cannot imagine what my father will plan to do with you if you remain."

Instantly persuaded by Simone's charms, Michael grabbed her into a tight embrace. "Simone, if we leave, we must leave now. But I don't leave to run away; I will return, with vengeance. You see, I met a few new friends while I was amongst the Ciatron. There are others that want nothing more than to put Navarre in his place." He chuckled darkly.

Simone's eyebrow shot up as she played with a button on his shirt. "These new friends, Michael, who are they?"

"Michael brought his lips to Simone's. He withdrew and smiled. "In time, lovely Simone. Now, let us go before the stable men are out with their morning duties."

Simone giggled with excitement; Michael was proving to be more of a man than she truly thought him capable. Maybe there was hope to remove Reece from Pemdas after all.

ABOUT THE AUTHOR

Award winning author, S.L. Morgan was born and raised in California. After 29 years of living in the Sierra Nevada Mountains there, she and her husband began their journeys of moving throughout the United States. She currently lives in California, where she and her husband are raising their three children.

In October of 2011, S.L. Morgan became inspired to write her new novel series, "Ancient Guardians." With her passion and love for Jane Austen and other classic romance novels, she was motivated to write a novel series of her own.

S.L. Morgan is currently anticipating five books in the Ancient Guardians series, and is very excited to bring her readers on more adventures and journeys with Levi, Reece and Harrison.

***Be sure to read the sequel to the Legacy of the Key. "Ancient Guardians: The Uninvited" (Book II, Ancient Guardians series.)** Please follow S.L. Morgan on her social media sites to keep up with the latest updates on the new releases of the upcoming novels in the Ancient Guardians series.

Sign up for our newsletter for information on new releases: http://eepurl.com/7_5I5
Official Website: www.slmorganauthor.com
WordPress Blog: http://ancientguardiansnovel.wordpress.com/
Twitter: https://twitter.com/slmorgan1
Instagram: http://instagram.com/slmorganauthor
Pinterest: http://www.pinterest.com/slmorganauthor/
S.L. Morgan Facebook page:
https://www.facebook.com/slmorganauthor?ref=hl
Goodreads: https://www.goodreads.com/slmorgan
Ancient Guardians Novel Series Facebook Page:
https://www.facebook.com/AncientGuardiansLegacyOfTheKey?ref=hl

From the Author:

Thank you for taking time to read the first book in the Ancient Guardians series. If you enjoyed Ancient Guardians: The Legacy of the Key, help spread the word by leaving your review. It is greatly appreciated and always helps other readers decide whether or not this would be a book that they would enjoy too.

Happy Reading!
S.L. Morgan

Made in the USA
San Bernardino, CA
20 September 2017